It Could Never Happen Here

Eithne Shortall studied journalism at Dublin City University and has lived in London, France and America. Now based in Dublin, she is editor of the *Home* magazine at the *Sunday Times Ireland*. Her debut novel, *Love in Row 27*, was a major Irish bestseller, and the follow-up, *Grace After Henry*, was shortlisted for the Irish Book Awards and won Best Page Turner at the UK's Big Book Awards. Her third novel, *Three Little Truths*, was a BBC Radio 2 Book Club pick.

Also by Eithne Shortall

Love in Row 27
Grace After Henry
Three Little Truths

It Could Never Happen Here

Eithne Shortall

CORVUS

Published in hardback in Great Britain in 2022 by Corvus, an imprint
of Atlantic Books Ltd.

This paperback edition published in 2022.

10 9 8 7 6 5 4 3 2 1

A CIP catalogue record for this book is available from the British Library.

Paperback ISBN: 978 1 83895 187 0
E-book ISBN: 978 1 83895 186 3

Printed in Great Britain

Corvus
An imprint of Atlantic Books Ltd
Ormond House
26–27 Boswell Street
London
WC1N 3JZ

www.corvus-books.co.uk

For my dad, Billy Shortall, who made me coffee while
I wrote and always served in a Seamus Heaney
'Inspiration' mug...

In case you thought I didn't notice.

1

• • • • •

ABERSTOWN GARDA STATION

The parents and staff filed into the police station. Pristine coats hung from their confident shoulders, and huddles quickly began to form. A few threw glances in Garda Joey Delaney's direction and he did his best to look authoritative from his position behind the reception desk. He lifted his blink-and-you'd-miss-it backside from the swivel chair, placed both hands on his belt and yanked it up, ready for action.

'Delaney, get in here!'

The young guard swung around to see his superior, Sergeant James Whelan, already disappearing back into his office.

He gave the belt one further hoist and quick-stepped it in after him.

'The first batch seem to all be here now, sir.'

Whelan lowered himself into the chair with a groan. The sergeant was forty-six – exactly twice Joey's age – but he moved like a man of far greater years. Garda Corrigan pointed this out to him once and Whelan snapped that being tethered to useless eejits such as him was slowing him down.

'Did you mark their names off the list?'

Joey had expected the parents to approach the desk and formally check in, but most of them had ignored him entirely. 'I'll go around now and do a roll-call.'

'You do that. I'll just finish up in here, and then we'll get started.' The sergeant lifted the remains of what looked like a chicken sandwich from his desk and took a bite.

'Do you think they'll know anything, sir?'

'If there's anything to know, that lot will be in the loop.' The sergeant nodded towards the door, to the staff and parents of Glass Lake Primary beyond. 'They pride themselves on it.'

Glass Lake was a sought-after school located one town over in Cooney. Curtains were due to go up on its annual musical tonight and even Joey had a ticket. He wouldn't normally be too keen on watching a bunch of twelve-year-olds perform *The Wizard of Oz*, but the other officers insisted the school's shows were always unmissable. 'West End quality at West Cork prices,' was how Corrigan had put it. Not that it mattered now. There would be no musical tonight, or any other night this week. Obviously.

Joey nodded, hands on belt, as he marched out of the sergeant's office and over to the desk where he had left the clipboard of witness names. He was determined not to be another useless eejit slowing the sergeant down.

He cast an eye over the list and then over the busy waiting area. Yesterday evening, this lot had been up at Glass Lake, getting the auditorium ready. Now, they were in Aberstown Garda Station preparing to give their two cents on the body that had been pulled from the River Gorm while they were busy painting the Yellow Brick Road and putting finishing touches to Munchkin costumes.

They were still waiting on the initial post-mortem results and

Joey knew the most likely cause of death was accidental. Eleven months he had been a qualified guard stationed at Aberstown and, until yesterday, there hadn't been a reason to switch on the siren of the station's sole patrol car.

This wasn't a part of the world where robberies happened, never mind murders.

Still, thought Joey, as he hitched up his trousers and strode over to the whispering masses, there was no harm in keeping an open mind.

Mairead Griffin, school secretary

It was pandemonium yesterday evening. It's been pandemonium ever since the parents learned this year's musical was going to be on television. They've been turning up in their dual roles of legal guardians and Hollywood agents, and God help us all if their child isn't standing right where the cameras are going to be. If a single one of them noticed anyone was missing – if they noticed anything other than how high their child's name was listed in the programme – then let me know and I'll keel over right here and die of shock.

Susan Mitchem, parent

I fully support postponing the musical – a mark of respect, absolutely – but I had a casting

3

agent coming to see my son and I've had no
clarity on when to reschedule the train tickets
for. I'm in serious danger of losing my money.
The whole thing is tragic, one hundred per cent,
but as the old maxim goes: the show must go on.

Mrs Walsh, teacher
It's just so sad, isn't it? Imagine how cold it
must be in the water, especially at this time of
year. A tragic, tragic accident – and this town
has had enough of those. My thoughts are with
the family. You hear about these things on the
news, but you don't really think about it, not
properly, not until it happens to one of your
own.

2
.....

The front door opened, and Christine Maguire leapt from the sitting room into the hallway, knitting needles and almost-completed teddy bear left languishing on the sofa.

She held her index finger to her lips and gestured up the stairs.

'Well?' she whispered. 'Did you find him?'

Her husband removed the thick thermal gloves the kids had bought him for his birthday. 'I've got four pieces of news,' he said. 'Three pieces of good news and one piece of bad news.'

'Jesus, Conor. Did you find the cat or not?'

Christine was the only member of the family who hadn't wanted a cat. Hers was the one vote, out of the five of them, for a dog. (Brian wrote 'porcupine' on his piece of paper, but given the options were 'dog' or 'cat', her son's ballot had been registered as spoiled.) The animal had sensed Christine's outlier position from day one and returned the disdain ten-fold. And yet here she was, unable to go to bed until she knew the damn creature was safe.

'I found him,' said her husband, undoing his jacket. 'Porcupine is alive and well.' (Such was Brian's aggrievement at being excluded from the democratic process that they'd allowed the seven-year-old to choose the pet's name.)

5

'Thank God.' Christine leaned back against the wall and glanced up the stairs. 'Maybe now Maeve will go to sleep.'

'They're the first two pieces of good news.'

She watched him jostle with the coat rack. 'What's the third?'

'He's being very well cared for in Mrs Rodgers' house.'

'Mrs Rodgers, of course! Why didn't we think of that?'

Rita Rodgers was an older lady who lived at the end of their street and spent a lot of time tending to her rose bushes – a real jewel in Cooney's Tidy Towns crown. The local pets were known to stop by and keep her company while their owners were out. She'd lived a fascinating life – literally ran away with the circus – and she exuded a worldly calm. Christine often said they were lucky to have Mrs Rodgers on their street; she was a reminder to stop and smell the (prize-winning) roses.

'Good old Mrs Rodgers, ay?' she said. 'We should drop her down a box of chocolates, to say thank you. I can pick something up tomorrow. I'll go tell Maeve that all is well.'

Their middle child had added Porcupine's disappearance to her ever-expanding list of things to lose sleep over. Other items included the teddy bear she was supposed to have finished knitting for school tomorrow (hence Christine currently committing late-night forgery) and a sudden, strong fear that she would not be involved in the Glass Lake musical.

Maeve didn't want to act in the production, which was a pity; she was the only one of Christine's children with the looks for stardom. (She wasn't a bad mother for thinking that. Maeve was her prettiest child, but Caroline was the most intelligent, and Brian the most likeable. Everyone went home with a prize.) Maeve wanted to work on costumes, but some other girl was already signed up to do that.

Christine didn't see the problem. It was a school show staged by a bunch of pre-teens. Surely the attitude should be: the more the merrier.

'Hang on,' she said, as Conor continued to mess around with the coat rack. It did not take that long to hang up a jacket, even if you approached things with as much precision as her husband. 'What's the bad news?'

'Hmm? Oh.' Conor frowned at the woollen collar as he attached it to a hook. 'She doesn't want to give him back.'

'*What?*'

'Mrs Rodgers, yes. I was surprised too. But she was quite firm about it. I always thought she was dithery, but I guess that was ageism. She's actually impressively sharp. She knows we're gone from the house for at least seven hours every day and that Porcupine is left on his own. She did this bit where she opened the front door wide and told Porcupine that he was free to go. *Go on now if you're going,* she said. And Porcupine looked up at her and meowed. Now I know he meows all the time, especially when he's hungry or when it's early and—'

'Yes, Conor, I'm familiar with the cat's meow.'

'Right. But this was different. This meow sounded like a word.'

'Excuse me?'

'A human word, I mean.'

Christine squinted at her husband, who was supposed to be the brains of the family. He raised his hands in a wait-for-it gesture.

She waited.

'And it sounded ... like, "No".'

Christine smacked her lips.

Conor nodded.

'*What?*'

'I know,' he said, still nodding. 'Crazy. Porcupine did not budge. I took off my hat, so he'd recognise me, but nothing. He just stood at her feet, loyal as you like. I have to say, it was very impressive.'

'What did you do?'

'What could I do? She was very nice about it. She explained that we were very busy – which is true, you said the same thing when we first talked about getting a cat – and probably didn't have a lot of time. But she has plenty of time and lots of space. She's an animal person, and she'd really cherish the company. I could almost hear her rattling around in the place, the poor woman. You know her husband died?'

'Yes, forty years ago, Conor! And they were separated. She left the man for a tightrope walker!'

'If we were separated and you died, I'd still be sad.'

'What? Conor, no! She stole our cat!'

Now it was her husband's turn to put his finger to his lips and gesture towards the stairs. 'Porcupine looked happy. I know it's only been a couple of days, but he looked fatter.'

'That cat couldn't get any fatter.'

'I don't know why you're so annoyed, Christine. You never liked him anyway.'

'She *stole* our cat! She cannot just steal our cat!' Christine caught her voice before it escalated to a full-on roar. That woman, their nice, old, butter-wouldn't-melt neighbour, had abducted their pet. How many times had Mrs Rodgers called out 'Busy today?' as Christine hurried past her house? When Christine called back 'Up to my eyes, Mrs Rodgers', she'd assumed she was making polite chitchat, not fashioning the noose for her own hanging. 'I should have known,' she raged. 'I should have known she wasn't the person she said she was. The Tidy Towns committee asked everyone on the street to leave some grass and dandelions in their gardens, but she just eviscerated it all. Animal person, my foot! She doesn't give a damn about the bees!'

'To be fair now, Christine, we're not too worried about the bees ourselves. I just haven't got around to fixing the lawnmower.'

'And how, exactly, could Porcupine look happy? That animal has one expression and it is smug.'

'Well,' Conor conceded, 'he looked sort of smugly happy.'

'Doesn't she already have a cat? A white and ginger thing?'

'I have a memory of seeing her with a brown one,' said Conor, 'but maybe not. That was a while ago.'

To think how many times Christine had stopped to compliment Mrs Rodgers on her 'organic' roses, knowing full well the charlatan was using chemical fertilisers. The Maguires lived on the same street, they had the same soil, and they could barely grow grass. But Christine never said a word. And when Mrs Rodgers won the intercounty garden prize, she'd written an article about it – she'd even pushed to get a picture of the old bat and her performance-enhanced bushes on to the front page.

'So, what? We leave him there? And then what? What are we going to tell the kids? What are *you* going to tell Maeve?'

'We'll just explain that Porcupine is an individual,' said Conor. 'He was a kitten but now he's a cat and he's decided to move out, like the three of them will one day ...'

Christine threw her head back and hooted.

She prided herself on being able to see her children for who they were. In Maeve's case, that was an anxious, conscientious little oddball. Dr Flynn had diagnosed her constant worries as 'intrusive thoughts' and said some children found comfort in prayer. But Conor was resolutely atheist – except when it came to ensuring their children got into Glass Lake Primary: then he was all for standing beside a baptismal fountain and shouting 'Get behind me, Satan' – so he bought her a set of worry dolls instead. Christine could have sworn their sewn-on smiles were already starting to droop.

Then, right on cue, their eleven-year-old daughter appeared at the top of the stairs.

'Why aren't you asleep, Maevey?' Conor called up.

'I was saying prayers for Porcupine. Did they work? Has he come home?'

'I've found Porcupine,' said Conor, ignoring the first portion of the question. 'And he's alive and well.'

Maeve gasped and started to run down the stairs.

'No, hang on, hang on. He's not here. He's at Mrs Rodgers' house.'

'Why is he at Mrs Rodgers' house?' Maeve directed this question towards her mother but, with a swing of the head, Christine lobbed it on to Conor.

'He's, well ...' Conor looked to his wife, then down at their daughter, his lips curled into a smile that didn't reach his eyes. That was his first mistake. Kids could spot a 'bad news' smile a mile away. 'When we got Porcupine, he was a kitten. But now, now he's all grown up. He's graduated from kitten college. He's passed his feline driving test. He's an adult, he's a cat ...'

Maeve's face shifted involuntarily.

'... and when people, and animals, grow up, they move out of home. When I was a child, I lived with your granny and grandad, but then I grew up and now I live here with you ...'

There it was again, a spasm just under the left eye. Christine winced in sympathy. A twitch. Wonderful. Just what the girl needed.

'... and when you grow up, you'll move out of this house too.'

'But I don't want to move out.'

'It won't happen for a long time.'

'I don't want to move out,' repeated Maeve, her voice creeping higher. 'I want to stay here. Mom? Do I have to move out? What if a baddie broke in or the house went on fire and I didn't know because I was asleep and there was nobody there to wake me or what if—'

'This is way, way in the future, Maevey,' explained Conor as the child's breathing grew louder. 'By then you'll be big, and you'll want to go. Caroline will move out first—'

'*Caroline's moving out?*'

Conor flinched. 'No, she's—'

'*Why is Caroline moving out?!*'

'I just meant because Caroline's older, she's fourteen and you're only—'

'Shush now, Maeve, breathe normally. It's all right. Caroline's not going anywhere,' said Christine, deciding her daughter's mental well-being should probably trump a learning opportunity for her husband. 'None of you are. We're all staying here, until we're old and grey and roaming around the house with walking sticks. All right? Okay?'

'And Porcupine is staying too? Until he's old and grey?'

'I'm not sure ... Conor?'

'Dad?'

'He's ...' Conor suddenly looked very tired. 'Yes. Porcupine is staying too. He's just having a sleepover at Mrs Rodgers' house.'

'A sleepover.' Maeve rolled the word around, deciding whether to believe it.

11

'Exactly. Like when you stayed at Amelia's house for her birthday and slept in sleeping bags and ordered pizza. I'd say Porcupine will have pepperoni, what do you reckon?'

Maeve smiled. 'He does like meat.'

'He loves meat,' said Conor, taking the reprieve and running with it. 'I'd say he'll ask them to bring a couple of portions of garlic sauce too, for dipping. Does that sound like Porcupine?'

'Cats can't dip, Dad.'

'No,' he agreed.

'He's having a sleepover?'

'Yes.'

'And he'll be home tomorrow?'

'Absolutely.'

'That's great news,' Christine chimed in, parodying her husband's enthusiasm. 'I look forward to seeing him then. Now, Maeve, back to bed.'

She followed her daughter up the stairs and into her room, which had the same animal wallpaper and curtains as when she'd first moved into it. Maeve had always been young for her age. She had an innocence that even Brian, four years her junior, was starting to shed.

The bedroom's centrepiece was a large noticeboard covered in drawings. Currently, it was dedicated to costume ideas for the Glass Lake musical and multiple, very similar pencil sketches of Porcupine. She'd done a good job of capturing his sly, soulless eyes. The noticeboard was always so singular in focus, and the artwork so concentrated, that it gave her daughter the air of an obsessive stalker. Maeve had got her single-mindedness (and her peculiarity) from her father. When Christine first met Conor – at a party in a squat in what felt like another lifetime – she couldn't believe anyone

12

grew up wanting to be a dentist. Yet by all accounts her husband's childhood bedroom had been much like this, only his noticeboard had been a shrine to teeth.

'Thank you for helping me with the teddy bear,' said Maeve as she climbed into bed. She took a tissue from the nightstand, wiped her nose, and pushed it under her pyjamas' sleeve.

'No problem.'

'And thank you for going to meet the Lakers tomorrow.'

Christine smiled tightly. 'No problem.'

The Lakers were the mothers, mainly alumni, who ran Glass Lake Primary from the shadows. The most ridiculous thing about the Lakers was that this was also how they referred to themselves.

'You can't be late, okay? The Lakers are never late, so I don't think that would go down well. If you're going to be late, you probably just shouldn't go at all.'

'I won't be late, Maeve.'

'And I was thinking maybe you could wear some legging things and a puffed waistcoat, maybe with fur on the collar …'

'Like the ones Amelia's mom wears?'

'Yeah, kind of like that.'

Amelia's mom was Beverley Franklin, a prominent Laker and director of this year's school musical. She used to work at a pharmaceutical company but now she sold jellies that were 70 per cent vegetables on Facebook and spent too much time on the sixth-class parents' WhatsApp group.

'I'm not sure I have one of those jackets,' said Christine diplomatically. 'But it'll be fine, I promise you. I'm going to charm the pants off those other mothers, and I'm going to get you a position working on costumes.'

Maeve didn't look wholly convinced. 'You do know Amelia's mom, don't you?'

'Yes, I told you,' said Christine, tucking the duvet in around her daughter. 'I was in her class at Glass Lake – just like how Amelia is in yours.' *I just don't pin my entire identity on it*, she added silently. 'Me and Beverley go back years. Okay?'

Maeve gave a small nod.

'That's my girl.'

The Lakers organised annual golf outings and reunions (For a *primary* school!) and lucrative fundraisers. They had no say in the academics, thankfully – going on some of the stuff sent into the parents' WhatsApp groups, there were a few anti-vaxxers in their midst – but they had a regrettable amount of input into extracurricular activities. They met at the Strand café on Cooney Pier every Thursday morning, and if you wanted your child to make the swim team or get a solo in the choir or to work on costumes for the annual sixth-class musical, you better believe you were pulling up a chair and ordering a flat white.

Conor couldn't understand this because Conor was a blow-in – meaning he'd only been living in Cooney for sixteen years as opposed to being born, bred and, crucially, educated here.

'It seems insane that you have to take a whole morning off work to meet some women in a coffee shop just so Maeve can maybe be involved in the school play,' he said as they climbed into bed that night. 'Surely the teachers decide who gets to work on it.'

'It is insane. But that's Glass Lake. The parents are far too involved; they were even when I went there. But if it eases Maeve's mind, I can put up with them for an hour or two.'

'And where will Derek think you are?'

Derek was her boss at the *Southern Gazette*. He'd been editor of a national tabloid in Dublin until a heart attack, and his wife, forced him into a slower pace of life.

'I've told him I'm meeting a source.'

Derek regularly talked about tip-offs and whistle-blowers and sources. Christine, who specialised in hundredth birthdays and local council disputes, found it best to just play along.

'Anyway,' she said, 'you've got your own morning to worry about.'

'My Thursday's looking pretty relaxed,' said Conor, sleep making its way into his voice as he nuzzled into her. 'Nothing but routine check-ups until a root canal at noon.'

'I'm talking about the morning-morning, dear husband, and what exactly you're going to say when Porcupine doesn't turn up for breakfast.'

....

Maeve Maguire didn't like getting out of bed in the middle of the night. The house was scarier and colder and sadder when the lights were off and everyone else was asleep. And she didn't like leaving her worry dolls unguarded. She lined them up under her pillow every night, and without her head to hold them in place, she worried they'd get up and run away.

In the daylight, Maeve knew they were only dolls and that dolls couldn't walk, let alone run. But at night, things were different. This was when the four tiny women in their bright dresses and dark pigtails would make a break for it. They would escape and tell everyone her secrets. She pictured them skipping along the streets of Cooney, avoiding the glow of the streetlamps and jumping over any deep cracks in the footpath (they were only teeny after all;

15

shorter than Maeve's middle finger) before they slipped into people's letterboxes, under their front doors and through any windows left ajar. She imagined them hopping up the stairs of these homes, sliding under doors and scaling the beds of Cooney's residents as they squeezed around pillows and climbed beside ears so they could whisper all the bad things that Maeve Maguire of Sixth Class, Glass Lake Primary, had done.

Maeve's biggest worry was that the dolls would achieve all this in the time it took her to get downstairs, do what needed to be done, and return to bed again. If Santa Claus could get around the world in a night, one little coastal town wasn't going to be much of an ask, especially when they could split it between four. If Maeve never knew they'd been gone, then she'd still go into school the next morning, where everyone would know her bad thoughts and bad deeds, and it would be too late to pretend to be sick.

She lifted her pillow and was comforted to see the dolls just as she'd left them. She looked away, then turned back extra quickly. They didn't move. She returned the pillow and slowly swung her legs out of bed. She crept out of her room and closed the door behind her. She grabbed a towel from the landing and pushed it against the gap under the door. She pulled the used tissue from under her pyjamas sleeve and squeezed it into the keyhole. Just in case.

Then, quick as she was able, and without making a sound, she snuck downstairs and did what she had promised to do.

3
· · · · ·

Beverley Franklin never wasted time. She did squats while brushing her teeth and jumping jacks when waiting for the kettle to boil. If suppliers placed her on hold, she put her phone on loudspeaker and cleaned a shelf of the fridge. She left floss beside her laptop and worked a thread of it around her mouth as she waited for the machine to load. And in the mornings, between shouting 'Rise and shine' and 'Let's go, let's go' at her two daughters, she did whatever household tasks could fit into the short window.

The first task this morning was to take delivery of the teddy bear. However, the taxi she'd ordered to collect the stuffed animal from Cooney Nursing Home had ignored either her precise timing instructions or the local speed limit and the driver was knocking on her door, package in hand, before she'd had a chance to deliver the first wake-up call.

'Twenty-six eighty,' said the driver, as she took the bag and removed the bear she'd commissioned several days ago. She'd read about the knitter in the *Southern Gazette*: an illustrious textiles career in Paris then London, where she made garments for the royal family. The article read like an obituary, but it had actually been to mark the woman's hundredth birthday. The centenarian played hard to get at first – retirement this, arthritis that, partial

17

blindness the other – but Beverley kept phoning the nursing home and upping the fee until she relented. And, credit where it was due, the woman had delivered. The bear was navy blue with button eyes, a large white belly and a right arm an inch longer than its left. It was perfect, but not too perfect – just as Beverley had requested. She carried the thing through the foyer up the main flight of stairs to Amelia's bedroom and knocked on the door, ready to rouse her.

'Rise and shine, *ma chérie*,' she said, pushing the door open to reveal the pleasant surprise of her youngest daughter already up and dressed and sitting at her vanity table.

Amelia turned from the mirror. 'He's so cute!' she exclaimed, arms stretched out towards the bear. 'Thanks, Mum. I didn't even know you could knit.'

'If you have a problem, I have the solution. Now. Are you ready to wish your grandmother a happy birthday?' A lifetime of grafting had taught Beverley that when making morning to-do lists you should start with the task you most want to put off. 'I'll stand by the window. The light is better.'

She crossed the room to the bay window and pulled her phone from the pocket of her next-season Moncler diamond quilted gilet. (Shona Martin's mother was a buyer for Brown Thomas, and she'd gifted it to Beverley when she was announced as director of this year's Glass Lake musical.) She scrolled to video.

'Do you want to wish her a happy birthday, and I'll record it?'

'That's all right, *chérie*. She'd much rather see your lovely face.'

Amelia, thankfully, understood nothing of difficult mother-daughter relationships.

The girl gave her ponytail a firm tug and stood poker straight by her pale pink wardrobe. Beverley nodded and Amelia flew into action.

'Happy birthday, Granny, I love you so much!' she gushed. 'I can't wait to see you again. Thank you for being the best grandmother in the world! You're amazing!' Most people's eyes would be engulfed by a smile that wide, but Amelia's exaggerated features could take it. '*Happy birthday*,' she sang, then she blew three gorgeous kisses to the camera and it was all Beverley could do not to reach out to catch them.

'*Parfait!*' she enthused, pressing stop on the video. 'Absolutely perfect. That could have come straight from the account of an A-list influencer.'

Amelia smiled modestly. She had more than 2,000 followers on Instagram – double that of any other child in her class. 'Thanks, Mum.'

Amelia had inherited more from her mother than high cheekbones and excellent hair. She was driven and hard-working. She wanted to be an influencer and she had what it took to make it. That wasn't Beverley being a deluded parent, either. She wasn't like Lorna Farrell, who was convinced the school choirmaster had said Marnie was a 'pre-Madonna' and now believed her daughter was destined for world domination. Beverley actually *had* experience of the entertainment industry.

'I promised my followers I'd post my everyday make-up routine,' said Amelia, switching on the ring light they'd bought for her recent birthday. 'It's more authentic if I do it in the morning.'

'Authenticity is very important,' agreed Beverley, who had read a lot about social media strategies before launching Sneaky Sweets, the health food start-up she ran online. 'Don't forget to take off the make-up when you're finished. Glass Lake rules. Ten minutes, then downstairs for breakfast. You don't want me coming back in and ruining your shot.'

Although actually, wouldn't it be kind of cute to feature some candid bloopers? Beverley had toyed with suggesting she take a cameo role in Amelia's socials. Followers responded well to glimpses into family life. Amelia could post occasional clips from her acting days and then Beverley could talk about what a fun time it had been but how family was more important.

If only all this technology had been around when she was younger, her career could have been so different. Magazines and newspapers had been obsessed with Beverley – and what were they, if not the social media of their time? (Ella was forever telling her she was obsessed with things – herself, Amelia, cleanliness, Glass Lake – but this had been *real* obsession. There was a two-month period where she'd appeared in the *Sunday Independent* every single week.) More people had heard of Beverley Tandon (as she was then) than Pauline Quinn, the young temptress she'd played on *Cork Life*. Beverley remembered her agent telling her this like it was a bad thing: 'You're not Julia Roberts, Bev. You're a soap actress.' Now, though, self-promotion was an asset. She ran Sneaky Sweets almost entirely through Facebook and it was doing well. There were a lot of desperate parents frantically searching the internet for ways to feed their fussy eaters. But however good Beverley might be at selling jellies made from vegetables, she'd have been so much better at selling herself.

'*Mum!*' chided Amelia.

'Nine minutes,' she said, stepping back out on to the landing.

Phone still in hand, she opened the last recorded video. She wrote 'Happy birthday' and deleted it. Then she wrote 'Happy birthday, Mam.' 'Happy birthday, Frances.' 'On your special day!' 'HB, Mama.' 'Peace and light x.' The last one was definitely the most

Her Mother. She deleted it too and just clicked send. The video was self-explanatory.

Mentally ticking the task from her list, she strode along the landing. This was usually when she delivered Ella's wake-up call. However, last night she had politely asked her eighteen-year-old daughter if she had any plans for the weekend – she wasn't even that interested; she was just waiting for the Duolingo update to load – and Ella had responded by asking why she was so obsessed with her. (If anyone was obsessed it was Ella; and she was obsessed with the word 'obsessed'. Beverley should have said that last night. She always thought of retorts hours too late.)

She paused at the bottom of the stairs that led to the next floor. Ella's first lecture was at 10 a.m. – Beverley had her university timetable linked to the Alexa family calendar, along with Malachy's work schedule, Amelia's after-school activities, and her own myriad appointments – and if she didn't get up soon, she'd be late. But Beverley kept walking. If that was how she was going to speak to her mother, she could sing for a wake-up call.

Next up was the toilet bowl in the main first-floor bathroom. There were, as Malachy had so eloquently described it a few hours earlier, 'stringy particles' stuck to the edges. She ran the hot tap and pulled the bleach and a pair of rubber gloves from the box of cleaning supplies Greta kept in the bathroom cupboard.

Ella accused her of 'Catholic guilt' for cleaning before Greta came, and 'white privilege' for having a cleaner in the first place. Whatever about being white (everyone she knew was white!), the Catholic guilt accusation was untrue. Greta worked for all the Glass Lake mothers, and Beverley cleaned before she came for the same reason the Franklins did their banking in Cork City rather than Cooney

21

and Beverley went all the way to Dublin to see her dermatologist. Because people talked. And she'd rather not give them anything interesting to discuss.

Pulling on the Marigolds, she grabbed the toilet brush firmly in both hands and applied brute force to the rim of the bowl until the debris came loose.

'It looks like bits of food,' her husband had said, as he stood at the foot of their bed at 5.30 that morning, stretching his glutes in preparation for his daily pre-dawn run. Malachy did not share Beverley's inherent drive – he'd been born wealthy instead – but when it came to his appearance, he found the motivation. 'I wouldn't be surprised if Ella has an eating disorder.'

'I doubt it,' Beverley had replied, as he placed his palms flat against the wall that separated their room from the second guest bedroom. 'It's probably just hard water build-up. I'll take a look.' Then, because he still wasn't appeased, she added: 'You look well toned.'

Flattery always settled her husband.

She carried the toilet brush over to the sink now and rinsed it under the flowing tap. It was important people thought she'd never dream of cleaning her own toilet, but the actual act of it was nothing. Hard graft and an eye on the future. That was how she'd secured such an enviable life.

Tick, tick.

The final item on Thursday's to-do list was admin. There were seventy-two unread WhatsApp messages. Being a Glass Lake mother was a full-time job and Beverley already had a full-time job, no matter what Ella thought. (It was hard to be a girl-boss role model for a daughter who dismissed your crusade to revolutionise

22

the food industry as 'refreshing your Facebook page'.) Beverley was sometimes tempted to let elements of school life slide, but there were parents and children counting on her, not to mention the reputation of Glass Lake itself. She skipped the Sixth-Class Parents group, the Wonderful Wizard of Oz group, the School Trip to Dublin group and opened the Lakers thread.

Lorna Farrell said, 'Is it terrible that Thursday is my favourite day because I get to have a Strand café flapjack?' Fiona Murphy said, 'That's how I feel about Friday – aka Wineday.' Lorna Farrell sent two cry-laughing emojis. Claire Keating said, 'Wineyay!' and sent a gif of a monkey drinking a bottle of Merlot.

Beverley went to put the phone away – they were meeting in forty minutes, for Christ's sake, no wonder she was the only one who ever seemed to get anything done – when a new message came through from Lorna.

'Today's meeting is going to be extra special – get ready for BIG news, ladies!! Isn't that right @BeverleyFranklin?' This was followed by a wink emoji, and then a cry-laughing emoji. Lorna ended all her messages like this, even when it made no sense.

The top of the screen alternated between telling her Claire was typing and Fiona was typing. 'What's the news??' said one. 'Spill spill!' said the other.

Beverley's grip tightened.

She was director of this year's Glass Lake Primary musical. *She* was the one who'd lobbied the national broadcaster. Everything Beverley had done, from selecting the highly visual *Wonderful Wizard of Oz* to thinking big on set designs and casting the leads early, had been to catch the TV station's attention. She'd sent in headshots of Amelia and Woody Whitehead. (If anything proved

23

Beverley's commitment, it was her willingness to cast a Whitehead. They were a scourge on Cooney, but even she couldn't deny the youngest son had a face, and name, for stardom.) And it had worked. Lorna Lick-Arse Farrell was not going to steal her thunder.

Beverley composed herself and fired off a response–

'BIG news, ladies. HUGE. I've a hectic morning on here, but I'll do my best to get to the Strand early. *Á bientôt.*'

– then she locked her screen and slid the phone back into her pocket. She shoved the bleach and gloves behind the cistern – Greta would tidy them away – and hurried out on to the landing.

On Thursdays, Beverley had Amelia at school for 8.40, dropped Malachy's shirts to the dry-cleaner's when they opened at 8.50, and was over at the Strand café on the other side of Cooney for 8.55. She would hang back in the car until she saw a few other mothers go in. Just because she no longer worked in the city didn't mean she had time to be sitting around waiting on people. This morning, though, she'd be in there first. Amelia could be a few minutes early and the shirts could wait.

She walked purposefully along the landing – let's see who was obsessed with what when Ella was late for college! – and headed for her younger daughter's bedroom.

Had she thought about it, she would have knocked. They'd talked about privacy last summer and agreed Amelia was entitled to some.

But she was in a hurry.

Her mind was full of Lorna Lick-Arse Farrell and how the Yellow Brick Road still looked bronze and the way Malachy had watched himself in the mirror that morning.

She was distracted.

She wasn't thinking.

She turned the handle to her daughter's room without any warning.

'*Chérie*,' she was saying before she was fully through the door, 'we've to leave early so maybe you can do—'

Amelia looked away from her phone. She was standing near the window, holding the too-large device aloft in her too-small hand as she angled it towards her body. Her entirely naked body.

'Mum!'

Her daughter – her beautiful, ambitious, *twelve-year-old* daughter – was wearing a full-face of make-up and not a stitch more.

Her skinny arms pushed against her sides, causing her barely-there boobs to move ever-so-slightly closer together and the skin at her sternum to dent. Beverley had never seen her do anything remotely like that with her mouth, her cheeks, her eyes. She barely recognised the expression as belonging to Amelia. The prominent hip bones and faint wisps of pubic hair came as delayed shocks, and the sticky, cherry-coloured gloss bleeding up on to the skin above her puffed out lips made Beverley's stomach lurch. But it was the pleading look on her daughter's face that would haunt her. It said 'like me' and 'love me' and 'reassure me' but also, and this was too much for Beverley because she was sure her daughter didn't even know what it meant and didn't want to imagine where she'd seen it, it said 'fuck me'.

This pushed Beverley over the edge.

Shock, upset and fury reverberated around her body, rattling against her ribcage and up her trachea, before launching themselves into the pale pink room in a high-pitched guttural scream.

No amount of chalky blusher could stop the colour disappearing from Amelia's face; a blackbird fled from the window ledge behind her; and a teenage boy awoke in a room upstairs where he'd been sleeping, all night, entirely unbeknownst to Beverley.

4
•••••

Arlo Whitehead's dream always went the same way. He and Leo and Mike were playing on stage at a massive stadium that was Madison Square Garden but also Cooney Parish Hall. Arlo had never been to New York (he'd never been further than Lanzarote) but he'd watched Tom Petty live at Madison Square enough times to know the venue. Sometimes Neil Young was watching from the wings, and sometimes it was the guy who'd driven their school bus. Whoever it was, he was always totally impressed. It was all going well – until the last song. Even though Arlo could never hear anything in his dreams (he wished he could; the crowd were totally into whatever they were playing), he knew they were falling out of time. When he looked over at Leo, ready to shout at him to sort it out, he noticed his best friend no longer had arms. Leo was just looking down at the guitar hanging around his neck, screaming. Leo screamed and screamed at the instrument until his face started to melt away.

Arlo had googled 'How to stop having the same dream'. The most common suggestion was to write down the details so he could interpret their meaning. But this was the only dream he ever had, and it didn't take Freud to work it out.

So, when he was roused by an almighty roar, he wasn't overly alarmed. He assumed it was Leo screaming about his missing limbs and was relieved to have woken before his friend's face started to run down his body.

But then he remembered where he was, and that there was never noise in his dreams.

He pushed himself up in the still unfamiliar four-poster bed and looked over at Ella. She was also awake, and though she wasn't screaming, there was a look of mild alarm on her perfect face. (Ella's perfection was beside the point, but it was difficult not to register, no matter the circumstances.)

'That's my mum,' she said, and suddenly he was completely alert.

'Your mom?' He scrambled further up, grabbing his T-shirt and navy jumper from the floor before climbing out of the bed. 'What time is it?' His foot caught slightly on the under sheet, which had come untucked. 'Shit, Ella! I knew I shouldn't have come over last night!'

Ella's parents did not know about Arlo. Well, they *knew* about him, in the way that everyone in Cooney knew about him: as Charlie Whitehead's son, a subject of suspicion, and the only teenager to have walked away from the Reilly's Pass crash intact. But they didn't know about him in the way that mattered: as Ella's boyfriend, as the love of their daughter's life.

'Where are my trousers? Why didn't the alarm go off?' he said, lying on his front on the floor so he could see under the bed. The Franklins' carpet had to be felt to be believed; it was softer than his own bed at home. 'Maybe someone saw me sneaking in last night? There are so many streetlights around here. I don't think there's more than three in our whole estate. I knew it was too risky.'

'Arlo, breathe,' said Ella, climbing out of the bed. She had a red mark on her left cheek from how she'd slept and was wearing the

28

E&A necklace he'd bought for her birthday and his favourite Dylan T-shirt. They had cover stories ready for where both items had come from, but Ella's parents never asked. Her hair was dark blond and cropped. She'd cut it short to piss off her mother, which Arlo didn't condone, but it was sexy. Although it was sexy when she'd had it long, too. Her eyes were pale blue and hypnotic, like an ocean. He'd written that into a song, but he hadn't shown it to Ella yet. Lyrics without music were cheesy. And with Leo gone and Mike gone-gone, he'd be waiting a while for someone to put it to music.

His trousers were not under the bed.

'Maybe your sister told her. Would Amelia do that?'

He was back on his feet and Ella was coming towards him. Already he felt happier. The mark on her cheek was a perfect circle. Half of him marvelled at how that was possible, and the other half thought, 'Ah, but of course'. Everything about Ella Belle Franklin was perfect.

He'd never been in love before and it was amazing. Sometimes he'd be working away, thinking about nothing but expanding pipes or shelf brackets, and then he'd be overcome by a giddy, nervous feeling, as if it was Christmas Eve or the day of some amazing gig, but it was actually just because Ella existed and she wanted to spend that existence with him. Wasn't that incredible? Love was better than all the songs said, even Leonard Cohen's. He wouldn't go as far as to say it was better than sex, but it was definitely equally good.

'Amelia wouldn't do that,' she said, standing in front of him. 'My mum doesn't know.' Ella was the only person he knew who said 'Mum'. He'd thought only English people said that. But then the Franklins were very wealthy, which was almost the same as being English. 'Not that I'd care if she did find out.'

29

'I know, but I care. I need more time.'

A couple more months of working hard and word would get around (as you could rely on it to do in Cooney) that he was a pretty decent lad and not, in fact, 'just like his father'. Then Arlo could look his future parents-in-law in the eye and tell them how wonderful their daughter was. The plan involved turning up early to every job, putting in long hours, doing good work and never saying anything rude no matter what was said to him. The plan did not involve getting caught in Ella's bedroom with no trousers on.

'Relax. There's no way she knows. Bev is too wrapped up in her own life to notice.' Ella also called her mother 'Bev'. She did it to annoy her, even when she wasn't there.

'She was yelling about something.'

'She probably spotted a blackhead in the bathroom mirror. Or maybe Amelia wasn't wearing the exact Glass Lake regulation knee socks. Who knows why Bev does anything? But there's no way she's coming near this room. I told you, we're fighting.'

Arlo tried not to come to Ella's house too often – getting caught sneaking up the Franklins' stairs was also not part of the reputation rehabilitation plan – but whenever he did, Ella picked a fight with her mother. This was apparently a watertight guarantee that Beverley would not come near her bedroom. 'Not until I apologise,' Ella explained. 'She wouldn't give me the satisfaction.' Arlo had grown up in a house where arguments were loud, instant affairs; Mom got annoyed at Dad, Dad charmed Mom, and then it was over. Ella's logic was alien. And he felt bad for Beverley.

Do not feel bad for Beverley Franklin. She's a head melt. Trust me. Who cares if she likes you or not?

It's all right for you, Leo. Everyone in this town loves you. They cross the road when they see me. They think I'm cursed or a bad omen or something.

Really, Arly? You really think it's all right for me?

Arlo pushed his best friend from his head – they could talk on the drive to work – just as Ella stepped forward and kissed him on the lips. She slipped her tongue into his mouth and he grinned. Then he remembered the current situation.

'What time is it? My phone is in my – there they are!' His trousers were hanging off the couch at the end of the bed, which Ella had informed him was actually a *chaise longue*. 'Give anything a French name and Bev will pay three times more for it.' He pulled on his jeans and found his phone in the back pocket.

8.28 a.m.

Not late, so. Not yet.

Good.

If there was one job he couldn't afford to mess up, it was this morning's.

....

'What are you doing?! Why would you do that?! *What is wrong with you?!*'

'I wasn't ... I'm sorry!' Amelia shouted back, whipping a blanket from the end of her bed. 'Don't freak out, Mum, please! I'm sorry!'

The reverberation in Beverley's head continued. She looked at her daughter, face caked in make-up, then down at the phone lying on the bed. 'Jesus Christ!' she cried. 'Jesus, Amelia! *Jesus Christ!*'

'I'm sorry!'

Beverley took a moment and shut her eyes, only as soon as she did, she was assaulted by the image of her daughter pouting into the camera. Where had she seen such an expression? They flew open again.

'Who was it for?'

Amelia's doe eyes were smothered in blue shimmery eyeshadow. Beverley had not known she owned anything so cheap.

She repeated herself. 'Who was the photo for, Amelia?'

'I don't … It wasn't for anyone.'

Beverley needed to think. She closed her eyes, but there it was again. Was the goddam image tattooed on to her eyelids for all eternity now?

'Don't lie to me.'

'Mum.'

'Do not lie to me!'

'I wasn't sending the photo to anyone,' she pleaded. 'I wasn't. I swear.'

Beverley took a deep breath but did not remove her gaze from her daughter.

'It was just for me. I just … I wanted to see what it would look like.'

The girl cringed, but she didn't look away. She was shivering, in spite of the blanket.

After what she'd found on Malachy's phone in April, Beverley was bound to be sensitive. But not everyone was as perverted as her husband. Young girls experimented. She was only twelve, for God's sake. Who would she be sending it to?

'Amelia.'

'I swear on your life, Mum.'

God help her, but the child appeared to be telling the truth.

'You swear you weren't sending it to anyone?'

'I swear,' said Amelia emphatically. 'I wouldn't. That's gross.'

Beverley agreed. It *was* gross.

Amelia's face was bright red, and Beverley struggled to tell where the excessive blusher ended and the embarrassment began.

'All right,' she said. 'Well, thank God for that.' She let out a loud sigh. Amelia looked equally relieved. 'You know you shouldn't be taking photos like that regardless? You don't know who could hack into your phone, or if it got stolen, where they might end up. It's a very stupid thing to do.'

'I know. I'm sorry.'

Beverley threw back her head. 'All right.' She leaned forward so her hands rested on her thighs, then she straightened up again. 'Okay. Get dressed, quick. And take off that make-up. We have to get going. I need to leave early.'

Amelia hurried back to her vanity table, where she'd thrown her camisole and school shirt.

'No time for breakfast. I'll grab some fruit,' said Beverley, heading for the door. 'And I'll meet you out at the car.'

'Sorry for giving you a fright, Mum.'

Beverley turned back to her daughter, who was attempting a smile. Of course she wasn't sending erotic photographs of herself out into the world at twelve years of age. Had she that little faith in her own parenting skills? These were the kinds of tender moments she never had with Ella any more. She should cherish them.

'And I'm sorry I thought the worst,' she replied, instructing her own face to soften. 'Forgive me?'

Amelia grinned. 'Always.'

'Good.'

Her hand was on the doorknob and she had one foot out in the landing when she heard it. A vibration.

Quick as a flash, she turned.

'Mum—'

But Beverley was back in the room and over at the bed before Amelia had thought to move.

She looked down at the screen.

Her daughter had one new message.

Beverley did not recognise the App logo, but she knew the sender's name. There was no need to unlock the phone. The reply was succinct.

Got it!!! Thanks!!!

For the second time that morning, Beverley emitted noises she had not known she was capable of making.

....

'Are you nervous?' asked Ella, sitting beside him on the edge of the bed as he pulled on his boots.

'About what?'

'Arlo.' She grinned.

'Oh, about Glass Lake!' he replied, bringing his hand to his forehead and generally making a joke of it even though he'd had an uneasy feeling in his stomach ever since he agreed to take on the job at the school. 'It'll be fine.'

'Of course it will.'

'I just have to be on time and do the best work I can.'

She kissed him on the cheek. 'I love you.'

She never seemed to mind that he didn't say it back. Probably because she knew he did love her – of course he did! – it was just that every time he tried to say it his tongue swelled in his mouth and his head got so hot that he thought it might actually go on fire.

'It's just part time, for a couple of weeks,' he said. 'I doubt I'll even see Principal Patterson.' His stomach flip-flopped. He *hoped* he wouldn't see her.

More yelling from the floor below. The only words he could decipher came from Beverley.

'Well, she's lucky to have you working there. You're so good with your hands.'

Arlo blushed, even though Ella hadn't meant it *that* way. Although, he hoped she did mean it that way too. He definitely put in the effort.

'This town, though. Some people can be real jerks.'

'I know.'

'They can be totally unfair and terrible ...' She was trying to make him feel better, but the flip-flopping in his stomach had turned to sloshing. '... and just tiny-minded gossip lickers.'

'Gossip lickers?'

'Or whatever,' she said. 'You know what I mean.'

People had only recently stopped sticking 'For Sale' signs in the Whiteheads' front garden. And two weeks ago, while he was walking down Main Street, a man spat at him. He hadn't told Ella that. He didn't tell her any more than he had to, in case it sowed seeds of doubt. 'Yeah. I know.'

'That's why we're getting out,' she declared, throwing herself back on the bed and pulling him with her. 'One more year. Less than a year. Woody will be finished primary school in June, and then we go. Right?'

35

'Right,' Arlo agreed, pretending to do the maths even though he knew exactly how far away it was. 'Eight months.' *One week and four days*. 'Then it's goodbye Cooney, hello Cork city.'

'We'll rent an apartment, overlooking the river.'

'Or maybe a little house, with two bedrooms,' he said, lying back beside her. 'One for us, and one for Woody when he comes to stay, or Amelia.'

'Amelia can only visit if she promises not to tell Bev our whereabouts.'

'We'll get a little dog ...'

'Called Wisdom,' said Ella.

'Or Cooney.'

'Why would we call our dog Cooney? We want to *forget* Cooney.'

'Okay fine, Wisdom,' said Arlo. 'And we'll grow our own vegetables and we'll have friends over for dinner, and when you come home from university, we'll sit in our garden—'

'Or on our balcony.'

'Right, and we'll be so happy that we'll listen to songs about heartbreak and we won't have a clue what they're going on about.'

Ella laughed. 'And then you'll go to college ...'

'Maybe.'

'Arlo!'

'Maybe I will, or maybe I'll be such a successful handyman by then that I'll have my own business with lots of employees and I won't need college.'

'You're still planning to re-sit your leaving cert next year, right?'

'You're ruining the daydream here, Ella.'

'Have you applied for the re-sits?'

'Daydream disappearing. Daydream disappearing,' he said in an automated voice, moving his arms in a robotic fashion.

'Have you?'

'I will.' He wouldn't.

He pushed himself up, stood on the bed and peered out the skylight. Beverley's Range Rover was still in the driveway.

'Shoes!' Ella swiped at his feet.

'Sorry,' he said, clambering down. 'Isn't your mom usually gone by now?' The only thing that made sneaking into the Franklins' after midnight slightly less of a gamble was that Ella's parents had schedules you could set your watch by. Her dad was always gone before they woke, and her mom left to drop Amelia to school at 8.24. Arlo checked his phone again. 'I need to leave.'

Ella jumped up from the bed and pulled a cardigan from the floor. 'I'll go down and distract her,' she said. 'And when the coast is clear, I'll give the signal and you make a run for it.'

She was grinning now. Ella loved the espionage.

Arlo could do without it.

'Sounds risky,' he said.

She shrugged. The beige knit slid down her left shoulder. How was her skin so perfect? Like silky milk. *Silk milk.* That might actually work as a lyric. 'Let's just wait it out then,' she said, throwing herself back down on the bed, 'and you can be late.'

The mere suggestion brought him out in a sweat.

Arlo groaned. Ella gave a gleeful grin.

'We just need a signal ...' She looked around the room. Her eyes landed on a poster by the door. 'Hang ten!'

'Hang ten?'

'Hang ten,' echoed Ella, gravely this time. 'When you hear me shouting "Hang ten", you make a break for it.'

'How are you going to casually yell "Hang ten" at your mother?' Arlo thought about this and burst out laughing.

'What?' demanded Ella.

'Beverley ... On a surfboard. In her furry jacket thing ... And her face ...' Arlo tried to rearrange his face into the mildly pained expression Ella's mother always wore, but he was laughing too much.

Ella furrowed her brows. Fits of giggles were her thing, not his.

'Ah, yeah,' he gasped, wiping his eyes.

'Okay, chuckles. Keep the bedroom door open, and when you hear me say "Hang ten", go!'

5
· · · · ·

Beverley saw Ella approaching and shifted her expression to indifferent. A crisis with one daughter did not automatically bring the other back into her good books. The eighteen-year-old was wearing her lovely 'Ella & Amelia' necklace and that mangy old T-shirt she always slept in after they had a fight: yet another punishment for Beverley, who regularly ordered expensive matching pyjamas from Anthropologie for the three Franklin women.

'Shouldn't you have left by now?' said Ella, less defiant than usual. Beverley took the tone, and eye contact, in the apologetic manner it was intended. Ella glanced behind her mother: 'You're going to be late for school.'

'Being late is the least of your sister's problems,' said Beverley. 'Do you know what I just caught her doing? Do you?' Beverley hoped that somehow she would know because she honestly wasn't sure how she could put it into words.

'Was she applying make-up with her feet?' said Ella, stepping into the bedroom and closing the door. 'There's literally no space between your lip gloss and your nose, Amelia.'

Why was Ella closing the door? Beverley needed air. She did not need a closed door.

'Amelia, tell her. Tell your sister what you were doing.'

Amelia went to take the phone from the bed.

'Do not touch that, I swear to God!' Beverley picked up the device and flung it across the room. She didn't want to look at it, never mind touch it, ever again. 'And get some make-up remover. Now!'

'Jesus, Amelia, what *did* you do?'

The girl shrugged. 'I took a photo.'

'Of what?' said Ella.

'Of myself.'

'A selfie. Yeah, I think I've heard of them.' Ella kicked her left foot back, so the sole was resting against the still-closed door.

'Open that please, Ella.'

The teenager didn't budge. 'Great to hear you're trying new things, little sister.'

'She took a photo of herself *in the nip*. A sex picture, a whatever you call them ...' The confined space was making Beverley a little breathless. Was this the worst thing that had ever happened to her? No. Of course it wasn't. *Get a grip, woman!* But it was the worst thing since the last time she'd stumbled across a naked photograph. 'Can you open that door? I'm feeling a little light-headed.'

'A dick pic?' suggested Ella.

'Gross!' shrieked Amelia.

'Who was the dick pic for?'

'It's not a dick pic! It's a nude.' Amelia stuck her tongue out at her sister.

A nude. Jesus wept. She made it sound like she'd been posing for an early Renaissance masterpiece.

'A boy at school,' replied Beverley, struggling to accept she was having this conversation. 'A sick little toerag who is going to regret the day he laid eyes on my daughter ... I'm going to see Principal

Patterson this morning and I'll have him expelled before the day is out. Open the door, Ella!'

'So, you're taking dick pics now ...'

'It's not a dick pic because I don't have a dick.'

'If you say so.'

'Mum, tell Ella to stop saying I'm taking dick pics! I don't have a dick!'

'Can you both *please* stop saying dick? Amelia, you're barely twelve. You shouldn't even know what a dick is.'

'I knew what a dick was when I was like eight, Mum.'

Beverley shut her eyes. 'Gah!'

'What?'

'Nothing, just my new internal screensaver.' She needed to get out of this room.

'It's not even a big deal.'

'Not another word, Amelia! Get your bag, get downstairs, and get in the car. We're going to the school. And bring the make-up remover. Sweet mother of God, Ella, if you do not open that door now, I am going to really lose it.'

'I'm doing it, I just ...' Ella opened the door a fraction and started shouting. Then she shut it again.

'What are you doing? What is Hang Ten? I said "open", Ella. Jesus! You're too old to be competing for attention. Amelia – take the bear, come on. Do not touch that phone!'

'But we're allowed—'

'I said leave it. Ella, open the bloody door! Now!' Beverley grabbed her youngest daughter by the arm, walked around her eldest and yanked the bedroom door open.

A faint bang echoed from the hallway below. Beverley might have questioned it if it wasn't for the accompanying, and oh so welcome, cool breeze that it sent gusting up the stairs.

....

'Sweet Jesus!'

Christine opened the bathroom door to find her daughter standing in the threshold.

'Is Porcupine back?'

Maeve had already gone through her mother's wardrobe, seeking suitable clothes for her meeting with the Lakers. She'd found skinny jeans that Christine had forgotten she owned, and which were now cutting off her circulation.

'That's nothing to do with me,' she replied, sticking her fingers into the jeans waistband as she tried to eke out some space. 'You'll have to ask your father.'

Maeve followed her down the stairs. 'He said to ask you.'

'And I'm telling you to ask him.'

'I can't.'

'Why not?' she asked, catching a glimpse of herself in the hallway mirror. She looked like she'd eaten Beverley Franklin.

'Because he already left for work.'

'He *left*?' Christine stuck her head into the sitting room and the study before marching down to the kitchen. No sign of the coward. His surgery did not open until 9.30. Conor never left before her.

'Yes, when you were in the shower. He said it was a dental emergency. So? Is he back?'

'Who?' asked Brian, slurping his cereal.

'Are those Frosties, Brian? You know you're only allowed Frosties at the weekend.'

'No, cornflakes,' said her son, lifting the bowl and necking the evidence.

Her daughter was down on all fours, peering under the table and making *psssh-psssh* sounds.

'Maeve, breakfast, come on.'

'But I don't see him.'

'Who?' asked Brian again.

'Porcupine,' came the voice from under the table. 'He was at a sleepover in Mrs Rodgers' house last night.'

Brian looked sceptical. 'Says who?'

'Mom.'

'I did not. Your father said he was at a sleepover. I never said a thing.'

'Mom, Dad, same difference.' Maeve was opening the back door now. 'Here, Porcupine! Heeeerrrrre, Porcupine!'

'Okay, that's it, time to go.'

'But I didn't have my breakfast.'

'No time. Here' – Christine opened the cupboard and threw two cereal bars at Maeve – 'let's go.'

'I want cereal bars!'

'Do not push me, Brian. I can smell the sugar off your breath from here.'

'But—'

Christine rounded on her daughter. 'Do you want me to be late for the Lakers?'

Maeve shoved the bars into the side of her backpack. 'Come on, Brian, let's go.'

Her youngest child slipped down from the table and they both followed Maeve out of the house to the car.

'He's not at a sleepover, is he?' said Brian, dragging his schoolbag down the path.

'I don't know anything about it. Ask your father.'

She unlocked the car from the front garden and threw a glance down the street, but there was no sign of life from number one Seaview Terrace.

Brian climbed into the back seat beside his sister. 'I'm sorry, Maeve, but Porcupine is dead.'

Christine whipped her head around. 'What?! No, he's not! Brian!'

'He's at a sleepover,' said Maeve, her face doing that involuntary twitch thing again, as she glanced to the front seat for reassurance. She looked tired and Christine wondered if it was worrying about the cat or the musical that had kept her daughter up.

She slowed down as they passed Mrs Rodgers' house, nestled behind a garden of perfectly pruned rose bushes. The cheerful flowers had masked the truth for so long. But no more. She would be getting that cat back, and an apology with it. In another life, one before children and beyond Cooney, Christine had attended demonstrations and sit-ins. Her activism was rusty – the last thing Cooney had protested was a Starbucks opening – but you didn't need to be a member of Amnesty International to know stealing a family pet was wrong.

'When Pablo's gerbil died, his parents told him it had moved to China.'

'Porcupine is not dead, Brian.'

'He's at a sleepover. Both Dad *and* Mom say it,' said Maeve. 'Right, Mom?'

Christine turned left onto Reilly's Pass, towards Franklin Avenue, though she had a good mind to swing by the dental surgery instead. 'Right,' she said through gritted teeth.

44

Gerry Regan, the town pharmacist, was stopped at the lights. He was dressed in full Lycra, lit like a scrawny Christmas tree and yelling up at the driver of an oil tanker. Articulated trucks were not allowed on this stretch. Local opposition had intensified since the crash last February, even though that had involved a single car.

Christine honked her horn and raised a fist towards Gerry in solidarity. (There was life in the old activist yet.) But now the carriage door was opening, and the driver was climbing down.

Brian twisted to catch a glimpse of the action as they sped on.

'A sleepover,' repeated Maeve, confirming the story to herself.

'Yes, Maeve, and one day we'll all be at that sleepover,' said Brian, placing a soft hand on his sister's knee. 'A big sleepover in the sky.'

....

Arlo had parked the van the next street over. He did this in case Ella's parents spotted it and started asking questions. After his dad went to jail, his mom wanted to sell the thing, and all the tools with it. But Arlo had been helping out since he was thirteen; he was well able to take over the handyman trade, or at least keep it going until his dad got out.

At the end of the road, he turned back and could just about make out Beverley Franklin bursting through her front door with Amelia trailing in her wake. He'd heard them talking as he skipped past the bedroom but hadn't hung around to get the details. Whatever it was about, he felt bad for Amelia. Arlo liked Ella's little sister. She knew about him and Ella but hadn't said a word. In exchange, she'd told him she fancied his little brother Woody and he'd promised not to say anything either.

45

Woody was the reason Arlo was still in Cooney. He'd have moved to Cork city the day Ella started university there, but his dad had made him promise one thing: to look after his mother and twelve-year-old brother. He couldn't say he was doing a great job of it, but Woody's entry into the moody teenage phase a year early was hardly his fault. Woody would be done at Glass Lake in June and heading to secondary school two towns over, where he might have a chance to be more than the son of a convicted killer.

Cooney didn't care that Woody was only a kid or that he'd had no say in what his dad had done or drunk or driven. People used to remark on how good-looking and fun Charlie Whitehead was and how he'd cut them a deal or done some extra job for free. Now they came up to his sons on the street and said their dad was a drunk and a chancer who had an eye for the women.

Arlo crossed the road towards his van. The path was carpeted in leaves and a woman was striding towards him, led by a cute dog in a fluorescent pink jacket. The woman swung her hips as she walked, and the dog waggled its butt, so that they kept perfect time.

Everyone hated Charlie Whitehead for what he'd done to Mike and Leo and their families, but also for what he'd done to the town. Cooney was supposed to be the home of Tidy Town wins and blue flag beaches, not a drunk driver who'd killed one teenager and left another in a wheelchair.

He smiled at the dog as it drew nearer, then up at the woman. She wore a sweatband around her head. It was an identical shade of pink to her dog's jacket.

'Shame on you.'

The woman was still in transit and Arlo didn't register what she'd said until she had passed.

He inhaled sharply and turned back, but she bustled on, hips picking up speed. Did she think he was going to run after her? Tackle her to the ground and demand she take it back?

It happened all the time, but it still knocked the wind out of him. He took three deep breaths, then opened the door of his van and climbed in.

He still had work to do, that was all. He just had to try harder.

He put his key in the ignition and tuned in the old stereo. He turned up the volume. Then he turned it up more.

Aren't you going to talk to me?

Can't. I need to keep my head in the game.

Pity you didn't do that the night my life was destroyed.

I'm sorry, Leo.

Or Mike's life. Do you spend enough time thinking about Mike's life? Do you spend enough time missing him?

I'm sorry. I'm really sorry, all right?

Not really, Arly, no. But I suppose it'll have to do.

Christine was at the top of the queue, jabbing around in her bag, when she was struck by an image of her Keep Cup relaxing on the top drawer of the dishwasher. She'd meant to pack it while Maeve was having breakfast.

Feck.

Her eyes flickered to the stack of disposable cups already decorated in cheery Christmas imagery.

The barista smiled, waiting.

'I don't suppose your cups are compostable, are they?'

'I'm actually not sure,' he replied with an enthusiasm usually reserved for helpful answers.

Their deep red background and delicate snow scenes were so inviting, not to mention how much better the proportions were for retaining heat than the Strand café's vast ceramic mugs. But Maeve had recently informed her that a disposable cup took five hundred years to biodegrade. Christine had been outwardly horrified and quietly guilty. (Ice caps melting! Polar bears dying! All so she could keep her coffee warmer a little longer.) That was when she'd bought the Keep Cup.

She sighed, grabbing a two-pack of waffle biscuits from in front of the register. 'I'll take a mug,' she told the barista stoically.

She paid and moved to the end of the counter to wait on her flat white. Beth Morton, who taught at a boys' secondary school two towns over, was already waiting. Christine lifted a hand to greet the petite woman. Beth had three sons in Glass Lake, one of whom was in Maeve's class.

'What do you think of Lorna Farrell's hairband?' asked Beth as Christine stood in beside her. 'Too much, or just enough?'

She followed her gaze to the corner alcove where a gossip of women was huddled around three tables scattered with cups and phones and car keys. Christine had been in school with half of them. The difference was she'd left; she'd lived in other places, had other experiences, and while she had ultimately ended up back in Cooney, she did not consider it to be the centre of the universe. It wasn't even the centre of West Cork.

'I've never been able to wear them,' said Christine, watching Lorna's head dip towards her notebook, the emerald stones of her hair accessory catching the harsh café light. 'They always end up going more headband than hairband on me.'

'Same,' said Beth, taking her coffee (served in a lovely, cheery Christmas cup). 'Last time I wore one, my husband said I reminded him of Axl Rose.' She took a sip and licked her lips. 'What are you in for?'

'School musical. You?'

'Same. Feck it, anyway. I knew I should have come last week. Maeve's not after lighting, is she?'

'No. Costumes.'

'Well, that's something, I suppose.'

'Flat white for here!'

Christine took her mug, which was more like a bowl – did the surface area really need to be *so* wide? – and added two sugars.

'I'm just glad Ethan doesn't want to be in the thing. Zero stage presence, that lad. He's the only one of my boys I ever left at the supermarket. There has to be less competition for the backstage roles, right?'

'You'd imagine. And it's a school play; there's got to be something for everyone.'

'In a perfect world, sure. But we're not in a perfect world. We're in Glass Lake,' said Beth, taking Christine's discarded sugar sachets and throwing them in the bin. 'At least you're one of them. Oh, don't give me that look, Christine. You know what I mean. You went to the school. I'm not even from Cork.'

'Well, I don't think I'm in the Lakers' good books either. Lorna has been thick with me since an argument in the playground last year. She refused to let Brian on the other swing because Annabelle's imaginary friend was using it.'

'I'm supposed to be in double geography right now. I told them the boiler burst.' Beth blew air through her lips as she shook out her shoulders. 'Christ on a bike. I feel like *I'm* the one auditioning. Why do we do this to ourselves?'

'I have no idea,' replied Christine, who should have been at her desk, working on an article about cuts to West Cork's bus service. She didn't know what she was going to do when she got back to the office after meeting her 'source' and had no juicy information to relay.

'There are other schools.'

'Absolutely,' agreed Christine, though they both knew that if you lived in West Cork and didn't at least try to get your kid into Glass Lake you were basically negligent.

There was a child in Brian's class who travelled out from Cork city every day. He only got into Glass Lake because his mother took a job as a special needs assistant. Halfway through his first year, she quit, and they couldn't very well kick him out. Heaps of parents gave grandparents' and third-cousins-once-removed's addresses as their own to secure places. Christine didn't feel wonderful about sending her children to such a privileged school, but they lived in Cooney, and she was a past pupil. This, combined with the baptisms, which *she* had no problem with, had made her lot a shoo-in. She wasn't about to send them further away just to prove her egalitarian credentials.

Beth took a deep breath. 'Right, come on. Before your coffee goes cold. You know if you get it in a takeaway cup, it stays warmer longer?'

When they reached the group, Claire Keating was holding court. Claire was well known in Cooney for having three sets of twins. If the Keatings so much as went to the supermarket together, a photo would appear in the *Southern Gazette*'s social pages.

Lorna Farrell was to Claire's left, taking notes in a Glass Lake copybook. She was dressed in a Lakers '92 hoodie (which she'd clearly had made as the school didn't sell merchandise) and bejewelled hairband. In front of her sat a flapjack cut into tiny chunks. Fiona Murphy was slouched on another chair, texting on a phone held up so the Little Miss Fiona case covered half her face. She had multiple bracelets dangling from her wrists and her fingers were covered in delicate gold rings.

Christine and Beth took the two available chairs.

'I would have backed you up in the WhatsApp group, but you know how difficult it is to say anything there any more,' Claire was saying to a vaguely familiar woman with an auburn bob. 'God forbid you question one thing about your child's education, without everyone accusing you of undermining the teacher. Which obviously you weren't doing.'

Christine placed her coffee on the nearest table. It was the only ceramic mug. She should have just got a festive cup. She wasn't going to save the ice caps single-handedly.

'Obviously not,' said Auburn Bob. 'I *want* Ben to learn about climate change. I just don't think they should be using the parents' literal cars as examples of the worst offenders. He point-blank refused to get in his booster seat last Friday. He wanted to get the bus.'

'Rosie's started going through our bin and taking out everything we forgot to recycle,' said another mother.

'I told Ben the bus also ran on petrol and he called me a climate change denier.'

'I've got three kids, two pets, and a mother-in-law who asked to move into our house but is actually residing up my arse,' said the other woman. 'I'm *sorry* if I don't always have time to rinse out every yoghurt pot.'

'It's not good for their mental health,' added Auburn Bob. 'Climate anxiety. Right? Isn't that a thing?'

'I've never liked how they teach climate change at that school,' said Claire, drawing air quotes around the words 'climate change'. Claire had some questionable views, which she liked to share on WhatsApp and Facebook, but Christine kept shtum. Her plan was to say nothing until the musical came up. It was best to go softly-softly with the Lakers. They took this whole thing very seriously. 'Lorna?'

'Yep, got it.' Lorna tapped the notebook with her pen. 'Have a word with Principal Patterson. See if we can't get the third-class climate change module toned down.'

'Great. Thank you. And welcome to our latecomers. Christine ...'

Christine dutifully returned the finger waggle.

'... and excuse me, I don't know your name ...'

'Beth. Beth Morton. My son Ethan is in sixth-class. He was hoping to work on the musical this year.'

'Whoa!' Claire whipped her head back as though Beth had just gone to throw her Americano at her. 'Jump right in there, why don't you? That's fine.' She exchanged a look with a few of the others that suggested it was not at all fine. 'I'm afraid, Beth, we can't discuss the musical until Beverley gets here. She's our director.'

'I could actually give everyone an update on the musical,' said Lorna, whose full schoolyard name had been Lorna Lick-Arse Farrell. Christine had a feeling she'd started that moniker. 'I'm across that with Beverley.'

'That would be great,' enthused Beth.

'No,' said Claire, holding a hand up to Beth and, by extension, Christine. 'We're waiting for Beverley. Now. What else is there?'

'The Halloween party,' said Lorna, recovering quickly. 'And actually, sorry, can I just check? Did anyone have an issue with the sixth-class knitting assignment? Anyone think it was a lot to ask of the kids, or too much pressure, or ...?'

'I thought it was great,' said Fiona Murphy, using the straw from her iced water to pull at her lips. 'Made me think the new teacher might be worthwhile, and not just as something to look at.'

A few of the others nodded and Lorna made a show of crossing something out. 'No issues. Roger that.'

'Right. Halloween. Talk to me,' said Claire. 'Where are we on decorations?'

The Lakers debated whether the proposed skeletons were *too* scary and if safety scissors would suffice for cutting through pumpkins. Lorna was experimenting with 'organic' papier-mâché cauldrons and would let them know how she got on. Then they discussed hiring a photographer for the Glass Lake first holy communions next May, and Claire passed around ring binders containing sample shots. Christine was tempted to ask what was wrong with Seamus McGrath, the school caretaker and general factotum who took the official class photos every year free of charge. Although she suspected the free bit was the problem. She caught sight of the 'pricing structures' in one of the ring binders and realised these women were willing to pay more for photos than she was for a car.

These were the times when she couldn't quite believe she'd ended up in the exact place where she'd begun. Sometimes, when she was quick-fire buttering bread and flinging it into moaning mouths, she wanted to turn to her children and say: 'You've no idea! Mammy once lived in a squat and wrote for the *NME* and slept with a member of Suede!' It had only been three articles, and he was actually the band's sound engineer, but the squat bit was entirely true. A squat! She doubted if any of these women had even been camping.

Someone got a text from Beverley saying she was running late. Beth made a tutting noise and when Claire's eyes darted in their direction, Christine made sure to turn her attention to Beth too. No need to be taken down with her.

She took another mouthful of coffee and grimaced. It was stone cold.

'I'm going up for a refill. Anyone want anything?' she asked, pretending not to see the daggers thrown by the mother who'd been in the middle of bad-mouthing another part of the curriculum. 'No? Okay.'

She joined the queue behind Butcher Murphy, who ran the butchers below the *Southern Gazette*'s office and was an unlikely candidate for a takeaway coffee. Butcher had a head like a ham and even though Christine had known him since childhood, she couldn't remember if it had always been like that or if it was a career version of how owners start to resemble their pets. His real name was Simon, but nobody called him that.

'Well, if it isn't the vegetarian,' said Butcher, who called her this because three years ago she'd asked if he ever stocked fish. 'Ordering a double shot of salmon, is it?'

'Just a regular, old-fashioned Americano. Presume you're getting a soya chai tea?'

'*Heee*-yah,' he scoffed. 'Three euro for some dirty water? They saw youse coming anyway.'

'Next!'

Christine waited but Butcher didn't step up to order.

'Next!' called the barista again.

'She'll have an old-fashioned Americano,' said Butcher, swapping places with Christine.

'In a takeaway cup,' she added. She'd forgo the avocados next time she did a shop. 'Aren't you ordering anything?'

'I'm just here to keep an eye on things,' he said, peering over her shoulder towards the Lakers.

'Ah.' She understood the situation now. Butcher and Fiona Murphy had separated a couple of years ago and, even if you went on the mildest of local rumours, he had not taken the split well. Fiona had swiftly started dating again and relished letting everyone, including her ex-husband, know. She'd cornered Christine at the Easter fundraiser to ask if the *Southern Gazette* would be interested in a column about modern dating. Christine had pretended her raffle number was being called and excused herself in the direction of the stage.

'What do youse be talking about at these yokes?'

'I'm not the best person to ask. I'm not a regular.'

'Clothes, is it? And men?'

'I think it's mainly about the kids ...'

'*Heee*-yah. Sex, I suppose,' he added, suddenly forlorn. Sixty to nought in no time at all.

'I better get back, Butcher. Look after yourself.'

He gave her the Cooney nod – sharp, fast, diagonal – and shuffled behind the next queuing customer. She returned to the Lakers just in time to hear that Beverley would now not be making the meeting at all.

'She just texted. Some sort of emergency,' declared Lorna, holding her phone aloft.

Bloody wonderful. Would she have to come again next week? How would she swing that? There were only so many 'sources' Cooney could realistically have to offer. And wouldn't it be too late? The musical was in a fortnight.

But then Lorna removed a second copybook from her handbag and started brandishing it about. 'I can fill everyone in on the musical,' she said loudly, the café light bouncing from her hairband to the crisp white pages and back up to her taut forehead. 'I've been across the show, in a sort of producer capacity.'

Claire waved a hand in her direction as if to say, 'Continue'.

'That's great because my daughter Maeve—'

But Lorna ploughed on. 'We've actually had some really exciting news. Like, really exciting.' She looked around the group, slowly nodding her head. 'This year's musical ... is going to be on TV!' Lorna gave herself a gleeful round of applause. 'We submitted the script to RTÉ and it has been accepted. They're going to film *several* segments for *The Big Children's Talent Show*.'

Other mothers were clapping now. Even Christine was impressed. *The Big Children's Talent Show* might be the only thing her kids watched on telly that was actually made for telly.

Everyone was talking at once and several women were making the case for why their child should be in the show. She heard Auburn Bob reminding Lorna how she'd canvassed for her husband Bill's councillor bid, while Beth was frantically offering the woman the use of their holiday home if she ever fancied a trip to Tuscany.

'People, people! The leads have all been cast. We only have smaller roles left to fill.'

'Lorna!' shouted Christine, hoping the woman had never figured out where the Lick-Arse nickname came from. She pulled her chair in towards Lorna, who was basking in the scramble for her attention. 'Can you give Maeve a job on costumes, please? She really wants to be involved.'

'I see she registered her interest with Mr Cafferty, all right,' said Lorna, glancing down at her notebook. 'Has she any experience?'

'She's eleven. So, no.'

'Well, Shona Martin's already down to do costumes and her mother's a buyer for Brown Thomas so ...' The woman shrugged apologetically.

'Oh, come on, Lorna. Two people can work on costumes. Isn't it the taking part that counts? It's a children's play.'

'A children's play that's going to be on national television,' she corrected. 'I'm sorry, Christine, but I don't think we can fit her in. We do have an opening if she wants to sell raffle tickets at the interval ...'

Auburn Bob was pulling her chair into the circle now, blocking off Christine and nearly stomping on her foot. 'How much are they going to film, Lorna? Will they be talking to parents, or just the children?'

'Lorna?' Claire interjected from across the circle. 'Max and Geoff are down to play Munchkins, yes? I know they're selecting a few extras from fifth class. I'm not sure if Beverley confirmed that.'

'I have their names here, Claire. No problem at all.'

Another woman arrived into the middle of the circle in what was turning into a rather aggressive game of bumpers.

Christine stood, so she could be seen in the growing bottleneck, but she was knocked off balance by Auburn Bob. Then her mobile started to ring. Christine stepped out of the scrum, her left leg almost getting caught between two seated women hopping into the centre.

'Derek, hi,' she said before her boss could get a word in. 'I know I'm running a bit late, but my source has some good information. I'm hopeful I can get a decent story out of it.' She could find her way out of this white lie later. The more pressing issue was that Lorna was scribbling down names, and Maeve's was not among them.

'Drop it,' came the thick Dublin croak. Derek had swapped his sixty-a-day habit for thirty-a-day as part of his post-heart-attack life overhaul, but his vocal cords were fried long ago.

'Sorry?' Christine swapped the phone to her far ear and edged back towards the Lakers. She had to get back in there.

'Drop whatever it is you're doing,' barked her editor. 'I've got a scoop, Christine. I'm talking front-page material, and I want you on it right away.'

....

Garda Joey Delaney

How would you describe the atmosphere at the school yesterday evening?

Claire Keating, parent

I fail to see what that has got to do with a beloved member of our community being found dead in a river.

Delaney

For now, everything is relevant.

Keating

Bustling. Everyone was busy. Some were busy-bodying, but one way or another, we all had something to do. I, personally, was proofreading the programme notes.

Delaney

A few people have mentioned that tensions were high.

Keating

This was going to be on national television. So yes, tensions were high. I wouldn't read

anything into that, though. It's Glass Lake.
Tensions are always high.

Delaney

I heard some parents were annoyed.

Keating

There was a lot to be annoyed about. I'm sure
you read the newspaper reports – they didn't
help either. But really, it was down to how
the school handled things. You live here long
enough, and you quickly learn: do not piss off
the parents. The Cooney Welcoming Party is only
ever one slow day away from becoming the Cooney
Vigilante Party. And the photos, well, they
pissed a lot of people off.

Beverley's husband hadn't had an affair. He'd said that when she found the photos, and she'd been repeating it to herself ever since. He'd handed her his phone so she could see the Audi he was planning to purchase, only her thumb slipped and she scrolled back too far. There were dozens of them: crude, unprofessional shots with terrible lighting and awkward angles. Beverley couldn't understand how he found them arousing.

'I never slept with her. It was only pics.'

Pics.

She'd never heard him utter that word before in his life.

Beverley had taken it in her stride, mainly. She wasn't naïve; she knew men would be men. When she had the space to think about it rationally, she was able to feel sorry for him – which was a lot easier than feeling sorry for herself. The idea of Malachy standing naked somewhere – their bedroom? The bathroom? His *office*? – as he pointed the phone at his naked body was deeply pathetic. And saying 'pics' was almost as childish as taking them. He was nearly forty-one, for God's sake.

Beverley came to a stop at the traffic lights beside the empty shop unit where a Starbucks had been for all of five minutes. The Keep Cooney Independent committee had formed a picket line and the multinational had slunk back to the city where it belonged. Lorna Farrell's husband Bill was a recently elected councillor (something she didn't let anyone forget) and he said an interiors studio specialising in louvre shutters was going in there now. Which was much more in keeping.

In the rear-view mirror, she watched her daughter rub at the last of the blue eyeshadow. A small mound of used cotton pads sat on her knee.

The light turned green, and Amelia looked up as Beverley returned her attention to the road. They hadn't spoken since they'd left the house.

They drove on past the newsagents and Regan's Chemist. Mrs Rodgers, who Beverley knew from the Tidy Towns committee, was heading into the pharmacy. She checked the mirror as the older woman disappeared inside, but it was hard to get an idea of what might be wrong with her. She hoped it was nothing serious. Mrs Rodgers had the most fabulous red roses; last year's judges' report had, quite rightly, singled them out.

She turned the car on to Franklin Avenue. Beverley was eight when she found out the meandering road that led from Main Street up to Glass Lake was named after Malachy's family. She'd immediately set about gathering intelligence on the boy in the year above. She learned that the long navy car that collected him every afternoon was driven by an employee and that his mother sat in the back seat, pushing the door open for him, but never getting out. She heard that at his tenth birthday party, the same driver was sent into Cork city to collect McDonald's and bring it back to Cooney, and that a woman who was not his mother had opened the door to the guests. As far as Malachy was concerned, Beverley knew nothing of him until they met at a local disco when they were sixteen. Even though she could have handed in a dossier by then.

Malachy had accompanied her to last year's Southern Pharmaceuticals Christmas party. This was before she'd quit that multinational cesspit and made a career pivot into health food entrepreneurship. (She had not been fired. She had *quit*. And she could not be happier about it.) Malachy had been in a foul mood until Benny from advertising asked if he'd ever considered modelling.

Her husband had laughed self-deprecatingly and blamed the Yuletide Slammers Benny was knocking back. 'I'm forty this month,' he'd said, patting his non-existent belly. 'I think I'll leave the acting to my wife.'

'Do you act, Beverley?' Tamara from development had asked, dragging her gaze away from Malachy's chest.

'I used to. A long time ago.'

In Cooney, Beverley's acting career was fundamental to her identity. She was the most famous person her friends knew, and she wasn't even famous. But she'd never mentioned it at work. Those people made fun of soaps.

'She was in *Cork Life*,' Malachy supplied. 'And she was phenomenal.' He was always so generous when his ego had been sated.

Beverley had looked at him and seen what the others saw. Sparkling blue eyes, a weather-beaten ruggedness, and thick sandy hair carefully cut so it always flopped to the left. Nobody could tell he'd had a small area transplanted from the back of his head. He looked like he might work on a yacht, but also like he could own a yacht – so that no matter what kind of man you were attracted to, you were always attracted to Malachy.

Tamara from development had mouthed *Wow* at Beverley and a slightly drunk woman from research shouted: 'The slutty babysitter! I knew I recognised you!'

'Not slutty. Sexy,' Malachy corrected, looking at Beverley in a way that said nothing – not even Tamara's ample cleavage and too tight dress – could compete.

That night, they'd stayed in a hotel in the city and made love on the bed, by the window, in the bathroom. Beverley's thighs throbbed and her heart soared. She'd instigated positions she wasn't aware could be done, let alone by her, and almost a year later, even while on a mission to defend her daughter's welfare, the memory still made her blush.

About ninety metres from Glass Lake, traffic ground to a halt. The Lakers had run a campaign to encourage parents to drop their kids off farther away from the school gates. It made little difference. Twice, she'd caught Fiona Murphy *parking* in the middle of the road, while she got Ciara out of the vehicle. What did they expect if they didn't lead by example?

The other Lakers didn't have the same loyalty to the school that Beverley had. Enrolling her at Glass Lake was the one great thing her parents had done for her – and even then, it was only because her mother had got a job in Cooney and the school was on the way. So much of her parents' lives had been about getting by and not drawing attention, that there was no space for big dreams. Her acting ambitions were never taken seriously. But Glass Lake had opened her eyes to a better world. Learning about the Franklins had given her a defined goal, yes, but one way or another she'd been working towards this life since she was five.

Of course, her own mother's life now was unrecognisable from the one she'd led when Beverley was small. As soon as Beverley's youngest sibling had finished school, her mother had left her father and their West Cork home for a retreat in India. Having endured years of her husband deriding her appearance, specifically her weight, Beverley had assumed it was a boot camp – sort of Eat, Pray, Love without the Eat – but no. It had been a hippy sex retreat. Now her mother, who lived in Dublin and was sixty-six *today*, could talk of little else, and Beverley was embarrassed by her in a whole new way.

She had made the mistake of confiding in her mother about Malachy's 'pics'. That evening she'd received a one-line email – Take the time to heal your relationship with yourself. Mam x – and a link to female-friendly porn. (Her mother. Sixty-six! Was *nobody* capable of acting their age?)

It was 9 a.m. Amelia was now officially late for school, which meant everyone ahead of them was late too. At least Beverley had a valid excuse. She blasted the horn.

'Mum!'

The car in front pulled into the right and she swerved around it, manoeuvring off Franklin Avenue and on to the short driveway that led up to Glass Lake.

When she read articles about the ubiquity of porn, she found herself wondering who all these viewers were. If it really was as prevalent as they said, then she must know a few of them. They couldn't *all* be in Dublin. She tried to imagine if her friends might be among the masses.

Claire Keating lived a heavily timetabled life. Three sets of twins was surprising, generally, but not given Claire's efficiency. Why do something six times when you could get the job done in half that? It was unlikely she saw sex as a leisure activity, and she certainly wouldn't make time for anything as discretionary as watching *other people* have sex. Lorna Farrell was far too won't-someone-think-of-the-children to be condoning smut. She couldn't even bring herself to use the correct terminology for genitalia. She had recently sent a message to the WhatsApp group seeking a recommendation for a 'good front bum doctor'. The only Laker who seemed a likely candidate was Fiona Murphy. Even if Fiona wasn't watching porn, she'd be delighted to know someone thought she was.

Beverley had never seen any. The idea made her sad. All those people who'd started out dreaming of Academy Awards and luscious costumes and ended up with harsh lighting and polyester nurses' outfits. Journalists wrote about it as if it was a foregone conclusion that the next generation – Amelia's generation – would be reared on the stuff. But that kind of thinking was what was wrong with parents. You had to fight for what you wanted. Nothing good in life was just handed to you. Even the most blissful moments of Beverley's life, when the midwife placed her daughters on to her chest, had been preceded by hours (days in Ella's case) of horrific pain. Being wealthy meant, as she'd known it would, that there was less resistance – but you still had to fight.

She pulled into a staff parking space, right by the entrance. She popped a Rennie out of its blister pack, threw the carton back on the passenger seat, and undid her seatbelt.

'Out. Now,' she said.

When it came to her daughters, Beverley was prepared to kick and scream.

....

Principal Nuala Patterson's only child refused to speak to her. Her only husband had left her, and her only working ovary had finally ceased production, resulting in night sweats and insomnia. Yet nothing, but nothing, made Nuala as weary as arriving into work to find a note on her desk saying Beverley Franklin had phoned ahead and was on her way in.

Given the Franklins' affluence, Nuala would argue that when Beverley lost her job at Southern Pharmaceuticals earlier in the year (the school grapevine said she'd been fired), it was actually her, as principal of Glass Lake, who had suffered the most. Before, it was phone calls; now Beverley came to see her every time she had an issue with Amelia's test results or one of Seamus McGrath's set designs.

Nuala dropped her bags on to her desk. She pulled out her heels, sat in her swivel chair and undid her runners. 'Did Beverley mention what time she'd be in?' she shouted through her open door.

'Didn't say,' replied Mairead. The school secretary appeared at the office threshold, eating a particularly milky bowl of cereal. 'But it sounded like she was phoning from the car.'

Nuala hooked her shoe strap at the last hole. (Dr Flynn was amazed by how she'd managed to experience almost every possible side effect of the menopause, from thinning hair right down to swollen ankles. Nuala was not surprised. It was the cherry on top of the worst year of her life.) 'How did she sound?'

Mairead raised an eyebrow. 'How does Beverley Franklin ever sound?'

When Nuala first came to Glass Lake – as a teacher, straight out of university, at the age of twenty-two – Beverley had been in second class. Nuala hadn't taught her, but she remembered the happy, pretty, not particularly well-off child. Now Beverley was one of the wealthiest women in Cooney and while still objectively attractive (the grapevine reported she went to Dublin to get her work done), her face settled in a faintly pained expression, as if she'd constantly just bitten her tongue.

'What else have we got on today?'

'The social worker is calling at around eleven; we still need to sort out those forms to hire two more SNAs; and Claire Keating has an appointment to see you this afternoon. It's about the sixth-class history curriculum; specifically, Edward Jenner.'

'The smallpox guy?'

Mairead raised an eyebrow. 'Claire has an issue with how the textbook describes his invention of the vaccine. She says it lacks balance.'

'There is no balance. It's facts.'

'Not according to Claire. According to Claire, it's big pharma propaganda.'

They were only seven weeks into the school year and already the parents, who had always been the hardest part of her job, were surpassing themselves. But then, everybody and everything was more irritating than it used to be. Nuala couldn't seem to pass a car without the driver texting on their phone, and every café she went into was packed with diners watching videos and listening to music without a set of earphones between them. Maybe it was the menopause or maybe it was her family skedaddling off to the other side of the country, but every now and again she feared she would have to stop leaving the house, lest she go on a murderous rampage.

And then, just as quickly as the rage came on her, the apathy took over.

Nuala sighed.

The first school bell had yet to ring and she could easily have taken to the bed.

'Ten minutes with Beverley then you knock on that door, okay? Any excuse will do. Someone's got a pigtail caught in a pencil sharpener, the Minister for Education's on the phone. Whatever. Just get her out of here.'

....

Beverley was out of the Range Rover and pointing the fob at it when she noticed the white van parked two spaces down from her. The older Whitehead boy – Argo? Anglo? Some made-up name like that – was unlocking the back of it.

'I don't believe it.'

'Mum,' pleaded Amelia, quickening her step to keep up. 'Please! Don't embarrass me.'

The older Whitehead boy was the one who'd been in the car when his drunken father got behind the wheel and killed Mike Roche Junior, not to mention leaving another minor disabled. He'd been in Ella's year, they all had, which meant he'd graduated in the summer. Why he was still in Cooney was beyond her. And what was he doing in Glass Lake, of all places? Clearly none of the Whiteheads had an ounce of shame.

'These parking spaces are for staff only,' she snapped. 'You've absolutely no right to park here.'

'But, Mum, you're not—'

Beverley yanked her daughter in closer, cutting her off. The boy continued to stand there, mouth open like a dead fish.

'Well? Have you anything to say for yourself?'

69

'I'm ...'

Beverley put her free hand on her hip. Charlie Whitehead's sons might have got his looks but neither had inherited his gift of the gab.

'I'm working here,' he said eventually.

Beverley guffawed. 'At Glass Lake? I doubt that very much.'

'Honestly, Mrs Franklin, I am.'

'You're telling me Nuala Patterson hired you? That's a barefaced lie and you know it.'

'Seamus McGrath hired me. I'm helping him out for a few days.'

'Seamus?' she echoed. The lad nodded dumbly. Yet another bone to pick with the school caretaker. Was a Yellow Brick Road really too much to ask for? Not bronze, not gold – yellow. She was asking the caretaker for a basic colour, not a utopian impossibility.

She peered into the van and saw a ladder and some buckets. The Whiteheads' vehicle had been spotted on the road over from theirs a couple of times recently and when Beverley found out which of her neighbours was throwing work his way, she'd be making a swift cut to the Franklins' Christmas card list.

'You ...' she said, steadying herself. He began to wither under her stare. '... and your *whole* family ...'

'Mum,' whined Amelia, tugging at her hand, '*please*.'

A scourge, that's what the Whiteheads were. Beverley had graciously cast Woody in the school musical, and how had he repaid her? By exploiting her daughter, that was how. She could have swung for his brother. But Beverley did not do out of control. She did poised and enviable. This morning had been a blip. She did not enjoy feeling so feral.

Without another word, she yanked her daughter towards the heavy double doors that led to Glass Lake's foyer.

8
·····

Mrs Rodgers pretended she didn't see the three people standing in line and walked straight up to the counter of Regan's Chemist. She slumped her shoulders as she did so, to remind the other customers that she was old. She didn't have as much time left for queuing as they did.

Gerry Regan looked from her to the small line and hesitated. She flashed her dodderiest smile, the one that exposed the upper right-hand side of her mouth, where she was missing a tooth. The other customers – who were all young and distracted by the phones in their hands – weren't going to make a fuss, so neither was he.

'Good afternoon, Mr Regan.' The bruise on his face was at the early stages but there was no pretending she couldn't see it. She allowed her smile to crumple into deep concern. She would permit two minutes for this exchange. 'Oh no, Mr Regan. What has happened to your eye?'

'Altercation with a lorry driver this morning, I'm afraid,' he said, bringing his hand up to what promised to be a significant shiner. 'I made some polite enquiries into the weight of his vehicle and whether it was permitted to be on Reilly's Pass, which of course it was not, and he swung for me.'

'That's shocking. You poor creature. Did you get his licence plate number?'

'I did. I was reciting it to myself, to ensure I remembered, when he hit me. I was on the bike, you see, no room for pen and paper in my cycling gear.'

'Well, of course,' said Mrs Rodgers, who had seen the pharmacist's cycling gear. There wasn't room for imagination, never mind a notebook.

'If he thinks I have concussion, he can think again. I've already phoned it in. And I've started a petition.' Mr Regan pushed the clipboard towards her. To live in Cooney was to be forever signing petitions.

Mrs Rodgers didn't like leaving Albert alone while he was still settling in. (She'd renamed the cat Albert, without any fuss. He was a clever so-and-so. He knew as well as anyone that Porcupine was a ridiculous name. The Maguires wouldn't have called their children Porcupine, and yet they wouldn't show a pet the same courtesy.) 'What is the world coming to, eh?' she said, scribbling her signature as illegibly as possible. 'Now, if you could lend me some assistance: I am looking to purchase hair dye.'

Mr Regan glanced at her white mane, which had never been dyed a day in its life. 'I see. Well, the hair colour is just here ...' He accompanied her to a small display with preposterously young women on the boxes. (Why would they need to dye their hair?) 'I'm afraid it's not my expertise.' He dipped his head slightly, acknowledging the loss of his own hair at a cruelly young age. 'But we have a few different shades and brands. What colour were you thinking?' He picked up a couple of boxes and read out the labels. 'Ashen blonde, maybe? Sandy brown?'

'Black.'

He paused. 'Black.'

Mrs Rodgers nodded. She removed a box from the shelf and scanned the back of it. 'Midnight Blackout. This will do. I'll take this one.'

'Are you sure?'

'I am.'

'All right ...' Mr Regan took the box and scanned it through. She caught him glancing at her crown again, no doubt trying to picture her with the hair of a moody, misunderstood teenager. She didn't have the time, or inclination, to explain. She'd told Albert she would be back for *The Chase*. When he used to visit her on weekday afternoons, that had been their show. He'd purred when she read out the TV listings this morning, so she wasn't about to let him down.

She handed over the money and waited for Mr Regan to bag the dye. He was very good at putting things in bags, slipping them in with sleight of hand and utmost discretion. She supposed that was an inevitable result of years spent selling piles suppositories and condom lubrication.

9
· · · · ·

'Mrs Franklin,' said Principal Patterson, rising from her desk, 'nice to see you. Again.'

Beverley pretended not to see the school secretary mouthing 'Good luck' as she quietly pulled the door behind her. She knew Nuala Patterson didn't like her, that she conveniently forgot about the thousands of euro Beverley fundraised every year and thought of her only as a nuisance and silly for being so invested in the goings-on of the school. No doubt she was counting down the days until Amelia graduated in June. *Both Franklin daughters finally gone!* But if she thought Beverley would let Glass Lake go to the dogs once she no longer had skin in the game, she needed to get out her dictionary and look up exactly what community was all about.

'I'm not here on pleasant business,' she said, pulling out the chair on the opposite side of the principal's desk.

'No,' agreed Nuala, retaking her own seat. 'What can I do for you?'

'I need you to expel Woody Whitehead.'

There was a faint sound of the principal sucking in air.

'This morning I went into Amelia's bedroom to call her for school ...' Beverley broke off. She produced a water bottle from her bag and took a swig. It turned out she didn't need to close her eyes

74

to get a picture-perfect memory of her naked daughter. 'I went in to call Amelia for school, and I found her taking a photograph of herself. Naked. She was taking a naked photograph of herself.'

Nuala's eyes widened ever so slightly. 'Right.'

'Not just a naked photo but a – a sexual photo. It was explicit. And she was sending it to Woody Whitehead.'

'I see.'

No, Principal Patterson, you did not see. Trust me.

'That can't have been easy.'

'No. It wasn't,' replied Beverley matter-of-factly. She did not want sympathy, she wanted action. 'That boy, that Whitehead boy, was soliciting sexual photographs from my underage child. And I want him expelled, Nuala. I want him gone today.'

'Did Woody send a photo of himself naked, too?'

'That's my understanding of it. Yes.'

The principal leaned back into her chair, causing her neck to disappear and the weight gain to become more apparent. Beverley tried not to notice – she was sure it was down to grief – but it wasn't easy.

'So, what are you going to do about it?'

'I understand this is very distressing for you. But I can't just expel Woody Whitehead.'

'Why not?'

'Well, for one thing, if I was to expel Woody, I'd have to expel Amelia too.'

'Of course you wouldn't. Amelia is a twelve-year-old girl. She didn't do anything wrong.'

'And Woody is a twelve-year-old boy. They're both underage. What we usually do in these circumstances is get both sets of parents in, talk to them, talk to the children, and make sure everyone understands how serious the situation is and that it shouldn't happen again.'

'What you usually do? Are you saying this usually happens?'

'Sometimes.' The principal corrected herself, 'Occasionally. Rarely.'

But she'd said 'usually'. Beverley had heard it, and she had not liked it.

'Sometimes, children can think they're in relationships, boyfriend and girlfriend, and they're playing at being grown-ups. They get the idea somewhere that this is what grown-ups do.'

'It is not what grown-ups do,' said Beverley, barely allowing the woman to finish her sentence. 'And they're not playing house, Nuala. This is not *normal* behaviour. My daughter is barely twelve, and now there's a naked photo of her out there in the world. I don't think it's too much to expect that the boy be punished. And I didn't expect you of all people to be sticking up for a Whitehead.'

'I'm not sticking up for anyone, Beverley.'

'I saw the older Whitehead brother in the parking lot. He says he's working here. Did you know that?'

'I didn't hire him,' replied the principal, her tone cool. 'I will talk to Woody, and to his parents, to his mother, I mean. I'll talk to Amelia, and to Mr Cafferty. The class teacher usually has an idea of what's going on.'

There was that word again. *Usually.*

'Mr Cafferty hasn't been here a wet week,' she shot back, though, actually, the new sixth-class teacher was fine. A little overzealous maybe – between after-school activities and running her socials, where did he expect Amelia to find the time to knit a whole bear? – but he was open to parental partnership. Some of the other staff acted like a weekly progress report was a massive burden. 'I'm not really interested in you talking to anyone except Woody's mother. I doubt she'd put up much of a fight. You think they'd be glad to move on to a different school, a different town.'

'What does your husband think?'

Beverley hadn't said a word to Malachy. The girls were her job. And in light of his own behaviour, she wasn't sure he deserved to know. Sending nudes was *not* something grown-ups did, not good grown-ups, and not when they were married to someone else. 'He agrees with me, of course,' she snapped. 'Neither of us think this is acceptable behaviour. I don't see how you can think it's acceptable behaviour.'

'I never said—' Principal Patterson cut herself off and sighed, as if Beverley were the errant child. 'If you want, I can get in touch with the Department of Education, talk to the district psychologist. They might have some advice, or they could talk to Amelia, if you're really concerned.'

Beverley leaned forward and banged the principal's desk (which the Lakers' 2017 Christmas extravaganza had paid for). She could feel her grasp on the situation weakening, her aim floundering. She took another swig of water. Her throat had been sore for months.

Poised and enviable, she told herself. *Poised and enviable*.

'My daughter doesn't need to see a psychologist, and certainly not a *state* one. I'm not concerned about her and you don't need to be either. What I'm concerned about is Woody Whitehead and how you don't seem to want to do anything about lewd behaviour in your school. I'm concerned that, instead of doing your job, you're trying to pass the buck.'

This wasn't just about her daughter; it was about Glass Lake. And Beverley was eternally loyal to this place.

Principal Patterson compressed her mouth in a way that did nothing for her lips. Beverley eyeballed her back.

'Technically, Mrs Franklin, none of this happened at the school.'

'That you know of,' she countered. 'And the school certainly didn't teach them *not* to do it, did you? The Lakers raised eighteen hundred euro last year to support the web-safety modules and I'm really starting to wonder where that money went.'

'We have done several web-safety modules with the students, and Amelia will do more this year. We also sent home an information booklet for parents on safe web use. It contained advice on restricting children's access to the internet as well as information on how best to monitor phone use. Glass Lake's advice is that parents refrain from giving children phones until they've finished primary school.'

'Oh, come off it, Nuala! School policy allows them to have phones in their bags in sixth class. Amelia is in sixth class. You can't wash your hands of this one. And a booklet isn't going to save you either. If you do not do something about this, I will be forced to take matters into my own hands, and I can promise you that will not be preferable.' She ignored the principal's raised eyebrows. 'Parents,' she stormed on, 'need to be made aware of what is happening at this school.'

'I don't think it is happening at the school.'

'And men – male students, I mean – need to be taught not to do it; not to make underage girls send them nude photographs and to generally have some decorum and class and self-respect!'

A sharp single knock on the office door. 'Sorry, Principal Patterson, there's a phone call for you.'

Beverley turned and glared at the secretary's head sticking around the doorframe.

'I've asked if they can wait, but I'm afraid it's urgent.'

....

Derek billed every story as 'front-page material'. A new heron in the park, trees felled without permission, a bicycle stolen from outside Connolly's supermarket; everything was a potential splash – until it was written up and he could no longer deny that it definitely was not. Christine admired his optimism. If only some big Dublin gangster would buy a holiday home in West Cork. It would make Derek's year.

'I'm on my way into the office this very second, Derek,' said Christine, who was still sidling up to the Lakers. Beth Morton was writing something into Lorna Farrell's notebook. She would need to get closer, but it looked like an Italian address.

'Forget the office,' came the thick Dublin croak. 'This is big, and I need my best reporter on it right away.'

There were only three reporters at the *Southern Gazette*, and Amanda was on holiday this week while Anthony operated a work-to-rule where he refused to cover anything but sport.

'I'm honoured.'

'This is juicy, Christine. It lives up to that great journalism mantra.'

'If it bleeds it leads?' Derek regularly shouted maxims at them. This one was a favourite. But it being Cooney, the nearest they'd come was when a Halal butchers opened on the outskirts of town.

'No,' said Derek. 'The other great mantra ... "Sex sells." And what sells even better is a sex scandal.'

'In Cooney?' replied Christine doubtfully.

'Right here in our own sleepy little town,' he confirmed. 'We had a phone call from an irate mother. She says some of the kids up at Glass Lake have been sending nude photos to each other, including her daughter. And since you've got a kid ... You do have a kid, right?'

'I have three kids, Derek. You've met them. Two of them are at Glass Lake.'

'Perfect! I knew you'd be the woman for the job. The mother wants to stay anonymous. She was gunning to name the boy involved, but obviously he's a minor so we'll keep that out of it. Still, pretty exciting stuff, eh?'

'Mmm,' said Christine, who thought it was a little icky and not particularly newsworthy. When Caroline was in sixth class, a girl had sent all the other kids a disgusting meme. Not for the first time, she'd been smug about holding out on giving her children phones until they got to secondary school. 'It isn't *that* unusual.'

'Yes, but we've got a parent giving out. And you know what that means? It means we've got a ...'

'A row,' supplied Christine reluctantly.

Beth and Lorna were now laughing. How had that turned around so quickly? Had Beth just bribed her son's way into the musical? Outrageous. Christine needed to get back there and see what she could barter for Maeve.

'A sexy row,' agreed Derek. 'And feel free to spice it up. Mention a few celebrities who've been caught sending around nudes and we can work a few of their photos in. Any of those Cork lads ever been caught out – Cillian Murphy, or Jonathan Rhys What's-it? That'll outrage the old dears. The letters will be flowing in.'

The previous editor of the *Southern Gazette* had heart palpitations any time someone complained about so much as a typo on the TV listings. But Derek relished the ire of his readers. 'Outrage means they're reading!' he'd shout with glee, slapping the missives down on Christine's desk. Christine oversaw the letters page as well as the local birthdays list.

The Lakers were packing up their stuff now. Lorna had slipped both notebooks into her Class of '92 tote bag and Beth was waving as she headed for the door.

'Can this actually wait until later, Derek? I was working on that story about cuts to the West Cork bus service and—'

'Forget buses. There's nothing sexy about buses. A bus accident, maybe. But cancelled buses? Definitely not sexy. No. I want you on this. Did I mention it's got front-page potential?'

Part of billing everything as a cover story was to incentivise them to work harder. But Christine had no interest in being on the front page, especially not for an underage sex scandal. She liked her comfortable life, down in the back pages of the newspaper, where she outraged nobody.

Now Lorna was heading for the door. Christine gave a silent moan. She could not return home to Maeve with no job on the musical and no sign of that Judas cat. There was no way the worry dolls would cut it; she'd have Christine and Conor up all night, encumbering them with her anxieties.

'I'll send you on the number,' Derek continued. 'The mother's name is Beverley. She lives in one of those McMansions on the southside of town. I said I'd get someone over to her today.'

'Beverley *Franklin*?'

'Ah now, don't tell me you're friends? This bloody town.

Everyone's someone's cousin! I'll have to see if Anthony will make a concession this once and—'

'No, no,' interrupted Christine, as the last of the Lakers packed up their things. 'I know her, but we're not friends. I can do it. Definitely. No conflict of interest.'

'Are you sure?'

'I am one hundred per cent positive.'

If Christine couldn't get Lorna to pencil Maeve in for costumes, she would have to take the matter up a level.

'That's the enthusiasm I like to see.'

She threw her bag over her arm and headed for the café door. 'So, you want me out there today?'

'This afternoon, yes. I'll send on her details. And remember, Christine: Outrage ...'

She caught the door just as Fiona Murphy swung it behind her. Butcher Murphy appeared from behind a nearby pillar.

'... makes a front page,' she chanted.

'Attagirl! Now go get 'em,' barked Derek.

....

Mairead placed the requested glass of water on Nuala's table and the principal chased down the Xanax rattling impatiently behind her teeth. When the secretary left, she popped a second tablet into her mouth. It was her recompense for not shouting at Beverley Franklin.

For years, Glass Lake had banned mobile phones. But parents had complained: what if they got delayed doing pick-ups? What if there was an issue with an after-school activity? So, the school amended its policy to allow, if necessary, sixth-class students to carry phones; they had to be kept in their bags and switched off for the duration of the school day. It was intended as an 'in exceptional circumstances' allowance, but instead students viewed it as the point at which they were *entitled* to a phone. So, every September, the sixth-classers returned with shiny new mobiles hopping about at the bottom of their backpacks and, within weeks, there was an incident. The staff referred to it as the Sixth-Class Curse.

Last year, two boys had watched porn and told their friends what they'd seen. It spread through the school like a virus, every student telling four more, the details multiplying and mutating as they went. Two years before that, a girl was sent an explicit meme by an older sibling and forwarded it to every student in her class. As sure as night follows day, parents had arrived at Nuala's office.

Never mind that none of it – the online bullying, the sexting, the viewing of inappropriate material – ever happened in the classroom. It occurred in the back seat of the car as the kids were driven home, or up in their bedrooms, or even when gathered together in the family room, the adults watching TV and the kids messing around on iPads, blocking classmates on TikTok as a joke or typing 'porn' into YouTube to see what would happen.

The parents had given their children the phones. But somehow, it was always the school's fault.

'Can you ask Mr Cafferty to come and see me at the end of the school day?' Nuala called after Mairead. The photos incident aside, she was due a check-in with the newest faculty member. Frank Cafferty, the sixth-class teacher, had come to them from an ultra-Catholic, rural, three-teacher school; she feared the Glass Lake parents would eat him for a post-workout snack. 'And can you get me the most recent sex and relationships curriculum from the Department, please?'

Nuala tried not to give in to the Beverley Franklins of her school. Nice and all as it was for the kids to have tennis rackets without holes and for the corridors to be repainted annually, the basic needs of the school, and Nuala's wages, were paid for by the state and she was not answerable to the Lakers. However, occasionally, and often accidentally, one of them had a point.

It had been a while since they'd updated the sex ed programme and, as far as Nuala could recall, there was currently no mention of online elements at all. It could be worth doing some contemporary modules.

Mairead appeared in the doorway. 'I've asked the Department for that.'

'Thanks,' replied Nuala, returning to the mound of paperwork on her desk.

The secretary didn't budge.

'What is it, Mairead?'

'Did you know Arlo Whitehead is working over in the auditorium?'

'Seamus hired him.' And she wasn't likely to forget with the whole world reminding her.

'Is that okay with you?'

The set designs for the musical had the caretaker swamped, and the gutters needed replacing. It was just for a week or two, he'd said. As if that made it any easier.

Nuala attempted a gracious smile, though she suspected it came out more like a grimace. 'I guess it has to be.'

The secretary nodded.

Nuala went back to her files. After a few seconds, she put them down again.

'You are now officially hovering, Mairead.'

'I presume you don't want me to send him in to you, for the usual greeting?'

Sitting on her desk, under the special needs assistant application forms and the folders for the social worker, were first-stage divorce papers. Nuala had printed off several copies in the weeks since she'd received them. There was an identical set spread across the back seat of her car and another sitting in an orderly pile on the kitchen table. But she couldn't bring herself to sign any of them.

The worst year of Nuala's life had many parts to it, but at the centre of everything sat Arlo Whitehead.

'No,' said Nuala, who hadn't spoken to the teenager since the day her only child lost the use of his legs in the Whiteheads' car. 'I don't think that's going to be necessary.'

10
······

ABERSTOWN GARDA STATION

Joey was standing at the entrance to the station, watching the last of his morning interviewees climb into a Range Rover, when the sergeant came up behind him.

'All done?'

'Yes, sir,' he replied, standing to attention. 'All done until the afternoon batch. Just have to type them up.'

'Anything of note?'

Joey pulled out the small notebook where he'd been marking down conversation topics all morning. Most of his notes consisted of half sentences – cut off at the point where he realised the tangent the witness had gone off on had nothing to do with the investigation. 'Not really ...' He flicked back through the pages. 'Someone saw the deceased in a heated debate with Principal Nuala Patterson a few hours before the body was found in the river.'

'Who said that?'

'A parent ... Lorna Farrell.'

'I don't see Nuala Patterson being caught up in this. She's about the only one of them who I'd give the benefit of the doubt. More likely that parent has a grievance against Nuala. I wouldn't be principal of that school for all the tea in China.'

'Is it worth following up on anyway?'

'No harm. Nuala's in this afternoon, so you can ask her about it. You've met Principal Patterson, haven't you? At that school information night you did?'

'Yes, sir.' Joey had met her once before that, too, the day her son was paralysed in a car accident.

It was early one February morning and the ambulance had just left the scene with Leo Patterson on a gurney in the back when Joey and the sergeant arrived at Reilly's Pass. They had to wait for a second ambulance to come for the boy who had died. His father was a star of the Cooney GAA scene, apparently. Joey didn't know much about Gaelic football, except that it was a big deal around here, but he'd committed the teenager's name to memory. Mike Roche Junior. His first body.

One of the remaining passengers had identified himself to Joey as the driver. He was distraught. His was another name he'd committed to memory. Charlie Whitehead. His first arrest.

It was five hours later, when the sergeant had gone to the hospital and Joey was left to guard the site until forensics arrived, that a car pulled up at the side of the road and Nuala Patterson got out. He tried to keep her away, but she was adamant. She explained that she was the injured boy's mother. He thought of his mam back home in Leitrim, and how if he was in a car crash, she'd probably turn up wearing a coat over her pyjamas too.

'The preliminary post-mortem should be back soon,' said the sergeant, lowering himself into the chair behind the reception desk.

'Do you think there's a chance of foul play?' asked Joey, trying to keep the hope out of his voice.

'There's always a chance,' said his superior. 'It's not likely around here, but I'm not ruling it out. The suicide risk on this one is low: gainfully employed, happily married – or as happy as any of us are. There's no sense of a desperate person teetering on the edge. Throw in the fact that we haven't got a plausible theory for why our DOA was out by the river when everyone else was up at Glass Lake. It doesn't make sense. And that makes me suspicious.'

Joey quivered. Half of him was giddy at the prospect of something exciting finally happening, and the other half felt guilty about it.

Lorna Farrell, parent
If tensions were high at the school, it wasn't down to the musical – it was because of the photos. I presume you know about that? The children were N-A-K-E-D in them. I was angry when I heard about it, of course I was. Show me a parent who wasn't and I'll show you a textbook example of negligence.

Beth Morton, parent
Glass Lake has always had feuds. One parent doesn't sign another parent's petition and suddenly people are getting kicked out of WhatsApp groups and children's birthday party invitations are being rescinded. But the stuff with the photos was different. Everyone was concerned. Personally, I don't think anyone should have handed in their resignation over it, but that's only an opinion.

Arlo didn't remove his head from under the sink, but he could feel the woman's eyes on his bent back. He tried to concentrate on the U-bend. He'd fixed this last week and somehow it was leaking again.

'Can I get you anything to drink while you're down there?'

'No thank you, Mrs Murphy,' he said, voice muffled as he reached behind him for a spanner. 'I'm fine.'

'What did I say about calling me that?' Her hand hit his shoulder and he gave a start. The Murphys' kitchen was so big, it echoed. It was disconcerting to never know how close she was. 'You're making me feel ninety,' she said. 'Anyway, it's *Ms* Murphy now.'

She laughed but Arlo could tell she didn't really find it funny, so he said: 'Fiona, I mean. Sorry. I'm fine for a drink, thank you, Fiona.'

'Are you sure?' She stepped away. 'A coke? Or a beer, maybe? I've some craft ale in the fridge, from this cool little microbrewery in Mayo.'

'No, thank you, Fiona, I'm fine. Thank you.' The heat rose in his cheeks. Could he not think of any new words? He wanted to reach behind and tug down the back of his T-shirt. But he didn't, in case she was watching.

The piping came away in his hand and Arlo peered up towards

the drain. How did he expect to win over the people of Cooney if the jobs they paid good money for weren't done properly? Word of mouth was everything in this business. His father had taught him that. He'd also taught him that, no matter how many adhesives you had in the van, charm was the best way to seal a deal.

But Arlo wasn't charming. His limbs were too long, and he blushed too easily. People said he looked like his dad, but no matter how much he studied his reflection, he never saw it. Sometimes he concentrated so hard on the mirror that his nose started to drift away from his face and he had to shut his eyes for as long as it took for the sensation to stop.

The footsteps halted. Arlo hoped she'd left the kitchen. Fiona Murphy was divorced, and she said it was a godsend to have someone to do 'manly things' around the house. She hired him a lot and always tipped. She was one of the few people in Cooney who was nice to him and he was grateful, but he made mistakes when he was also trying to guess if he was being watched or not.

She fancies you, boy.

Don't be stupid, Leo. She's like forty.

Remember that time she pressed her leg against your back?

She was reaching for a pillowcase.

Must have been a hard-to-reach pillowcase.

She's probably just afraid I'll steal something.

During the summer, a family out by Cooney Pier had hired Arlo to fix their boiler. They'd been so torn between not trusting a Whitehead and needing to go to work that they'd locked the doors to every room before they left, giving him access only to the hallway. It was the hottest week of the year and he couldn't open a window or get to the kitchen for water. He'd sweated so much he left a stain on the patch of carpet outside the boiler room and they'd docked him the cost of cleaning. The final payment hadn't even been enough to cover parts.

'I heard you were up at the school this morning.'

Arlo jumped slightly, banging his head off the exposed pipe. He scrunched up his face and cursed silently into the darkness until the worst of the pain passed.

'You know what some of those Glass Lake mothers are like,' Fiona continued. 'Keeping an eye on everyone's comings and goings, sending the details into WhatsApp like it's the Interpol messaging service.'

She laughed but the knowledge that people were actually discussing him, and it wasn't just in his head, made Arlo feel so exposed he could no longer resist the urge to emerge from under the sink and make sure his T-shirt hadn't ridden up his back.

'Mrs – Fiona – I would actually take some water, if that's okay?'

His shirt was still where it should be, but it was clammy, as was his face. He felt sweat around his eyes and he blinked.

Fiona, who was leaning against the far wall, walked over to the fridge and removed a bottle. 'Is it totally awkward?' she asked, crossing the room towards him. 'With Nuala Patterson?' She lowered her voice even though they were the only people in the kitchen. 'Does the woman just *hate* you?'

She unscrewed the water bottle and left it on the ground beside him, brushing her hand across his back as she straightened up.

Definitely looking for the ride.

Fuck off, Leo. She's talking about your mom.

Arlo spoke to his best friend in his head because Leo would no longer talk to him in real life. He'd sent him messages on Instagram and SnapChat, he'd even sent him a long email, but Leo ignored them all. Then a few months ago, he blocked him. So, the last thing he'd ever said to Arlo was still, 'You're a fucking wimp.' Two seconds later the car skidded off the road, and Leo and Mike were thrown up against a 200-year-old oak tree.

They'd been on their way home from a gig in Cork city. Donovan was playing, so they had to go. But Leo, Mike and Arlo were only seventeen, and the Triskel was strict on ID; they needed an adult. Arlo convinced his dad to take them. Arlo was supposed to drive them there and back, only he got drunk. People blamed his dad for that, but Mike was the one who snuck in the whiskey. His dad had only bought them one pint each, but it was true he'd bought himself several more.

What they should have done was left the car. They should have paid for a taxi. Arlo imagined this scenario all the time. In reality, nobody would have gone for it. It was an hour and a half's drive so a taxi would have cost at least two hundred euro, plus the hassle of coming back for the car the next day, and his mom needed it to get to work in the morning. Now, though, two hundred quid seemed like a pretty good price for his dad to avoid seven years in jail, Leo to keep his legs, and Mike to still be alive. Mike was the funniest fucker Arlo had ever known, and now he was gone for ever. And without Leo around, there was nobody he could really talk to about that.

'Nuala Patterson should be grateful,' said Fiona, watching him carefully from her seat at the kitchen table. 'At least her child is alive. I heard she didn't want to hire you. Is that true?' Her stare burnt into his skin and he knew he was going red again. 'That's discrimination. You could sue, you know? Does she ever speak to you? I bet she says *awful* things.'

There were people in Cooney who refused to hire him because of what had happened. But there were a few, like Fiona Murphy, who saw it as a bonus: your sink fixed by the one who escaped unscathed. Ella said they were like hyenas, tossing around his intact carcass, desperate for any remaining morsel of gossip. But it didn't help Arlo get through the day to think of them like that.

'We don't – she doesn't talk to me,' he said finally.

'Is that right?' gasped Fiona, as if he'd revealed something far more interesting. 'How *terrible*. You hardly made your father get behind the wheel drunk, now did you? And your little brother got a lead role in the musical – I'd say Nuala Patterson just hates that.'

Without thinking, Arlo lifted a wrench and placed the cool metal against his burning cheek. He switched it to the other side. Fiona caught his gaze and raised an eyebrow in a way that made him drop the tool. It clattered on the pale blue tiles and he quickly shoved his torso back in under the sink.

'I should get on with this,' he said into the airless dark.

'Absolutely, Arlo sweetheart.' He could hear the smile in her voice. Under his T-shirt and heavy jeans, his skin prickled. 'I'll be as quiet as a church mouse,' she said. 'I'm just checking in on my socials. Pretend I'm not even here.'

....

Frances Tandon was having a lovely sixty-sixth birthday. She'd started the day with scrambled eggs from her hens, who had been on strike for the past week but were now back laying with gusto, and some deep meditation where she came as close to reaching bliss as she had all week. She'd received several cards in the post and the students who rented the house next door had dropped in a box of 'special birthday brownies'. They'd underlined special a few times, lest they accidentally drug an unsuspecting, and newly minted, pensioner. Frances was saving them for this evening.

Then she'd hosted a particularly successful workshop for beginners. She knew it had been successful because ten of the twelve participants had signed up for Tantric Sex level two before they left, and everyone had removed at least one item of clothing for the concluding gentle touch session. While she had been slightly concerned about the man who started taking notes – 'How do you spell "solar plexus"?' – that same student got so into the shaking off his inhibitions portion of the afternoon that he'd knocked over the altar and sent the Shiva statue and incense burners crashing to the floor. So, all in all, excellent feedback.

Having seen off the students, extinguished the candles and gathered up the bedsheets from the floor, Frances was now making the ten-second commute from the renovated shed that served as her tantra studio to the main house, where she had happily lived alone for more than twelve years. She threw the sheets into the washing machine and placed a saucepan of soup on the hob's back-left ring. Her favourite ring.

She poured herself a generous glass of kombucha and tore a corner off one of the brownies; just a nibble while she waited for the soup to heat. Then she checked her phone for the first time that day. There were missed calls and birthday greetings from her children and grandchildren. Even Beverley, she was glad to see, had sent a message.

Frances opened the WhatsApp from her daughter. There was no text, only a video. She pressed play.

Happy birthday, Granny, I love you so much! I can't wait to see you again. Thank you for being the best grandmother in the world. You're amazing. Happy birthday!

Frances watched as Amelia blew three kisses to the camera. That was it. No sign of Beverley. Presumably she was holding the camera.

Frances pulled another chunk from the brownie – they were deliciously moreish and the hashish not at all noticeable – and watched it through again. It was, ostensibly, a lovely message. What grandmother didn't want to hear she was the best in the world? What person didn't like to be told they were amazing? Yet despite Amelia's exaggerated, effusive way of speaking, it was oddly hollow. It was like the camera had turned her granddaughter into a shiny, unauthentic version of herself. Frances would have preferred an awkward but simple 'Happy birthday Granny' and then for Beverley to turn the camera on herself and say the same. Better yet, a phone call, so she could have an old-fashioned interaction with her daughter and granddaughter. Ella was the only Franklin who ever actually phoned.

It wasn't that Frances was lonely. Far from it. She talked to her other children on the phone and saw a wide circle of friends in Dublin regularly. She had a busy and fulfilling second career, having given up badly paid pen-pushing at the same time she gave up her husband. She held tantric sex and massage workshops in her studio and travelled the country hosting retreats and classes. She took a lover, a retired chiropodist named Geoffrey, about once a week. They had sex and played Scrabble and generally succeeded in ensuring the lovemaking lasted longer than the board game.

So no, it wasn't that she was lonely for her daughter, it was just that she yearned to help her. Beverley reminded Frances of her former self. Her daughter would balk at that; she was slim and wealthy, things Frances had never been, and Beverley didn't allow her husband to call her names in front of her children. But it wasn't about external traits (a possibility Beverley would struggle to comprehend); it was about being so tangled up in yourself that you didn't realise you were your own prison guard, let alone that it was possible to be free. Her daughter had always been chasing the wrong things for the wrong reasons, and she accepted her role in that. She should have left her husband a lot sooner.

Frances had given birth to five children, but it was only when they were grown and she had travelled to India and discovered tantra – specifically, in the middle of a vigorous shaking session just outside Mumbai – that Frances felt she had finally given birth to herself. She was a woman renewed, freed from cultural baggage and people pleasing and western expectations. She had achieved bliss. And she desperately, oh so desperately, wanted even a sliver of that for her daughter.

Of course, Beverley had no truck with tantra. She acted as if Frances had chosen this path in order to continue a lifetime of embarrassing her. (Now her mother wasn't just fat – she was fat *and* she removed her clothes for a living!) But tantra wasn't only about delayed orgasms and pleasing a sexual partner – although Beverley's sex life didn't bear thinking about; Frances doubted if her son-in-law found anyone as attractive as himself – it was a spiritual practice that helped people to heal. It healed the relationships we have with ourselves. After an adulthood marred by verbal abuse, Frances had learned to love her body. Her daughter was so thin, so afraid of ending up like her mother, and yet she didn't love herself half as much.

Frances felt a faint tremor and took a deep breath, opening her channels and allowing the energy in.

Only it wasn't her body vibrating. It was her phone.

Her granddaughter was calling.

'Ella, my love, how wondrously cosmic to hear from you.' Frances leaned back in her chair and watched the evening light reflect off her glass wind chime and explode across the ceiling. 'You'll have to speak slowly. It seems your dear old grandmother has accidentally scoffed an entire hash brownie.'

....

Ella Belle Franklin had intended to go to Dublin for university. Her dad offered to pay for accommodation wherever she wound up, but Ella had planned to live with her grandmother. Her parents were surprised and delighted when, at the last minute, she swapped University College Dublin for University College Cork. They were even more delighted when she decided to live at home for her first year. Her father was rarely there, and her mother was perpetually disappointed in her: her hair, her clothes, the close bond she enjoyed with her grandmother. But her parents were controlling people, who liked to be in charge, and this way they knew where she was. Most of the time.

Ella had stayed in Cork, and Cooney, because of Arlo. Her parents would never have guessed that, and this fact delighted Ella. They could only see their daughter in their own image and so couldn't even consider that she might fall for someone they would deem wholly unsuitable. Not that she was with Arlo because it would annoy her parents. That was only a bonus. She had loved Arlo since fifth-year religion, when they all had to write about someone important to them. Most of the boys had picked footballers or YouTubers, but Arlo wrote about his little brother. Sister Tracey read out his essay and Arlo went so red that Leo Patterson threw cold water on him. This only made the boys laugh more, but Ella had felt this ache in her chest, like she needed to know everything Arlo thought as soon as humanly possible. She made more of an effort with her friendship with Leo then, because she knew they were close.

Arlo had stayed in Cooney for Woody, and she had stayed for him. Now, though, she couldn't wait to get out of the place.

On Thursdays her lectures were done by lunchtime, but she was reluctant to come straight home. Arlo worked long days so there was nothing to rush back for. Sometimes she went for lunch or coffee with classmates, but mostly she drove to the car park of the Lidl superstore just outside the town and sat and listened to music and watched as Cooney residents snuck into the chain outlet while pretending not to see each other. There was a very active Keep Cooney Independent campaign, and locals were supposed to shop at Connolly's supermarket. But Connolly's was extortionate, and their vegetables were shite.

Today she parked in front of a gigantic billboard advertising special offers on monkey nuts, skeletons and large, plastic cauldrons.

She had declined her parents' offer of a new car in favour of her grandmother's old Peugeot, even though the heater didn't work – Ella was currently wearing gloves and a scarf – and it often leaked oil. She loved this car because it reminded her of good times. Frances Tandon was the only woman who could make driving over a pothole, at speed, fun. Ella, however, never drove at speed.

The last time she heard from Leo Patterson was April. She and Arlo had been trying to contact him since the crash but neither had got a response. Then, out of the blue, he sent her this long email. He called her a slut and a tease and told her about the fight he and Arlo had been having when the car left the road. They'd been fighting about her and this was what had distracted Charlie Whitehead. She was the reason they'd crashed. She, he wrote, was the reason Mike was dead.

Sometimes, when she was driving, she thought about this so much that she could no longer be sure she was in control of the car. So, she'd pull over and do something else. Today, sitting in the Lidl car park, she'd called her grandmother.

Then she sat back, listened to loud hip hop and watched as Lorna Farrell, one of her mother's many frenemies, rolled a trolley laden with jumbo packs of toilet paper, shopping bags, several skeletons and a cauldron out of the supermarket in a pair of oversized sunglasses and a large floppy sunhat.

Ella gave an involuntary shiver. She checked the thermometer on the dashboard.

It was seven degrees outside.

12

A few weeks ago, Maeve went to a sleepover at Amelia Franklin's house. She was so excited to be asked, it didn't matter that every girl in the class had got an invitation. Christine hadn't slept properly that night. She kept waiting for the call telling her Maeve was homesick and sobbing in the Franklins' bathroom or walk-in wardrobe and to come get her. But her phone never rang. Maeve had a great time and arrived home the following morning with a goodie bag for herself and some interior design suggestions for her parents. Their nice but not particularly remarkable semi-D could do with more. More marble, more rooms, more gym equipment, and definitely more chandeliers.

'Even one would do. We could put it in the foyer,' the eleven-year-old had said, not a hint of irony as she gestured to the tiny damp porch with the peeling paint where the Maguires kept umbrellas, mucky shoes and Porcupine's kitty litter.

So, while Christine hadn't been inside Beverley's home since they were children, and she'd lived somewhere a lot less glamorous than this, she had an idea of what to expect.

The winding staircase, expansive foyer and entirely marble kitchen were all as to be expected from a neo-classical, *nouveau riche* home. Not that the Franklins were new to money – they'd made their fortune in printing two generations back and were as close to a dynasty as West Cork came – but Beverley was. The ostentatious light fixtures and shoe room – where Christine reluctantly left her ankle boots – were also predictable. Indeed, nothing in the vast pile took Christine by surprise until Beverley put her sitting at one of three marble breakfast bars and continued to yammer on about how her daughter had been wronged. As she glanced back across the floor, convinced her threadbare ankle socks had left sweat marks on the gleaming slabs, she spotted the fish.

An artificial pond, measuring about 3ft by 3ft and topped with a glass ceiling, had been built into the kitchen floor. Two colourful fish were swishing around the water feature, which had been made flush with the marble slabs. It was so decadent and so surprising – nothing about Beverley said 'quirky' – that all journalistic enquiries and representations on behalf of her daughter flew from her mind. All she wanted to ask was, *Why?*

'Apologies,' said Beverley, interrupting her own lengthy diatribe, the gist of which was: sexting is bad; Woody Whitehead is worse. 'My mind is in a million places. Would you like a coffee?'

'Sure, but I can make it.' Christine slid down from her stool. 'Where do you keep—'

'Alexa,' said Beverley, so sternly and decisively that Christine was sure the woman had forgotten her name despite being classmates for *eight* years, 'make coffee.'

A flicking switch echoed through the uncluttered room and on the countertop (also marble) over beside the silver oven, a stainless-steel coffeemaker started to gurgle.

Beverley pressed a cupboard door that, up to this point, Christine had assumed was a wall. The thing popped open and she removed two mugs.

'It's not even really about Amelia. Well, it is, of course, but I'm not *worried* about her, not in any greater sense. She's confident, you know, very talented, her own person. Have you seen her Instagram page? She's going to go far. I'm more worried about what this says about Glass Lake and that Principal Patterson doesn't seem to care. What might the Whitehead boy get some other young girl to do, someone more impressionable, with less attentive parents? Not everyone is as well-adjusted as Amelia. And we all know what the father was like. A drunk. You know about the crash, right? Out on Reilly's Pass?'

Christine nodded. Everyone knew about the crash. She had reported on it. She'd also written about Mike Roche's horrendously sad funeral and Charlie Whitehead's sentencing. Derek was livid when he pleaded guilty immediately – 'Do you know what a local manslaughter trial does for newspaper sales?!' – but Christine was glad they'd been spared a court case. It had been a grim few months in Cooney as it was. The *Southern Gazette* received a lot of letters and emails from people calling for the Whiteheads to be run out of town. Christine had chosen not to publish them. Connie Whitehead was getting a hard enough time of it in the real world without having to see the hatred in print. She'd be lying if she said she hadn't been slightly concerned when Maeve was put sitting beside Woody Whitehead at the beginning of the school year. But Maeve liked Woody, and Charlie's children were as much victims as anyone else. Plus, she'd googled it, and according to some study in Arizona, a criminal mind was not hereditary.

'So,' Beverley continued, 'you wouldn't exactly keel over from shock if his sons turned out not to be the greatest citizens either, would you? An expulsion would be the quickest, fairest and most discreet solution, but Principal Patterson just isn't on the ball like she used to be. I think she needs it pointed out to her that Woody is not the kind of student we want at Glass Lake.' She yapped on and on, her perfectly manicured feet stepping on the fishbowl's glass cover as she crossed the kitchen, turned on the cold-water faucet and filled a jug. 'I watched Woody at pick-up today – nobody there to collect him, *quelle surprise* – and you can tell, just by looking at him... It's his expression, or the way he walks or something. It's weird. *He's* weird. You know when you can just tell?'

Christine half felt like sticking up for the boy. Maeve made Woody sound like a sweet if slightly peculiar kid. The peculiarity was probably why they got on so well. And who was to say Amelia hadn't started the whole thing?

Still. Sexting.

Even the word was unpleasant. It was like something a snake might say before it lobbed its head forward and gave you a fatal bite. *Ssss-exting*. Kids would be kids; but she wasn't so sure she wanted them 'being kids' while sitting beside her overly naïve daughter.

Beverley put a jug – complete with mint leaves and slices of cucumber – and a glass tumbler in front of Christine. 'Nuala Patterson wouldn't even entertain the notion of expelling him. She basically said if he went, Amelia was going too. She threatened me, essentially. You'd think the Whiteheads would be her least favourite Cooney residents, given what happened to her son, but I guess I still win out. And that's it. It's a *fait accompli*,' she said, sounding out each syllable. 'Who made her judge and jury of Glass Lake?'

The Department of Education, thought Christine, as the goldfish continued to whip their tails around the dimly lit rectangle. Was it soundproofed? Could fish even hear? And how did they get the food into them?

'He is not the kind of student we want at Glass Lake,' Beverley said for what must have been the fourth time now. 'We don't want a junior pornographer representing us on national television, for God's sake. I don't know if you've heard, Christine, but I've got this year's musical onto *The Big Children's Talent Show*.'

'I did hear that, actually, at the Strand this morning,' said Christine, pulling her attention away from the fishbowl and back to the rather tedious conversation. This was her chance. 'Well done. Seriously. It's such an impressive achievement. It's great to have Glass Lake represented on the national broadcaster.' Christine lifted the tumbler to her mouth and resisted the urge to blink. She needed to convey she was genuine – and not just a genuine suck-up.

'You were at the Strand this morning?'

She nodded as she swallowed. 'Mm-hmm.'

Beverley leaned forward. 'How did Lorna break the news about the TV appearance? Did she make it clear I was the one who organised the whole thing? Because I was. Her only idea was to send the director general of RTÉ one of her weekly thank-you cards. Have you ever got one of those? Awful things. Now that her husband's a councillor, she stamps the back of the envelopes with the Cork County Council crest. If you ever see one coming in the letterbox, bin it straight away. It doesn't matter how good your cleaner is, she'll never get the glitter out of your carpet.'

'I'll bear that in mind.'

'I was the one who—'

'I was actually at the Strand to talk to you,' Christine interrupted, unwilling to let the conversation move on. 'About the musical, as it happens. Maeve wants to work on costumes. She's very enthusiastic and she has loads of ideas already. I gave her name to Lorna Farrell but I'm not sure she heard me ...'

'Lorna Farrell is a lapdog,' said Beverley dismissively. 'That's fine. Maeve Maguire for costumes. I'll remember. Woody, though, Woody is a lead.'

Christine let her shoulders drop. 'Great,' she enthused.

'Excuse me?'

'No, I mean, about Maeve, great. Just about Maeve.'

Beverley put her hand to chest. 'He's playing the lion. My God, I hadn't even thought about that. How does Nuala Patterson expect me to work with him now? No way. Absolutely no way.' She lifted the coffee pot and poured. Even the Franklins' technology could only do so much. 'For the sake of everyone in Cooney, he needs to be named.'

If one of the fish died, was there a way of getting the carcass out? Or did it just lie there decomposing under the LED lights until construction professionals came and pulled the whole thing apart? The Franklins had this place built, so presumably the fishbowl was their idea. It was just so hard to imagine that when they were drawing up the designs for the kitchen – plug socket here, gas line there – they'd thought to draw a little rectangle and write 'Fake Indoor Pond'.

'Named publicly,' clarified Beverley. 'As in, in the *Southern Gazette.*'

'We can't name him,' said Christine, as firmly as she could. 'I can write the piece without names, as I think my editor explained. But Woody's a minor. We've got to be careful around that. We wouldn't name Amelia either.'

'Well, of course you wouldn't name Amelia. She didn't do anything wrong.'

Christine took a slow sip of her coffee. 'Delicious. Thank you.'

'So, fine, no names. I don't think it'll take much for people to guess, anyway. Who else *would* it be?'

Beverley was deluded if she thought people would only be interested in the male party. Cooney was a small town. Christine ignored Derek's voice screaming in her head – 'Outrage Makes a Front Page! Outrage Makes a Front Page!' – and said, 'Are you sure you want to do this, Beverley? Children do silly things. Before she reaches adulthood, I'm sure Amelia will have done a lot worse.'

In her head, this sounded empathetic, comforting even, but from the expression on Beverley's face, it was clear that was not how it came out.

'Has your daughter done a lot worse than this?'

'No,' said Christine, before quickly adding, 'Not that I know of. But I mean, possibly.' She wanted to say that Maeve didn't have a phone but thought it might sound like she was gloating, which she was a bit. 'It's a full-time job, worrying about kids,' she said instead. 'My eldest is a vegan who doesn't like vegetables, so I have nightmares about her being diagnosed with scurvy and me having to explain myself to a team of doctors. And my youngest says everything that comes into his head. He goes up to complete strangers and asks why their face is so red or tells big burly truckers that his mom says tattoos are for criminals. I have disowned him in public more times than I care to admit. And Maeve' – Christine chortled. She talked fast as she tried to coax Beverley around – 'Maeve has to confess every bad thing that enters her head. She regularly tells me she worries she wouldn't be sad if I died, and I just have to smile and say it's fine. And then we've got this cat who abandoned us for a neighbour and ...' She shook her head. 'Anyway, trust me, it's a lot. My family, I mean. Not yours.'

Beverley's bottom lip protruded, and her eyebrows lifted. (And they did go up, even though her forehead didn't budge. Whoever did her Botox was very good.) 'Thank you for the concern, but I know what I'm doing.'

When they were at school, Christine had been paired with Beverley for a project on the *Titanic*. They were meant to go to Christine's house to work on it, but her mom got food poisoning, so they had to go to Beverley's over in Aberstown instead. It had been nothing like this place. As Christine recalled, they'd been given big plates of chips for dinner, which Beverley insisted they eat in her room while the rest of her family ate together downstairs. Beverley had shared a bedroom with two older sisters who painted their nails and taped songs off the radio. Christine, who never had chips for dinner and was an only child, thought it was amazing, but when her dad came to collect her, Beverley made her promise not to tell anyone in school about her house. They'd got on well working on the project, but they never hung out again after that. As an adult, she got that Beverley had been embarrassed, but she'd never understood of what.

Christine produced a Dictaphone and notebook from her bag. She didn't really need both, but they were good visual aids to remind people they were talking to a newspaper. 'Why would you want to remind them?!' she could practically hear Derek shouting. But Christine, like her daughter, needed a clear conscience to sleep at night.

She pressed record and flipped back the notebook cover.

'What was the school's response when you told them about the photo?'

13

Mrs Rodgers had to bribe Albert with a promise of two more episodes of *The Chase* to get him to sit still while she ensured he was thoroughly rinsed. She gave him a quick towel-dry and carried him into her bedroom where he stretched out on the eiderdown.

She took a hand mirror from her dressing table and held it up to him. 'What do you think? New home, new you?'

But Albert just yawned laboriously.

Mrs Rodgers ran her hand along the dressing table and idly picked up the hairdryer. She did a slow, exaggerated yawn of her own, so as not to rouse his suspicion (Albert was a very intelligent animal; he could have been on *The Chase*, and that show was so rapidly running out of gimmicks that a pets special was only a matter of time), then she pointed the contraption at the cat, pulled the trigger, and blasted him out of it. Albert gave a high-pitched whine and leapt up and out of the room. Mrs Rodgers sighed. It would have to do.

She turned the thing off, just as the doorbell went. Pulling back the net curtain from her bedroom window, she peered down on to the thinning crown of Conor Maguire from number seven.

Mrs Rodgers was surprised to see him back again. They had settled this last night.

She made her way slowly down the stairs, scooping up Albert as she went. Remembering at the last minute to hunch herself forward – frailty was her greatest weapon – she slowly allowed the front door to creak open.

'Hello?' she said, forcing her voice to croak. 'Who goes there?'

'Conor Maguire, Mrs Rodgers. Sorry to disturb you.' He was standing on her path, prancing on the spot like a boxer warming up for a fight, except he was wearing slacks and a shirt. 'I'm here about the cat. I talked to my wife and we'd really like him back, if that's all right. You see, the kids are missing—' He stopped jigging. His eyes had dropped to her chest. It was a while since a man's gaze had rested there. 'Is that Porcupine?'

She looked down, as if noticing the animal curled up in her arms for the first time. 'Hmm? Oh, no. This is Albert.'

Albert purred at the sound of his name.

Good cat, thought Mrs Rodgers.

Conor blinked.

'I haven't seen your cat in days, I'm afraid. But I will let you know if he comes calling again.'

'Mrs Rodgers, I was here last night. You had Porcupine then. That *is* Porcupine.'

'Al-bert,' she said, slowly, kindly.

'What happened to his ...?' Conor's brow furrowed as he inspected the cat. When he looked at her, his face was flooded with a sort of horrified respect.

She smiled vacantly.

'Mrs Rodgers ... did you *dye* his fur?'

'Whose?'

'Porcupine's! Our cat. The cat you're holding!'

'As I said, I haven't seen Porcupine. Maybe you should put up some Missing posters? I hear they can be very helpful.'

Conor opened his mouth, but no words came out. It took two more attempts before he spoke, though it was hardly worth the wait. 'That's my cat,' he said meekly. 'Please give me back my cat.'

'This is *Albert*,' she said again, patiently, though she needed to get back inside. It was chilly and Albert was still damp. Plus, it had been at least forty minutes since his last meal. 'Albert is *my* cat. I suppose he does look a little like Porcupine, but you couldn't get them confused, not really. Albert's fur is so distinctive, with this big patch of black on his back. See?' She nodded down to the animal, then looked back up at Conor. He had reverted to opening and closing his mouth.

She hoped he wouldn't cry. Animals were very sensitive to human emotions.

'If Porcupine has any similarly distinctive features, it might be an idea to mention them on the poster. You're a dentist. Maybe you noticed something unusual about his teeth?'

Albert purred, more insistently this time.

He was right, of course. It was getting late, and she had promised him two more episodes before bed.

'Well, thank you for the visit, Conor dear, and best of luck with the cat. Tell the children I was asking for them, and Christine. I do hope they're not working her too hard at the paper. Busy, busy!'

....

They were wrapping up the interview when Beverley heard Ella's old Peugeot sputtering its way up their porcelain-paved driveway. They had offered to buy her a new car, as a reward for doing so well in her exams, but she had taken her grandmother's banger instead. This had succeeded in pissing off both parents: Malachy because he did not like having a piece of junk in his driveway, and Beverley because it was a constant reminder of the close relationship Ella had with her mother, and not with her. She gave her girls everything she never had, and Ella just kept finding new ways to throw it back in her face.

Beverley picked up Christine's cup, and her own. She was halfway to the sink when she realised the journalist still had coffee left. But she couldn't bring them back; she'd look ridiculous. She was never at ease when an outsider was in her home, even though she'd spent years getting it just right for showing off. It was a hangover from childhood.

Her jitters were not helped by the fact that Christine was the only person from school who'd ever been in her house as a child. And of course, she'd had to be there for dinner.

Beverley's dad was constantly making comments about her mother's weight: lamenting that she was 'too good a cook' in front of strangers and calling her an embarrassment in front of the kids. But mealtimes were the worst part of Beverley's childhood. When her mother was eating, he said nothing. He would lay his own cutlery to one side, making it clear her consumption had his undivided attention. He refused to eat a morsel until she was done. He just sat there watching her. Beverley had watched too, not out of meanness, but because he made it seem so enthralling. Her mother never lifted her eyes from her plate. The day Christine came for dinner she'd insisted they eat in her bedroom, but she was sure she'd noticed anyway. How could she not?

Ella strolled into the kitchen, tapping away on her phone.

Beverley carefully moulded her lips into a smile: not too wide as to be needy, but not too tight as to be antagonistic. She never knew where she stood with her eldest daughter these days, and she did not want to have an argument in front of someone whose only familial complaint was that her daughter confided in her *too* much.

That had been a humble brag worthy of Lorna Farrell.

'Hello, darling,' said Beverley. 'How was college?'

Ella looked up from the screen and, though it took her a second, she returned the smile. If nothing else, the Franklins knew how to keep up appearances.

'Good,' she said. 'Grand.' She looked at Christine. 'Hi.'

'Hi,' the woman replied, raising a hand. Ella's gaze lingered on the Dictaphone.

'Ella, this is Christine Maguire. She's a journalist with the *Southern Gazette*.' Her daughter's face remained blank. 'That's the local paper. You know newspapers, darling? The physical things with words printed on them.' She'd meant it to sound jovial, a little ribbing, but playful was not a tone she excelled at. 'And Christine, this is my elder daughter, Ella. She's studying psychology at UCC.'

'I know what newspapers are, Bev. You've shown me your scrapbook enough times, all those articles from your time as an actor that never actually mention your acting.'

Beverley held on to her smile. 'It's not a scrapbook, darling,' she said, with just a hint of a warning. 'It's a few cuttings I happened to hang on to.'

'And laminate,' Ella muttered. 'Are you writing something about Bev?' she asked, louder. 'Has she told you about the time she nearly got Minnie Driver's part in *Circle of Friends*, but the director said she was too young and too thin?'

It was actually the casting director – her agent had been far too lazy to get her in front of the actual director – and those hadn't been his exact words, but years of auditions had taught Beverley to read between the lines.

'Christine is writing about Glass Lake and its complete rejection of any responsibility for how its students communicate with each other.'

'Is this about Amelia's nude?'

Beverley's nose wrinkled.

Still, at least 'nude' was better than 'pic', or indeed 'dick pic'.

'Yes. Although I'm an anonymous source – so you never saw Christine here, all right? And we will not be naming Amelia' – she turned to the journalist for confirmation – 'and you're not to tell anyone else about what happened.'

'Just the newspapers.'

'It's anonymous.'

'Nothing's anonymous in Cooney,' said Ella, pulling open the fridge.

The strained relationship with her eldest daughter pained Beverley more than she cared to admit. Ella had once referred to her mother as her best friend. That changed when she hit adolescence, which was fine, Beverley knew the importance of letting your children be who they wanted to be. She'd thought they'd have more time together after she left Southern Pharmaceuticals, but the sporadic bickering and animosity had only got worse. At first, she worried her daughter had been traumatised by that horrific car crash. Ella was in the same year as the boys and it must have been quite the shock to attend the funeral of a classmate. She had been friendly with Leo Patterson, and Beverley half-thought they'd been dating. She hadn't minded. It was slim pickings in Cooney and the son of a school principal and an accountant was at least a respectable first boyfriend. Anyway, Ella had laughed at the suggestion. They weren't even that friendly any more, she'd said. But if it wasn't the crash, then what was it? What had turned her into an argumentative teenager at the very point she should have been exiting that phase?

'So not a word to anyone else,' repeated Beverley. 'Got that, Ella?'

'Mmm.' Her daughter's head disappeared into the fridge. 'Except Granny.'

'No, including Granny.'

'Yeah, well, too late. I already told her.'

'*What?*'

Beverley brought her hand down hard on the marble worktop and waited for her daughter to show herself.

'You know, I think I have everything, so I can just—'

'Don't go on my behalf,' said Ella, emerging with a yoghurt, and speaking to Christine as if she was the only person in the room. 'I'm going upstairs now.'

'Ella Belle Franklin. What do you mean you told Granny?'

'I rang to wish her happy birthday, which I hear is more than you did.' Ella opened the yoghurt and slurped a bit from the carton. She did this to annoy her. Beverley resisted the urge to throw a spoon at the ingrate. Ella shrugged. 'Granny asked.'

'My mother asked if Amelia had sent any naked photos lately?'

'No,' said Ella, heading for the door. 'She asked how Amelia was, so I told her.'

'You couldn't just have said "Fine", no? You had to ...' From the corner of her eye, she could see Christine starting to gather her belongings. She still had to ask about copy approval and to see if they could get some vague reference to the boy's 'troubled family background' or how the family was 'known to gardaí' into the piece. 'We'll talk about this later, Ella.'

'Whatever you say, Bev,' sang her daughter, as she swung out of the door, and disappeared back into the foyer.

'**A**rlo? Is that you?'

He followed his mother's voice into the living room where the Nine O'Clock News was on mute. The house was always quiet now. Connie Whitehead was sitting on the couch, remote by her side and mobile in her hand.

'Hi, Mom.'

'How was today?'

'Long,' he said, throwing himself down beside her. 'And grand,' he added. 'Today was grand.'

It actually had been. He'd had an easy introduction to Glass Lake. Seamus had given him the tour and Principal Patterson hadn't been mentioned let alone sighted. Fiona Murphy's was a bit awkward but she'd added a sizeable tip. He'd had two jobs outside the town after that; neither family seemed to have feelings on him one way or the other.

'How was your day?' he asked. 'How was work?'

'Work was fine.'

His mother was a teller in a bank on Main Street. Arlo had wanted her to ask for a backroom position after the car crash, but she refused. She said people were welcome to bad-mouth her husband; she'd probably agree with them. But it wasn't just Charlie

Whitehead they bad-mouthed. After the trial, a man had come in, thrown a carton of eggs at her counter and demanded to know when she was going to get the fuck out of Cooney. Arlo only knew about it because the man, an uncle of Mike's, had come up to him in Connolly's and gloated about what he'd done. His mother hadn't said a word, which made him wonder what else she didn't tell him.

'Really?'

'Yes, really,' she said, throwing an arm around his shoulders. 'I had a call from Glass Lake, though ...'

Had he done something wrong? Had someone complained? Surely, they wouldn't ring his mother. He was eighteen. If Seamus had a problem—

'... about Woody.'

'Oh, right.' But the relief was short-lived. 'What about Woody? Is he okay?'

'He's been sending naked photos of himself to a girl in his class. And this girl has been sending them back to him. Amelia Franklin, you know, of *the* Franklins.' His mother shook her head. 'I've to go in and talk to Nuala tomorrow, which, you know, is not ideal, but it's fine.' She looked at him. 'Arlo, it's fine.' This was how it worked now; both trying to make the other feel better, both failing miserably.

'Amelia Franklin?' He hadn't spoken to Ella since he left that morning. He'd barely looked at his phone. But the clogs were turning now, things slipping into place. 'How did the school find out?'

Connie sighed. 'Well, that bit's even worse. The girl's mother walked in on her taking a picture. A picture of herself, like.' She winced. 'God help me, but the first thing I thought was, Rather her than me. Can you imagine if I'd walked in on Woody doing the same? Mother of Jesus. Anyway, Beverley – you know Beverley

Franklin? – was beside herself, which is fair enough. And she went up to the school.'

His mother didn't know about him and Ella, but for different reasons to the Franklins. Her husband had just been sent to jail and he didn't want to rub her nose in his happiness. Or at least that was how he'd reasoned it to Ella. He also liked having another world to escape to, one that was just for him, one where he didn't have to feel bad whenever he started to feel good.

'Did this all happen today?' asked Arlo, recalling the argument between Amelia and Beverley that morning.

'This morning. And I've talked to Woody, before you start. I've taken his phone off him. George says he's probably just acting out, missing his father's influence. He's offered to take him fishing or hiking or on some other male-bonding activity.'

'George from the bank?'

'My friend George, yes.'

'He doesn't even know Woody.'

'It was just a suggestion.'

'I can take Woody fishing.'

His mother gave him a look. 'Since when do you fish?'

'Since now, if it's what Woody needs.'

'George and I are just friends, Arlo.'

'I know,' he said defensively.

'George is happily married. Very happily.'

'So are you.'

A beat. 'Right.'

'I'm going up to talk to Woody,' he declared, sounding more confident than he felt. He was no longer sure how to speak to Woody. As a brother? As a father? As a friend? 'Is he in his room?'

118

'He is.' Connie watched her eldest son make his way towards the door. He was never comfortable being observed.

He could smell his own stale sweat. If he stank last night, he really stank now. He desperately needed a shower.

'There's a letter for you on the kitchen table. From your dad.'

'Did you open it?'

'No, I did not open your post.' Her gaze drifted back to the muted screen, where a beaming weather forecaster was now standing beside a massive map of Ireland. 'I just assume he's the only person writing to you from Cork Prison.'

Arlo moved out into the hallway. He didn't like the turn the conversation had taken.

'You don't have to visit, whatever he says,' she called after him. 'You don't owe him anything. None of us do.'

....

'So, you want to report a missing cat?'

'No, not missing,' said Christine, pacing the kitchen with her mobile stuck to her ear. 'Abducted. He's not missing because I know exactly where he is. He's at number one Seaview Terrace, probably stretched out on the couch, licking himself.'

Conor looked up from his seat at the dining table, where he'd been nursing a tumbler of whiskey since she'd arrived home from the Franklins' and poured it for him. He had relayed his latest attempt to retrieve their cat like a soldier detailing atrocities witnessed at the front.

'Seaview ... Are you at Seaview Heights? Did you already phone this in?'

'No. We're the next road over. This is my first time calling.'

119

'I have a record of a missing cat from Seaview Heights, in June.'

'The cat has only just been swiped. And I'm at Seaview Terrace, not Heights, number seven. Look, can I just speak to the sergeant?' She knew Sergeant Whelan through work. He was always good for an off-the-record quote.

'The sergeant really is in a meeting, Mrs Maguire. If I interrupt him for a missing cat, I'll lose my job.'

'But the cat's not missing!'

Conor caught her sleeve. 'Tell them about the fur.' He mimed his fingertips being stuck together, then slowly he pulled them apart. 'It was all ...'

'Listen, Garda Delaney, wasn't it?'

'Yes, Ma'am.'

'Our cat has been abducted by a woman called Rita Rodgers. She's our neighbour. If you send a guard out to have a chat with her, I'm sure she'll give it back. That's all it would take.'

'Have you tried asking this woman to give you back the cat?'

'My husband tried mediation but she's refusing to return the animal, so I felt I had no choice but to get the guards involved. She coaxed him into her house with food and treats, and then she assigned him a new identity.'

'It was matted together,' whispered Conor. 'You should have seen ... All these great big clumps ...'

She pushed his glass closer.

'So, can you send someone out? Get a guard to have a word? Tell her to hand over the animal?'

'Oh, hang on, is it Seaview Crescent? I have a missing cat here: brown, last seen in August. Is that yours?'

'It's Seaview Terrace. Terrace!'

Conor flinched. The line went quiet.

'Hello?'

'One second, Mrs Maguire.' There was a harsh rustle against her ear as the officer put his hand over the receiver. She could hear him explaining the situation to a co-worker: 'Missing cat ... abducted ... no, seriously ... I can't ... I don't think I should ...' She thought she heard someone laugh.

When he came back on the line, the phone was on loudspeaker.

'Look, I know this isn't exactly blazing-sirens stuff, but I'm phoning on behalf of my kids. They're distraught without Porcupine.' This wasn't entirely true. Only Maeve had enquired about his whereabouts when Christine got home, and even then, she had been distracted by news of her costumes position on the musical.

'Porcupine?' repeated the officer. 'I thought it was a cat.'

'It is a cat. That's his name.'

Some sort of snort came from further away, then someone else hissed, 'Shhh!'

Christine clenched her free hand into a fist. 'Our son chose it. And now our deranged neighbour is calling him Albert. The name isn't really the point. The point is that our neighbour has stolen our cat and is pretending it's a different animal.'

'Why would she dye his fur?' said Conor to nobody. 'Why would a human being do that?'

'Okay, well, we'll get an officer on this as soon as one becomes available. Thank you for the call, Mrs Maguire.'

'What if it's a case of animal cruelty?' she said, before he could hang up. 'Then would you take it seriously?'

'I can assure you we take all complaints seriously, and in line with procedure, I have created a file and—'

'Yes, yes, yes, I know. But this is animal cruelty. This woman is abusing our cat.'

The line went completely silent as she was placed on mute. She could just imagine all of Aberstown Station enjoying a hearty chuckle.

'Animal cruelty?' said Garda Delaney when the line returned.

'Yes. She dyed his fur.'

'Excuse me?'

'He used to be a sandy colour but now he has a big patch of dark brown on his back—'

'Black,' whispered Conor. 'It was pitch black, like her soul.'

'I mean, black, a huge patch of black on his back, and all the hair was matted together from the dye.'

Conor took a large gulp of whiskey.

'She never sought his consent,' said Christine. 'Or ours. She just did it.'

The line went dead again.

'Hello?'

More silence.

'Hello? Are you still there?'

The background noise returned. '*Yes,*' said the officer, his voice now high and breathless.

Then the line went silent again.

'Oh, for feck sake.' She lowered her own phone. 'He's putting me on mute,' she hissed at Conor. 'So he can have a good laugh.'

A couple more seconds and the line returned. Christine rolled her eyes.

'I'm sorry,' said the young officer. 'We're hav— we're having some technical difficulties here.'

'I'm sure,' said Christine coolly. She wanted to read him the riot act, but she knew she was on loudspeaker and she needed to maintain some shred of respectability with the guards she occasionally dealt with for work.

The officer cleared his throat. 'I'll be sure to ... to add that detail to the file, Mrs Maguire. Thank you.'

More whispering in the background. 'Say it!' 'No.' 'Go on!'

Garda Delaney's voice returned. 'And, ah, I'll forward it on to the ISPCA, to, ah, to the hair and beauty department.'

The last bit tumbled out so fast and so squeaky that she barely caught it.

Then the line went dead.

'Well?' asked Conor, the whiskey entirely drained.

'Well, he had to get off the line before he gave himself a hernia from the hilarity.' Christine sighed. 'We need a Plan B.'

....

When Arlo opened the bedroom door and stuck his head around, Woody pulled his hand away from his mouth.

'Hey,' he said.

'Oh, hi. Hey.' Woody threw down the controller and turned away from the old TV set. 'I thought it was Mom. How – how are you?'

Arlo laughed, relieved. His brother could still be his old pre-teenage mutation self, awkward and earnest. 'Grand, thanks. How are you? You weren't just sucking your thumb there, were you?'

'No.' Woody went a shade of red that was familiar to Arlo, and he instantly regretted saying anything.

'Sorry,' he said, still standing in the doorway. 'How are you?'

'Fine.'

'Mom told me about the photos.'

'Oh.'

'Yeah,' said Arlo. The screen behind his brother was paused on a computer game image of two men in army combats firing at someone else. The gamer tag in the corner said 'Ruth'. If that was another girl from school, he didn't want to know.

'Are you mad at me?'

'Of course I'm not mad at you. But like, you know you shouldn't have done it, don't you?'

'Yeah, I know. I'm sorry.'

'Why did you do it?'

Woody shrugged.

'Do you want to talk about it?'

'No.'

'Okay,' said Arlo, relieved. His own cheeks were starting to burn at the idea of discussing his little brother's naked body – or worse, Ella's little sister's naked body. 'It'll be all right. Mom will calm down, and it'll blow over. If she can get past the car crash ...'

But Woody didn't smile, and Arlo stopped forcing his.

He didn't know why he'd said that. It wasn't funny.

'Amelia's mom is really mad.'

'Yeah ...' Of all the students Woody could have been messaging, Beverley Franklin's youngest daughter really was a bad choice. 'Maybe stay away from Amelia for a while.'

'I am staying away from her. She told me that, about her mom being mad. I didn't ask.'

'Good. That's good.'

Woody looked at him. Arlo nodded emphatically.

Neither of them had any more to say.

124

'Do you want to play with me? I'm in the middle of a mission but I can leave if you want?'

'I better have a shower. I stink.'

'Okay.' His brother turned back to his game and the screen started to move again.

He wanted to tell his little brother he loved him, but it seemed too dramatic for a Thursday night; it might sound like he was dying of cancer or off to kill himself or something. So instead he said 'Goodnight' and headed for his own room, ignoring the guilty sense of relief.

When their dad told them he loved them, he made it sound like the obvious next line in whatever mundane conversation they were having. How did he do that? Arlo couldn't even bring himself to say it to Ella, though he did love her, and he knew exactly what he wanted to say.

I love you, Ella Belle Franklin. You saved my life.

I'm going to stop telling you things if you're going to mock me.

Sorry, Arly, but that's not how it works. I live in your head now. I know everything you think.

He lowered himself down on to the pale blue sheets of his single bed and examined the envelope. His name and address were scrawled across the front, while Cork Prison was stamped on the reverse.

Leo hadn't come to Charlie Whitehead's sentencing. After the crash, he went to a physical rehab facility in Dublin and hadn't set foot in Cooney since. Mr and Mrs Patterson had been in the court gallery. They'd sat near the back, beside Mike Roche's parents. Arlo felt uncomfortable that he and his mother were in the front row, as if they were saying they were more important or something. When the sentence was handed down, Mr Roche had shouted, 'Is that justice? Is that justice?' Nobody had answered and sometimes Arlo still heard the question hanging in the air. Mr Patterson moved to Dublin shortly afterwards, and when Leo was able to leave the rehab unit, he moved in with his dad. Several of the women he did jobs for told him the Pattersons were getting a divorce, as if, somehow, Arlo might enjoy that piece of information.

Mike's parents had moved too. That really upset people. Mr Roche was the best coach Cooney GAA had ever had, and now he was gone. But the Whiteheads, who'd never added anything to the local football team, were still here. His family's only contribution to the town, if you listened to the current gossip, was death, misery and dodgy plug socket fixtures. He could appreciate why they were so annoyed.

Arlo's chest ached like it sometimes did when he thought about his dad. He tried to imagine him sitting down – in a cell? At a desk? – to write to him. Was he sad? Lonely? Nervous? Scared? Did he have friends in prison? Did people like him? Did they still laugh at his jokes and ask for his opinions? These were the things Arlo wanted to know but they were too childish to ask. He had spoken to his father twice by phone since May. Both times, he had felt like he was choking. He couldn't get the words out. Nothing seemed important enough to say. The more he thought about these calls the worse he felt and the more he avoided speaking to him again. But he wanted to talk to him – and talk about him. Nobody else did, though, not his friends, not his neighbours, not even his wife.

Or me. I don't want to talk about him either.

And I don't want to talk to you about him, Leo, so don't worry. Are you going to open that letter, or are you too scared?

Why would I be scared of a letter?

It's you, Arly. You jump when people look at you.

Sometimes it seemed impossible that Cooney would ever like him. He was breaking his back for people who would never let him be unremarkable again because they needed someone to discuss and the Whiteheads were still the best offering.

He thought of Ella and felt both better and worse.

If she spent a day in his head, she'd understand why he couldn't study.

Are you actually feeling sorry for yourself? You're the only one who walked away with your former life fully intact.

It's not exactly intact. People literally spit at me on the street.

Boo fucking hoo. And you got the girl. Fuck knows you didn't deserve that.

His bedroom was suddenly all out of proportion. It felt like he was reclining in a matchbox. Everything was tiny while he remained the same size. Slowly, he stretched out his right arm, convinced it would touch the opposite wall, but of course it was several feet away. He closed his eyes and counted to twenty. He breathed in and out.

He would keep trying, keep working hard, and everything would come right.

It just had to.

15
......

ABERSTOWN GARDA STATION

Joey knocked on the sergeant's door and waited for the bark instructing him to enter. The man was sitting at his desk, eating another sandwich. This one appeared to be tuna.

'Sorry to disturb you, sir ...'

'Are the second batch of parents here already?'

'Not yet. I just wanted to drop in the transcribed statements from this morning – before we have to start round two.'

'Very quick, Delaney. Good job.'

'Thank you, sir. My mother taught me to type. I could do fifty-five words per minute by the time I was ten; sixty-five by the time I was twelve.'

'Did I ask for your life story, Delaney?'

'No, sir,' he said, dropping the pages on to his boss's desk and pulling up his belt. 'No, you did not.'

'Anything noteworthy in here?'

'A lot of talk about the kids sending naked photographs.'

'Yah, that came up with me too.' The sergeant caught a large dollop of mayonnaise with his tongue before it splashed out of the sandwich and on to the freshly typed-up pages. 'Anything else, though? Anything that might actually explain why we were fishing a body out of the Gorm yesterday evening?'

'It's hard to say.'

'I'll take that as a no.' The sergeant sighed, wiping at his mouth then throwing the half-eaten tuna sandwich down on to the crisp paper. Joey tried not to wince. 'They're an opinionated bunch, aren't they – the Glass Lake parents?'

'They are, sir,' he agreed. 'Very, ah, strong willed. I got that impression from the information night.'

'Yes, that came up a few times too,' said his boss, moving both hands to his lower back as he stretched it out. 'Is it true two of the fathers almost came to blows, right in the middle of the assembly?'

'It is,' said Joey, as the sergeant reached for his food. 'I gave the main speaker a police escort home. A few of them looked ready to charge the stage.'

....

Sally Martin, parent
On at least three occasions, I saw Mr Cafferty
slipping files to parents. I don't know what
was in them and I can't say if it's related
or not, but it's worth looking into. I'm not
exaggerating when I say 'slipping'. He was not
just handing them over. There was something in
there that he did not want anyone to see. I'm
not telling you how to do your job but that, to
me, is worth investigating.

Fiona Murphy, parent

I say this from a place of respect, friendship and concern, but Beverley Franklin has been acting unhinged for a couple of weeks now. I'm her friend; Lakers for life. But if I was looking for someone who might be capable of pushing someone to their death, that's where I'd start. And I wasn't the only one who noticed. Ask anyone who was at the parents' information night, for a start. That was when she began to unravel.

16

TEN DAYS EARLIER

'Sexting' row at Glass Lake Primary

By Christine Maguire

A concerned mother has lodged an official complaint with Glass Lake Primary after her daughter was involved in a 'sexting' exchange with a male student.

The mother, who cannot be named to protect the children's identity, has called for the male student to be expelled and described the school's response to the situation as 'wholly inadequate'.

The male student, who is in sixth class, sent a nude photograph of himself to the female student, also in sixth class, and asked that the gesture be reciprocated. The girl did so shortly afterwards.

'Glass Lake has a responsibility to keep its students safe,' the mother said. 'It needs to ensure the children receive adequate education about the internet, and it also needs to remove any students who are a threat to the well-being of everyone else at the school.'

Nuala Patterson, principal of Glass Lake Primary, said the school did not comment on individual students, but that an information night is being organised for parents, with fifth- and sixth-class students due to receive two additional sex education workshops this week.

••••••••••••••••••••••••••

It was impossible to say what a typical autumn evening was like on the tree-lined stretch that wound its way from Franklin Avenue up to the main Glass Lake building because, typically, nobody was here to experience it. Arlo imagined it was very still; the only light coming from whatever stars were not blanketed in clouds sent inland by the Atlantic, and the only sound the wind working its way in and out of the branches of the 200-year-old oaks.

He and Ella should walk up the avenue some night, see what the quietness was like. He'd bring his warmest coat, in case she got cold, and if they heard something rustling amongst the trees, he would walk on that side, an arm thrown protectively around her waist. And maybe, if they found a clearing, and the mood took them, they—

The short, sharp blast of a horn brought Arlo back to the present.

A man's head appeared out the driver's side of a year-old Merc. 'Oi, space cadet! Any chance we can hurry this up?'

Tonight was not a typical autumn evening on Glass Lake's avenue. Tonight was a parents' information night.

A cacophony of purring engines, tyres on fallen leaves, and honking horns ran the length of the private avenue that led up to the school. Dozens of impatient parents were waiting to be told where to park. The headlights and backlights were dipped, but still they created a glow in the sky above like the aurora borealis.

He tugged at the reflective jacket that kept slipping down his arm and gestured for the Merc to approach. The fluorescent stick Seamus had left for him was already starting to malfunction.

Arlo had never seen the aurora borealis. He wasn't even sure what country it was in or, come to think of it, what exactly it was. But still. Beauty was beauty. And it would make a good lyric. It had the bonus of rhyming with Alice.

Eh ... who's Alice?

Who was Eleanor Rigby? It doesn't matter. We'll write a song about her and then she'll be someone.

I'm pretty sure there are already a few songs about people called Alice.

And they'll all be sick that they didn't think of rhyming it with aurora borealis.

Go on so, Lennon and McCartney, what are you thinking?

Aurora borealis, a door for Alice.

Abbey Road, here we come.

Shut up. I'm brainstorming.

The Merc came to a stop beside him. The driver gave him a look.

'Here for the information night?' asked Arlo, cutting the father off at the pass. 'Are you fifth- or sixth-class parents?'

'Fifth,' said the woman in the passenger seat, and Arlo watched her face do the thing parents' faces had been doing all evening.

'Fifth, okay, so just park by the sports hall. There should be plenty of spaces. If you could keep in line with the other vehicles, that would be great. Thank you.'

He pointed his semaphore rod in the direction of the sports hall with such conviction that it flew from his hand.

He caught the beginning of the woman's comment to her husband – 'That's the boy who' – as their window rolled up and they drove on.

....

'Oh, for heaven's sake,' Beverley muttered when the young man in the fluorescent jacket pulled his head away from the window of Tony Moran's Mercedes and threw his traffic baton on to the path, causing it to extinguish.

'What is it?' Malachy glanced in the rear-view mirror and slowly moved the car forward. The gravel caught on the wheel underneath.

The entirety of the Lakers' summer fundraiser just two years ago had gone towards repaving the yard. This was what happened when they let Principal Patterson hire the contractor herself.

'That's the Whitehead boy, the older one,' she said, pointing through the front windscreen. 'The one from the car crash.'

'From Ella's year?' Malachy squinted into the darkness where Arlo had recouped the broken baton and was brandishing it furiously, as if trying to cast a difficult spell. 'Not exactly setting the world alight, is he?'

Malachy put the car into first and inched forward. Then he was rolling down the window and opening his face into a broad smile. In the generous, confident voice he always used with the people of Cooney – his dynasty voice, as Beverley thought of it – he said, 'All right, son? Cold evening to be standing about outdoors.'

If Beverley had been hoping for a show of paternal protectiveness when she told Malachy about Woody soliciting photos from their daughter, she hadn't got it. 'They're young,' he'd said. 'Young people don't think.' Beverley was tempted to ask what his excuse was so, since he was forty. But she didn't, of course. They never spoke about the photos she'd found on his phone. It was dealt with, over, nothing more to say.

'I hope they're paying you a princely sum for this,' Malachy continued, as Arlo stared dumbly into the car, his broken baton hanging by his side.

'Yes, sir,' the boy mumbled, glancing from Malachy to Beverley. 'It is cold.'

Beverley leaned out slightly so she could be seen. She raised her eyebrows. 'Are you going to grant us permission to drive on?'

'Yes. Yes, sorry. The sixth-class parents are in the far yard, up by the swimming pool. You can head on up.'

'Very kind of you.' There was something especially irritating about a Whitehead telling them where to park in the yard they had built, or at least paid to have resurfaced.

She didn't need to look to know Malachy was making his apologetic face. It was the one he used with waiters. It said: 'If you think not accepting tagliatelle as a substitute for linguine is bad, you should try living with her.'

The engine started again. 'Thank you, son, and try not to get frostbite. You're doing a great job.'

Beverley focused her eyes on the space just above the dashboard. It was about the only way she could stop them from rolling.

The window closed and Malachy released the handbrake. 'Those looks are wasted on that kid,' he said, as the car rolled forward. 'Not really at the races, is he?'

Beverley had had a bad feeling about this information night ever since she'd received the To-All-Parents email on Friday afternoon. When she said she wanted something done, she meant she wanted Woody Whitehead gone. She did not want free cheese and a lengthy lecture.

Malachy's priority was that nobody know their daughter was the girl being discussed. Of course he wasn't going to drive over to the Whiteheads and start pounding on their door; he had no interest in making a scene. It was for the best that the *Southern Gazette* article had ended up as a small piece on page nine, overshadowed by an obscenely large photo of the town pharmacist straddling a bike in Lycra and holding a hefty petition above his head with such pride you'd swear he'd won the Tour de France. Ella had agreed to keep quiet about a journalist being at their house, though Beverley knew the payback for that favour was still to come. And Malachy didn't read the local papers. Not unless he was in them.

'Go right here. We're not parking by the pool.'

'The boy said—'

'I don't care what he said. I'm not parking in a yard. Go up to the staff spaces. We paid for that car park; we can at least get some use out of it.'

As soon as the Audi was stationary, there was a tap on Malachy's window. He opened the door to reveal Fiona Murphy, dressed in a bright pink bomber jacket.

'Hi, Mal; nice scarf. Hi, Bev.' She bent over slightly and wiggled her fingers into the car.

Fiona had been particularly irritating the past few weeks. She kept grinning at Beverley and giving her the exact same knowing look that was currently plastered across her face. She was acting like she had something on Beverley. It had started long before the incident with Amelia and the photo, so at least it wasn't that.

'We better get inside, Malachy.'

'We still have a few minutes,' said Fiona, taking a half-step back so Malachy had just about enough space to exit the vehicle.

Beverley smiled at the lower-ranking Laker. 'You can squeeze in anywhere, Fiona – a real benefit of being on your own. It's much harder when you're in a couple.' She linked her husband's arm, aware of how enviable it and every other part of him was. 'We need to find two seats together.'

<hr>

'Oh God,' said Christine, slouching down in the passenger seat. 'Can we park somewhere else?'

'Why?' asked Conor, eyes on the side mirror as he reversed slightly to better approach the parking space. 'Is this not where the young fella meant? It was hard to tell. A black stick in the darkness; not very helpful, is it?'

The Franklins were out of their Audi and talking to Fiona Murphy. Butcher Murphy was probably lurking somewhere nearby. She had been in for steaks that afternoon, and still he'd referred to her as The Vegetarian.

'I don't want to talk to Beverley Franklin. She'll be raging about the article. She probably thought it would be on the front page – complete with a cowboy-style Wanted poster for Woody Whitehead.' She watched Beverley link her husband, catching her hair with her other hand and tucking it into her sleek mac. 'I suppose it's hard being that wealthy; you must struggle to find things to worry about.'

'Everyone has their worries,' said Conor, eyes still trained on the mirror as he shifted the steering wheel ever so slightly to the right, then back to the left.

'Not Beverley Franklin. You don't know her. You should see their house. Literally fish in the floor.'

'I do know Beverley.'

'You're her dentist, Conor. You know her teeth.'

'You can tell a lot about a person from their teeth.'

'Well, I sat in the same classroom as her for eight years, and I'm telling you she expects to be the centre of attention, always. She will not like having been relegated to the bottom of page nine by Gerry Regan's crusade to stop trucks driving through Cooney.'

Christine was delighted the article had been relegated. She'd got a frosty response when she phoned Nuala Patterson for a comment. The principal had been more welcoming about her covering tonight's event. A story she'd been working on had fallen through (the local estate agent finally admitted it might not have been *that* Cillian Murphy he'd sold the house to) and Derek had gone for the sex education evening as a replacement. 'We can do spin-off lists,' he'd enthused. Derek loved lists. 'Five Signs Your Kids Are at Risk Online. Ten Things the Youngsters Aren't Telling You. Sexting: Six Ways to Tell if You're Doing it Right.'

'How's the alignment your side?'

Christine peered out into the pitch black where she couldn't tell the colour of the car beside them, never mind see the lines on the ground. From the glow at the school entrance, though, she could see that the Franklins had stopped to talk to someone else. 'I dunno, Conor, maybe another inch to the left.'

'On it,' he mumbled, rounding his shoulders.

She relaxed back into the seat, rubbing the condensation from the windscreen with the cuff of her coat sleeve. Malachy Franklin was probably the best-looking father at Glass Lake, though he was too suave for her. She preferred them gauche and earnest – or at least she had done the last time she stopped to consider how she liked her men, which was probably fifteen years ago.

Conor pushed his thin-rimmed glasses up and moved his face closer to the glass. 'Aim for perfection and you might just achieve it,' he muttered. He'd rather drive around all night than park a car that was even a degree off straight. It was the dentist in him.

The engine died, and he tapped the steering wheel with a satisfied sigh. 'Beautiful,' he said, before unbuckling his belt. 'Right, let's go.'

The Franklins were still chattering away. Christine could hear the echo of Malachy's big, hollow laugh.

'Do you want to phone Caroline and make sure everything's okay at home?'

Conor gave her a look. She was not the type of parent who spent the evening away from her kids worrying about her kids. Out of sight, out of mind was more her motto.

'I left my phone at home, charging,' he said, opening his door.

'I can do it?'

'No. Let's go.' The door swung shut after him.

Conor rapped on the window. Christine groaned.

'Fine,' she grumbled, pushing open her own door and clambering out.

The Franklins were standing in the entranceway talking to the Farrells, who also had a daughter in sixth class. Lorna Farrell was wearing a jacket identical to Beverley's and her husband Bill was sporting a large 'Farrell No. 1' badge on his lapel, even though he'd been elected to the council several months ago.

'Conor, how's it going? How's the teeth business?' bellowed Bill, as the whole group turned in their direction.

Beverley caught her eye, then immediately looked away.

'Fine, Bill, just fine. Thanks.'

'I must get in for a check-up soon. Hahaha.'

Bill was a patient with both dentists in Cooney, just like he bought meat from all three butchers and declared every pub his local. A true politician.

'We were just saying how much we're looking forward to being told our children should be playing with abacuses and spinning tops until they're eighteen,' boomed Bill. 'It's a brave new world, and we'd rather not be parenting in it, but here we are.'

Malachy smiled conspiratorially at Christine, who was mortified to find herself blushing. Was standing at the entrance to Glass Lake all it took to turn her into a schoolgirl again?

'How are you, Beverley?' she said, as Bill asked Conor something about rates subsidies and the group became divided along gender lines.

'Fine,' said Beverley curtly, as if this was a bizarre question to be asked. Had she really expected them to run an 'Off With his Head' type article? He was a twelve-year-old boy.

Lorna squeezed her lips into a wide, tight smile. 'I see you managed to get Maeve down for costumes, Christine. Weren't happy to accept my answer on it?'

'Well, I was talking to Beverley anyway, so I just asked if there might be space ...'

Lorna turned to Beverley. 'I thought you said the request came from the school.'

'I'm sorry, Lorna. Are you director of this year's musical, or is that me?'

'You.'

'Right, so stop asking stupid questions. Malachy' – Beverley reached for her husband's arm – 'we should get inside.'

The Franklins left and Lorna glowered at Christine as if she were the one who'd reprimanded her.

'Ready?' asked Conor, side-stepping over to her.

'Very,' she said, and gratefully accompanied him inside.

• • • • • •

17

The parents trooped in and selected their seats: not too far back as to appear uninterested, not too near the stage in case they were asked a question to which they didn't know the answer. The perimeter of the auditorium was lined with long tables topped with tablecloths and refreshments. These were manned by teachers and volunteers – that curious breed who attend parents' nights, even when it doesn't affect their own children. Most of them were Lakers.

Christine took out her notebook.

Some 100 parents attended the information night held at Glass Lake Primary on Monday.

Which wasn't surprising. Glass Lake parents had better attendance records than their children.

Maeve's new teacher, Mr Cafferty, unstacked cups and saucers from plastic pallets and arranged them in four neat rows on a table in the far-right corner.

Teachers were on hand to help. Refreshments were served ...

At the adjacent table, a younger Laker was removing the lid from the large tea urn and peering inside while Mrs Walsh, who'd been teaching Junior Infants and making tea for parents' nights since

Christine was at Glass Lake, watched on nervously. The Laker stuck in a cup, scooped out some liquid, swirled it around and sipped, like she was completing her sommelier qualifications. Across the room, Mr Peoples, the choirmaster, was laying out sandwiches and cakes, while another Laker clipped at his heels. Every time he finished a platter, she swooped in and rearranged it.

... with military precision.

She could have written this in her sleep.

'I'll get some tea,' she said, pulling Conor to one side as Fiona Murphy barrelled past, making a sound somewhere between a hush and a hiss as Butcher Murphy hot-stepped after her. 'You find the seats.'

'Here?' said Conor, gesturing to two empty chairs beside them, in the second last row.

'Are you insane? No. Somewhere in the middle.'

Mr Cafferty was taking tea and coffee orders while Mrs Walsh filled them, under the watchful eye of the designated Laker. Lorna Farrell and the Auburn Bob from the Strand last Thursday were in front of Christine in the line, interrogating the new teacher.

'You could come along the Thursday of the Halloween mid-term. You wouldn't have school then,' Lorna was saying, taking a cup without looking at it. 'There's no mid-term from parenting. And it is parents, usually, but we'd make an exception for a brand-new teacher. We meet every Thursday morning, all year.'

'Except Christmas,' added Auburn Bob.

Lorna nodded. 'The Strand is closed at Christmas.'

'I would love to come –' began Mr Cafferty.

'Excellent.'

'It's a date!'

'– but I'm away for mid-term.'

'Really?'

'Are you actually?'

'Yes,' he said, taken aback by the follow-up question. 'I promise.'

'That's a shame,' said Auburn Bob. 'It's just you teach our kids and we know so little about you.'

'We know you're married.' Lorna nodded towards his wedding ring. 'What does your wife do? Is she from around here?'

'What's your background?' added Auburn Bob.

'Do you have children?'

'Oh, well. Okay.' The man swallowed nervously but managed to retain his smile. 'I, I worked in tech before retraining as a teacher. This is my second school; I was in the midlands before. Jess is a wedding planner ...'

'Jess,' repeated Auburn Bob. Christine could almost see her opening a new mental folder and filing it inside.

'We don't have children.'

'Yet.'

Mr Cafferty laughed. 'Right,' he said agreeably.

The women's eyes lit up at this.

'So, you do want them?'

'Soon?'

'Sounds like soon to me. It's never worth waiting. You must be what, late thirties? How old is your wife? The same age, I imagine. You don't want to hang around too long.'

'That's right. Just ask Una Rawle.'

Lorna made a '*Mmm*' sound, as if Una Rawle was recently deceased of shrivelled ovaries, rather than a living and perfectly happy (as far as she could tell of the local physio) mother-of-one.

'Okay, ladies,' said Christine loudly. 'There are several parched parents here, desperate for a cup of tea.'

Lorna looked around at her with that same psychotic smile. 'I'm surprised you're queuing, Christine. Why don't you just bypass the whole system and go back there and make your own tea? Isn't that how you like to do things?'

Christine no longer regretted the Lick-Arse moniker. One more comment and she was going to tell her, with relish, that she was the one who'd started it.

'Two teas please, Mr Cafferty,' she said instead. 'One with lots of milk, one with a dash.'

'If your mid-term plans fall through you know where we'll be,' said Lorna, giving the sixth-class teacher a meaningful look. 'And you'll throw me into the mix for those weekly progress reports, right? Beverley spoke very highly of the one you did on Amelia. Whatever you're doing for her would be perfect.'

The teacher nodded, and the woman moved on.

'Don't give them anything.'

'Sorry?'

'Don't tell them a thing about yourself,' she elaborated, as Mr Cafferty glanced at his phone then stuffed it back into his pocket. He took a tea from Mrs Walsh and passed it forward.

'Oh, it's fine, I don't mind,' he said.

'There'll be a pool going on your first offspring's date of birth by the end of this evening. And the most popular Google search in Cooney tonight will be Jess Cafferty wedding planner.'

His face twitched. 'We kept our own names.'

'Well, lucky for you,' said Christine, leaning forward to take the second cup that the teacher seemed to forget he was holding. 'And for her.'

The reverberating echo of a throat being cleared brought Christine's attention to the stage. Nuala Patterson was standing in front of a lectern embossed with the school crest. Balancing the two cups, Christine worked her way back across the hall.

There were three chairs set up on the stage. The principal had vacated one, while another was occupied by a young guard, presumably from Aberstown Station. (Cooney did not have its own police station. While this could easily have become a petition issue, residents embraced it as proof of Cooney's low crime rate.) The third chair was filled by Dr Cian O'Sullivan, a child psychologist from north Cork. The *Southern Gazette* had run several articles on him. He was also a second cousin of Nuala Patterson.

She slipped into the chair beside Conor and handed him his tea-y milk.

Principal Patterson welcomed them all and set out the evening's running order. She looked tired, but then maybe Christine was projecting. She'd heard rumours Leo Patterson and his dad weren't coming back. She couldn't imagine the strain something like that must place on a family.

The principal listed Dr O'Sullivan's many accolades – though only his local address got a round of applause – and said he would be talking about the parents' role in keeping their children safe online. He had agreed to do two workshops as part of the Relationship and Sexualities Programme with the sixth-class students, this coming Thursday and Friday, and would explain what they entailed. A few rows in front, Lorna Farrell blessed herself at the word 'sexualities'.

The guard would talk to them about the legalities of uploading and sharing images online. And finally – you could hear the defeat in the principal's voice already – there would be time for questions. Glass Lake parents never waited until the end to ask questions.

She did not recognise the guard and so suspected it was the same one who'd found Porcupine's abduction so hilarious. They'd told the children the truth now. Or the half-truth, in Maeve's case; Porcupine was on his holidays at Mrs Rodgers. Conor wanted to leave the cat – he still wasn't the better of being gaslit by a woman twice his age. But Christine wasn't giving up. She had a plan – working title: Operation Liberation – and currently had all three kids marking down Mrs Rodgers' movements in a notebook she'd left on the windowsill in the front room.

Principal Patterson retook her seat and Dr O'Sullivan approached the podium. He rested a few pages on the lectern and pushed his thin spectacles down his nose so his brown eyes were smiling over them. 'Everyone sitting comfortably enough to talk about sex?'

A nervous energy sparked through the auditorium as parents shifted in their seats. Lorna folded her arms as if to say, 'That sex talk's not getting in here.'

Christine wrote down the doctor's opening gambit, even though it would never make it into print. Derek talked a good talk, but they all knew the typical *Southern Gazette* reader was over seventy, politically conservative and mainly bought the paper for photos of their grandkids and death notices of their friends. The only time they were sitting comfortably enough to read the word 'sex', never mind talk about it, was in a highly serious context, preferably criminal.

The doctor talked about how technology and discussing sexual health had the potential to make us feel foolish. This got a low rumble of recognition, including from Conor, while others, such as Lorna Farrell, remained stony-faced.

'But your children are technology natives,' he said. 'So, let's gather up those awkward emotions and place them, at least for now, under our chairs.'

Across the room, a man mimed putting something under his seat. His wife yanked him back up.

Slides flashed up on the whiteboard and Dr O'Sullivan talked through them: sexting; inappropriate social media pages; explicit chatrooms; mislabelled videos; grooming; exposure to pornography, both accidental and intentional. Lorna's hand was flying up to her forehead with such regularity now that she should have just left it there. Her husband Bill cleared his throat loudly.

The doctor focused on sexting. He explained that some young people saw it as part of relationships or friendships. Others were mimicking what they'd seen in porn.

A dry cough spread through the hall.

A graph explained that five per cent of children had sent a sexually explicit image by the time they've finished primary school. 'If your child has engaged in sexting, process the information carefully,' he said, as a slide titled 'How Parents Should Respond' flashed up. 'Remember: they will be aware of your reactions.'

The Farrells were no longer the only people squirming. The collective murmur was now colliding with a faint titter and the sound rippled through the hall. Christine took down some of the bullet points as the doctor worked his way through them. These were more palatable and should work for one of Derek's beloved lists.

'I'm sorry,' came a voice from the back of the hall. A woman in a wine-coloured fur coat rose from her seat. She neither looked nor sounded particularly sorry. 'Can you stop, please? We're talking about children here, not teenagers. They're eleven and twelve. This isn't relevant. And, frankly, I don't think it's appropriate.'

A hubbub of agreement went up around the woman and she folded her arms defiantly.

Dr O'Sullivan leaned into the microphone. 'While sexting is concerning amongst primary school children, it's not uncommon. Remember five per cent have sent an explicit photo by the time they leave. That's one in twenty of your children.'

The woman's response was lost in a general swell of discontent. Bill Farrell was on his feet now.

'That's a country average,' he shouted up at the stage, chest puffed out. 'We're talking about Glass Lake.'

A sea of heads bobbed in agreement. Dr O'Sullivan frowned. He didn't understand the distinction. Which showed that while he was from near Cooney, he wasn't from Cooney.

'Isn't this the school's responsibility?' said a man near the front. 'Teachers are meant to teach. They just need to tell the students what is acceptable behaviour and what is not. That's it. We don't need to start talking to them about grooming, for Christ's sake!'

This got a small smattering of applause.

'I'm not suggesting I talk to the children about grooming. These slides are for the adults—'

But Fiona Murphy was on her feet now. 'It's not up to teachers to control what our children do online,' she said to the father near the front. 'Parents need to check their kids' phones. It's up to us to make sure they're not doing anything they're not supposed to. Right, Doc?'

'I'm not sure checking their phones is the best idea,' said someone else. 'It's better to talk to them. It builds trust.'

'I'm sorry,' said the not-sorry woman at the back, 'but we're here because of one incident. One boy and one girl sending each other pictures. At least, that's what the *Southern Gazette* said.'

Christine slouched in her seat.

Dr O'Sullivan looked to Principal Patterson, who nodded. The woman looked exhausted. And Christine was sure she wasn't projecting this time.

'That's right,' he said.

'Right,' echoed the woman. 'So why can't the school just talk to those parents, of the two perpetrators, and stop tarring everyone else's kids with the same nasty brush? It's ridiculous that we all have to come here for a telling-off. This has nothing to do with my daughter. She knows not to send naked pictures of herself. We raised her better than that.'

....

How dare Imelda Dargle call Beverley Franklin a bad parent? It didn't matter that Imelda – who was still wearing her coat even though the auditorium was warm, and it was hideous – didn't know she was talking about Amelia. She was implying the parents of *both* children involved had done a bad job. And after Beverley had cast Imelda's daughter as the Good Witch of the North. She made a mental note to cut some of her lines.

The so-called doctor was talking again now. More blame, no doubt, all directed at Beverley. Was he a real doctor, or just one of those people who'd spent too long at university? He had the air of the latter.

She could almost laugh at the irony of this man telling them not to judge or blame their children, while he was standing up there, judging and blaming her. His 'How Parents Should Respond' guide could have been re-titled 'How Beverley Got It Wrong'.

What should she have done, in the heat of the moment, when she walked into her baby's room to be confronted by ... *that*? Told Amelia to carry on? Offered to hold the phone for her? Suggested she try the bathroom, for better light?

Across the room, Christine Maguire was scribbling into a notebook. She must be reporting on this, too. What had the woman been thinking, talking to her on the way in? She might as well have got up on stage and pointed to Beverley: 'Ladies and gentlemen, my anonymous source!'

She did agree with Imelda on one point, though. It was ridiculous that they were having a public conversation. This could have been solved with a swift expulsion. Nobody was going to lobby to get Woody Whitehead back into the school. She'd spotted Connie Whitehead on her way in, seated in the back row – a sure sign that she didn't give a fiddler's about what was happening on stage.

The so-called doctor was now explaining how aside from sexting (who knew the man could talk about anything else?) he'd be giving the children the 'tools' they needed to stay safe online. Were the Lakers paying for this guff? Nuala Patterson was remarkably good at wasting other people's money.

'Shouldn't we name the children involved, so as to stop suspicion falling on the innocent kids?' said a voice from the front. 'Or at least name the male student. It's always the boys who start it.'

Beverley gave this a loud round of applause. Finally, someone was speaking sense.

'Spoken like the mother of a girl,' retorted someone else, to another smattering of applause.

'Hi, mother of a boy here,' came a familiar voice from the back of the hall. 'I'd be happy to hand over my son's mobile, should the school decide it does want to monitor phone use.'

'Well, we're not handing over our son's property to anyone!' retorted a father in Beverley's row.

'I'm just saying my son has nothing to hide.'

'I don't know who you are, lady, but that's not how it works here.'

'Sorry,' said the woman, whose voice Beverley recognised but couldn't place. 'I should have introduced myself. I'm new here. My name is Tamara Watson.'

Beverley froze.

It couldn't be. Surely.

She turned in her chair, eyes travelling up the aisle until they hit on the woman sitting at the edge of the second-last row, legs sticking out to the side, crossed and swinging.

Tamara Watson. In the flesh.

She looked exactly as she had when Beverley last saw her six months ago. She hadn't seen Tamara since she left Southern Pharmaceuticals, which was also the last time she'd felt this humiliated. And that time, it had all been Tamara's fault.

....

Nuala Patterson tried to muster up the vigour required to keep the Glass Lake parents in line. The young Garda Delaney had an odour of deep-fried chips. Leo had smelled like that sometimes, when he refused to change out of his football gear. She hadn't realised how much she'd missed it. She took her time crossing the stage to the podium, breathing it in deeply. But guilt-free thoughts of her son were impossible now, and before she had exhaled poor Mike

Roche was also in her mind. A lot of people in Cooney had spent more time mourning Mike Senior moving away than they had Mike Junior dying. Even Nuala felt she didn't give the late teenager the reflection he deserved.

'You try taking my son's property off him and I will have you charged with theft so fast you won't have time to open the photo gallery,' one of the school's older parents was saying to the new woman. 'You can't tar all boys with the same brush. Our son knows right from wrong.'

'I'm really not suggesting we check anyone's phones,' said the doctor, though nobody was listening to him any more.

'Our boy has never done anything like sexting,' the father continued, his bald head growing red and shiny.

'That you know of,' said Fiona Murphy, who was seated between Butcher and the new woman, Tamara. 'Kids are very good at hiding stuff.'

'We check his phone regularly,' shouted the father, jabbing his finger in Fiona's direction. 'Check his messages, check his Facebook. That's how I know my son's not up to anything.'

'Kids don't actually use Facebook, John. Maybe that's why you're not finding anything.'

'Also, children can have two accounts on any given social media platform,' came the voice of Claire Keating. 'One for their friends to see, and one for their parents.'

'I'm guessing you've never heard of Finstagram, John?' said Fiona. 'Fake Instagram. No? It's the cover account; the one they want adults to see. John Junior probably has about six of them.'

'I know exactly what my son has and exactly what he's up to. He's not even that interested in computers.'

Fiona made a half-arsed attempt at coughing. 'Okay, Boomer.'

The father's chair scraped against the floor as his wife's (much younger) hand flew up from the chair beside him and held him in place.

Butcher Murphy was also on his feet now, ready to defend his former spouse.

'He finds the internet distracting,' retorted the father.

'Get away out of that!' scoffed Fiona. 'I gave John Junior a lift home from summer camp this year, and the boy barely registered the car had windows.' Fiona mimed some sort of ape pushing buttons with his thumbs.

'How dare you!'

'He thought I Spy was a new Apple tablet!'

'You take that back,' the man shouted, fighting to break free of his wife's grip as Butcher pushed his way out into the aisle.

'Just try it, Slaphead!'

Nuala stepped in beside Dr O'Sullivan, who readily backed away from the podium. In the middle of the stage, Garda Delaney was looking worried. One didn't expect a parents' night to require riot gear.

Nuala pulled the mic towards her.

'Okay,' she said, as Butcher Murphy pretended to play bongo drums, 'let's take a break.'

Beverley moved both ham sandwiches to her left hand and reached out to the passing platter with her right to take a slice of fruit cake. The teenager carrying the tray was Arlo Whitehead. Did he now do everything around here? Would he be teaching Amelia's class next?

'The language the doctor used,' Lorna Farrell was saying, as she held a teacup in one hand and a saucer in the other. 'You wouldn't get it in a brothel. And I didn't care for his tone one bit. He's talking like the students are a bunch of criminals.'

'Taking or sending an explicit photo of a minor is a criminal offence,' said Beth Morton, who was also standing in their circle. 'We deal with this kind of thing regularly at secondary school.'

'But they're taking the photos of themselves,' said Lorna.

'If they're taking photos at all,' clarified Bill.

Sandwiches consumed, Beverley stuffed the fruit cake into her mouth. But the unsettled feeling in her stomach refused to be buried. She surveyed the room, turning her head as far as it would go without making it obvious she was looking for someone.

'It's still technically illegal, even if the images are of themselves,' said Beth.

'Well, I doubt that's true,' scoffed Bill, taking a bite of his own fruit cake.

Beverley had lost sight of Tamara Watson when everyone got up from their seats. She wouldn't fully believe the woman was here until she was standing in front of her. What would Tamara be doing in Cooney? And at a Glass Lake parents' night? Did she know someone else in this town? She had been sitting beside Fiona. Was that why Fiona was acting so smug lately? Did they know each other? Had Tamara told her what happened at Southern Pharmaceuticals?

The Whitehead boy passed them again, and she grabbed another sandwich, taking the opportunity to glance swiftly over her left shoulder.

Lorna caught her eye and smiled conspiratorially: 'Someday you'll have to tell me where you put it all.'

....

Arlo tried to wipe his forehead with the cuff of his shirt, whilst still balancing the two trays. Seamus had asked him to help with parking. Before and after the event. During it, he was supposed to be free. If he'd known he'd have to get up close with the parents, he'd have declined the job. He'd been sitting outside, alternating between trying to get the baton to work and rereading his dad's letter, when some woman had shouted at him to come inside and make himself useful. The torch from his phone must have given him away, not that he needed it. He didn't even need the letter any more. It was short, eight lines in all, and he knew it by heart. Charlie Whitehead wanted him to visit.

It was warm in the hall and he was bad at carrying things. He was trying to pass unnoticed by everyone whilst also making sure he was never gone from any group long enough for someone to complain. He'd made two failed attempts to get over to his mom, the well-thumbed letter in his pocket egging him on: *Look after your mother and your brother.*

'I see Susan Mitchem was at the wine again last night,' said a stocky father, taking an iced bun from Arlo's tray without looking at him.

'Saw that,' said the other man, also taking a bun. 'She must have sent that last meme five times. Doesn't she know the old maxim? If you can't identify the alcoholic in your parents' WhatsApp group, it must be you.'

Arlo waited for the men to each take another bun, before turning back towards the Franklins. He didn't want them of all people to think he was skiving. Beverley had taken several snacks from him already, which he chose to take as a good sign. He'd travelled about two metres when he was yanked to one side.

'Arlo!' exclaimed the woman, knocking one of his platters as she pulled him towards her. He managed to catch the tray but not before a row of sandwiches were sent flying to the floor. 'Oops, sorry about that.'

'Mrs Murphy,' he said, placing his trays on the ground and quickly gathering up the bread before anyone could stand on it.

'What did I tell you about calling me that?'

'Fiona, sorry.' Arlo glanced up at the woman.

'Let me help you,' she said, getting down on her hunkers. The women she'd been talking to stood in a huddle behind her, grinning.

'It's fine,' he said, stuffing the soiled sandwiches into a bunch of serviettes and then stuffing those into his pockets.

'This is *Arlo*,' said Fiona, elongating his name in a way that made him want to spontaneously combust. She placed a hand on his arm. 'He's my handyman.'

Arlo desperately needed to wipe his forehead, but he couldn't risk knocking any more food. 'Ah, hi,' he said, trying to move his neck away from the fabric of his shirt. 'Nice to meet you all.'

'If you ever need anything seen to around the house, Tamara, he's your guy.'

'I can see that,' said one of the women, glancing at his bulging pockets.

'I know you, don't I?' said another woman.

'I don't think so ...'

'I do. You're the guy whose dad killed Mike Roche's son.'

'He – he didn't ...' Arlo looked to Fiona, but she was still smiling at her friends as if they hadn't mentioned anything more inappropriate than the weather.

'Charlie Whitehead,' said another of the women, nodding. 'He did the wiring in our house. It kind of makes sense that he was a drunk; half the switches were upside down.'

'Is that the light in your hallway?'

'Mmm,' said the woman, watching Arlo.

'Sorry about that,' he said, pathetically, the sweat tickling his temples now.

'Stop, Sally, you're embarrassing the boy,' chastised the second woman, the one who'd breezily asked if he was the son of a murderer.

'He looks like him,' said the upside-down switches woman. Then, more accusatorily: 'You look like him.'

Arlo blinked. Fiona's hand was on his arm now and he was so warm he thought his head might burst into flames.

'Now, now, ladies,' she said, moving her hand up and down.

'There's absolutely nothing wrong with looking like Charlie Whitehead.'

Beyond the women, Nuala Patterson was working her way towards them. She approached the tray, reached for a sandwich, saw who was holding it and pulled back her hand like it had been bitten.

'Oh,' she said. Arlo caught her eye for the first time in months. Then she turned on her heels and disappeared into the crowd.

All the women, and Arlo, watched her go.

The upside-down switches woman gasped. 'Unbelievable.'

'Told you,' said Fiona.

'Oh my God, you were right.' The woman turned to Arlo, eyes shining with sheer delight: 'It's like you don't even exist.'

....

Malachy was regaling the group with a story about the time Ella and Amelia baked a lemon cake for his mother's birthday, only for their grandmother to slice the thing open and find congealed, raw egg.

'They didn't realise you were supposed to whisk them. *You never gave us that instruction, Daddy!*'

Everyone laughed. One mother even nudged him playfully. Women loved to touch Beverley's husband.

He did make it sound charming, even if it had actually been a sponge cake and neither Malachy nor his mother were laughing at the time.

'Beverley. Coo-coo. Beverley.' Fiona Murphy was approaching them, and she sounded positively gleeful. 'I've got someone here I believe you know.'

Bill Farrell moved to one side as Fiona and her little posse joined the group.

'I've been meaning to reacquaint you guys for ages,' Fiona was saying, though Beverley only had eyes for the dark-haired woman standing behind her. 'I helped Tamara here find a house to rent in Cooney, and we just got chatting. She mentioned that you used to work together. Isn't it a small world? She has so many interesting stories about you, Beverley.' Fiona wriggled her eyebrows, or at least that was what she was trying to do; but she got her Botox done locally, and cheaply, so nothing above her eye sockets budged. 'It's been so interesting to hear about you as a co-worker, when of course we only know you as a friend. I believe you were a real go-getter. Tamara says you really *attacked* whatever task you were given.'

Beverley tensed. Her hunch was correct. This was why Fiona Murphy had been so insufferable of late. She'd met Tamara Watson and Tamara had told her how Beverley came to lose her job.

'Hello, Tamara,' said Malachy, stepping forward to kiss the woman on the cheek. 'Long time, no see.'

'Hi, Mal,' she said, receiving the kiss graciously before giving Beverley a smile. 'Hi, Bev. You're looking well.'

When Beverley didn't respond, her husband spoke again. 'Everyone, this is Tamara Watson. She and Beverley were colleagues at Southern Pharmaceuticals.'

Tamara lifted a hand in greeting.

'And you live in Cooney?' asked Lorna.

'Yes, just moved here. Myself and my husband separated. He got the house, but I got the kid. Fiona here was my estate agent. She found us a lovely little rental out by the pier.'

'I said she must come to a coffee morning at the Strand, Beverley,' added Fiona, still beaming. 'Her son is starting in sixth class this week.'

'Absolutely,' gushed Lorna.

'Yes, we're both very excited. I remember you telling me how good the primary school was out here, Bev. I couldn't believe it when there was a space.'

'You must have got Marcus Birch's place. His dad got a job in London. The whole family just moved over.'

'So, you used to work together? That's fun,' trilled Lorna. 'You can tell us all Beverley's secrets.'

'Oh, she really can,' said Fiona.

Tamara smiled demurely.

'If you'll excuse me,' said Beverley, dumping a half-eaten salad sandwich on a passing tray. 'I must use the bathroom before Principal Patterson has us all back in our seats.'

....

Arlo was hiding in the corridor beyond the main auditorium. He'd come out to dump the soiled sandwiches, which he still hadn't done. Every time the double doors swung open, he jumped, convinced another parent was about to give him a task. Occasionally, he glanced in through the windows. He was keeping an eye on things, and by things he meant Nuala Patterson. He wondered if Seamus understood just how awkward he had made matters when he decided to throw a few weeks' work Arlo's way?

He stepped away from the window and took his phone from his shirt pocket. He was sending Ella updates, detailing the breakthroughs he was making with her parents, particularly her dad.

She responded:

> Trust me, Mal acts like he likes everyone.

He hit reply:

> I'm telling you I have cracked him. He called me mate. And
> he winked at me. He tipped me a fiver!

It was slightly annoying how Ella automatically thought the worst of her parents. They were old and conservative, but they were there for her. Last summer, her dad offered to buy her a new car. And yet she had only contempt for them. She didn't appreciate how lucky she was.

He pulled the napkins from his pockets and began to empty them into the bin. The double doors swung open and Beverley appeared. She did not look happy to see him.

He stalled for a moment, then he flung the last bits of bread into the trash, gave her a sort of awkward bow – he didn't know why; it just came out – and walked on down the corridor, not having a clue where he was going.

When he rounded the corner, he kept walking until he could no longer hear the hustle and bustle from the hall. He pushed his back against the wall and took a few breaths.

His phone beeped again.

> He tipped while people were watching, right? I'd say Bev
> just loved that.

·······················

Beverley could hear Malachy coming after her, but she didn't quicken her step and she didn't turn back. She couldn't bear to see the others gently interrogating Tamara, who would be only too delighted to tell them all about the time Beverley Franklin attacked her.

She exited the auditorium to see Arlo Whitehead chucking a pile of sandwiches into the large bin.

He bobbed his head awkwardly and hurried away.

Beverley marched over to the bin and, without really thinking, pulled the sandwiches from the top of the mound. She shook her sleeves down over her hands to hide the food and headed into the girls' bathroom, past the line of grown women hunched over child-height sinks, and into the only free cubicle. She locked the door and began to stuff the bread into her mouth.

Bread was always best.

The last time Beverley saw Tamara she'd been standing beside the microwave in the first-floor kitchenette of Southern Pharmaceuticals laughing at something a colleague had said. Beverley saw red and lunged for her. The fall wouldn't have been so dramatic if Tamara had been wearing appropriate lab shoes – or if she'd had her cleavage strapped down. The woman was a teetering inverted triangle waiting to topple.

Principal Patterson's voice echoed through the speakers out in the main hall.

If everyone can take their seats, we'll wrap this up as quickly as possible.

One by one, the other cubicles opened, doors banging back against the stalls. Faucets squeaked on and off and hand driers blasted. A final pair of heels clip-clopped out of the bathroom and the main door swung shut again.

The only remaining sound was the buzz of the two long fluorescent bulbs.

Beverley counted to ten, just to be sure.

Then she leaned over the miniature toilet bowl and vomited.

....

Frank Cafferty was doing his best to stack the dirty cups without making a racket. The acoustics in the auditorium were phenomenally good. His last school didn't have acoustics, or an auditorium for that matter.

He'd insisted Mrs Walsh, the Junior Infants' teacher, sit down; he'd clean out the tea tanker and stack the crockery. The Glass Lake mother who'd been supervising the pair of them all night had got distracted by some misaligned mini quiches across the hall and disappeared. Frank was grabbing the opportunity to tidy up unobserved.

Principal Patterson was back on stage, addressing the audience.

He told himself to concentrate on what she was saying, on the dirty cups, on the four additional weekly student reports he'd somehow already agreed to this evening – on anything but the buzzing in his pocket. Five missed calls now, and all from a withheld number.

'Are you sure you don't need a hand?' Mrs Walsh asked from the plastic chair where she sat massaging her knees.

'Not at all,' he replied, flashing his widest smile. 'You have a rest. I'll fly through the rest of this.' Sometimes he forced himself to smile the whole drive to work, and when he arrived at the school, he really did feel happier.

As the buzzing stopped, Frank looked around the hall for a hand disappearing into a breast pocket or a phone being dropped into a handbag, but there was none. All his parents were here. Which meant it wasn't one of them tormenting him. He took some comfort from this. It wasn't exactly the same as what had happened at his old school, so.

He stacked the cups carefully, mindful of the superior echo. Then he transferred each stack into the plastic crate.

'Look at you go, Mr Cafferty. You could have taught my husband a thing or two. Lord have mercy on his useless soul.'

'I'm used to tidying, Mrs Walsh. Don't mind it at all. I do all the housework at home.'

'I'd well believe it,' marvelled the older woman, shaking her head in awe. 'I hope your wife knows how lucky she is. Sure, you're as good as two women.'

ABERSTOWN GARDA STATION

Why hadn't their man been at Glass Lake? He was supposed to be at the school, helping with musical preparations, but instead he was out walking by the River Gorm. Why? This was a puzzle at the centre of the case and one Joey was desperate to crack. Imagine if he came up with an answer. The sergeant couldn't possibly mistake him for a useless eejit then.

Joey took out his notebook and considered the possibilities. There was no way their man had gotten lost – he knew how to get to the school, they all did. The officers had been instructed to leave the car for forensics to examine, but it was parked neatly nearby. No signs of a crash or that it had broken down.

'Was there any unusual action on his mobile phone yesterday, sir?'

'One call to the wife at lunchtime, just as there was every day this week and every other week. Nothing else. Nothing unexpected.'

Joey brought his pen to his lower lip and tapped. 'Curiouser and curiouser ...'

Whelan frowned.

The younger officer dropped his hand and cleared the embarrassment from his throat.

'Don't you have a second round of witness interviews to get started on?'

'Yes, sir. I'm just going in now, sir.'

'Well, don't let me keep you.'

'Right you are,' said Joey, as gruffly as he could manage. 'I'll let you know if there's anything of interest.'

....

Fiona Murphy, parent

The whole thing with Mr Cafferty and the quote-unquote mystery files was just progress reports. He was giving a few of the more interested parents updates on how their kids were doing. Nothing sinister about it. Of more relevance is the fact that Beverley was fired for anger management issues. She has form on lashing out, so who knows what else she might be capable of? She attacked Tamara Watson - just ask her. They used to work together.

Bill Farrell, parent

Of course I knew the man. I'm a public representative; it's my job to know all the men, and women. It was a terrible, tragic accident. He slipped and fell. It's awful, and I will be raising the need to rebuild the fence along the Gorm as a matter of urgency at the next council meeting. But you lot asking questions - looking to find out if the man had any enemies - you're

needlessly dragging our community's reputation
through the mud. Cooney has a Tidy Towns
competition to concentrate on.

Tamara Watson, parent
I don't want to land poor Beverley in it, and
like this all happened months ago, long before
I came to Cooney or anyone drowned. But yes,
it's all entirely true. Beverley attacked me
in the office kitchen. She shoved me right into
the recycling bin. I sprained my ankle. And
before you ask, Officer, I haven't a clue why she
did it. Not an iota. I was more surprised than
anyone.

20
· · · · · ·

SEVEN DAYS EARLIER

In her teens and early twenties, Beverley had made herself vomit. Being a thin person who didn't eat was dull and obvious but being a thin person who put away vast quantities of calories was exciting and commendable. Where possible, she did media interviews over dinner, knowing the journalist would write about how she'd consumed a whole pizza (Hollow legs! Where *does* she put it? Not your typical actress!) but wouldn't waste ink on her going to the ladies' room afterwards to touch up her lipstick. What started as an alternative to dieting soon became a source of comfort. When she was upset or uncertain or anxious, she'd eat too much, and almost immediately start to panic. But she knew that if she kept going, she would get to the point where she could easily expunge it all: the calories, the panic, the niggling possibility that she was nothing special. She'd stopped when she got pregnant with Ella. Nineteen years ago. And she hadn't done it again, not once, until she found those photos on Malachy's phone in April.

At first, she hadn't recognised the woman – her face wasn't exactly the focus – but eventually there was a wider shot that took in the familiar flared nostrils and thick dark hair falling either side of her neck.

'Tamara Watson? From development? From *my* job?' she'd yelled, standing in their pristine marble kitchen, waving the phone at her husband.

Malachy had been more taken aback than panicked. He'd pushed the door shut and told her to calm down. 'The girls are upstairs.'

'You don't know Tamara! She lives in the city. You've never even met ...' And then she remembered. 'The Christmas party? Are you serious? Has this been going on since then?!'

'It hasn't been going on at all. It's just pics. So please calm down.'

And Beverley had calmed down, as she always did. Malachy slept in the guest room that night, but the following evening, he was back in their bed. 'That's enough now, Beverley,' he'd said, undoing his cufflinks, and she'd rolled onto her side without another word. She wasn't going to leave him, so what was the point?

'Beverley?' said Claire Keating now, sitting in her usual chair in the alcove of the Strand, a disposable cup in her left hand. 'What do you think?'

What Beverley thought was that Malachy had phoned her three times in the ninety minutes she'd been here and still hadn't got the message. This happened whenever he worked from home, but today she would not be answering questions about the whereabouts of coffee filters (same cupboard as always) or why Alexa was ignoring him (because Beverley had been so pissed off after Monday night's school meeting that she'd deleted his voice profile). She pressed decline, again.

'Beverley?'

Claire's voice was sharper now, and Beverley let the phone fall back into her bag.

'Yes, Claire,' she said, just as curtly. 'I was checking my notes.'

169

The Lakers did not have an official chair. Given she'd been a parent the longest – Ella was three years older than anyone else's child – Beverley was the obvious honorary leader. But since Claire had her last set of twins, she'd been acting as if quantity, rather than quality, gave her seniority. 'What I *think*,' she continued, 'is that we need to go big on marketing.'

Lorna Farrell was cutting a flapjack into tiny pieces, and Fiona Murphy was idly tapping on her phone. She'd given Beverley an overzealous welcome when she arrived and made some pointed, apropos-of-nothing comment about Lorna *attacking* her dessert. Beverly couldn't tell how much Fiona knew, or what, if anything, she'd told anyone else. None of the others were acting like they had anything on her. Which was something, at least.

'We need every seat in that auditorium filled and people queuing up outside for returns. Nothing's as desirable as something you can't have – and all those bodies will look great on TV. So, we need to get the word out. Let's pitch the musical as a feel-good story to local media: radio, newspapers, websites. Have we any leverage there?'

'We got Buddy Reilly's son on to the spelling bee team last year,' said Lorna.

'That's right.' The local radio mogul's youngest had cost Glass Lake a place in the semi-finals and made them a temporary laughing stock on the Cork spelling circuit when he forgot the 'e' at the end of 'heroine'. 'Let's hit Buddy up for a couple of free radio ads, and a bit of editorial coverage.'

'And my sister works at *Cork Now* magazine,' offered someone else.

'Fine,' said Beverley, shaking her head as Lorna proffered the decimated cake around the group. She'd had nothing but coffee since dinner the night before. Things were back under control. 'Who wants to make some calls to the papers? You.' She pointed to the woman who'd come to the Strand to secure her son a place on Glass Lake's soccer team and had clearly zoned out of all other conversations. 'You can ring around the local press.'

'I'm actually not great on the phone,' said the mother of the aspiring soccer star. 'I have a bit of an anxiety disorder ...'

'It's the twenty-first century. We all have anxiety disorders,' snapped Beverley.

She never stuck her finger down her throat. All she had to do was a sort of internal lurch, like she was burping from her stomach, and everything came gushing back up. Apart from a couple of dentists, who could see the erosion on her teeth, the only person to ever remark on it was her mother. But then Frances did not understand the desire to be thin. Her mother had been absent the day that memo was sent to all women.

Still, she'd never done it anywhere as public as the Glass Lake bathroom. The lack of self-control had frightened her. It no longer made her thinner. It didn't even make her feel good any more. So, yes, that was it. She was done with it.

'What position did you say your son was interested in?' she asked, turning to face the mother.

'Goalie.'

'Yes, I think goals is actually oversubscribed at the moment ...'

'For what age group?'

'For *all* age groups,' said Beverley, who had little time for fair-weather parents who came to Lakers meetings when they wanted something for their individual child, but had no interest in the greater, holistic well-being of the school.

Fair-Weather Soccer Mom looked around the group. Lorna and Claire nodded. 'Always a lot of competition for goalie,' said Lorna. Nothing bonded the Lakers like a mother with no community spirit.

'Actually, you know, it's fine, I can make some calls.' The woman reached into her tote bag for a biro. She grabbed a napkin. 'So, *Cork Now* ...'

'*The Examiner,* the *Southern Gazette* ...' Beverley watched as she took down the details. 'No harm in trying the nationals either.'

Tamara had propositioned Malachy at that Christmas party, but he'd turned her down. (He'd paused after telling her that. *Well done, Malachy!* she hadn't said. *Well done on not falling into her bosom right there in the middle of the Southern Pharmaceuticals function room!*) They did, however, swap phone numbers. 'Not with any ulterior motive,' he stressed, though what sort of above-board reason there could possibly have been he didn't say. Tamara started texting him (he said) and a month later, with no coaxing (again according to him), she sent a pic.

A *pic.*

She spat the word from her brain.

'You okay, Beverley?' asked Lorna.

'Fine,' she replied, turning the grimace into a smile.

'You could get Christine Maguire to write something,' Claire told Fair-Weather Soccer Mom. 'She works at the *Southern Gazette*, and she's got kids at Glass Lake. Did you all see her article this morning? About Monday's information night?'

Lorna put down the eighth of a flapjack she was slowly nibbling. 'I could not believe they got a quote from Orla Smith, of all parents, giving out about kids accessing technology. I mean, come on.'

'What's wrong with Orla?' someone else asked.

'Surely you heard what her son did on the first day of Junior Infants? No?' Lorna's eyes widened as she jumped her chair forward. 'He picked up a book and ...' She lifted her left hand and dramatically dragged the air to the right. '... he swiped!'

'*No!*'

'Yes. He swiped *a book*! As if he'd never seen one before. Oh my God, Orla was *mortified*. She's been trying to make up for it ever since. Every afternoon, she's there shouting at Reuben to go back in and get a more difficult book to bring home. *Get a red one, Reuben. You know your level's RED.* And she's eyeballing all the parents as she shouts it. Annabelle's in his class and by the sounds of it the poor boy can't even spell "red" but she's making him bring home *War and Peace*, or whatever. I mean, Annabelle *is* reading at red level, but I wouldn't scream about it. It's nobody else's business if she found *Animal Farm* obvious or not.'

'Parenting's not a competition,' agreed Fair-Weather Soccer Mom.

'Exactly,' said Lorna. 'When Marnie was nine, and she was rereading *Romeo and Juliet*, Bill wanted to post a picture on Facebook but—'

'You said no because you didn't want to be boasting,' interrupted Claire. 'Yeah, you've mentioned it.'

What had hurt Beverley was that Malachy hadn't been remorseful. He'd acted like Tamara had just sent him the number for a good mechanic, and she was making too much of it. 'You don't even like Tamara,' he declared, and while it was true – Tamara was loud and cheap and brash – she had never told him that, which meant Tamara had. 'I don't like my friends either,' she'd snapped. 'But that doesn't mean you can send them a picture of your penis!'

'Any joy with getting a copy of the syllabus for what this quote-unquote doctor is going to be teaching our children, Lorna?' asked Claire.

'I managed to corner Principal Patterson after school yesterday, but she was less than courteous. She told me I could download the syllabus from the Department's website. But that's hardly going to tell us anything, is it? We were there Monday night. The man is clearly a renegade.'

'I had a snoop on Twitter,' said Fiona.

'And?'

'He has his pronouns in his bio.'

'Now? See?' said Lorna, looking around the group with an air of inevitable doom.

'I check Ciara's phone,' said Fiona. 'Girl or boy, you have to know what they're up to. You need to get to kids early, before they learn about sex from porn.'

Lorna spluttered, losing several precious flapjack crumbs. 'Fiona!'

'It's the reality, Lorna. Kids watch porn.'

'Stop saying that word.' Lorna looked around, lest anyone else might be listening to their conversation. 'Jesus! We don't even let Marnie watch *Friends*!'

'If someone started talking to my boys about pornography, I don't know how they'd cope,' said Fair-Weather Soccer Mom.

'Oh, come off it,' guffawed Fiona. 'Your eldest is twelve. Of course he's heard of porn.'

'If we're going to keep talking about this, can we at least call it something else?' squeaked Lorna. She took another morsel of flapjack and composed herself. 'Beverley and I are in the school this afternoon for musical rehearsals. I can snoop about a bit, see what I can find out about what Dr O'Sullivan is teaching.'

Beverley had agreed to have Lorna as an assistant director because it was Glass Lake tradition to have one and because she hadn't realised the woman would turn up to every run-through dressed like a has-been ballerina and deliver the 'fame costs' speech to any child who stood still for more than two seconds.

'But we still don't have an answer to the big question,' added Lorna.

'What question?'

'Who are the two kids that were sending the photos?'

'Well, I know we have a few sixth-class parents here, so let's not put anyone on the spot,' said Claire, drawing out the last word, so her conversation shutdown sounded more like a question.

'Not my kid,' said one mother with such immediacy that, had she not known the truth, it would have made Beverley suspicious.

'Or mine,' said Fiona. 'Though if Ciara was involved, I wouldn't be ashamed.'

'I'd say you're raging Ciara's *not* involved,' said Claire, and a couple of the women laughed.

Fiona shrugged, lifting her coffee cup. 'I can neither confirm nor deny.'

They weren't taking it seriously. It was because it was still a faceless – bodyless – act. If they knew who was responsible, they wouldn't find it so amusing. Beverley knew she couldn't identify Woody without casting suspicion on Amelia, but she comforted herself with the fact that he was the most obvious candidate. They would get there eventually.

'That new kid turning up just when this all happened is pretty suspicious,' said Lorna eagerly.

'What new kid?'

'The boy who took Marcus Birch's place. You were talking to his mother at the information night, Fiona. What was her name?'

'Tamara Watson,' said Fiona, answering Lorna's question but smiling at Beverley. 'I helped them find the house they're renting.'

'And?' pushed Lorna.

'And what? Does she seem like the mother of a sexual deviant? How would I know?' Fiona shrugged. 'Beverley might, though. And actually, Beverley, on the subject of Tamara ... Ciara would really love to have a bigger role in the musical. Something with lines? Would that be possible?'

'What's the musical got to do with the new woman?' asked Lorna.

Beverley did her best to keep her tone light. 'As you know, Fiona, all the roles have been well cast by this stage. The show goes up in one week.'

'It's a bit of a tricky one, I know, but I was thinking you could throw some ideas around?' Fiona smiled sweetly. 'Tamara said you were good at that, in work, I mean, throwing things around.'

'That's right,' enthused Lorna, taking another piece of flapjack. 'You used to work with the mother, Beverley. Any insights? Do you think it was her son?'

'I don't think it was the new boy.' Beverley tried to minimalise the authoritative tone that came so naturally to her. She continued to eyeball Fiona. The woman was as thick as two planks and yet somehow she was blackmailing her.

Lorna was crestfallen. 'Do they not seem the type to be up to something inappropriate?'

'Oh, they do,' replied Beverley. 'They absolutely do seem the type. But it wasn't him.'

As much as she would love to have the Lakers blacklisting Tamara Watson before she'd even received the Cooney welcome basket, suspicion could not be allowed to shift from Woody Whitehead. It annoyed her that he was still walking around, free of blame, and that his mother had sat in the auditorium on Monday night without anyone challenging her.

'How do you know it wasn't the new boy?' asked Claire.

Lorna lowered the flapjack square. Claire raised an eyebrow. The whole group was looking at her now. Faking self-doubt was harder than it seemed.

'Well, I don't *know* ...' Beverley picked up her own coffee. 'I just think there might be other candidates.' How could they *not* suspect the Whitehead boy? His father was literally a murderer!

'My money's still on the new fella,' said Lorna.

Fiona nodded.

So did Claire. 'I mean, it makes sense—'

'It was the Whitehead boy!'

Suddenly everyone was gasping and saying 'What?' and 'No!' and 'How do you know?' She had hoped they'd get there by themselves, but if they needed a little push, so be it.

'I can't say how I know, but I do.'

'The girl's not Amelia, is it?' asked Fiona, still grinning like she knew more than she did. It was highly unlikely Tamara had told Fiona *why* Beverley had sent her crashing into the recycling bin in the Southern Pharmaceuticals kitchenette. It was much easier to identify yourself as a victim than a homewrecker.

'No,' lied Beverley. 'How dare you, Fiona Murphy?'

The woman held up her hands. 'Just wondering ...'

'Christine Maguire has a daughter in sixth-class,' mused Claire. 'She's written two articles on the whole thing now. Where better to get the inside story than from inside your own house?'

Lorna gasped. 'Maeve Maguire? Do you think?'

Claire shrugged. 'It's one possibility.'

'I think you might be right,' said Fiona excitedly. 'Ciara is always giving out that Maeve gets to sit beside Woody. I think Ciara has a bit of a crush on him. Don't look so appalled, Bev, the Whiteheads might be criminals, but they're very handsome criminals. Anyway, yeah, apparently, they're friends, maybe *good* friends.'

'Beverley?' said Claire, and the group's collective head turned in her direction again.

She should contradict them, but what sacrificial lamb could she offer up in place of Christine's girl? She was rolling through the various parents that had crossed her recently – if only Tamara had a daughter! – when her phone started to buzz at her feet. 'Sorry. I have to check this.' She reached down and pulled the thing from her bag. Malachy's name flashed on the screen. She pressed decline. Although now she had no reason to avoid answering. And they were all still looking at her.

'Well? If the boy's Woody Whitehead, is the girl Maeve Maguire?'

Lorna was biting her lower lip. It may have been a coincidence, but her index and middle fingers were crossed. Claire's coffee hovered in front of her face. Fiona tilted her head slightly.

'It wouldn't be my place to say,' said Beverley eventually, her tone more knowing that she'd intended.

The Lakers exchanged smiles and loaded glances, while the Fair-Weathers – there were three in attendance today – looked as clueless as usual. Why have children if you weren't going to keep up with what was going on in their world?

At least Christine wasn't a member of the group. If people were going to talk about you, it was best to be in the dark about it. Beverley didn't have that luxury. Everyone in Cooney knew her, and she knew everything that went on.

'Can we discuss sets now, please?' she said, feeling mildly uncomfortable despite knowing she hadn't said or done anything wrong. (Could she help it if she was an assertive person? It was just how she spoke. It didn't *mean* anything.) 'Lorna, have you spoken to Seamus McGrath again? The man keeps presenting bronze bricks and insisting they're yellow and, honestly, I am running out of patience.'

There was a lot of musical business to get through. Despite her many reminders that he was made of heavy metal, the tinman kept flying across the stage in his rush to get his scenes over with, while Woody was still tiptoeing around the stage when he was supposed to be a lion. Their glaring faults highlighted just how good Amelia was in the real lead role, but they were dragging down the overall quality. Mr Cafferty was helping with movement; she'd be on to him this afternoon.

Fiona brought up a speaking role for Ciara again and, through gritted teeth, Beverley said she would see what she could do. As it happened, the girl playing the Wicked Witch of the West had just come down with a bad case of tonsillitis, but Beverley wasn't going to deliver this good news just yet. She didn't want Fiona thinking she could hold the Tamara incident over her head for ever. One fair-weather mother, who had been trying to 'augment' her son's role since Beverley cast him as Munchkin Number Seven, started talking about character development, but Beverley cut her off. This was what happened when people found out television crews were coming. *Me, me, me.* They were so transparent.

'Beverley!'

The holler came from behind, and the familiarity stopped her mid-sentence. A hush fell over the group as they shifted in their seats to see where the commanding voice was coming from.

'Isn't that ...?' Lorna trailed off and Beverley turned to see what the rest of the Lakers saw: a heavily overweight woman with grey hair slicked behind her ears making her way towards them. The woman moved as though she was wading through mud rather than skirting a few tables. She was dressed incongruously in a girly pink kaftan, rimmed with silver foil and beads. A large purple gemstone hung from a necklace, banging against her ample chest.

'Beverley, *a stór*! Hello, hello, hello! And oh my days, is that Claire Potter?'

'Keating, now,' replied Claire. 'Hello, Mrs Tandon.'

'Miss, now.' The older woman winked. 'But I've kept the Tandon because it goes so well with tantric.' She put her hands on her hips and surveyed the group. 'Aren't you a fine-looking group of girls? A bit on the thin side, but great hair all round.'

A few of the women tittered with delight.

'What are you doing here?' said Beverley through gritted teeth.

'I'm here to see you, of course. I'm doing a workshop in Cork city for a few evenings. You weren't answering Malachy's calls, so I said I'd come on over. And wasn't it great that I did? Now I get to meet your friends! I see the puffer waistcoat is still in fashion, anyway.' She beamed at the seated women in amazement. 'If I didn't know one of you was my daughter, I'd swear you were all sisters. Like the

Corrs, but blonder, and without the conspiracy theorist brother.'

'Who is that?' whispered Fair-Weather Soccer Mom, and Fiona, who could hardly contain her delight, said, in a far louder voice: 'That's Beverley's mom.'

'What are you thinking about?' asked Ella, as they lay side by side on her bed, the rain pounding the skylight above.

'Nothing.'

Arlo was thinking about the crash.

It was almost noon. They hadn't moved in hours, not since Ella's grandmother turned up at the house without notice and Ella went downstairs to investigate. The drops exploded against the window above his head and he was right back in the car, watching them collide with the windscreen.

'You always hold my hand like that.'

Arlo turned his head and looked down at the narrow space between them where his fingers were curved around her palm and vice versa. 'Like what? That's how you hold hands.'

'Mm.'

'Ella, that's a standard hand-hold right there.'

'Sure, if you're a businessman.'

'Excuse me?'

'Glad the merger worked out, old boy,' she barked. 'A pleasure doing business with you.'

'All right then, show me how you'd do it.'

The mattress shook as Ella separated their hands, then reconnected them. 'There.'

Arlo glanced down. Their palms were perfectly aligned, fingers interlocked.

'That's how lovers hold hands.'

Arlo had had his driver's licence four months by the night of the Donovan gig. He'd been looking forward to chauffeuring them in and out of the city – and he had driven in without a hitch. Mike kept joking about how smooth his transitions were, but Mike hadn't a clue what he was talking about. He couldn't even start a car. Leo didn't comment, but only because he was jealous. He'd started lessons ages before Arlo and only recently passed his test.

He turned his face towards Ella, reassuring himself with her presence. 'It does feel more secure,' he conceded.

'The other way is a bit platonic. A bit ...'

'Business meeting.'

'Yes, or a father and daughter crossing the road.'

'Well, that's not what we're going for.'

'No,' she agreed.

The rain continued to fall, and Arlo heard the skid and screech and surprisingly low thud of Mike's body being crushed.

'What are you thinking about now?'

'Still nothing.'

'You must be thinking about something.'

If only Mike hadn't snuck in the whiskey. If only Arlo hadn't drunk it. If only they'd all stayed sober. If only his dad had stayed sober. If only the rain hadn't been heavy. If only the roads had been dry. If only the bend hadn't been sharp.

'I'm not.'

He was supposed to be at a job this morning, assembling furniture for a new woman called Tamara, but on the way to Ella's last night, she'd texted him to 'reschedule'. He wondered who she'd spoken to, and what they'd said.

A bit of being bad-mouthed is getting off lightly, Arly. Wouldn't you say?

Arlo concentrated on the rain.

Arrrr-leee … Hello?

Bam-bam-bam went the drops.

Hello? Are you just going to ignore me?

'Are you thinking about the visit to your dad?'

'No.'

'But you're booked in for tomorrow, right?'

'Doesn't mean I have to go.'

'I thought the prison already confirmed.'

'I got an email this morning confirming the time for tomorrow afternoon, but I don't *have* to go. I can just not turn up. Dad said he'd understand if I didn't feel like it and what's he going to do anyway? It's not like he can come after me.'

He hated how defensive he sounded. He would love nothing more than to talk about his dad, to tell someone about the real Charlie Whitehead. He wanted to tell Ella how his dad had taught him to affix a plug socket – the right way up! – and how readily he said he loved him and Woody and that it came so easily because it was true. Ella would listen because she loved him, but he knew she didn't want to hear. She didn't understand how he could say good things about the man who killed Mike and maimed Leo. And Arlo was caught between what he wanted and what everyone else wanted.

'I'll decide tonight,' he added, relaxing his tone.

'Your mum's right, you know,' she said carefully. 'You don't owe him, like, at all. He owes you and Leo and everyone else.'

I knew the girl still thought about me. Tell her I said hi, Arly. Tell her when she gets bored of you, she should give me a call. She knows I'm funnier and smarter and much better craic.

Arlo's stomach began to churn. 'It's not that simple.' He pushed himself up from the bed. 'I'd better go. I'm at the school for the rest of the day and I've to pick up paint on the way. Your mom has been on Seamus's case about the sets again. This is our fourth tin of yellow.'

Ella rolled her eyes. 'The woman's insane.' She held out her arms and he pulled her up to standing. 'You know Bev hasn't said a word to Amelia about the photos in the week since she walked in on her taking them? She's talked to the press and she continues to hound Principal Patterson, but she hasn't said a word to Amelia. She went straight back to being Bev's golden girl. And Amelia's so blasé about it I honestly wouldn't be surprised if she instigated the whole thing. How's Woody? Did he get into trouble?'

'I haven't spoken to him much since it happened.'

'Yeah, give him space. He'll come to you if he needs to.'

'Yeah,' agreed Arlo, ignoring the niggle in his chest.

'I'll go distract Mal,' she said. 'I'll ask him about that time he completed a triathlon in less than four hours. That should keep him talking.'

'Is your granny definitely gone?' Arlo had heard a lot about Ella's grandmother, and apparently, she'd heard a lot about him. This had worried Arlo, but Ella insisted that just because her granny knew about him, it didn't mean Beverley did. 'Their mother-daughter relationship is even worse than mine and Bev's,' Ella had explained. 'Bev acts like Granny's the embarrassment, when really it's her.'

'She's gone to track down Bev, who will hate that,' she said now, delighted. 'So, the path should be clear.'

....

'You didn't have to leave on my account,' said Frances, pink kaftan billowing as she followed Beverley out of the Strand and across the road to where the Range Rover was parked, right by the pier.

The wind made the rain worse, drawing it in on them from all directions. Beverley caught the driver's door before a gust took it. She absolutely did have to leave on her mother's account. Five minutes after she'd shown up at the café, Frances was pulling up a chair and reading the Lakers' sexual fortunes.

'This line here? This means you're going to have a long sex life. Actually, you're probably already in the middle of it.'

Fair-Weather Soccer Mom had roared with delight at this. 'Don't be telling them all my secrets, Miss Tandon.'

Beverley had tried to bring matters back to the musical, but Claire waved her protestations away. She wanted to know if she was going to have more children.

'Beyond my expertise, I'm afraid,' Frances had said, inspecting Claire's palm. 'But I can tell you're putting the effort in.'

'We are,' giggled the woman formerly known as Claire Keating, but who had clearly been invaded by some sort of body snatcher. 'We actually are.'

They'd all lost their minds.

They were howling and shrieking as if they'd downed a bottle of Bacardi as opposed to a couple of Americanos and low-fat flat whites. Her mother was sitting in the middle of it, oblivious to how she was making a complete fool of herself – and, by association,

Beverley. When Lorna divulged that she called Bill 'Councillor' in bed, Beverley had made their excuses and left.

Her mother had this effect on people. They automatically opened up to her, and it was all the more incomprehensible because Beverley's reaction was always the complete opposite.

Frances went around the other side of the car and clambered into the passenger seat, Beverley snatching away the half-empty Rennie packet and bottle of water before they were flattened. She opened the glove box and fired them in.

'Why do the seats need to be so far off the ground? It's not as if we're going cross country. Would you consider getting yourself a nice Mini, *a stór*?'

Beverley grimaced at her mother's pet name for her but said nothing.

'Do you remember the Mini we had when you were small? The five of you piled into the back, screaming at us to speed up anytime there was a bump in the road.' Her mother laughed to herself. 'You'd all beg us to go faster so youse would go flying up and bounce your heads against the ceiling.'

'That wasn't me,' said Beverley, bringing her hand to her chin. It barely seemed possible but, yes, there was another spot.

'Of course, that was before the EU introduced its nanny state rules.'

'Seatbelts are basic safety. We should have been wearing them. There were seatbelts in the car.'

'Yes, but only for three of you. And what were we going to do? Pick our favourite kids?' Frances chuckled lightly. 'Anyway, it was more fun without the seatbelts. I can still hear you roaring: *Faster, Mam, faster*!'

Beverley couldn't speak for her siblings – although childhood brain trauma would explain a lot – but she knew for a fact she had never goaded her parents into giving her a concussion. Her mother loved reflecting on their childhood as if it had been this idyllic time, and if Beverley interjected with the truth, she was the uptight party-pooper.

'Your friends seem nice. That Claire is a howl. And Lorna. I only ever met them once or twice when you were a child, but I remember you speaking about them. It's wonderful you're still friends.'

Beverley motored on along the seaside stretch, her jaw clamped shut. Her main memory of the Mini was the day they'd arrived home to find her dad had sold it. She now knew he'd sold it because they needed a vehicle with space for all the children, but that hadn't stopped him making the same cutting joke over and over: 'Your mother's too maxi to be driving a Mini.'

Beside her, Frances quietly exhaled. 'It's breathtaking around here,' she said, gazing out the window. 'I'm so truly happy for you, that you get to live somewhere so tranquil. I love my life in Dublin, but I miss the Atlantic, and all the open space. Of course, Aberstown was never as nice as this, but it had its charms. In the countryside, the rain makes everything greener. In Dublin, it just accentuates the grey. It's much harder to keep your doshas balanced in a city.'

Beverley felt a short surge of acid reflux, but she was not about to reach over her mother for the glovebox. Nor was she going to give her the satisfaction of asking what doshas were. She did her best to swallow down the reflux.

Her mother rolled down the window and took some dramatically deep breaths. The rain splashed in, hitting Beverley at the side of her eye.

'Does Ella know you're coming?'

'I saw Ella when I called to the house this morning. I like the short hair. She's such an impressive young woman. So many opinions on so many things. I haven't a clue where half the countries she talks about are. What's that election she's obsessed with at the moment? Bangladesh? Or Barbados? I can never get them straight. Is Barbados even a country? It's great to see that passion. You've done a wonderful job with her. I hope you know that.'

She hadn't a clue what her mother was talking about. Ella never instigated conversation with her any more. 'Ella should have been at university,' she said, knocking on the indicator earlier than necessary.

Her mother hit her gently on the arm. 'I don't remember you sticking to your lecture schedule too diligently.'

The difference, she desperately wanted to respond, *is that Ella's mother cares.*

'She told me about this business with Amelia and the photos. I can imagine that had you very worried, *a stór*. I'd love to help if I can.'

'So *that's* why you're here. Of course. That makes much more sense.'

'I really am doing a workshop in the city. Tantric sex, three nights, starting tomorrow. You can look it up online. I just thought, while I was in the area, I'd see if I could be of any service.'

Beverley nodded to herself, tightening her grasp on the steering wheel. 'You don't think I can handle this. You thought this would be an opportunity to remind me that I'm a big old prude.'

'I'm receiving your negative vibrations, *a stór*, but I'm finding it difficult to track the origin.'

189

'Why didn't you stay in a hotel, so? I'm sure the workshop organisers would have put you up.'

'They would,' Frances agreed. 'But I'd rather see you. And I thought I could speak to Amelia too, if you wanted.'

'To give her some pointers, is it?'

The wipers swished over and back, fighting a losing battle with the rain. The wind rattled in the branches as they began the incline up to the Franklins' street.

Her mother pulled the seatbelt away from her chest and sat straighter. 'I'm sorry you have such a low opinion of me, Beverley. And I mean that genuinely. Amelia is only twelve. I take this seriously. And if you're concerned, then I'm concerned.'

Frances opened the beaded handbag on her lap and removed a bottle of what looked like silage. She took three large, loud gulps. Beverley's reflux surged.

She dropped to second gear as they approached the house. Ella's car was still in the driveway. Was she planning on going to classes at all today?

'Maybe we could spend some time together this afternoon?'

'Can't,' said Beverley, killing the engine. 'I've rehearsals for the Glass Lake musical shortly. I'm directing this year.'

'Of course! *The Wizard of Oz*. No better woman for it. You always loved putting on plays.'

'I was a professional actress, Mother.'

'Oh, I know, I know. Amn't I always telling people? But it's the love of it that counts, not whether you once made money from it. I'll come along to that. Rehearsals! So glamorous.'

'No way,' said Beverley as they exited the car, her mother doing an unnecessary jump down on to the recently resurfaced driveway.

190

'Oh, go on, Beverley. I'd love to see Amelia in action.'

'No.'

'All right. I'll just stay here so.'

'Yes, you will.'

'Give me a chance to talk to Malachy. I never did get to give him a good dressing-down about his own nudes. Speaking of which, did you ever watch those erotic films I sent you? Some exquisite shots in there. I suppose I could root out a bit more of that for you while I'm home this afternoon too—'

'All right, all right! Fine! You can come. But you cannot say a word and you must remember I'm in charge and it's not a game, it's a school musical that is going to be on national television.'

Beverley was almost at the front door when she turned back to point the fob at the car. Her mother disappeared from sight.

'Mother?'

A sudden loud warble came from the far side of the car and Beverley rushed over. Frances was on the ground, her pink kaftan gathered up at her waist as her black-legginged legs splayed outwards.

'Mam!' She tried to help her up. 'What happened?'

'I lost my ... my footing ...'

'Mam? Are you okay?'

'Just give me a moment,' said Frances, her voice faint.

Her mother's gaze settled somewhere behind her. Beverley snapped her fingers. 'Mam? Can you focus? Can you see me?'

And just as suddenly Frances was back. 'Sorry, *a stór*. I'm fine,' she said, gently pushing her daughter away and getting to her feet as nimbly as a cat. 'The damn rain. I must have slipped. These tiles are a bit slippy, aren't they?'

Beverley exhaled loudly, sending her eyes skywards. 'This is porcelain paving, not tiles, and it's not slippy, it's expensive. You're carrying too much weight, Mam. That's the problem. It's not good for your balance.'

Frances dusted off her leggings and readjusted her bosom so the large gemstone sat right in the middle. 'Oh, my darling girl,' she said cheerfully, 'don't you know my vastness is one of the most spectacular things about me?'

....

Arlo didn't dare turn back until he was at the very end of the street. Even then, it was only a surreptitious glance. The rain blurred his view. He hoped it would blur Beverley Franklin's too.

So that was Ella's grandmother.

One of Arlo's grannies only wore black (her husband died when she was forty, and she wasn't going to let anyone forget it) and the other still worked the farm and dressed as such. Ella's granny didn't look like either of them. And she certainly didn't look like Beverley. Ella's granny looked like she'd been to Woodstock.

As Beverley disappeared inside the house, the older woman stopped and looked around. Could she see him? Should he wave his appreciation for her brave act of diversion? He hoped she hadn't hurt herself.

He'd thought he was done for when he opened the front door to find the woman looking right at him, and Beverley on the cusp of turning back in his direction. He was about to say something – 'Sorry' was the word that had been forming on his lips – when suddenly the grey-haired hippy was throwing herself on to the tarmac. (She was sort of how Janis Joplin might look, if she'd had a chance to grow old.) Arlo didn't hang around for directions. He legged it.

His dad had a pirated DVD of Arlo Guthrie playing Woodstock. He'd rooted it out of the attic for him and Leo one Saturday night. They'd watched it over and over until they could mimic every gesture Guthrie made on stage. Arlo's brother was named after Woody Guthrie, and he was named after his son, Arlo, who was also a folk musician and who Charlie Whitehead regularly argued was as good as, if not better than, his father.

Leo had thought Charlie was so cool, all Arlo's friends did. Their parents had never even heard of Arlo Guthrie. Leo had once told him, in the deepest confidence, that he was named after Leo Sayer. Arlo had never heard of the singer, so he looked him up. Then he rolled around his bedroom floor laughing for at least an hour.

Jogging up to his van now, Arlo laughed again. 'When I neeeed you, I just close my eyes and I'm with you ...' he sang softly, as he opened the driver's door.

The fuck you bring that up for? Haven't I suffered enough?

Leo Sayer! He's even naffer than Cliff Richard. You should have just lied, boy. Leo Varadkar would have been cooler than that!

So you're talking to me again, then? I thought you were throwing me under the bus for your girlfriend. Or should that be my girlfriend?

She was never your girlfriend, Leo.

She almost was, and she would have been if it wasn't for what happened. And that's why you don't like to talk to me when she's about. You're a wimp.

Don't call me that.

Wimp, wimp, wimp. It all worked out really well for you, didn't it, Arly?

That's not true.

You were never exactly competition. You had to butcher me just so you could stand a chance. You're scrawny and gangly and anytime anyone speaks to you, you look like a fucking tomato – a tomato with a wonky nose. I'd have won hands down.

Arlo started the van.

You know I'm not real, right? As in, I don't actually live in your head? These are your own thoughts.

I know, Leo. I'm not fucking insane.

He turned the radio up so loudly and so quickly, that the speakers vibrated. But Leo's voice was still clear as a bell.

Then you really need to work on your self-confidence, Arly. Like fucking pronto.

The Glass Lake auditorium was unrecognisable from the hall Christine had sat in at the start of the week for the Parents' Information Night. Gone were the orderly rows of seats, the tables topped with tablecloths and carefully arranged finger-food platters, and the parents dressed in suits and autumnal coats. When Christine entered the hall now, just before 1 p.m. on Thursday, she was greeted by colourful pandemonium.

A large group of children stood on the stage, half of them dressed in orange and the other half decked out in blue, but all committing to their chosen colour from the bobble at the top of their hats down to the toes of their socks. Beverley Franklin stood in front of the coordinated children. She had her back to Christine, but it was clear she was reading them the riot act.

Amelia Franklin was standing off to the side of the stage, holding her long blonde ponytail aloft as Maeve pulled at the back of her sky-blue 'Dorothy' dress. A measuring tape and several yards of ribbon hung around Maeve's neck and Christine was relieved that this, at least, had worked out for her easily stressed middle child.

About two dozen more students were milling around the main hall, under the supervision of Mr Cafferty and a couple of other teachers. The students sported a mixture of fantastical costume and

Glass Lake uniform. One child, presumably the tinman, was having large sheets of silver cardboard attached to his body by a woman in her sixties who wore a bright pink kaftan and who herself looked like she could play one of Oz's good witches. Seamus McGrath, the school caretaker, was taping mesh to a tall, wire structure that was already identifiable as a tornado.

Lorna Lick-Arse Farrell was the only other parent present. She was dressed all in black, save for a coffee-coloured wraparound cardigan, and she was holding some sort of stick, which she periodically banged on the ground, adding to the cacophony of noise and making the small circle of students gathered before her leap with fright. Woody Whitehead was among them, dressed in his uniform but with whiskers painted on to his face.

Derek had pitched this article as 'on-the-ground reporting'. 'Our Glass Lake correspondent embeds herself in the trenches of rehearsals and reports on what's *really* going on,' he'd said in the action movie trailer voice he used to spice up rudimentary stories. Christine had written several such pieces in her time with the *Southern Gazette* and knew that the key was to mention as many students as possible, so they could use plenty of photographs of them dressed in adorable costumes.

She pulled her notebook from her handbag and jotted down a few quick observations. She was trying to remember the name of the boy playing the tinman when she felt a tug on her jacket.

A small girl in orange leggings, sweatshirt and woolly hat was standing at her side.

'Director Franklin says you're to wait in the stalls.'

Christine looked up to the stage and waved at Beverley, but she was already turning back to the blue and orange children.

'Wait where?'

'In the stalls,' repeated the child-sized satsuma. 'That's what you call the seats in the auditorium. Director Franklin says she'll be with you as soon as she solves the problem of mass ineptitude.' She paused. 'Do you know what that means?'

'Not a clue.'

The satsuma nodded. 'She also says you're late.'

'Only slightly,' Christine shouted after the girl, who was running back towards the stage. 'I had some cat trouble!'

Christine had been due to arrive at the hall half an hour ago, but she'd finally seen an opportunity to retrieve Porcupine. The three Maguire children had been watching Mrs Rodgers' house from the front-room window for the past week, noting her movements in the notebook Christine had left on the sill and, besides her Tidy Town meetings on Mondays, the one constant was her late-morning walk. The cat thief left the house in a pair of Asics runners every day at 11.30 a.m. She returned between 12.22 and 12.37 and stopped to detangle her beloved roses before disappearing inside. That gave Christine fifty minutes to get in and out of number one Seaview Terrace, cat in tow.

'We are not breaking into our neighbour's home,' Conor had said when she ran the plan past him last night.

'Of course we're not.' Christine had already considered this option. But a few surveys of the perimeter (thank you, Brian) suggested Mrs Rodgers never left so much as the bathroom window ajar. 'We're going to use a key.'

Father Brendan O'Shea, who lived at number twelve, had a key to all Seaview Terrace homes in case of emergencies. Christine was going to call to him, explain that Porcupine had got trapped in their neighbour's home, that they had tried phoning the elderly woman to no avail, and that they were now very worried about her safety. The cat being only an afterthought.

Conor had been against it. 'Porcupine has changed.'

'He has not changed, Conor. He's just had his fur dyed.'

'It was more than that. It was in his eyes. It was like he didn't know me.' Her husband shivered. 'Or didn't want to know me.'

In the end, none of it mattered anyway. After a good five minutes knocking on his door, Christine had gone around the back to try the small shrine Fr O'Shea had built in his garden – the previous owners had installed a goldfish pond; it had only taken a woman's head to convert the water fountain into Our Holy Mother – where she was spotted by his next-door neighbour. Fr O'Shea had left for Medjugorje the day before. There'd been another sighting on Apparition Hill, apparently. 'Says he won't be back until the Virgin Mary shows herself,' relayed the neighbour. 'Or until Ryanair close the Bosnia route in late November. Whichever comes first.'

Now, Christine headed for the small cluster of plastic chairs in the centre of the auditorium where the tinman was having bonus bits of tinfoil wrapped around his forearms. Lorna was leaning on her stick, watching her, and Christine smiled over.

Conor reckoned she should give up – 'The kids don't even mention Porcupine any more' – but it wasn't about the stupid animal, it was about right and wrong, and Christine would find another way into that house, even if it was through the goddam cat-flap.

She took a seat and watched as the tinman wobbled off awkwardly, tripping slightly on his new shin guards.

'That'll help get him into character anyway,' she said to the older woman in the bright kaftan who'd been helping with his costume.

'He probably should have been cast as the lion, poor child. Seems to have a lot of fears. The flying monkeys are giving him nightmares, and his mother came in with him this morning to see if Beverley could eliminate the bit where he kills a swarm of bees by having them bounce against his armour.' The white-haired woman pulled a bottle of something mud-coloured from her bag and took a swig. 'There are no actual bees, of course, just sound effects, but that didn't seem to make a difference.'

'I don't remember a swarm of bees.'

'Oh, it's in the original book. You better get that right, or my daughter will be very cross,' she said, nodding at Christine's notebook. 'It's *The Wonderful Wizard of Oz*, like the book, not *The Wizard of Oz*, which is the movie. You don't want to make that mistake, trust me. I got a twenty-minute lecture on the subtle but important differences on the drive here. I assume you're the local journalist?'

'Christine Maguire, hi. I'm basically here to write a very long picture caption. The more kids we can feature, the more family members guilted into buying a copy.'

'Frances Tandon,' said the woman, extending a hand. 'I'm Beverley's mother – and Dorothy's grandmother.' She held out the bottle to Christine. 'Kombucha?'

'No, thank you.' It looked like what you might find at the bottom of Beverley's kitchen fishpond. 'I actually met you once, about thirty years ago. Beverley and I were in the same class here, and I was at your house working on a school project.'

'Were you?' said Frances, amazed. 'That must have been a first, and a last. I don't remember Beverley ever bringing friends home. I'm afraid my daughter has always been rather embarrassed by her family – and me, in particular.'

Her tone was breezy but Christine glanced around for a change of subject. Maeve and Amelia were gone from the stage, and Lorna Farrell appeared to have broken her stick in two.

'Rehearsals seem to be in full swing,' she said. 'Are they going well?'

'Oh, I'm sure they are. If you want a job done properly, put Beverley in charge. I'm not sure where she got her determination from. I've never had an ounce of it,' said Frances cheerfully. 'Though there does seem to have been some crossed wires with the Munchkins. Half of them have turned up as Oompa Loompas.'

....

Three of the Oompa Loompas were now crying, and another (one of Claire Keating's boys) was trying to make the case for how the Wizard of Oz was Willy Wonka's father based on a 'thread' he'd read on the internet. Beverley was ignoring the boy, who she'd long suspected had an attention deficit disorder, but he kept talking.

'... and the Munchkins actually showed Willy Wonka how to grow magic sweets, especially lollipops, because they have a lollipop guild, and so Oompa Loompas and Munchkins are basically the same thing, and if you watch the film backwards ...'

Another boy, who was at least dressed in blue, kept suggesting ways in which he could enhance his role. He had been doing character development at home with his mother and, having watched the Judy Garland film and spotted a Munchkin mayor, had turned up to today's rehearsals with a gold chain around his neck.

'We're basing our production on the book, where there is no mayor,' said Beverley. 'You're a Munchkin, James. You don't need any more development than that.'

'But why do we have to be blue?' asked a fifth-classer who'd gone as far as painting her face orange.

'Because you're Munchkins.'

'Can I at least keep the hat?' said one of the orange snifflers. 'My granny knit this hat.'

'But who says Munchkins can't be orange?' The face-painter.

'Me. And L. Frank Baum. And no, you can't keep the hat. Maybe your granny will knit you another one.'

'Who's Frank Bum?'

'*Baum*. He's the author.'

'But my granny's dead.'

'The author of Willy Wonka or the Wizard of Oz?'

'Of *The Wonderful Wizard of Oz*! And there's no such book as Willy— It doesn't matter. I say it. All right? Me. I say Munchkins must be blue and I'm in charge.' Beverley took a deep breath. 'Okay?'

The children nodded slowly.

A hand went up.

'Yes?'

'Maybe I could sing a song explaining *why* Munchkins are blue?'

'No, James. No extra songs! No gold chain! No conspiracy theories about fictional characters' parentage! No orange costume pieces, made by the living or the dead! None of it. You all wear blue, sing "Ding Dong the Witch Is Dead" and that's it. You got it?'

Even the Keating twin stopped babbling now. The other brother's lip started to quiver. She couldn't tell which one he was, since the boys had identical haircuts and (incorrect) costumes.

Jesus, don't let them all start crying.

'I know this is stressful,' said Beverley, more calmly. She was in danger of having to get up on stage and sing 'Ding Dong the Witch Is Dead' herself. 'But show business always is. You all know I used to be a professional actress, yes?'

The children nodded glumly.

'So, trust me. We're nearly there. One week to go.' A *week*, and they still couldn't get their colours straight! She did her best to smile. 'But we need to keep going, because currently we are behind schedule.'

It wasn't just the schedule that had her stressed. It was the presence of numerous unwanted people at rehearsals, namely Tamara Watson's son, who had been given a chorus role as a flying monkey; her own mother, who was allowed to attend on condition that she not tell Beverley to take it easy, breathe, or anything similarly dismissive; and Christine Maguire, who had been sent to write about rehearsals, and who was half an hour late.

She felt marginally bad that she had arguably planted a seed that may or may not have people suspecting Maeve Maguire was the girl involved in the sexting episode. But she didn't have time for such frivolities as remorse. They were halfway through rehearsal time and had yet to run a single scene.

'We need to do the arrival to Oz scene, pronto.' She looked around her. 'Amelia?' Her daughter was standing alone in the wings. 'Over here, now. And where's Ciara Murphy? James, go down there and get Ciara Murphy.'

'But I don't want to miss any notes!'

Beverley took a deep breath. 'Oh, for God's sake ... Ciara! Ciara Murphy!'

Fiona Murphy's daughter emerged from the chorus of flying monkeys currently getting the 'fame costs' speech from Lorna.

'Yes, Director Franklin?' she said, running towards the stage.

'You're now the Wicked Witch of the West, congratulations.'

The girl gasped, pushed her hands to her chest and started to bounce manically.

'Yes, yes, well done. Alison O'Hagan has come down with tonsillitis. That's the reason you've been promoted, got it? Ciara!'

The girl stopped bouncing.

'If your mother asks, that's why you got the part, no other reason.' Beverley loathed herself for giving in to blackmail. But what was she to do? She could not have the whole town whispering about her, saying she'd been fired (She had quit!) and casting doubt on her enviable marriage. And she had not been fired! *That* was the most important thing.

'Yes, Director Franklin.'

'Good. Now, up on stage, let's go. Gordon, get her a script.'

Gordon was Beverley's PA. He had crippling stage fright that meant he couldn't even cut it as a cornstalk. But he was a whiz with a spreadsheet.

As a script was found and Ciara came around the side of the stage to the stairs, Beverley cast a cold eye over the auditorium. Her mother was talking to Christine, which was not something she needed right now. God knows what Frances was saying, and to a journalist.

'Got the script.'

Beverley took the stapled pages from the boy. 'Page seventeen,' she said, throwing it to Ciara. 'Gordon, who else do we need for this scene?'

The kid checked his notes. 'Munchkins, Dorothy, Wicked Witch of the West.'

'Check, check, check. Props?'

'The Cyclone. Silver shoes. The broom.'

'You,' she said to another of the Munchkins, 'go down there and tell Caretaker Seamus I want to speak to him. The shoes we have, and ...' She rotated to where her assistant director was psyching up a new batch of supporting cast with her talk of sweat payments. 'Lorna! Lorna! We need the broom! Now!'

But as the Laker made her way to the stage, Beverley could see that the Wicked Witch's broomstick, which Seamus had made especially, was snapped in half.

'For God's sake, Lorna. I told you to stop hammering the thing off the floor. What are we going to use now?'

'It was shoddy craftsmanship. I was going to get a replacement from the storage closet ...'

'Well, go on, so. What are you waiting for?'

'It's locked.'

Beverley put a hand to her chest and swallowed. This was not good for her heartburn.

'You called,' said Seamus, appearing at the foot of the stage. She ignored the caretaker's tone. Here was another person who struggled to comprehend primary colours.

'Seamus, do you have a key for the storage closet?'

'Not currently,' he said. 'But Principal Patterson does.'

Beverley turned back to the children, picking an Oompa Loompa at random. 'Go and ask Principal Patterson for the key to the storage closet. Tell her we need a broom as a matter of urgency.' There wouldn't be any Munchkins left to greet Dorothy at this rate. 'Go on. Go!'

The girl ran off, the bobble of her orange hat bouncing.

'Was that it?' asked Seamus, as Ciara started mumbling her new lines to herself. Out of the corner of her eye, she saw the ambitious Munchkin whip the gold chain out again and throw it around his neck.

'No,' said Beverley. 'I want to talk to you about *that*.' She pointed at the set design Seamus had been working on. 'We have a problem.'

'With the tornado?'

'Exactly. I did not ask for a tornado.'

'You did. It's in the script. It's what carries Dorothy to Oz.'

Beverley shook her head. 'Gordon?'

'According to *The Wonderful Wizard of Oz*, by L. Frank Baum, published in 1900, Dorothy is carried from Kansas to Oz by a cyclone.' Her sidekick looked up from his notes.

'A cyclone,' agreed Beverley.

'They're the same thing,' said Seamus.

'Gordon?'

The boy flicked to the next page. 'A tornado is a collection of strong winds that spiral around a central point, creating a funnel shape. A cyclone rotates around a centre of low pressure. They move slower than tornados and are generally accompanied by rain.' He looked up at Beverley. 'Technically, if we're setting the musical in Cork as opposed to Kansas, it should really be a hurricane. They're more common along the North Atlantic Ocean.'

'Gordon,' warned Beverley, 'what did we agree?'

'No unsolicited opinions. Sorry, Director Franklin. Won't happen again.'

They both regarded Seamus.

The caretaker sighed loudly.

'Can you talk to the kids about the sets? They're meant to be in charge. I'm only supposed to be helping out.'

Beverley spotted the sixth-class teacher heading for the double doors at the rear of the auditorium. 'Eh, Mr Cafferty! Mr Cafferty!' The newest staff member turned back towards her. 'Seamus,' she said, before the caretaker could slink off, 'can you please take another look at the Yellow Brick Road? I appreciate you've gone over it, and there have been some improvements, but it still looks gold at best.'

'Yes, Beverley?' said Mr Cafferty, approaching the stage. He smiled at the caretaker, but the older man ignored him as he sighed again and headed back to his tornado.

'Have you fixed the lion's movements yet? Lorna said he was still creeping about the stage like a burglar last time she ran scenes with him.'

'I'm trying,' said the teacher. 'But it's proving difficult. Woody's ... he's not that open to instruction, at least not from me. Maybe you'd have a better shot at talking to him yourself?'

'I don't talk to Woody Whitehead.'

'Excuse me?'

'Gordon?'

'Director Franklin does not talk to Woody Whitehead,' the boy confirmed.

'Why not?'

'I just don't.'

'But he's playing the lion. That's a lead role. I don't see how that could work.'

'Lorna!' called Beverley. The assistant director scurried over to join her. It had taken thirty-five years, but she'd finally found something useful for the woman to do. 'Go and tell Woody he needs to start stomping on the stage. If he needs more details, Gordon here has an animal information sheet. But tell him to think clubfoot, not twinkle-toes.'

'Right you are,' said Lorna. 'Oh, and Bev,' she lowered her voice, 'did you see who's here? Christine Maguire! *Maeve Maguire's* mother!' Lorna's eyes widened. Her whole face was brimming with implied meaning, but Beverley pretended not to hear.

'And I'll need him up here in about half an hour; we'll be rehearsing the lion's arrival after this. So, you'll need to be up here too, in case I have any further notes to relay to him.' Beverley swivelled back to her assembled leads and clapped her hands. 'Okay, ensemble, let's take this from the top. Dorothy to the left; Munchkins in the middle; and Wicked Witch of the West to the right. Lights, camera—'

'Beverley?' Ciara Murphy was raising her hand. 'I mean, Director Franklin?'

The girl was cut out of her mother. On stage two minutes and already acting like she had a God-given right to be here.

'Do you think we could drop the "wicked"? It stigmatises women. And it goes against the school's bullying policy as regards name-calling.'

Beverley clamped her teeth together so aggressively that she bit her tongue.

'So, okay? The Witch of the West? It's just "wicked" ...' The girl scrunched up her face. 'It might impact my self-esteem.'

....

Lorna Farrell delivered the instructions to Woody Whitehead; gave him a brief, and highly accurate interpretation of a lion walking on two feet; and granted him permission to go to the bathroom. Then she scurried over to where Christine Maguire and Beverley's mother were sitting.

While she wasn't happy any child had been subject to such terrible parenting that she'd resorted to sending naked photos of herself out into the world, she wasn't entirely distraught that the girl involved was Christine's daughter. She was assistant director (an important role!) and she did not take kindly to this glorified copywriter going over her head to Beverley to get her daughter onto the musical. She'd never liked Christine. She'd always suspected she'd started that god-awful Lick-Arse nickname, which continued to plague her to this day. It was particularly hurtful because it wasn't at all true.

'What are you ladies gossiping about?' she said, pulling a third chair up beside them.

'We're not gossiping,' replied Christine, just as Frances said, 'The school's new sex education classes.'

'They start today,' said Lorna, who'd always had great gossip timing. 'I was going to see if I could track down the doctor, actually, and find out what exactly he's teaching. I don't know if you've heard, Frances, but he's quite controversial. What do you think of him, Christine?'

'I don't know much about him.'

'Mmm,' said Lorna. Then she took a deep breath and went for it. 'I heard Woody Whitehead was the boy who sent the nudes.'

'Who told you that?' said both women at the same time. Frances sounded curious, but Christine was livid.

'So, it's true?'

'No comment,' said Christine.

'It doesn't really matter who it was,' said Frances. 'It's great all the kids will get these classes.'

'I think it's too young,' said Lorna, not taking her eyes off Christine. 'Just because two children were sexually deviant, the rest of the class shouldn't be stripped of their innocence. If the girl's parents want these classes, they should organise to have them privately.'

Christine gave a hollow laugh. 'The girl's parents did not want these classes. I can tell you that for nothing. It was not their idea.'

Lorna's face erupted. 'And how do you know that?'

Christine was suddenly flustered.

'You interviewed the mother, didn't you?' coaxed Frances. 'For an article. That's how you know ... I presume?'

'Yes, exactly. That's it. I interviewed the mother under the promise of anonymity, so I can't say another thing about it.'

But Lorna didn't need her to. She had all the confirmation she needed. It was blatantly obvious.

Woody Whitehead and Maeve Maguire.

Lorna removed her phone from the black bumbag she had tied around her waist and discreetly fired off a few correspondences.

'**Rehearsals can** be a tad noisy,' said Nuala Patterson as she led Dr O'Sullivan down the corridor, past the auditorium. She did not throw her head around the door; the longer she could avoid Beverley, the better.

The woman had already called by her office that morning. She wanted to make it clear that she remained 'deeply unhappy' with Nuala's decision to lecture the parents and toss a couple of vague sex ed sessions at the children instead of eliminating the root of the problem: Woody Whitehead.

'They'll be done with rehearsals before two, and then you should have forty-five minutes for your first session. There'll be more time tomorrow. Is half an hour enough for you to set up now? You'll have the classroom to yourself. The whole of sixth class and Mr Cafferty are in the hall.'

'That's fine. I'm all ready to go – except for this,' said Dr O'Sullivan, swinging the black metal box he was carrying in his left hand.

The doctor – a second cousin on her mother's side that she only ever met at funerals – had arrived at the school early because he needed some help welding a hinge on the container.

'Seamus will sort that out for you in no time.'

The doctor nodded.

'His office is just down here.'

'Great.'

Nuala slowed as they passed the younger classes. Mrs Walsh was winding down the Junior Infants with a bit of afternoon story time and Nuala recognised the cover without being close enough to read the title. *Run with the Wind*. Leo had loved that book.

'What's the box for, can I ask?'

'Anonymity,' said the doctor, switching the heavy-looking item from one hand to another. 'It allows the children to ask things or tell me things in the strictest confidence. Sometimes the presence of their peers makes them too embarrassed to speak, so instead, they can write it down and stick it in here.'

There was no mention of that on the departmental curriculum, but it was a clever idea. Still, she'd probably neglect to mention it if Lorna Farrell cornered her again in the schoolyard.

They rounded the final corridor corner.

'How's your son, that was in the accident? My mother told me he was in Dublin?'

'Leo,' said Nuala, the name sounding strange. How long since she'd spoken it aloud? 'Yes. He's been discharged from rehab there, but he still has regular sessions.'

'You must miss him.'

'Yes,' she said, relieved to be placing a hand on the door to Seamus's workshop. 'Well, here we are.' She peered in the window and the growing light-headedness escalated. There was no sign of Seamus. Only Arlo Whitehead, hunched over a table, reading some sort of letter. 'Seamus must still be in the auditorium,' she said, taking a step away from the door. 'But Arlo will look after you.

211

And he'll show you to the sixth-class room afterwards.' She took another step back. 'I've a million and one things to do, so I'll leave you to it.'

'Okay,' said the doctor.

'I'll speak to you after.'

Then she turned and left. But instead of heading back to her office, Nuala made her way through the next available fire exit.

She stood outside for a full five minutes, waiting for the cold wind to blow the unsettled feeling away. When her fingertips started to go numb, she curled them into balls and went back indoors.

....

It took Arlo twelve minutes to fix the hinges on the large black box.

It helped that the doctor hadn't sat there watching him. He seemed to get the message when Arlo offered him the choice of two plumbing manuals to read, and instead walked around the workroom looking at the various kids' drawings of Seamus that adorned the wall. Arlo's personal favourite was the one of the grey-haired caretaker playing Xbox while standing on a surfboard.

Arlo had been staring at his dad's letter since Seamus left for 'five minutes' to check on rehearsals. That was an hour ago. He was relieved to have something to do. He tightened the screws on the other hinge while he was at it. No point doing a half-arsed job.

Arlo led the doctor down the corridor towards Mr Cafferty's classroom. Sixth-class students had been sitting in the same corner of Glass Lake since he was a student.

The corridor was clear except for Mr Cafferty and a student, who appeared to be arguing. Except it wasn't any student, it was—

'Woody?'

His little brother turned, whipping his arm down by his side, and the teacher looked up.

'What's going on?' asked Arlo.

'Hi, there. I'm Mr Cafferty,' said the teacher, smiling broadly as he held out a hand.

'Arlo Whitehead,' he said, shaking it. 'I'm Woody's brother.'

'Dr Cian O'Sullivan.'

'Of course,' said Mr Cafferty. 'I enjoyed your talk on Monday. I'm delighted you'll be speaking to the students.'

Arlo looked at his brother, but he was busy glaring at his feet. 'Aren't you supposed to be at rehearsals in the hall? Woody?'

'Your brother was a little mixed up about where he should be,' said Mr Cafferty. 'I came back to the classroom to get something and found him out here. He must have got confused about the timetable. Was that it, Woody? I'd say it was.'

'I was going to the toilet,' mumbled the boy, avoiding eye contact with all three adults.

'Well, on you go,' said the teacher, watching Woody slouch off in the direction of the bathroom.

Arlo watched him go too. 'I was just showing the doctor to your classroom,' he said.

'Yes, yes, go on in,' enthused Mr Cafferty. 'There's a staff toilet right next door, and the kitchen is just to the left around that corner. I've to get back to the hall – I'm helping with movement, and the tinman is having some issues with staying on stage – but go ahead and make yourself at home.'

....

'He asked if he could go to the bathroom and I said yes. But that was twenty minutes ago.'

'So, where is he?' One cast member, that's all Beverley had asked Lorna to look after. She just had to keep an eye on one student while Beverley looked after the remaining thirty or so, and she couldn't even manage that. 'We need Woody. I can hardly do the Dorothy, Scarecrow and Tinman meet Lion scene without the lion, now can I?'

Lorna was pulling a watery-eyed expression not dissimilar to the one the Oompa Loompas had threatened her with earlier. 'I could go and look for him,' she said. 'He can't have gone too far ...'

'No, forget it. Forget it. We'll do something else.'

The Arrival to Oz scene remained on hold while she waited for word on a replacement broom, but they were running out of time and they needed to perform something so Christine Maguire could write about it. This was their second-best scene, and a central piece to the story, but Woody Whitehead was, of course, nowhere to be found. How Principal Patterson couldn't see that the boy did not deserve to be a Glass Lake student was beyond her.

'Gordon, what other scenes are in reasonable shape?'

Beverley's PA frowned as he read down through the list. 'Dorothy and Scarecrow meet Tinman, maybe?'

'No Munchkins in that one, right?'

'Right.'

'Fine. Dorothy and Scarecrow meet Tinman, it is. You three ready?' Beverley turned to her daughter, who really did look radiant in blue, and the two male students.

'Yes, Director Franklin,' they said.

'You okay, Henry?'

The tinman nodded nervously.

'The armour on my left arm is a bit loose. What if the bees attack me and it comes off?'

'We're not doing the bee scene yet. And, as I told you, they're not real bees, it's just going to be sound effects, and you pretending, okay?'

'Maybe the bees could attack Scarecrow instead?'

'No way,' said the boy playing Scarecrow. 'I'm allergic.'

'Again: they are not real bees. So nobody needs to worry. But let's get your costume fixed, Henry. Where's Shona Martin?' Beverley asked Lorna, as she searched the room for their head of costume.

'Shona's out sick today.'

'Right. Who else is doing costumes?'

'Maeve Maguire.'

'Maeve!' Beverley looked around the stage and then out into the auditorium. 'Maeve! Maeve Maguire! Has anyone seen Maeve?'

Lorna gasped. 'Woody *and* Maeve missing?' She lowered her voice slightly. 'You were so right, Beverley. First photos, now this ...'

'I never said anything about Maeve Maguire,' hissed Beverley.

'No.' Lorna nodded solemnly. 'Of course you didn't. Mum's the word.'

An orange child ran back into the hall and up on to the stage.

'There are no Munchkins in this scene,' said Beverley. 'Please clear the stage.'

'You sent me to get the key to the storage cupboard off Principal Patterson,' said the little girl, panting slightly in her woollen hat.

'Oh, right. You can give it to Lorna.'

'I couldn't find Principal Patterson. She wasn't in her office. I ran down all the corridors but there was no sign of her.'

Beverley did not have time for this. She needed a broom. 'Where's Seamus?'

'He left a few minutes ago,' said Gordon, checking his watch. 'Eight minutes ago.'

'You,' she said to the out-of-breath Oompa Loompa. 'Go down to Caretaker Seamus's office and tell him we need access to the storage cupboard. He must have a bolt cutter or something. What are you waiting for? We don't have all day!' The girl took a big gulp of air, spun around, and sped off again. 'Will you go and get Christine please, Lorna? Tell her we're ready to go if she'd like to watch.'

'Roger that.'

Lorna ploughed off towards the back of the hall and Beverley took a minute to gather herself. She threw a glance in the direction of her mother, who had a group of sixth-classers in stitches. As always with Frances, Beverley did not want to know.

Just then, Woody appeared through the main doors.

'There he is,' muttered Beverley. 'Gordon?'

The boy nodded. 'I'll go and get him.'

24

......

'That bloody woman,' said Seamus, bustling back into his workroom and throwing tools down on the floor inside the door. 'I build her an entire cornfield, travel the length and breadth of the country collecting glass for her Emerald City, and what do I get? A fecking lecture on weather phenomena. Stick on the kettle and crack open the emergency Jaffa Cakes, before my blood pressure really takes off.'

'I heard the racket all right,' said Arlo, flicking the switch.

'It's not the kids. You've no idea how much I love those kids. It's the parents.' Seamus considered this. 'Occasionally the teachers, but mostly the parents.'

Arlo took the only two mugs from the draining board of the small kitchen unit and threw in teabags. Then he pulled the jumbo packet of biscuits from under the sink.

'You know what Principal Patterson says? She says the Glass Lake parents make her wish she was principal of an orphanage.' Seamus chuckled. 'You can imagine what *Director Franklin* would have to say if she heard that.'

Arlo pretended to study the row of old baseball cards Seamus had framed and hung above the sink. They were all of the same guy in a striped uniform and New York Yankees cap. Mostly, they managed to get through the day without mentioning Nuala.

'Which of the teachers don't you like?' he asked, carrying the mugs from the counter to the worktable.

'Thanks, son. Hmm? Ah, they're grand, mostly. I'm just giving out. Ignore me.'

Arlo went back for the biscuits and then sat himself on the stool opposite Seamus.

'Mr Cafferty? You were giving out about him last week.'

'Arra, he's just a bit up in your business. I can't stand people like that. Does Woody like him?' The way the caretaker's eyes flickered up from his cup threw Arlo, and he thought back to his brief encounter with Woody and Mr Cafferty in the corridor earlier.

'I don't know,' he admitted.

Seamus dunked a Jaffa Cake into his tea. When he'd caught the soggy biscuit in his mouth and swallowed, he said: 'Didn't you want to ask me something about tomorrow?'

'Oh, yeah,' said Arlo, as casually as he could muster. 'I might need the day off. You said you weren't sure if you'd need me, so I thought it would be okay.' Half of him hoped Seamus wouldn't allow it, that he'd suddenly have too much work on and need his help. 'I was thinking about visiting my dad, you see, and I have jobs on most days, but tomorrow is pretty much free and there are visitor hours in the afternoon ... Would that be okay? If it's not, it's fine. I'm not even sure if I will go. It's just ... It was just an idea.'

Seamus went to say something but a knock on the door cut him short. 'That's grand, son. No bother,' he said, as the door pushed open and a small child dressed head-to-toe in orange appeared in the office.

'Caretaker Seamus?' said the girl, panting. Arlo wondered what role she was playing. Part of the rainbow, maybe?

'Director Franklin said—'

'No.'

The child blinked. She tried again. 'She said to ask if you can—'

'No,' repeated Seamus.

'To ask if you can come back and—'

'No, no, no.'

'But—'

'Sorry, Amy, but no. I am not going back there. I am on my tea break now, and then I have a mountain of work to get through. You tell Director Franklin that if she wants to clear out the gutters at the back of the building, then fine, I'll go and see to her sets.'

Orange Amy looked doubtful. 'I don't think she'd want to do that.'

Was there a rainbow in *The Wizard of Oz*, or was that just the song?

'No,' agreed Seamus. 'Nor do I.'

'But we need a broom from the storage closet, and we can't find the key. She said you might have some sort of cutter to break the padlock.'

Seamus took a loud, long slurp of his tea.

Orange Amy didn't budge.

'Please, Caretaker Seamus. Us Munchkins are already on thin ice. If I go back again without the key, she might get rid of us altogether.'

'Are Munchkins orange?' asked Arlo, who wasn't sure if he'd ever seen the film, or just a few stills.

But suddenly Orange Amy's big eyes were filling with tears and Seamus was pushing himself up from his seat to pat the girl gently on the shoulder. 'Shhh, now. It's all right, Amy petal. Arlo will go and help. Won't you, Arlo?'

219

'I'm not sure if I'd really be wanted there … I think I'm better out of sight.'

'Principal Patterson will be nowhere near rehearsals. She's far too clever for that,' said Seamus, offering the girl a Jaffa Cake.

But it wasn't just Principal Patterson Arlo was avoiding. Director Franklin was Beverley Franklin, and Arlo's success rate with her remained at zero. He'd decided he was better off focusing all his efforts on Ella's dad.

'Go on down and sort it out, Arlo. It's a cheap warded lock. I've some picks and a tension wrench somewhere in the filing cabinet if you need them, but you should be able to jimmy the thing open. Okay, Amy, you're okay. It's going to be all right. Here. Have another biscuit.'

....

Beverley had sent the girl to get Seamus McGrath, not Arlo bloody Whitehead. She would have demoted her to a flying monkey there and then, only the last scene, the one they'd performed for Christine Maguire and the wider readership of the *Southern Gazette*, had gone very well, so she was feeling generous.

'Come on, then,' she said to the lanky teenager who remained incapable of eye contact. 'Let's go, let's go. Christine – you can come too. We'll walk and talk.' She led the pair of them to the storage closet beside where her mother was seated. Lorna Farrell, who never needed an invitation to ride Beverley's coattails, was clipping at their heels. 'Where were we?'

'You were talking about your own acting background,' said Christine.

'Ah yes. Well, I'm sure you know the basics. A few high-profile adverts, a prominent role in *Cork Life*, a couple of theatre gigs – do you want to stop while you take this down?'

'I'm fine.'

'But then, you know, I had kids, and family won out. So, it's great to be able to get back to my roots, to tap into that creative energy again. And of course, I still have some contacts in the business, so I just made a few calls, sent in some footage of Amelia, and boom: TV cameras in Cooney. I see a lot of what I had in Amelia. She was the only choice, really, to play Dorothy. I've built the production around her.' They came to a stop at the storage door. 'This is the lock. What are you going to do about it?'

Arlo stepped forward and tilted the silver padlock in different directions. He pulled down sharply on it. Nothing happened. He gave it two more strong tugs.

'Is that what your expertise gets us – some brute force?'

'Give the boy a moment, Beverley,' said Frances, who was smiling kindly at him. Her mother's ability to irritate her was incredible. It was like she had a sixth sense for the people Beverley most disliked and made it her business to be nicest to them.

Arlo's face was now such a shade that he could have been an Oompa Loompa. He gave the lock another pull.

Beverley sighed. 'Right. Well, it seems we'll be doing the broom scene without a broom. Wonderful. Lorna, tell the children we're going to use an old-fashioned thing called imagination.'

The teenager inspected the keyhole again. 'Has anyone got a hairpin or a paperclip?'

Beverley rolled her eyes. 'We're not the Famous Five.'

'Oh, I loved those books!' gushed Lorna. 'And there are five of us here. Bagsy George.'

'No, Lorna. I do the casting around here, and you're clearly Timmy the dog.'

'I have a hairclip,' said Christine, pulling a brown slide from the back of her head and handing it to Arlo. 'Are you going to pick the lock?'

'I'm going to try.' He started to bend the clip out of shape. 'Do you mind?'

Christine shook her head, her eyes following Arlo's hands.

Of course the boy knew how to pick a lock, thought Beverley. He'd probably learned it from his father.

Once he had the clip in an L-shape, he shoved one end into the keyhole and started to push it in all directions.

Fifteen or so seconds passed, and nothing happened.

'Time to admit defeat, I think,' said Beverley.

'You need a plan, crumpet,' said Frances, stepping closer to the boy. 'It's a very male approach to just shove the thing in there, poke around and hope for the best. Believe me, I've seen it a lot.'

Dear God, let her mother not tell Arlo what she was referring to.

Frances took the straightened pin from the boy and gently laid it flat on his palm.

'What you need, Arlo' – how did her mother know his name? – 'is to go in there with intent and respect. Think of the padlock as a sacred place, somewhere that should be cherished and worshipped. Know what sensation you wish to achieve and keep that in your mind's eye.' Frances nodded encouragingly. 'Give it another try.'

The boy reinserted the pin.

'Start with some gentle circles – smaller, then larger – that's it, now vary the pressure ...'

'I'm not great when people are watching me,' Arlo mumbled, his face glowing.

'No,' agreed Frances. 'Most people aren't. Although I don't mind it myself ...' She shook her arms out and wriggled her fingers. 'Just reject the shame, reject the judgement, focus on the pleasure that will come with reaching your goal ...'

'You've a very soothing voice, Frances,' said Christine. 'I should get you to record meditation tapes for my daughter.'

'Yes, Maeve!' said Lorna, far too excitedly. 'Have you seen Maeve? We couldn't find her earlier.'

'Couldn't you?' Christine looked around the hall with mild concern.

Lorna's face was pinched. 'Yes. It was around the same time Woody went missing. That's a coincidence, isn't it?'

'Is it?'

'Don't mind her,' said Beverley, throwing daggers in Lorna's direction. 'Nobody's missing. Maeve's around here somewhere. And look. There's Woody over there.'

A sudden click and the bolt came away from the lock.

'Hurrah!' shouted Lorna.

Arlo grinned.

Frances joined her hands together and bowed slightly. 'Bliss.'

'Very impressive,' said Christine. 'Have you done that before?'

'Once or twice,' said Arlo, his face starting to cool now. 'It's not that hard.'

'Not once you know how,' added Frances.

'All right, Mother. You can go back to your seat now,' said Beverley, who did not think they should be praising the boy for being a dab hand at breaking and entering. She grabbed a brush from the cupboard. Lorna and Frances moved away but Christine was still watching the teenage boy with fascination.

'You wouldn't have a business card, would you, Arlo?' asked Christine, inspecting the hairpin that he'd returned to her. 'I might have a bit of work for you.'

....

Maeve Maguire finally stood and stretched out her legs. Her thighs were throbbing. She'd been crouched under Mr Cafferty's desk for something close to forever. She'd leapt under the table when she heard the teacher's voice in the corridor – talking to Woody – and she'd been about to crawl back out when the classroom door opened. She could only see the bottom half of the man who entered (she knew it was a man because of his big shoes and legs) but it wasn't Mr Cafferty because he wasn't humming. Mr Cafferty was always humming. This man was carrying a big black box, which he left on the ground. Then he'd started writing things on the whiteboard. He made that squeaky noise with the marker and more than once Maeve almost shrieked. Then he'd spent forever flicking through a notebook. She couldn't see what he was doing, only hear the pages. She might have fallen asleep with the boredom, if she hadn't been so uncomfortable.

And now he was gone. She had to get out of here quick. She'd been missing from rehearsals for ages and the man could return any minute. Or Director Franklin might come looking for her. Or Mr Cafferty. Or God – even her mom.

She wasn't mad at Woody for not turning up. She'd heard him getting stopped in the corridor. She was worried about him.

She grabbed what she'd come for, stuffed it in her bag and legged it towards the door.

Arlo came to an abrupt stop at the lights. He'd just missed them, again. All the lights were against him this afternoon. How was it four o'clock already? Time kept disappearing, while the commitments kept multiplying. He'd managed to move the only two jobs he had scheduled for tomorrow to today and Seamus had let him go early so he could get them done.

I don't see how you're going to get everything done, especially now your Sugar Mama wants you to come and see her too.

He had been in the school car park, climbing into his van, when a text message came through from Fiona Murphy requesting that he call to her house today. She said it was an emergency.

She's not my Sugar Mama, Leo, so will you please fuck off.

It's her you should tell to fuck off, boy. She calls, you come running. You're a wimp. I don't care how many extra twenties she leaves on the nightstand; you don't have time for this today.

I'm not going to leave her with a leaking sink, am I? Anyway, I'm not going running. I told her it would be tonight.

Right on cue, his phone beeped. He glanced over to where it lay on the passenger seat. One new message from Fiona Murphy.

| This evening is perfect xx

A horn beeped and Arlo looked up to see the lights had gone green. He took his foot off the brake and the van lurched forward.

'Don't say it, Leo, don't fucking say it,' he said, out loud, in the van, well aware as always that he was talking only to himself.

Say what, Arly? That if it can wait several hours it doesn't sound like much of an emergency? I wouldn't dream of it. Now come on, we've places to be; move that gearstick down to fourth.

·····························

Frances observed her daughter, standing at the marble kitchen counter with a beetroot, some fancy lettuce and an open recipe book. She saw Beverley as she was now but also all the versions that had come before. A profound loneliness emanated from her daughter's past selves and she felt sad for how easily they had been discarded.

She was in Cooney because her daughter needed her. Beverley would scorn the idea but, as her mother, Frances knew it intuitively. She had been sitting at her kitchen table last Thursday, as the sun set on her birthday, and it came to her as clear as day: she must go to Cooney. And the urge had still been there the following morning, when the special brownies had worn off.

Her daughter's face was dark as she chopped the vegetables.

They'd been talking about Glass Lake's refusal to expel Woody Whitehead. Again. Frances had spoken to Amelia that evening and she seemed fine; no lasting damage appeared to have been done.

'You think I'm ridiculous,' said Beverley. 'You think I'm over the top. I'm uptight. Go on, just say it.' Beverley's hand went to her chin, where the make-up was starting to wear away and two angry inflamed pimples were breaking through.

'I love you to distraction, *a stór*. That's why I'm here.'

'That boy should not be in Glass Lake. Glass Lake means something and that's not the sort of behaviour it accepts. You don't know Glass Lake. That's why you don't understand.'

'I understand what that school means to you. I know you credit it with all the things people usually credit to their parents. And I'm sorry you were unhappy with my mothering, but it wasn't a coincidence you were sent there,' she said, taking the first batch of chopped beetroot and laying it out on the roasting tray. 'I took that job in Cooney *because* I wanted you to go there. And since you're determined to resent me, I might as well say this now too: I do not believe you are upset with a twelve-year-old boy. At least, not as upset as you think you are. You're annoyed at Malachy. And maybe yourself. You're embarrassed, and you've never dealt well with embarrassment. But nobody expects you to be perfect. You're good enough.'

'You think I'm good ... *enough*?'

'Well now, you've taken my words and given them an entirely different meaning. That's not how I said it.'

'People loved me,' declared her daughter, banging down the knife. 'Everyone else wanted to know about life on set – which actors were bitchy, who was nice – but you never asked. You weren't proud of me.'

'I am immensely proud of you. You're so self-sufficient and capable. They're traits I've been working on for years and they come so effortlessly to you. But you being on television didn't make me any prouder. All I ever wanted was for you to be happy. And I don't think acting made you happy. I certainly don't think that window of fame did. You weren't in it for the right reasons, *a stór*. One

227

day soon, you'll be dead, and it will no longer matter what anyone thought of you. Having people think you're better than them doesn't make you better than them. And no matter what happens, you will always know that and so it will never truly feel good. All that'll matter is that you were impressed by yourself. That you did what you believed was right, that you loved your children, that you cared for those who were vulnerable, that you were the best version of yourself. You're always trying to prove yourself and you're trapped in this image you've created. You're good enough, Beverley, you always were.'

Frances took a deep inhale.

Beverley picked up the knife and resumed chopping. When the beetroot was done, she started on the fancy lettuce.

Whenever Frances started to think she knew her daughter inside out, she reminded herself that there were two goldfish swimming around the floor of what was an otherwise perfect white cube. Beverley still had the ability to surprise.

'I know I'm good enough,' she said, her voice so small it could only have come from her inner child.

It was as much as Frances could ask for.

'Good,' she said, rolling up her sleeves and glancing around the kitchen for a potential source of pots. It was impossible to discern the walls from the cupboards in here. 'What say I make a system-cleansing turmeric grain bowl to go with this? That spice does wonders for the complexion.'

....

Arlo got through the afternoon's work as quickly as he could. He put up shelves for the new woman, Tamara, and he tiled the splashback in Mrs Regan's kitchen without taking a break. When Mrs Regan started talking about how a radiator his dad had installed in her husband's pharmacy was already leaking, he didn't fight it. He just accepted the reduced fee, thanked her politely and left. It was 9 p.m. when he got to Fiona Murphy's house. Depending on the scale of the emergency, he might still have time to see Ella.

Arlo parked the van in Fiona's driveway and took his toolkit from the back. He had a bad feeling that the problem with her sink lay with the water supply line. He'd replaced the drain, examined the pipes, tightened the nuts and bolts. He'd even redone the putty last time he was out. But a leak in the water supply line was a much bigger problem. If that was why she kept having difficulties, he'd be here all night – and even then, there was a good chance it would be beyond his expertise.

When Fiona opened the door, she was dressed, as she sometimes was, in a long silk dressing gown. It was wrapped tightly around her, but it still parted at the bottom and Arlo could see nothing but leg. He crossed the threshold, already blushing and already annoyed at himself.

'I'm sorry I couldn't come sooner,' he said, following her through to the kitchen. Her feet were bare, and he thought for the first time that he should offer to take off his grubby work boots. Maybe this was one of those houses where people didn't wear shoes.

'Not at all,' said Fiona. 'I hope I didn't tear you away from anything important. You weren't on another job, were you?'

'All finished for the day now.'

'Well, that's even worse. Am I interrupting your evening plans? You were probably going to meet someone, go out. It is a Thursday, after all. I know that's the new Friday.'

229

'No plans,' he said politely. 'Nowhere to go. Nobody to meet.'

'I find that hard to believe,' she said in that sing-song way that made him think she was teasing him. 'You don't have a girlfriend?'

Fiona was friends with Ella's mother. 'Nope,' he said.

'No one?'

'No girlfriend.'

Fiona grinned. 'Good.'

Arlo got down on his hunkers and opened the toolbox. 'I was thinking the problem with the sink might actually be in the supply line,' he said, glancing up, only for his eyeline to be level with the split in her dressing gown. 'I'll have to take up a bit of the skirting to have a look,' he continued, head back in the box. 'Even then it might be hard to say for sure, but if I can't sort it, I have the number for a plumber who owes me a favour and—'

'Oh Arlo, darling. The sink's fine. You did a wonderful job on it last time.'

He blew air up into his face and removed his head from the box. 'Right. Okay, well that's good.' He stood, taking a step back from Fiona and trying not to think about what was or was not under her gown.

'It is,' she said, smiling. 'You always do a wonderful job.'

He did his best to return the smile, but he was starting to get that constricting feeling in his chest. 'So what's, em, what's the emergency?'

Fiona leaned back slightly, her arms reaching behind her so they gripped the edge of the kitchen table. This caused her chest to push against her dressing gown and he was embarrassed to find himself light-headed. He didn't like her. He knew he didn't. So why was he dizzy?

'It's about Woody,' she said.

'Woody? My brother Woody?'

'I'd be surprised if there was another Woody in Cork, wouldn't you? Let alone in Cooney.' She turned around briefly and picked up a phone from the kitchen table. Her phone, Arlo knew, had a Little Miss Fiona cover, but this one had a shiny yellow back plastered with stickers. 'Ciara's at her father's house tonight. He doesn't usually have her on school nights, but I thought it would be better if we could talk about this privately. Where is it?'

She frowned at the screen of her daughter's phone and Arlo felt like every resident of Cooney had their hands around his lungs and they were squeezing at once.

'I heard Woody was the boy involved in the sexting scandal up at the school.'

She made it sound off-hand but of course it wasn't. He said nothing. He couldn't. He just stood there, and she went back to the phone.

'There's been a bit of chatter about it, you probably won't be surprised to hear. I swear Cooney was built on sand and gossip. And petitions. If you went back through the annals, I doubt you'd find any acts about the founding of this town, just a whole load of rumours passed around the various high kings and monks of Ireland.' She looked up again. 'Woody Whitehead and Maeve Maguire. It's only ever a matter of time before the word gets out, isn't it?'

Arlo could not place that name. Maeve Maguire. Fiona said nothing about Amelia Franklin. If they only had the details half right, maybe they weren't so sure. If nobody knew for certain, maybe they'd be reluctant to spread it around.

He could feel Leo pushing to deliver some smart-alecky comeback to that, but he refused to let him in.

'That's not,' he began. 'It's not ... That's not right.'

'Look, don't worry, you don't have to say anything about it. I didn't ask you here to catch you out. We're friends. Right?'

She was a customer and he was an employee. He couldn't even bring himself to use her first name.

He nodded.

'Good,' she said, still smiling. 'Which is why I thought you should see this.' She held out the phone. 'I check Ciara's phone every week. Usually it's a cursory check. But after Monday's meeting at the school, and then I heard some things, well, about your brother, at coffee this morning, I thought I should do a deeper dive. I found this in her deleted images. I'm not sure when it was sent exactly but it was saved on ...'

He was no longer listening. So much of his attention was trained on the image on the screen that he was barely in the room any more.

'Arlo?'

Fiona's voice was muffled and at a distance. The only thing he heard was the throbbing in his ears.

'Arlo? Arlo?'

He looked up from the screen to where Fiona's mouth and nose were suddenly too large for her head. They were starting to pulsate.

'That is Woody, right?'

The more he looked at them, the more her features no longer seemed to belong to her face. They were coming apart, like the Picasso poster that hung in Ella's bedroom.

'I thought so,' she said, nodding, as he realised he was doing the same. 'I couldn't quite remember what he looked like but the boy in the photo just looked so like your dad and like you.' Fiona laughed. 'His face, I mean. I couldn't speak to the rest.'

'What are you ...? What will you do with this?'

'Oh,' said Fiona, as if it hadn't occurred to her that she might do more with this naked photograph of his little brother than show it to Arlo. 'Well, I'll be talking to Ciara again. She insists it was unsolicited' – Fiona rolled her eyes – 'but I find it hard to believe she didn't send anything in response. She has a bit of a crush on your brother, you know. I think a lot of the girls do. I haven't shown it to her father yet, though I really should. It's just that with him being in the shop all day and trading as much in gossip as meat, I might as well take out an advert in the *Southern Gazette*. The whole town would know by lunchtime tomorrow. I don't really mind people knowing – you know me, I'm an open book – but for you and your family ...' She made a pained expression. 'You've already been through so much. And then, of course, Butcher has such a temper, he'd be up making a show of himself at your door or screaming at your poor mother in the bank. And I wouldn't want that. It's always the mothers who get the blame.'

'So don't tell him.' Arlo's voice squeaked, making it sound more like a question than an order.

Fiona scrunched the lower half of her face in more pained confusion. 'Oh, but I have to. He is her father.' She took the phone back and put it on the table. 'I'd have thought Woody would be more careful, after what happened with Maeve Maguire, and all the attention and drama that brought.' She took a step closer and placed a hand on Arlo's arm. 'I'm sure he's not a *bad* kid, no matter what people say. And I hardly see how this is your mother's fault, or even your father's.'

Arlo's head was spinning. He knew the room wasn't swaying, but he couldn't seem to get that through to his inner ear, or wherever it was that controlled his balance. He had been breaking his back trying to turn around the Whiteheads' reputation. He was exhausted from it. His face ached with the constant smiling. It always felt like one step forward, two steps back, but he was still trying. If this got out, that Woody was sending naked photos to multiple girls, they'd be driven out of town with pitchforks.

'Please don't tell him. Please.'

Arlo moved his hands so he was holding her right one in the space between them. There was a flash of surprise, but she didn't pull back.

What was wrong with Woody that he would do this? The parting line of his father's letter swam in his head. *Look after your mother and your brother.* He'd said the same thing the day he was taken away.

He squeezed her hand and implored her: 'Please don't. Please. Just don't say anything, Mrs Murphy – Fiona, Fiona, sorry, Fiona. Don't tell your husband. I'll do anything.'

'My ex-husband.'

'Your ex-husband.' Arlo was nodding too quickly, the dizziness getting worse. This must be what it felt like to float in space, and suddenly have your helmet disappear. 'Don't tell your ex-husband. Please, Fiona. Please.'

'Oh, Arlo, sweetheart. Hush now. It's okay.'

'I'll do whatever you want up here for free for a whole year. I'll clear out your back garden. And I'll talk to Woody. I'll make sure it never happens again, not with Ciara or anyone. But please don't tell anyone. It … It would kill my mom.'

Fiona's brows nudged ever so slightly closer. He was finding it difficult to look her in the eye; everything on her face seemed too big, almost grotesque, and the more he looked at it, the more stressed he felt.

'I am a sucker for a man who loves his mother,' she said. 'Butcher hated his mother – she is an absolute weapon, but still – that should have been enough to send me flying for the hills.'

'Please,' he said again. 'Please don't say anything.'

'Well ...' Fiona stared into the middle distance over his shoulder, her left hand coming up to join the right so they were clasped around Arlo's. Only where his grasp had been beseeching, hers was gentle. 'I suppose we are friends.'

'Yes,' he replied quickly, his heart pounding. 'Yes, we are.'

'And I wouldn't want you to start getting a hard time in Cooney. I do like you ...'

'And I like you.' He spoke quickly, barely registering that she had taken a step closer and was now moving her fingers ever so slightly against his.

'Do you?' She was in his face. Her nose about three inches from his mouth. She tilted her head up slowly, and it was only at that point that the strangeness of their set-up – standing so close together, holding hands – hit him. She wasn't going to ... Surely she wouldn't—

And then her lips were on his. They pushed his apart and something hard jabbed to get in. It shook him from his daze. Was that Mrs Murphy's *tongue*?

'I'm sorry, no,' he said quickly, as he put his hands on her shoulders and stepped back. 'I have a girlfriend. I'm sorry I said I didn't, but I do.'

A flash in her eyes, an emotion he couldn't quite identify.

'You – you're an attractive woman, Mrs Murphy, Fiona, and maybe if I was older, and didn't have a girlfriend ...'

There was that look again.

For a moment, nobody spoke.

'I was only joking, Arlo,' she said, suddenly breezy, as she returned to her default expression of being in on a private joke. 'You're the one taking it seriously.'

'Right, okay, sorry.'

He was confused, embarrassed, and not sure how the kiss could have been a joke, but fully trusting he was the one who'd misread the situation.

'Sorry,' he said again.

'I suppose you should go see your girlfriend, so.'

'Yes,' he said gratefully. 'Please don't tell anyone.'

'About what?' she asked. 'About Woody, or about our little frisson?'

Arlo had meant about his girlfriend but faced with this choice he wanted to say both. He didn't know what a frisson was, but he was pretty sure whatever had passed between them wasn't it. 'About Woody,' he said, picking a priority.

'I won't.'

He exhaled heavily. 'Thank you, Fiona. Thank you so much.' He picked up his toolbox and felt for the keys in his pocket. 'And I'm sorry for the misunderstanding, if I gave you the impression that I liked you – not that I don't like you, I do like you, but I mean like *that* ...'

Her lips tightened. 'It's fine, Arlo,' she said coolly. 'You really need to stop making such a big deal out of it.'

Ella Belle 9.30 p.m.

Hey. You still planning to call over tonight? My granny might be meditating in the back garden so try not to scare her. X

Ella Belle 11.02 p.m.

It's 11 now so I'm gonna take it you're not calling. I hope you're not working too hard. Good luck tomorrow. Give me a call on the drive to the prison if you want. X

26
· · · · · ·

I'**m going** out to see the wife,' announced Sergeant Whelan.

'Do you want me to come?' said Joey, hands on his belt once again. 'Or I could go instead?' He pictured himself motoring out to Cooney, making a key discovery and speeding back out to the station with the siren blaring.

Whelan shook his head. 'You've got a second round of interviews to type up. I'm just going to check in. She doesn't appear to have many friends in town. I don't know if anyone is keeping an eye on her.' He pushed himself up, laboriously, and pulled on his jacket. 'The poor woman. Your husband goes to work one day and never comes home. I doubt she thought much harm could come to him. It's got to be one of the safest places to work, doesn't it? A primary school. My eldest is studying to be a teacher and when I think about how he wanted to enter the guards, I'm constantly relieved. Schools, I used to think; nothing all that bad can happen at a school.'

'But his drowning may not have anything to do with the school.'

'Which is another reason I'm going to speak to the wife,' said Whelan, heading for the exit. 'Maybe something has occurred to her – someone with a grudge, or even a reason for him to have been out there. For now, his workplace is just the place he was supposed to be at the very moment that he lost his life.'

'So you don't think there's a connection?'

'That's for us to find out,' replied his boss, one foot out the door. 'I'm hoping we will know, one way or another, today.'

....

Beverley Franklin, parent

I spoke to him the day before. He was helping with the musical – most of the staff were. It was just about that, work stuff. I didn't get the impression he was worried about anything. There was no sense that something bad was about to happen. Is it possible he was having problems at home? Men aren't always the best at addressing their personal issues.

Orla Smith, parent

I'm not as, shall we say, involved as some of the other parents. So I can't exactly say I knew him. Most of my Glass Lake interactions are with my own children's teachers. He seemed nice, though. Are you treating the fall as suspicious? I can't imagine anyone having it in for him.

Ms Cunningham, teacher

It's not the norm to give out progress reports, no. I heard Mr Cafferty was doing it and I told him it wasn't a good idea. You agree to one, and next thing you know you're doing twenty. He said he didn't mind. He was really trying with the parents. Because he was new, I suppose, and because of the discipline issues. I share a classroom wall with him, and the truth is they'd been going on a while. He was doing his best, but the students just don't want to listen.

SIX DAYS EARLIER

Most of the Glass Lake teachers had a 'yard coat', a heavy-duty jacket worn only when it was their turn to do break-time supervision. The rest of the time, the bulky garments lived in their classrooms. There was no reason yard coats had to be ugly – there were jackets that were both warm and stylish – and Frank Cafferty refused to give in to this trend. His yard coat was a cream trench with tartan lining that Jess had bought him for their second wedding anniversary. He thought of it as his geezer coat.

When the bell went for lunch on Friday afternoon, the sixth-class students leapt from their desks, grabbed their school gaberdines and lined up by the door; it was the one time of day they did what they were supposed to without Frank having to ask, or more often beg. He removed his own coat from where it hung behind his desk. He was on yard duty today.

'Okay, okay, nice and quietly, please,' he called, as the students hopped from one foot to the other, waiting to be set free. Things would be better after lunch, he told himself; they'd settle down once they'd burnt off some energy. 'James,' he said to the child at the top of the line, 'you're going to lead everyone out, all right?'

The tall boy grew taller as he absorbed the temporary responsibility.

A wave of laughter rose behind him and Frank turned, embarrassed to find himself willing it to be aimed at another student, rather than him.

Before he could ask what was so amusing – something he always tried to do in an equally amused voice that suggested he was already in on the joke, so they couldn't turn it on him – Ethan Morton was raising a hand.

'Teacher, what's a ped-oh?'

The sniggering students, mainly boys, laughed louder.

'It's not a ped-oh, you dope,' said one of them. 'It's a pee-do.'

Ethan didn't look any more enlightened. 'What's a pedo?'

'That's not a suitable discussion for right now,' said Frank, the words catching in his throat. 'Right now, we're going out to the yard.'

'Is it a bad word?' asked another student.

'A pedo is someone who fancies children, isn't it, Teacher?'

At the start of the year, he would have engaged them in conversation. But he had learned that the students weren't always asking innocent questions. Often, they were messing with him. He searched the line for the usual suspects, but none of them were laughing. Even Woody was expressionless.

'It's short for paedophile,' said Amelia Franklin. 'That's in the dictionary. It's the same as pedo.'

'I don't want to hear the word again, please,' said Frank. The one time of day he felt any semblance of control over the class and it was slipping through his fingers. 'If you want to know the definition, ask your parents, or check your dictionaries. But I don't want the word used again in this classroom.'

Frank refused to let his mind wander. The students were just testing him, as they always did. The prank calls had subsided – that had been a coincidence too. He made a mental note to phone the parents of the boys who had asked. It was generally best if such things were explained at home. He glanced down the line to Woody, but the boy was messing with the zip on his coat.

'But, Teacher, you're the one using the word.'

He ignored this nonsensical statement and went to open the door. They were forever last out at break-times, often for reasons like this. The more effort Frank made, the worse they seemed to get.

'Yeah, Teacher,' said someone else. 'If you don't like the word, then why is it written on the back of your coat?'

....

Ella Belle 12.13 p.m.
WhatsApp says you haven't read any of these?? U ok? Don't be nervous about today! He's your dad and you've got the moral high ground! I. Love. You. X

....

Lorna Farrell was just contorting herself into the Half Moon Pose, when Fiona came jogging into the studio. She bowed her apologies to Paul, the hot yoga instructor, and Paul smiled as he bowed in return.

'You're late,' whispered Lorna, who was never late for anything. Today, as with most days, she had helped to lay out the yoga mats. She joined her hands together above her head and stretched to the left.

Fiona took the free mat beside her and began to warm up.

'Thought I'd give you a few minutes before I came in and stole Hot Paul's attention.'

Lorna ignored this comment. He was called Hot Paul because he instructed his class in a room heated to above 40 degrees, and because he was attractive. But she had Bill. Who was a *councillor*. And nothing was hotter than power. When Lorna's gaze followed Paul around the room, it was only in search of praise.

'You never turned up last night,' she whispered, as the class stretched out their arms and lowered themselves onto their hunkers. 'I saved you a mat and everything.'

'I told you I mightn't make it.'

'Yes, I know. But you never said for sure, or why. Had you a date?'

'Of sorts.'

Paul passed them now. 'Good, Lorna. Very good.'

She beamed.

He straightened Fiona's arms slightly and moved on.

'Did it go well?' she asked, feeling more generous now. 'Who was it with?'

Fiona tipped her nose as she brought her arms out straight in front of her.

Lorna glanced at her friend, causing her own Awkward Pose to sway. 'Since when are you shy about that stuff? Usually you're singing it from the rooftops.' She gasped, coming down from her tippytoes with a thud. 'Was it *Butcher*?'

Fiona made a face.

'The banker from London?'

'That's long over.'

'Maybe it didn't go well, and that's why you don't want to tell me,' said Lorna, as they crossed all their limbs down into the Eagle Pose.

'Of course it went well,' shot back Fiona. 'I'm just saying it wasn't the banker.'

Lorna made an 'Mm-hmm' sound as she struggled to hold the final step of the pose. It was like vertical twister.

And then, because she could not stand to have her allure questioned, Fiona added: 'If you must know, I've traded him in for a much younger model.'

....

Ella Belle 12.48 p.m.
Are you pissed off with me? Is it about yesterday morning? I'm sorry if I didn't come across as supportive of your decision. I think it's great you're visiting your dad. I think you're great. Please write back.

....

A girl in the front row raised her hand, giving Nuala Patterson a moment's hope that this wouldn't be a drawn-out, painful process.

But alas, the girl had not put her hand up to confess.

'Maybe that word was already there when Teacher bought the coat, but he didn't notice because the shop didn't have one of those mirrors where you can see your back?'

'Thank you, Shona, but Mr Cafferty is perfectly capable of looking in mirrors.'

This drew giggles from the rest of the class and Nuala chanced a glance at Frank Cafferty, who was sitting quietly at his desk, arms wrapped tightly around himself.

Despite her foreboding presence at the top of the room, there was a giddy energy in the class. The children snuck furtive glances at each other and grinned. Ciara Murphy turned her head to the side and nodded vigorously at Ethan Morton. It was, she recognised, an impression of Mr Cafferty.

These were not students who respected their teacher. How had she not noticed? She was slipping this year, and Glass Lake standards were going down with her. *Pedo*. It was such a nasty word, and not one she often heard students use, even in hushed voices. This story was already as good as going around the parent WhatsApp groups and there would be those who, for no reason but their own enjoyment, would speculate on whether there was something to the accusation. It was the sort of rumour that could kill a career. She felt a deep swell of sympathy for the man, and a hard flash of anger at the students sitting before her.

'That's enough,' she shouted, relieving Ethan Morton of his effort to stem the giggles. Ethan, Ciara and every other student looked at her. 'That is absolutely enough. In Glass Lake, we show respect to our teachers and to each other. We do not laugh at anyone. Do you understand?'

The room was silent.

'I have all day,' she said, by which she meant she had forty minutes before the final bell went and she was legally required to send them home. 'And I can wait as long as you can. We'll stay here all night if we have to.'

The suggestion was so ludicrous, she was surprised nobody laughed.

Her eyes roamed the room, looking for a guilty face. A small movement caught her attention. Woody Whitehead was shaking his head at Maeve Maguire, who was seated beside him.

'Maeve?' she said, as the girl gave a start. 'Have you anything to tell me?'

'No, Principal Patterson.'

Another flicker of action, and her gaze moved to the desk right in front of her.

'Amelia? How about you?'

'No, Principal Patterson,' said the pretty girl, as her neighbour smiled.

'What's so funny now, Ciara?'

The child stopped giggling and looked straight ahead.

Nuala paced in front of the whiteboard as the students sat staring at their desks or out the window or into space. In her twenty-two years at the helm, Nuala had dealt with countless incidents of bullying and many horrible words scrawled across bags and coats and even shoes, but none of those items had ever belonged to a teacher. Had Mr Cafferty been too nice? Too soft?

Time passed and nobody spoke. So settled in the silence were the children that when Ethan Morton knocked a pen on to the ground, several of them jumped.

Nuala decided to go for broke. 'As I'm sure you know, we have CCTV cameras in this classroom.' She pointed to the ceiling. The students turned to look at the high-tech sprinkler that hung a foot from the fire alarm. 'And if I do not get a confession in the next five minutes, we will be checking that, and I can guarantee you the punishment will be much more severe.'

Again, they exchanged glances. There was less smirking this time. Several of them looked worried. Perhaps this was a story worth rolling out more generally, like the threat of Santa's omnipresent elves.

The students shifted in their seats and murmurs of a disagreement rose from Woody and Maeve.

'Maeve?' said Nuala. 'Something to say?'

The girl's voice quivered. But it was Woody who finally spoke.

'Say that again, Woody? I didn't hear you.'

....

> Ella Belle 1.55 p.m.
> I know you're probably in there now, but I'd really like to talk to you. Maybe it's a problem with your phone. If not, can you ring me back when you get a chance? XXX

....

Lorna was trying to figure out what sort of coffee would feel like a treat but not completely undo all the good work done during hot yoga. She burnt off an estimated 500 calories during a session and did six sessions a week. She needed to lose 42,000 calories in order to drop a dress size before December. She tried to hold these numbers in her head while she counted backwards to when she first bought a 'bundle' of Hot Paul classes.

'I only drink Americanos,' said Fiona, who'd already ordered hers. 'If I don't know what the other stuff tastes like, then I can't lust after it.'

Lorna found it impossible to do maths and maintain a conversation, so she ordered the same. She would console herself with a generous dollop of full-fat milk.

'Is that the woman Beverley used to work with?' she half-whispered, as they collected their beverages from the end of the counter.

Fiona followed her gaze to the window seat. 'It is. Tamara Watson. You know I found her a house? Nice woman. Let's go and say hello.'

Lorna wanted to talk to Fiona alone, to grill her about this new mystery man. She was being uncharacteristically coy. But before she could object, they were heading towards the small circular table where the woman was reading a magazine and enjoying one of the Strand's legendary flapjacks. This cheered Lorna up slightly. Perhaps she'd offer them a piece.

'Tamara? Hi.'

She looked up from her magazine. 'Fiona! How are you? I've been meaning to call you.'

'Tamara Watson, this is Lorna Farrell. Lorna, this is Tamara.'

'We met briefly at the parents' night, hi. I love your dress,' said Lorna, who liked to start every new acquaintance with a compliment.

'Thank you,' replied Tamara, sitting up straight and closing over the magazine. She had an enviable figure. The breasts of a twenty-year-old.

If Lorna got to know her better, she'd ask who did her work.

'Fiona, I wanted to thank you for recommending that handyman. Arlo? I find flat-pack furniture more painful than childbirth, but he put my bookcases together in record time yesterday evening. He even managed to get a few extra shelves up. He's amazing.'

Lorna did not agree with hiring Arlo Whitehead. She was with Beverley on this entirely and would never let the lad set foot in her house. Charlie Whitehead was the reason the Roches had moved away, which was the reason Cooney GAA had been relegated at the quarter finals. As far as any right-minded resident was concerned, hiring a Whitehead was a betrayal of the town.

'I wanted him to do my son's desk too, but he'd another job to get to – at nine on a Thursday night,' Tamara continued. 'He must be in demand.'

Bill did, very occasionally, get Arlo to do jobs in the garden, but that was entirely different; he never came *inside*.

'That was me, I'm afraid,' said Fiona. 'I took him away from you.'

'Last night?'

Fiona nodded, dipping her chin slightly as she brought her coffee cup up.

'Well, it's fine,' said Tamara. 'He was busy today too, but he's coming back to finish the job next week.'

It took Lorna a moment, but eventually she caught up.

'Wait. Last night?' She turned to Fiona. 'Last night when you should have been at yoga? I thought you said you didn't make it because—' Her friend's eyes were trained on the white lid of her disposable cup. 'Oh my God. Oh. My. God! Is *Arlo Whitehead* the younger man?'

Fiona shook her head as she pulled her fingers across her mouth. 'My lips are sealed.'

....

Ella Belle 2.45 p.m.
Okay, I'm kind of worried now. I'm going to try you on email

28
· · · · · ·

Arlo had been sitting outside the prison for forty minutes. His visitor timeslot was for 3 p.m. If he didn't get out of the van soon, he was going to miss it. He looked in the rear-view mirror and told himself to take three slow breaths. Things must have been bad because even Leo was trying to help.

Inhale ... Exhale ... Inhale ... Exhale ...

Where did you learn that?

Just shut up and breathe.

This vat of guilt sat on the bed of his stomach and every time he tried to identify its origin – neglect of Woody? Betrayal of Ella? Betrayal of his father? – another possibility popped into his head.

His phone beeped.

Four missed calls, eight new messages, and now, an email notification.

He unlocked his phone, careful not to click into WhatsApp. Until he figured out how to explain himself, he couldn't let Ella know he had read them.

Is this the first email I've sent you since school? Weird. I think there's something up with your phone. Or at least I'm hoping that's the problem. I can't get through to you.

Is everything okay? Have you seen your dad yet?

Even if you're annoyed at me over something, will you just get in touch to say you're okay? It's stupid I know, but I'm worried.

So, get in touch – by phone or email or like messenger owl. Whatever!

El x

The vat threatened to overflow.

Arlo needed to explain to Ella, in person, what had happened with Fiona Murphy. He was supposed to call to her last night, but for some reason he couldn't do it. He'd gone straight home and had a long shower. *She* kissed *him*. He hadn't started anything; he hadn't done anything wrong. He didn't even like her! He had taken her hand first, but that was different, he hadn't done it in a ... in a *sexual* way. Maybe Fiona thought he had? He'd been trying to save Woody. But the way she teased him, the way she smiled ... Had it been his fault?

He couldn't bring himself to respond to Ella, to make casual chitchat, until he'd explained what had happened. He needed to be honest with her; it didn't feel good otherwise. He would go straight from the prison to her house. She'd understand why he hadn't replied then, and hopefully she'd admire him for not being a fraud.

It was five to three now. He had to get out of the van.

Out on the tarmac, he checked the pits of his shirt for sweat stains and fixed the tie that he'd last worn to Mike Roche's funeral. He followed the signs out of the car park, turning left to the visitors' entrance of the modern, white building. He pushed his way through the glass doors into a waiting area and presented himself at the reception desk. The guard took his details, checked his driver's licence, and gave him a sheet of paper. He asked him to empty his pockets and pointed him towards a locker where he could leave his phone and keys. He made a joke about young lads not liking to be parted from their phones, but Arlo had never been happier to see the thing go. He placed his boots into a plastic tray and walked quickly through the full-body scanner. He was given a once-over with a hand-held device, and then again with another. 'It's like the airport,' he said nervously.

One of them smiled. 'It's looking for drugs.'

Around the next corner was a big dog that sniffed at his trousers and boots. And even though he knew he wasn't carrying any drugs, had never carried any drugs, he could feel the sweat forming on his brow.

A different guard led him down a tiled corridor, past cameras and thick doors. It had the same smell as his secondary school, that peculiar mix of must and chemical cleaners. The guard stopped at a small desk and pushed open a heavy cream door.

'Here we are now, the family room.'

Whatever Arlo had expected, it wasn't this.

The room was bright and airy, with a large colourful mural painted on to three of the walls. There were boxes filled with toys and a play kitchen, which was missing one of its hobs but otherwise in good nick. The fourth wall was taken over by a fortified Perspex hut, where two guards sat, laughing at something. That bit was more what he'd had in mind.

One other group was already waiting: a woman and her two young sons. They sat on low green chairs at a matching children's table.

The guard nodded him towards a similar set-up, only red, then waved to the two men in the little hut and left. The chair was so low that Arlo's knees almost came up to his face. When nobody was looking, he brought his head down and sniffed both armpits then straightened his tie again. He'd had the whole morning to think about it, and he hadn't a clue what he was going to say.

The youngest son in the other group took a tentative step towards the kitchen, but his mom shook her head. His elder brother went and brought him back, catching Arlo's eye and nodding solemnly. He nodded back. They were both just sons, waiting on their fathers.

Then the door opened, and two more prison guards appeared, accompanied by his dad.

'That's him,' said Charlie Whitehead to one of the men. 'That's my son.'

He said it with such pride, such admiration, that Arlo instantly pinked, but he also grinned.

Before he could ask if touching was allowed, his dad was across the room, engulfing him in a bear hug. 'Oh, I have missed you,' he said in his big, deep, reassuring voice, the words slightly muffled against Arlo's ear. 'I have missed you something awful.' He pulled back, looked at his son. Arlo did his best to arrange his awkward face, but Charlie was already reaching for him again. This time the hug was tighter, longer. Arlo felt a tingle in his throat. He was relieved when his father let go. A second longer and he'd have erupted into tears.

'Come on,' said Charlie, pulling him back down on to the bright red plastic chairs. 'I asked for the family room. You're probably a bit old for all of this but it's the nicest room, and you'll always be my little boy. And' – Charlie brought his head forward to rest on his right knee – 'these seats come with built-in chin rests; handy, eh?'

Arlo laughed. It was pathetic how comforting his father's presence was, even though he was visiting him in a medium-security facility where he had power over absolutely nothing.

All possible conversation topics vanished from his head. 'How ... how are you?'

'I'm a lot better for seeing you. Thanks for coming. I know it can't be easy to see your dad in a place like this.'

Arlo shook his head. 'Nah,' he said, clumsily, awkwardly. He didn't want his dad thanking him. 'I'm sorry I didn't come sooner. I know I should have. I meant to. I just ...'

The door opened again, and another prisoner was brought in. This man had none of the bonhomie or presence of his dad. He walked over to what was presumably his wife and children. He shook the boys' hands, even though the eldest couldn't have been more than eight.

'So, tell me all the news,' said Charlie, rubbing his hands together. 'How are you? How's the business going? Your mom said you were working all hours. Although that was a while ago now. Is it still going well? Tell me everything. I want to hear it all.'

He noticed now that his father's hair was parted to one side, slicked down with gel or wax. This display of effort increased the pressure.

Arlo told him about work, doing his best to match his dad's energy as he spoke. He omitted all tales of the less courteous clients and the complaints about Charlie's previous supposedly shoddy work, instead discussing the details of certain jobs and asking for advice on others.

'The van's been acting up,' he said. 'Just the last few days. It goes to give out just before I bring it to a stop.'

'Could be the brake pads. Have you had them looked at recently? I don't think I had them changed in a while. Yeah, could be that.'

'Okay, I'll have it looked at. Thanks.'

'Bring it to Dodger's place, tell him you're my son.'

Arlo nodded. Dodger had called to their house three weeks after his dad was sent away and said that if they didn't pay the €400 Charlie owed him, he'd take the wheels off the van himself. 'I'll do that. Thanks.'

'He'll see you right.'

Charlie smiled. So Arlo did too.

'How's Woody?'

'Good,' he said automatically. 'He's fully transitioned into moody teenager and spends most of his time playing computer games in his room, but he's in the musical this year, so he's not a total hermit.'

'Woody's in the musical? Good boy, Woody. That's great. And is he still hanging out with his friends? Ethan and James?'

'I don't think they're in the house as much,' Arlo said, struggling to recall when he'd last seen his brother hanging around with either boy, or anyone else. 'There was the incident in the school with the photos, but I think that's going to blow over. Mom's probably told you all that already.'

Charlie shook his head. 'I haven't spoken to your mom in a while.'

'Oh.' His face started to heat up. 'It's nothing to worry about. He was sending photos to another girl in his class – and she was sending them to him – but it's all fine.'

'You're looking after it?'

'Yeah,' said Arlo, still feeling hot. 'I'm sorting it.'

Charlie nodded. 'Good. How is your mom? Is she seeing her friends?'

'I think she sees some people from work ...' Arlo wasn't going to tell his dad that the only person his mother ever mentioned was her boss, George. If he were the one in jail and someone told him that about Ella and Leo, he would drive himself crazy thinking about it.

'And how about you?'

'Oh, I'm good, great, grand.'

'Have you heard from Leo?'

'I ... no. I haven't heard from him. I don't think I will.'

'That's understandable.'

'Yeah,' said Arlo breathlessly.

'And are you hanging out with anyone else?'

'Why are you so concerned about who we're seeing?'

Charlie shrugged. 'I guess I just want to know youse have support. So, are you? Anyone else from school? A *girlfriend*?'

He looked at his grinning dad in shock. How could he tell? Arlo felt a fresh wave of guilt that he should be embarking on the great love affair of his life while his dad sat in jail, married to a woman who could barely find the will to say something good about him, never mind take his calls.

'Nobody serious,' he said eventually.

'Playing the field? That's my boy. It's the only way to have it when you're young.'

'Yeah.' Another breathless scoff.

'Ten minutes, folks,' called one of the guards, sticking his head out from the hatch.

Arlo wanted to tell his dad all about Ella and her perfect face and how smart she was and how funny. He wanted to get his advice on

257

Fiona Murphy. His father would put it in perspective. He'd tell Arlo he had nothing to feel guilty about, and Arlo would believe him. Even on the worst night of their lives, when Arlo could do nothing but sob, he'd had a plan.

'I'm really sorry you're in here,' he said, suddenly, keeping his gaze on his father's hands, which had always been so solid and manly. His own fingers were long and thin and devoid of hair.

'It's not your fault, Arlo,' replied his dad calmly.

'Except that it is. We both know that it is.'

29

Beverley Franklin had to read the message twice. In her quest to be first with news, Lorna had a habit of getting things arseways. But this, bizarrely, made a lot of sense.

'What is it?' said her mother, who was hunkered down on the kitchen floor, watching the goldfish chase each other. Ella was sitting on the opposite side of the kitchen island to Beverley, a chicken sandwich in front of her. Her daughter had been glued to her phone since dinner the night before. She'd skipped her morning lecture, again, supposedly to spend time with her grandmother, but she'd barely looked up from the screen. They were having lunch late because it had taken this long to coax Ella around to eating. Although she'd yet to have a bite.

'A friend, she's done something ridiculous,' said Beverley, before waving a hand. 'It doesn't matter. You don't know her.'

'You can't say "ridiculous" and then not tell us. You've got our attention now, hasn't she, Ella?'

'Mm.'

Frances puckered her lips and blew a kiss to the fish, before standing and returning to the island.

Beverley hadn't meant to put a mini aquarium in the middle of her kitchen, *obviously*. She'd written 'fishbone', indicating the zigzag pattern she wanted for the marble, but the moronic builder had read 'fishbowl'. She'd have made him rip the thing out, only Malachy had wanted her to hire an interior designer from day one, so she had to pretend two stinky, slimy creatures in the middle of her pristine kitchen was exactly what she'd been dreaming of all along.

'Well, you have my attention anyway,' said Frances, retaking her seat. 'Come on, tell us.'

She was trying to make more of an effort with her mother, now that she knew the trip was finite – she was leaving Monday morning – and dinner last night – just her, her mother and the girls – hadn't been completely awful.

'Fiona Murphy,' she said eventually. 'She was at the Strand café yesterday, lots of cheap charm bracelets and more mismatched gold around her neck. "Friend" isn't actually the right term. She's a Laker, and a particularly silly one.'

'Yes, the woman who ran after us when we were leaving to ask if her daughter could have a solo in the musical. She has quite an aggressive aura, I have to say. Green and tan. You don't often see that.'

'That's her.' Fiona was still trying to leverage whatever sordid details she knew about Beverley's pivot away from Southern Pharmaceuticals, but Ciara Murphy hadn't a note in her head and Beverley would not allow the musical to suffer. 'She's quite an aggressive person generally. She used to be married to one of the butchers in town. He's the same. But that ended a couple of years ago. She's had a few relationships, if you could call them that. Anyway, now it seems she's got a new man. Well, a new boy would be more accurate. She's making a fool of herself.'

'Nothing wrong with a younger lover,' said Frances, a glint in her eye that Beverley chose to ignore.

'It's not just his age,' she said, rereading the message for a third time. 'He's not the sort of person you want in your life full stop. His dad was the one who killed that boy out on Reilly's Pass in February, and his brother was the one soliciting photographs from Amelia.'

Well, there you go. Miracles were possible. Ella had finally looked up from her phone.

'Arlo Whitehead,' Beverley extrapolated for the benefit of her mother. 'You know, the boy you tantric-ed into opening the storage closet at Glass Lake. He does a lot of work for Fiona, out at her house. It seems that's not all he does for her.'

'No,' said Ella softly.

'Of course,' said Beverley. 'He was in your class. Sorry, darling, this probably isn't appropriate conversation. I don't think it's a relationship or anything. But yes, they seem to have had some sort of *liaison* last night. Fiona could never keep something like that to herself, much as we might like her to. But knowing her, it will all be over before …'

Ella climbed down from her stool and left the room.

'…we know it.' Beverley sighed. 'Don't say goodbye or anything, darling.'

'Beverley,' said Frances.

'What? I've given up understanding that girl's moods.'

'Arlo Whitehead?'

'Yes.' Beverley paused. 'Why? Do you know something more about him?'

'Do you not?'

Beverley frowned. 'Is this a cosmic thing? Had he a pink aura or something?'

'Beverley.'

'*What?*'

'Arlo Whitehead is the love of your daughter's life. He's been sneaking in and out of your house for months.'

'*Excuse me, what?*' said Beverley, in a voice so high-pitched she sounded like Lorna Farrell. 'No.'

'Yes.'

'There's no way. No way. You're getting mixed up.'

'Beverley.' Her mother laid a hand on hers. 'I've been here less than two days and I've seen him. How have you not?'

·························

'It's not that bad in here. The food is pretty good, and my cellmate used to be a roadie for the Stones. Or at least that's what he says – he's not the kind of man you challenge. Either way, he's got good stories.' Charlie flashed him the grin that had once made him so popular with the women of Cooney. 'You really don't need to feel bad for me, Arlo.'

They might be in the family room, but he was not a child. Prison was always bad. That was the whole point of it. 'I see it happening in slow motion,' he said. 'I've heard people say that, in films and stuff, but I never really believed it, that you could actually see a memory that clearly, but I do. Now it happens when I'm drifting off to sleep, or when I'm driving and my mind is empty. It jumps back in. And I hear Leo's voice in my head. Sometimes I think I'm going crazy.'

'I know,' said Charlie, legs pulled back into him on the low plastic chair. 'I see it too.'

Arlo shook his head. 'No, but I see the road. The rain splattering on the tarmac, bouncing off the bonnet, the wipers on Mom's Volvo going ninety and getting nowhere. The music is playing and the chorus has just cut in – I can *hear* it, Dad, and the "Welcome to Cooney" sign is up ahead, and I see all this in one micro-second, and then in the next we're gone, the car is swerving off the road and there's nothing I can do. I know this terrible thing is happening, but I can't stop it. I can't get a firm grasp on the steering wheel. It's too late. It's all dark grass and sky. Even when I'm lying in bed at night, I feel my body turning.'

His dad was nodding. He'd been nodding the whole time, and Arlo felt himself getting annoyed.

'I know,' said Charlie. 'It happens to me too, especially when I'm falling asleep. I hear the wheels skidding. I see Mike flying up against the side of the car. It's okay.'

'But it's not the same!'

'Why isn't it?'

He leaned in, even though the guards weren't remotely interested in their conversation. 'Because we didn't have the same view, Dad. You weren't even sitting in the front seat.'

'Arlo.'

The tingle in his throat and nose again. He swallowed it down. 'You were in the back. You weren't the one driving, so just for a second stop pretending you were and let me take some responsibility.'

'Arlo,' he repeated more softly. 'I was driving. We agreed that on the night. I was driving.' He dipped his head down to catch his son's eyes.

To Arlo's horror, tears started trickling down his cheeks. 'I shouldn't have got drunk.'

His dad laughed. 'None of us should.'

'It was my responsibility and I fucked up. I'm so sorry, Dad. I'm so sorry you're in here. It's my fault. It's all my fault. I should have told you we'd all been drinking, that Mike had snuck some in.' He rubbed at his face with the back of his hand. He couldn't bring himself to look around the room. 'I lied to you and I ruined your life and I'm so fucking sorry.'

When he managed to look up, his dad was shaking his head. Gently, kindly. He was looking at him with unabashed love and Arlo was jealous of his ability to express emotions and still be a man. Arlo was capable of neither.

The guards were making moves now and the other prisoner had said goodbye to his family.

He hoped he hadn't shaken the boys' hands again. He hoped he'd given them a hug.

'Arlo?'

'No, don't say something nice. I know you're going to say something nice.'

'Arlo?'

'No.'

'Arlo?'

He looked at his dad and he felt the guards moving and suddenly he was frightened. This was all about to be over. His dad was going to go and Arlo would be right back where he deserved, all alone, scrambling to rescue something from a mess entirely of his own making.

'I love you.'

'Dad,' he pleaded.

'I look at photos of you in here sometimes and I get a fright. I think, Jesus, am I having a heart attack? That's how strong the feeling is. It's like my heart physically lurches forward, trying to get closer to the image of you. I love you and I feel it so keenly that I'd happily die of it. I'd be fucking honoured, actually.'

Arlo laughed in spite of himself, snot threatening to escape now too. He bit the inside of his cheek and blew air up into his eyes.

'It doesn't matter who was driving, Arlo. It was still my fault. I was the adult and I was drunk. You were all underage.'

'You shouldn't have to cover—'

'Shhh!'

'Come on now, Charlie, time to finish up.'

'No bother, Steve. Just saying goodbye to the young lad. Did I tell you he was a musician?'

'Is that right?' said the guard, whose nose hovered in front of his face, just as Fiona's had done last night. 'What do you play, son?'

Arlo had to look away.

'The bass,' said Charlie. 'He's very good.'

He could barely play three consecutive cords when his dad went away and he'd probably gotten worse since.

'Very good,' echoed the guard, shifting his weight. 'Right, so.'

Charlie stood, and Arlo did the same.

His dad engulfed him in a final embrace. This time Arlo hugged him back. Charlie's voice was at his ear again, muffled and insistent. 'You look after Woody and your mother. Let me do the rest.'

....

Nuala Patterson hadn't spoken a word to Connie Whitehead for more than eight months and now she'd had to phone her twice in as many weeks. As soon as Nuala explained why she was calling, Connie was overcome with concern.

'Are you sure it was Woody? I don't think I've ever heard him utter that word. The teacher's jumper? No, his jacket. When did this happen? And you're sure it was him?'

They made an appointment for Connie to come and see her on Monday and then Nuala hung up. She was tired. She had spoken to Leo for the first time in weeks last night. He'd finally agreed to take her call, and he had been worse than she feared: bitter and angry and completely incapable of counting his blessings. Three times, he'd reminded her he was in a wheelchair, as if it excused everything else. If she was any sort of mother, she'd drive to Dublin and give Leo a good talking-to, remind him how other people's lives had ended up – or just ended. But she wasn't a good mother. She was a coward. And he knew that, which only made his anger towards her worse.

The last bell rang, and the students left the building. She powered off her laptop and gathered up several files to tackle over the weekend, though in her heart-of-hearts she knew she'd be returning on Monday with the same folders unopened.

She was just lacing up her runners when there was a knock on her door.

'Oh, Cian, hello.'

'Do you have a moment?' asked the doctor, who was carrying a couple of sheets of paper in one hand and his black box in the other.

'Of course, come in,' she said, hurriedly looping a knot and standing. 'Oh, shoot. I was meant to come and fix up with you, wasn't I? I completely forgot. I have your payment here.' She rustled through the loose pages on her desk until she found the envelope Mairead had labelled 'Dr O'Sullivan'. 'Thank you so much, again, for doing this. We're very appreciative. How was your second session? Fruitful?' She leaned forward and removed a couple of the pages that had spilled from her desk on to the chair on the far side. 'Do you want to sit?'

'I'm fine,' he said, placing the box on the seat instead.

'Did that work?' asked Nuala. 'Did they tell you all their secrets?'

'Yes.'

'Well, good.'

'That's why I'm here.'

She frowned.

'This afternoon I spoke to the class about the dangers of putting images online or sending them to someone else. Not explicitly about sexting but generally about privacy and how they might think they're sending a photo to one person, but they can never be sure of that. The focus is really on feeling comfortable and keeping themselves safe and happy.'

'Okay ...'

'I asked if they had ever shared material that they wouldn't like to get out into the wider world. Nobody put their hand up. That's pretty common among pre-pubescent and pubescent children, particularly in a mixed class.'

Nuala nodded. She had no idea where this was going, but she knew she wouldn't like it.

'So, I invited them to use the box. It worked well yesterday for any questions they had. I asked them to write down whatever they would like to tell me on this subject and to put it in the box. I'd marked the corners of the slips of paper, so I knew who they were coming from. I didn't get to look at the slips until the class was over. And now I'm thinking I should do a third session.'

'Oh, well, I'm not sure we have the funds, but I can check ... Why, though? What did they say?'

'Maeve wasn't the only girl who sent Woody a nude photograph.'

Nuala blew air out through her lips. She'd had enough of Woody Whitehead for one day. For one lifetime.

'Let me guess ... Ciara Murphy?'

He looked down at his sheets of paper. 'Yes.'

Nuala nodded. This was all she needed. 'Thanks for letting me know. I'll call her parents.'

'Any other guesses, or shall I just tell you?'

'How do you mean?'

'Several girls said they sent him naked photos of themselves.'

Nuala frowned. 'How many is several?'

The doctor looked at the piece of paper again, which she now saw was a list.

'Three? *Four?* I refuse to guess more than four ...'

'Seven.'

'*Seven?*'

'And three others received photos of him but didn't send any in return.'

'Ten students! He sent nudes to *ten female students*? Jesus Christ. That must be some sort of record. There can't be more than fifteen girls in the whole class.'

'Fourteen.'

'Fuck. Fuck! Sorry, Cian.'

The man shook his head. 'It is worrying behaviour.'

That was a lot of parents to phone. And as soon as she did, they'd be ramming on her door, be that at school or at home. Could she put that off to Monday morning? She could certainly do her best.

Ten, though. *Ten*. Was there something wrong with the boy? A chill ran through Nuala. When the Lakers found out about this, there would be war. There was no way Beverley Franklin would let it go now.

Woody Whitehead. Of all the students. Would she never be free of that family?

'Are you sure they were all from Woody?'

The doctor nodded. 'Every single one.'

ABERSTOWN GARDA STATION

J oey had finally finished typing up the entire day's statements and was reading back over them. He kept hoping the pathology office would call with their initial findings and, in the sergeant's absence, it would be up to him to handle it. But the phone hadn't rung since Whelan headed off to see the wife.

He finished one transcript and began reading over the next. Halfway down the page, he noticed something. He flicked back a few files and saw the same thing again. Different witnesses referring to different instances, but they were both making the same point. He allowed himself a dramatic gasp, then jumped to his feet. He hiked his trousers up so far that he gave himself a mild wedgy. Ignoring the pain, he lunged across the table for the phone.

'What is it?' barked Whelan, answering on the squad car's Bluetooth system after the first ring.

'Sorry to disturb you, sir, but I'm just after noticing something and I think it could be important.'

'Spit it out, Delaney. I'm about to go into the house.'

'A couple of our witnesses mentioned there being animosity between our man and another Glass Lake employee. Seems there was a bit of bad blood, though I'm not sure why.'

Down the line, Joey heard the muffled sound of wind and the low beep of the squad car being locked from the outside.

'Is that worth investigating?'

'How the bloody hell would I know?'

'Sir?'

'Call them in, Delaney!'

'So, I have permission to conduct supplementary questioning?'

'Yes, you have ... Jesus wept. Just get to the bottom of it and leave me alone!'

The line went dead but Joey felt only triumph. Finally, he had a lead.

••••••••••••••••••••••••••

Christine Maguire, parent
If you'd told me a few days ago that I'd be in here speaking to you about something terrible happening to someone from Glass Lake, I'd have put money on Woody Whitehead. Isn't that awful? He's only a child. But try telling that to the Lakers. I presume you heard what happened at the school on Monday? Absolute anarchy. You'd have a real whodunnit on your hands if Woody was the subject of your investigation, because the suspect list would be long, and the Lakers would be top of it.

Lorna Farrell, parent
It's a blessing he doesn't have children. I'm not saying being a parent always makes you a

better person, but let's be honest: it would
make his death more tragic. I saw him earlier
in the day, talking to Nuala Patterson down by
Cooney Pier. It looked like they were arguing,
which I thought was strange. I gave the horn a
little toot to say, 'hello', and I saw Nuala see
me, but she didn't so much as wave. That's the
only bit that wasn't suspicious. The woman has
always been doggedly rude.

Nuala Patterson, principal
We were discussing school business, all entirely
mundane. So mundane, in fact, that I can barely
remember a word of it. Lorna Farrell told you
that, didn't she? She still hasn't forgiven me
for what happened at Glass Lake on Monday.

31

THREE DAYS EARLIER

'**L**ights, *a stór*! Lights!' Frances cried from the passenger seat.
      Beverley Franklin brought the Range Rover to a sudden stop, causing her body to strain against the seatbelt and the burning sensation to return to her chest.

The traffic control had never flashed orange. It had gone from green to red with absolutely no warning. She could have sworn it.

Frances exhaled just as her suitcase rolled on to its side on the back seat and tumbled down on to the floor.

'Good thing I put my vagina in the boot,' she said cheerfully.

The students of her three-day tantric workshop had been so invigorated by Frances' teachings ('Invigorated' was her mother's word) that they'd clubbed together and bought her a large glass sculpture shaped like a vagina. Frances said it was abstract, but there was nothing abstract about the raw flesh tones or the wide, open slit. It was hand blown, which surprisingly was not more innuendo but an actual term for how the glass was moulded. Frances offered to leave it with her daughter as a thank-you for her hospitality – 'You could put it on the hall table, throw your keys into it' – but Beverley had packed it up this morning and left it by the front door with the rest of her mother's things.

'I must get Bill Farrell to check these traffic lights,' she muttered. If there was something wrong with the colour filter, it would need to be fixed. Cooney did not want another traffic accident.

The lights went green and she started the engine again. 'Isn't it amazing, how one family, or really one boy, can wreak so much havoc and cause so much destruction in one town?'

'Oh, now. You're not talking about Arlo Whitehead again, are you?'

'It's Monday. That means it's three days since Ella stepped foot out of her bedroom.'

'It's not quite that bad. She has used the toilet, and she came down to say goodbye to me this morning ...'

'She's miserable. And it's all that gigolo's fault. Fiona Murphy's the same age as his mother, for Christ's sake!'

'It's hard to stand by when your daughter's in pain, I know. And it's hard to offer help and have it rejected at every turn. But at least Ella knows she's hurting, and that is the first step to healing. Now you said you were going to leave it alone.'

Beverley had said no such thing. She had no choice but to leave Ella alone. Her daughter had locked herself away after Friday's accidental revelation about her cheating boyfriend.

Boyfriend! The word wailed in her head. How could Ella have a *boyfriend* and Beverley not know? They used to tell each other everything. She was hurt and bewildered by her daughter keeping the relationship secret, and maybe a little disappointed – a Whitehead! Of all people! – but she wasn't angry at her. That was reserved entirely for the gangly lothario.

'Lights, Beverley!' Frances screamed, as the car came to another sudden stop, the suitcase bouncing about in the back. 'Sweet heavens above!'

'I'm going around to his house after I drop you to the station,' she said, as her mother groaned.

'Beverley, no. He probably won't be there.'

'Well then, I'll talk to his mother. When we're done discussing Arlo, we'll move on to her other depraved son. So many daughters to exploit; so little time.' She brought her right hand to her chest. 'You don't have any Rennie on you, do you?'

'You know I only use home remedies, crumpet.'

'Well, have you any hocus-pocus potions for heartburn?'

'Afraid not.'

Beverley straightened her back. Righting her posture helped. 'I'll drop you at the station, swing by Regan's Chemist, and then it's on to the Whiteheads for a little *tête à tête*.'

'Ella won't thank you for it.'

Beverley lived in constant fear of losing her daughters, of one day waking up to find they no longer wanted to have anything to do with her. It wasn't just a fear, it was an expectation. This was why she'd wanted to have several children – to increase her chances of being loved. Malachy had dismissed the idea entirely. Franklins had two children, no more no less. He said large families were trashy, which meant Beverley was trashy, although she'd known that already.

'I can't get my head around her stubbornness sometimes,' she said, turning on to Station Road. 'Amelia is so much easier; she's a lot more like me.'

Frances laughed and Beverley, who felt exposed enough already, threw her a look.

'I'm sorry, *a stór*. I'm not laughing at you; it's just the idea that you're more like Amelia than Ella.'

'I am. Ella's so headstrong, it's impossible to tell her anything.'

'I agree,' said Frances, the smile audible. 'I haven't met a teenager as single-minded since you turned thirteen.'

The train station came into view. Her mother would take a commuter train into the city, and then on to Dublin. Beverley had bought her a first-class ticket, only for her mother to remind her she had the travel pass.

'I was listening to an item on the radio the other day,' said Frances. 'They had this doctor on and she was very interesting.'

'A real doctor?'

'Yes.'

'A medical one?'

'Yes, of course a medical one. I'm not about to give you a report on tribal cures from the depths of the Amazon rain forest.'

Beverley shrugged as she turned her head from side to side, looking for a parking space. 'I never know with you.'

'Anyway, she was talking about eating disorders in older people, particularly women. You won't fit in there.'

'Yes, I know.'

'This doctor was saying how there's been a huge increase in diagnoses among over thirty-fives in the past decade. While teenage rates are pretty constant, older demographics have seen a surge. They can't be sure if these women are developing eating disorders for the first time, or if they're flaring up again after years of being dormant, or if maybe they were active all along but the women are finally seeking help.' She felt her mother's eyes on her. She kept her own trained on the parking lot. 'Traumatic life events can trigger them. You know, divorces, or deaths, or even a marital infidelity.'

She stalled the car again, closer to the station. It would be a bit of a squeeze, but she'd manage it. She started to reverse slightly.

'Crumpet, you might get the car in, but you won't get me out. I don't know if you've noticed, but I need a bit of wiggle room.'

Beverley drove on.

'What really surprised me was that eating disorders are more dangerous when you're older. Did you know that? You don't have the reserve of nutrients and the bone density you have in your youth, and your heart finds it more difficult to cope with the weight loss.'

'I haven't lost any weight, Mother,' said Beverley. 'I've been exactly the same weight for the past eight years.' Nine stone, two pounds. It was annoying that she had stalled so close to a nice round number, but it refused to go any lower. It would happily climb, of course, not that she'd let it.

'I didn't say you had,' replied her mother. The breezy innocence made her want to throw Frances and her collection of ornamental reproductive parts out of the car. 'And actually, weight loss isn't a huge symptom in older people. The metabolism starts to stall.'

Finally. Two empty spaces side by side. Beverley pulled in.

'Things like bad teeth, acne, indigestion, even heartburn' – Frances allowed the word to linger – 'they are all far more common.'

Beverley turned off the engine. She wanted to round on her mother and tell her that, actually, she had it wrong; Beverley *had* slipped, yes, but she was past it. She hadn't made herself sick since she'd frightened herself in the Glass Lake bathrooms. And she would have been telling the truth, if they'd had this exchange a few hours ago. But she'd slept so badly last night – she couldn't stop thinking about Ella, no doubt lying face down in her pillow, sobbing over that useless creature – that she'd been exhausted this morning and couldn't stop eating. She'd had Bran Flakes, then toast, then yoghurt, then more toast. Malachy, who'd begrudgingly skipped his morning run to wave off Frances, had wanted to know why Ella hadn't been at dinner the night before and why she wasn't appearing for breakfast. Beverley didn't know what to say. If she told Malachy, it would be her fault. She was at home every day – how had she not noticed a highly undesirable suitor breaking in and stealing their daughter's heart? Instead, she ran upstairs to get her car keys for the school drop-off. Only they were already in her bag. She locked herself in their en suite. She was anxious and twitchy and uncomfortably full; she barely had to do more than lean forward.

She searched her handbag now for the printout of the train ticket. Her phone was aglow. Forty-two new WhatsApp messages, which was some feat given she'd checked her mobile before they left the house. Something must have happened. 'Here you go,' she said.

Her mother didn't take the ticket. She reached past it and covered Beverley's hands, the pudgy skin instantly making hers clammy.

Beverley's father had made her see her mother through his eyes and she hated him for that. What was harder to admit was that she also resented her mother. If she'd lost the weight, everything would have been better. If she'd got thinner, he would have stopped. Why couldn't she have just done that? Hadn't she cared about them enough?

'If you need me, *a stór*, you just call, and I'll come running.'

Beverley pulled her hands free. 'Isn't that a song?'

'The way you feel about your girls, that you'd kill to protect them, that's how I feel about you. And I'm proud of you, always and for ever.'

Beverley cleared her throat. She would pick up some lozenges at the pharmacy too. 'Take the ticket before you forget it. I've paid for the upgrade, so you might as well use it. I'll help with your luggage. I'll carry the ... box up to the platform.'

She crossed the car park, glancing around for who might be watching the unlikely duo of Beverley Franklin and the obese woman wearing a sarong, and instantly hating herself for it.

'Thanks, Mam,' she said, when they were in the small waiting area and she'd placed the bubble-wrapped sculpture at Frances' feet.

'For what?'

For being a role model, she wanted to say. But she couldn't bring herself to do it. She dreaded sounding foolish. 'For telling me about Ella and Arlo,' she said. 'Thank you. It's important information to have.'

....

Christine Maguire's phone was hopping. News of what Lorna Farrell was calling a 'Glass Lake s*x scandal' was spreading through the social networks like wildfire. Even a WhatsApp group for a school tour three years ago had come alive.

Christine was at Cooney Nursing Home, attempting to report on West Cork's oldest citizen turning 106.

'I think you left your torch on, pet,' said the birthday girl.

'Hmm? Oh, no. No, that's just...' She reached into her handbag and turned the phone over, so the screen was faced down. 'Anyway, I think I've got everything I need.'

She'd gathered all her quotes and badgered the woman for her top tips on living longer, as per Derek's request. ('Old people are depressing! At least get me a list!')

'You must stay for cake. It's low sugar, given half of us could keel

279

over from diabetes at any moment, but it's still good, I promise.' The woman wiggled her eyebrows, so her birthday crown tipped slightly to the left. 'It's Black Forest Gateau.'

Christine smiled. It was always Black Forest Gateau. 'How could I say no? Happy birthday again, Muriel.'

She could hang on a few minutes but then she had to get home to Maeve, who was off sick today. As she waited for a care assistant to slice up the cake, she scrolled her way through the onslaught of facts, gossip and everything in between.

Principal Patterson had contacted several sixth-class parents this morning to tell them their children had also been exchanging nudes with Woody Whitehead. With so many informed, any hope of keeping his name private was gone. Christine had phoned the school on her way to the nursing home and the secretary assured her Maeve was not one of them. But something was up with her daughter. Maeve's sick days were always caused by worries that wormed their way so far into her anxious body they made her physically ill.

Someone shook the man at the keyboard awake and he guided the group in a boisterous rendition of 'Happy Birthday'. Christine clicked her phone shut and dutifully joined in.

'*For she's a jolly good fellow ...! For she's a jolly good fellow ...!*'

They applauded the blowing-out of the candles. It took six goes, but Muriel got there in the end.

Christine ate her slice of cake quickly, then she headed for her car. She had to check on Maeve and, after that, she had Operation Liberation to oversee.

....

By the time Beverley had left the train station, called to the pharmacy, and made her way across town to the Whiteheads' house, she had 213 WhatsApp messages and six missed calls, mostly from Lorna, The couple of messages she'd caught flashing up on the screen suggested there was some sort of meet-up this afternoon. She couldn't make it anyway. Her mother's visit meant she was behind on Sneaky Sweets orders. Whatever it was about would have to wait. She couldn't afford to lose her nerve.

Out of the Range Rover and up the path she went. There were two 'For Sale' signs pitched in the small lawn at the front of the house. She'd heard people were doing that. She'd never had reason to drive out this side of town herself, but she believed a few other parents had made an exception.

The door opened before Beverley had a chance to ring the bell. The startled look on Connie Whitehead's face meant it had already been the correct decision to call.

'I'm here to speak to your son.'

'Oh, well, I'm afraid he's at school, and I was just heading up there ...' The woman switched her car keys from her right hand to her left.

'Not that son. The other one.'

The woman glanced behind her. From inside the house, there was the sound of someone coming down the stairs.

'Have you seen my tools?' asked a male voice.

Then Arlo appeared in the doorway.

'Mrs Franklin.' He wiped his hands on his trousers. 'Hello.'

'Beverley is here to see you,' said Connie, giving him a meaningful look. 'But I was just saying I've to get up to the school and that you have a job to get to.' She turned back to Beverley. 'I'm giving him a lift, you see. His van is on the blink. Maybe you could call back another time ...'

'It's fine, Mom,' said the teenager, taking hold of the door frame. 'Go on. You can't be late. I'll take my bike.'

'With all your tools?'

'It's fine.'

Connie looked from Arlo to Beverley before conceding. 'Your toolbox is under the kitchen table,' she said, heading down the path. 'Nice to see you, Beverley.' She looked back at them as she climbed into a car that, according to the licence plate, was older than Amelia.

'The brakes are acting up on my van. I'm having it serviced.'

He said it as if she'd asked – as if she cared. 'Heard from my daughter lately?'

His mouth opened, then shut. Open, shut. Open, shut. 'I don't ... I'm not sure ...'

'I know all about you creeping into my house at all hours, without my say-so. That's trespassing. Did you know that? I could have you arrested.'

'I didn't ... It wasn't ...' He was the colour of one of her tomatoffees (trademark pending). What had Ella seen in him?

'How could you do this to her? Do you know how wonderful Ella is? How lucky you were to get to spend any time with her? You ... You lanky string of piss.' Beverley never cursed, at least not beyond the confines of her own home. It felt wonderful. 'And Fiona Murphy?' She thought of her daughter's pale perfect skin and of the crêpe texture of Fiona's sun-bedded chest. Why were men allowed to exist? 'Have you no respect for yourself? She's heartbroken, you know. She's barely left her room. You're just some cheap cliché gardener, tending to the lawns and sexual desires of his old customers. Just like your father.'

Beverley eyeballed the boy, daring him. It felt good to be defending something she really, deeply cared about. Was this what her mother meant when she said that ultimately all that mattered was that she did what she believed was right?

'Did Mrs Murphy say something happened?' the boy said finally. 'Is that what Ella thinks? Is that why she's ignoring me?' His face was flaming red. Did he really expect her to fall for the innocent act?

Two cars drove past. One of them pulled in a few doors down. With nothing to fan the flames, her fire began to die.

'Stay away from my family and my house. And tell your brother to do the same.' She turned on her heels, before pivoting back. 'You're a plague, you Whiteheads. A plague on this whole town!'

She barrelled back down the path, zipping up her fitted jacket, fob pointed at the car. Safely inside, she watched Arlo reappear from the house in a jacket, carrying a toolbox. He paused in front of the 'For Sale' signs. Then he reefed them out of the grass and flung them over the side gate into their backyard.

Beverley unlocked her phone and started to go through the messages. As she scrolled back to the start – 264 messages! – she watched Arlo throw his leg over an old Raleigh and precariously balance the toolbox on the handlebars. He kicked off and freewheeled down the hill and out of the estate.

There were nine different threads, but they all said the same thing.

'Zut alors,' whispered Beverley as she took in the details.

This afternoon's get-together was happening at the school. Only it wasn't a meet-up they were planning at all. It was a full-on riot.

32

Arlo cycled as fast as he could across town. The toolbox jangled on his handlebars, and Beverley's rage rang in his ears. He'd put so much effort into her not finding out about him and Ella, but now he found himself in a situation where that was the least terrible bit.

He'd felt oddly buoyed after visiting his dad and had texted Ella from the prison car park to apologise for not responding and to say he was on his way back to her to explain. He'd never felt so much like he was driving home. When he got to Cooney, he had a reply. All it said was: Don't call. Despite follow-up messages, voice notes and even phone calls, that was the last he'd heard from her. He though she was mad at him for ignoring her messages; now he knew it was much worse.

Flying down Main Street, he checked the clock over Regan's Chemist. Christine Maguire had been very precise about time when she hired him, and it would take twice as long on the bike. But when would he get a chance to contact Ella? He needed to tell her that whatever she'd heard was wrong. Nothing had happened between him and Mrs Murphy. The increased speed kept his mind from spiralling. Every time he imagined a scenario in which Fiona Murphy had somehow told Ella an exaggerated version of events, the wind bellowed in his ears.

When he made it to Seaview Terrace, Christine and a girl he took to be her daughter were waiting outside. He climbed off his bike and they led him back down the street.

'As I said on the phone, our cat is trapped, and we need you to get him out,' said the Glass Lake mother, coming to a halt at a very well-maintained garden.

He tried to keep his thoughts on the job. 'Your roses are lovely.'

'Oh, this isn't our garden. Our house is up there.' Christine pointed back the way they'd come. 'This is our neighbour's house. A sweet old woman who has gone away on holidays – to visit a dying relative, I believe – and our cat has got trapped in her home.'

'When did this happen?' he asked, swiping at the sweat along his hairline.

'When was it, Maeve?'

The girl looked up at her mother in mild terror.

Christine tapped her chin. 'Let me see now ...'

'You phoned me on Saturday.'

'That's right,' said Christine. 'It was Saturday. Porcupine has been trapped in there since Saturday.'

Arlo ran the back of his hand along his brow as he looked up at the house. When he was done with this job, he would send Ella another text. But this time he would make it clear that there had been a huge misunderstanding. 'How did the cat get in there?'

'How does Porcupine get anywhere?' mused Christine. 'He roams the street, calling into neighbours. Nobody minds, we're a close little terrace. I guess he just got stuck in this one. Porcupine's a free spirit, isn't he, Maeve?'

Maeve Maguire. He knew the name.

'Okay, well, Mrs Maguire, I thought I was here to get him out of a shed or a storage unit or something. Was that not what you said on the phone?'

Christine stuck out her bottom lip and frowned. 'No, I don't think so.'

'I couldn't break into this house, even if I wanted to. I'm sorry.'

She looked at him blankly.

'This is a pin and tumbler,' he explained, pointing to their neighbour's door. 'It's a totally different kind of lock. I'd need a tension wrench, at the very least, and probably a rake. I don't have those tools with me.'

'So, where are they?'

'Well, there's a lock pick kit up at the school, but—'

'Perfect. We'll wait.' The woman checked her wristwatch. 'We have an hour until she … until I have to leave for work, I mean. That's enough time to get up to Glass Lake and back.' She smiled. 'You go, and Maeve and I will wait here.'

'I don't—'

'And I'll pay you double for the effort.'

'Mrs Maguire, I really can't afford to get into any trouble. And to be honest, I don't feel comfortable about breaking into someone else's home.'

'I completely understand, but you wouldn't get into any trouble, I promise. If it wasn't for Mrs Rodgers' dying sister – did I mention she was dying? – I'd phone her myself and ask her to come back. I know she'd be heartbroken to think a cat was wasting away, starving to death, in her home. Ask anyone. She's a real animal lover.'

He looked at the house again. The curtains were open and the lights off, which told him precisely nothing. There was no car in the driveway but maybe the resident didn't drive or was just away for the day. It seemed unlikely a Glass Lake parent would want to break into a neighbour's home for immoral reasons, but he really didn't want to get caught up in criminal behaviour. He had enough to contend with as it was.

'Look! Look! There he is!' Maeve ran to the front-room window.

Arlo moved closer to the house, still reluctant to touch it – though he'd already noted there was no alarm – and peered in through the glass to see a rotund cat with the strangest fur colouring padding into the sitting room. In the middle of the rug, he lay on his side, and started licking his paws.

'He doesn't look like he's starving to death.'

'Oh, he is,' said Christine. 'See? He's so hungry he's considering eating himself. Cats do that, you know. Self-cannibalism.'

Maeve moved her face closer to the window. 'Pssh,' she hissed. 'Pssh, pssh, pssh.' But the animal just rolled on to his other side.

'You should have seen him before, honestly. He's wasting away.'

Maeve turned from the window, so the two of them were looking at him.

'I don't have my van,' he said, remembering his trump card. 'It'd take too long to get up to Glass Lake and back again on the bike.'

'No problem,' said Christine. 'I'll drive you. It won't take ten minutes to get there, especially at this time.'

He was working hard to put obstacles in their path, but she was equally determined to remove them.

'Please, Arlo, we really are desperate.'

He was out of excuses. 'All right. All right, let's go.'

He fired off a message to Ella as soon as he was in the passenger seat, and they drove to the school with the radio doing most of the talking.

The car turned on to the tree-lined avenue that led to Glass Lake. 'When we get to the school, Maeve, you'll wait in the car, all right?' said Christine. 'She's supposed to be off sick today, though as you can see, she's not exhibiting many symptoms of illness.'

She brought the car to an early stop. The parking spaces reserved for visitors' cars were full, and about a dozen adults were standing on the grassy verge in front of the school. They were wrapped in jackets and scarves and a few of them were brandishing signs.

'What are they …?'

Christine trailed off. One of the protestors turned to the side, his banner rotating with him. It said: NO SEXTS AT OUR SCHOOL.

'Is this about Woody?' Arlo said, rubbing condensation from the window. 'Is it to do with the jacket?' Their mom had been called up to the school this morning to talk to Principal Patterson about Woody graffitiing a teacher's coat.

'I'd wager it's got more to do with the nudes,' said Christine, veering the car to the right as she gave the protestors a wide berth and headed for the back of the school.

'From a couple of weeks ago?'

Christine frowned. 'Didn't you hear anything today?'

'No.'

She glanced into the back seat and lowered her voice. 'Woody's been accused of exchanging nudes with other students. Principal Patterson phoned the parents this morning. We'll park up by the pool. You have an access card, right?'

That's why the 'For Sale' signs had reappeared this morning after a month's reprieve. People were back to wanting them gone, because now they thought Charlie's youngest son was some sort of sexual deviant. Was his mother here yet? He'd forgotten to look for her car. He twisted against the seatbelt. Had she seen this?

'Arlo?'

'Yes?'

'Have you got an access card?'

'Yes, I have one.'

They pulled in between Frank Cafferty's Skoda and Principal Patterson's BMW. Christine pushed open her door and, somehow, he followed.

Though they were on the other side of the building, they could easily hear the chants.

'*What do we want, what do we know?*' cried a woman who must have had a megaphone.

The crowd sang back: '*Woody Whitehead must go!*'

Arlo rested a hand on the roof of the car.

'Come on,' said Christine, her voice suddenly soft as she took him by the arm. 'We'll go in the back way and avoid the crazies.'

....

Nuala Patterson walked Connie Whitehead out to the entrance of the school. She did not enjoy spending time in the woman's company, but she was a professional. She'd made it clear that Woody was being punished for the graffiti incident and not the sexting, which was technically not the school's business – although she didn't know how much longer she could maintain that line. It was certainly starting to affect school life. Woody was to be suspended for a week, starting tomorrow, and he would be removed from the musical.

'He'll miss *The Wizard of Oz*. He's been working so hard on it,' said Connie, breaking the hypnotic sound of Nuala's work shoes clip-clopping along the corridor.

'He'll be all right, I'm sure,' she replied, pushing her way through the first set of double doors, and then the ones that led outside.

When she thought of the photo fallout as affecting school life, she meant the sheer number of students now implicated. Foolishly, she'd forgotten about the parents.

'*What do we want, what do we know?*' Lorna Farrell was shouting into some sort of control panel, the amplified words blaring from a megaphone in her other hand.

'Woody Whitehead must go!' replied a crowd of ten or so other parents.

A father at the rear held up a banner that said NO SEXTS AT OUR SCHOOL, while someone else had a placard calling for LESS LETCHING, MORE LEARNING.

There wasn't a bad situation that Glass Lake parents couldn't somehow make worse.

'Sorry, Principal Patterson,' said Mairead, jogging up behind her. 'I was in the staffroom making a cup of coffee. I just saw them now. What do you want me to do?'

The crowd had caught sight of Connie Whitehead and was now aiming the chants at her.

'*Marnie Farrell, say her name!*' yelled Lorna.

'Marnie Farrell! Marnie Farrell!' came the reply.

'*Ciara Murphy, say her name!*'

'Ciara Murphy! Ciara Murphy!'

Nuala could barely believe it. They were going through the list of female students who'd sent explicit photographs of themselves. When Nuala had contacted the parents of the implicated students this morning, she'd asked them to respect the children's privacy. And now they were literally shouting their names through a megaphone.

'Tanya D'Arcy, say her name!'

Nuala turned to Mairead. 'Take Mrs Whitehead back to my office,' she said. 'And then ask Seamus to roll out the power hose.'

....

If Frank Cafferty could just get Woody to listen, they would sort this whole mess out. He only wanted the best for the boy. He cared about him. Couldn't he see that? There was no reason to be acting out in class and destroying his teacher's possessions.

He had taken Woody out of the classroom for a moment so he could explain this. But the child kept turning his head away. He couldn't get him to understand.

'Fuck you,' muttered the boy.

'Woody! You can't speak to me like that. I'm still your teacher!'

Behind him, there was a loud sound of metal clattering to the floor.

Frank jumped.

Seamus McGrath appeared from one of the storage rooms, wheeling a coiled-up hose behind him.

'Seamus ... hi, hello.'

But Seamus just stared at him.

The same thought as always crossed his mind. The caretaker knew.

But no, of course not.

How could he?

Woody took the opportunity to disappear back into the classroom. Frank tried and failed to swallow. Seamus kept staring.

'I was just talking to the boy and—'

'I know what you are,' said the caretaker.

Frank did some version of a smile, as if Seamus had just made a mild-mannered joke, then he too vanished back into the classroom.

....

Lorna Farrell watched Connie Whitehead retreat and felt a rush of victory. She'd been worried she wouldn't have what it took to lead the crowd but, if she did say so herself, she was doing a stellar job.

'*Whose children?!*' she shouted into the voice box, as Principal Patterson stepped out onto the lawn and folded her arms.

Lorna would have folded her own arms, if either had been free. Instead, she held the megaphone higher.

'Our children!' the crowd replied.

That was right. They were here on behalf of their children and as parents, as guardians, they would not be intimidated.

'*Whose children?*' she yelled into the voice box again.

'Our children!'

Lorna had assumed Beverley would take control of the rally, as she did everything. But she hadn't responded to any of this morning's WhatsApp messages. Bill was the one who'd encouraged her to step up, to become leader of this movement. If her husband was going to be mayor one day, she was going to be first lady, and she wanted to be one who used her powers for good. Like Michelle Obama. Lorna was a great admirer of Michelle Obama.

She wasn't glad her daughter had got caught up in this mess, absolutely not, but it did strengthen her right to lead. Plus, they had the megaphone left over from Bill's election campaign.

'*Children's lives ...*'

'Matter!' came the response.

'Children's lives ...'

'Matter!'

As well as being a fan of the Obamas, Lorna bought all her soap from a woman in Aberstown who was one-quarter Asian (not that Lorna saw colour), so she was sure the Black Lives Matter movement wouldn't mind her borrowing a few chants. They were very catchy.

'Hey!'

Before she could stop it, Principal Patterson was reefing the megaphone off her, causing the cord to detach from the voice box she was still holding in her left hand.

'We will not be intimidated, Nuala! We will not be silenced!'

'We will not be intimidated, Nuala! We will not be silenced!' echoed the group.

Lorna hadn't meant it as a chant, but good to know they could continue without amplification. It felt particularly defiant to have so many parents referring to Principal Patterson as 'Nuala'.

'Enough,' said the principal. 'What do you all think you're doing? Not only are you in breach of some serious data protection, but you are violating the privacy of a collection of minors.'

'We're their parents,' asserted someone behind Lorna.

'Some of you are. Moira Gaffney – your son is only in Junior Infants; and Gerry Regan, you haven't had a child at Glass Lake in half a decade.'

Gerry let his NO SEXTS AT OUR SCHOOL sign drop slightly. If you needed someone to get involved, you could always count on the pharmacist. He was a great man for a petition or a planning application objection.

'Those of you who are parents of affected students, I have already invited you to come here this afternoon to talk to me, and I expect to see you at those prearranged meetings. But this is not talking. I'm asking you to please leave the school premises. Seamus is due to water the grass, and I would hate for any of you to get wet.'

The school caretaker appeared behind Principal Patterson wheeling a heavy hose reel. He began to unravel it.

'We're parents,' Lorna shot back, 'and we deserve to have a say in the welfare of our children. We were patient. We tried your workshops idea. We went to your information night. I heard that doctor is your cousin, by the way.'

'Second cousin once-removed,' said the principal coldly.

'Mmm.' Lorna paused. Did she dare? 'It's interesting that the Lakers fundraised money for you to spend in the best interest of the school and you spent it on a family member.'

'I hired the best—'

'We did some workshops and they didn't work,' Lorna interrupted. Megaphone or no megaphone, she would be heard! 'The following week, we find out we have a s-e-x pest in our midst. And, according to my daughter, a lewd graffiti artist too. Who knows what will be next? We want the boy gone.'

The crowd cheered and she couldn't fight the smile. This was how the British queen must feel every time she stepped out on to her balcony.

Nuala Patterson looked at her with unmasked irritation.

'This is a place of learning. We have several hundred children here trying to get on with their lessons, in silence. If you want to form a lynch mob, I suggest you take your nooses elsewhere.'

As an opponent to slavery – she had been first to sign Claire Keating's petition to get it removed from the history curriculum – not to mention her well-known Obama admiration – she had organised the bus to Dublin the time Barack came to visit – Lorna found the racially charged comparison pointed and insulting.

'For now, as I said, we have grass to keep alive. Good to go, Seamus?'

The caretaker was gripping the mouth of the hose in both hands.

Reluctantly, the crowd began to disperse. There was some chatter about heading over to the Strand. Gerry had a copy of the 'Ban Articulated Vehicles in Cooney' petition saved to his laptop; he could rework the template.

'You're on my list, Nuala Patterson,' said Lorna, narrowing her eyes as the principal took a step back into the porch. 'And I'll tell you this – it is *not* my homemade thank-you card list.'

33

'This is different,' Christine explained to her perpetually concerned daughter as they waved farewell to Arlo.

After the teenager got Mrs Rodgers' front door open, he'd offered to stick around, but she told him there was no need and he hadn't argued. He'd headed off on his bike with an expression not dissimilar to Maeve's.

'How is it different?' asked the girl, still standing on their neighbour's porch.

Christine, who was just beyond the threshold, didn't know if she should keep trying to coax Maeve in, or concentrate on coaxing Porcupine out. They had very little time before their neighbour returned from the Tidy Towns committee meeting and the loud clock in the woman's hallway – which she now realised had pictures of cats where there are usually numbers – was not helping.

'We're not robbers because we're not stealing anything,' she said decisively. 'We're just taking back what is already ours.'

'But we're still breaking and entering.'

'No,' said Christine, shaking her head slowly, waiting for a rebuttal to reveal itself. 'We didn't *break* anything. Entering, maybe. But not *breaking* and entering.'

'Why can't we just wait for Mrs Rodgers to come home?'

'Because she might stop us.'

'How?'

Christine threw her arms up in the air. 'I don't know, Maeve. She might wrestle us to the floor.'

The child was doubtful. 'If Caroline's too old for wrestling, then Mrs Rodgers is definitely too old.'

'Or she might phone the guards on us. Who knows? All I know is we need to find this cat.'

'My tummy doesn't feel good.'

'I know, but it'll feel a lot better when we're home and Porcupine is lying across it, purring away. Now, you can wait there if you like, but I'm going in.'

Mrs Rodgers' hallway was shadowy and smelled faintly of dust balls. The sitting room, where they had seen Porcupine earlier, had a similar odour and was just as dark. She turned on the light.

'Porcupine,' she called. 'Here, kitty, kitty. Here, Porcupine. Here, kitty, kitty. Come on, Maeve! Give me a hand!'

'He's there,' said her daughter, appearing in the living-room doorway.

'Where?'

'By the fireplace. See?'

Christine walked over to the cat, who was at least fifty per cent larger than the last time she'd seen him up close. What had the woman been feeding him? She reached down just as Porcupine pushed himself up and arched his back. He remained as unenamoured of Christine, his rescuer, as ever.

'You pick him up and we'll get out of here.'

'*Me?*'

'It's okay, we're not doing anything wrong. If anyone did a bad thing here, it's Mrs Rodgers. Now, come on, pick him up.'

Her daughter took a step forward. Christine glanced out the window, but her view of the road was obscured by the rose bushes.

She reached out and gently inched her daughter forward until she bent down and scooped up the cat. He purred contentedly. Christine exhaled.

She steered Maeve and the animal out the front door, softly closing it behind them. She pushed against the door, but it didn't budge. No sign of tampering.

'Hang on ...' She held a hand up to her daughter as she jogged down the garden path and threw glances up and down Seaview Terrace. 'Okay, let's go. Let's go, let's go, let's go!'

She ushered her daughter down the garden path and up the road as if this was a hijack situation and she was shepherding the hostages to safety. Which, in a way, she was. 'Keep going. Don't look back. Do not look back,' she said, as she did just that. The road remained clear. A few cars whizzed past the bottom, but none turned up.

When they made it to their own garden, she pulled the key from her shirt pocket and got the door open in double time.

'Mission complete!' she cried, leaning down to kiss her daughter's head and even ruffle Porcupine's hideous fur. 'First thing we're doing is getting that dye out. What sort of psycho ... Maeve? Are you okay?'

Her daughter's eyes were big and pained, and the left one was twitching again.

'I did a bad thing.'

Christine crouched down and brushed her hair back from her face. 'No, you didn't. Honestly, love! You did a very good, a very brave thing. You rescued Porcupine.'

Maeve shook her head. 'I mean before.'

Christine nodded. It might take a while for Maeve to tell them what was up, but the confession always came. 'Is this about why you couldn't go to school today? Because you did a bad thing and you felt too bad, in your tummy?'

Maeve nodded.

'Is it to do with Woody?'

She nodded again, and Christine felt a plunge in her own stomach.

'But it's not photos. I never took any photos.'

'Okay,' she said, head already spinning as the euphoria of being a feline emancipator evaporated. 'Why don't we just start at the start?'

....

Frank Cafferty stared at the blinking cursor on the blank Word document. He had never written a letter of resignation before and wasn't sure where to start.

He hadn't had the chance to resign from his last school. As soon as parents started to complain, he was placed on sick leave, and never taken off it. He'd had two blissful years there before a father confronted him in the playground. Frank had been collecting the cones after PE; he hadn't been expecting it at all.

'I know about you,' the man had said, spat really, head jutting out as his hands bunched into fists.

Frank played dumb.

When the same man approached him at his home, he acted outraged and insulted. He threatened to sue for slander.

'You shouldn't be working with children,' the father shouted, as Frank shut the front door on his tirade.

Then notes started to appear under his windscreen wipers, each one nastier than the last. He'd ignored them all, until the final one. It contained that same four-letter word, as crude in writing as when uttered.

Pedo.

That's when he'd started to get scared.

School management didn't say why they were placing him on leave, just that parents had raised concerns and it was for the best. Frank had agreed in a bid to shut off any further questions. After a few weeks, he started looking for a job in a bigger town.

He had hoped it would be different in Cooney. He had promised Jess it would be. But he couldn't change who he was. The best he could do was keep it to himself, until the rest of the world became more open-minded.

Everyone on the chat forums said he was playing with fire opting for a job that involved working with children. He couldn't help it. He loved being around them too much. But he was done with teaching now, that was it. He was going back to tech.

'Are you sure about this, Frank?' said Jess, appearing in the doorway behind him. 'You didn't do anything wrong.' It sounded more like a plea than a statement of fact. Was he imagining that? He hoped so.

'We'll move to Dublin, start afresh,' he said, with trademark enthusiasm. He'd be a better husband there, a better person, a better version of himself.

....

'I got Mr Cafferty's coat from the classroom last Thursday when I was supposed to be at rehearsals, and I gave it to Woody. We were supposed to get it together but he got stopped in the corridor so I put it in my bag and brought it back to the hall and gave it to Woody and he wrote the bad word on it and now Woody will probably be thrown out of school for ever and ever.'

'Well, I don't think that's going to happen,' said Christine, who hadn't had a chance to fully catch up on the latest WhatsApp goings-on, but the word seemed to be that Woody was suspended for a week.

'It's all my fault.'

'What you did wasn't *good*, but it wasn't that bad either. You didn't have anything to do with writing on the coat, right?'

Maeve shook her head.

'Good.'

'But I did call Mr Cafferty's phone lots of times and hang up without saying anything.'

'*What?* Maeve!'

'I know. I'm sorry.'

'You prank called your teacher! How? You don't even have a phone!'

'I used Dad's phone, when you were both asleep or when you were out. And then I deleted the calls because I didn't want Dad to see and get cross.'

'Where would you even get a teacher's number?'

'Woody gave it to me.'

'Where did he get it? I don't ... Why would you do all that?'

'Because Woody is my friend.'

'So?'

'Woody needs to make Mr Cafferty quit. He needs to make him leave the school and go away and never come back.'

'Why does Woody need to make your teacher quit?'

Maeve shrugged, turning her attention to Porcupine, the absolution of the confession already having an effect. It was amazing how quickly children recovered, while their parents were left reeling. 'I don't know why he wants to make Mr Cafferty quit,' said the eleven-year-old, tickling the cat gently. 'He just does.'

There was one more set of quick breaths before Tuesday morning's class was dismissed, but Beverley rolled up her mat, bowed to Paul and quickly left the overheated studio. Usually, after a hot yoga session, she went straight to the bathroom and drenched her face with cold water, waterboarding her pores into submission. But today she lingered by the reception desk.

She'd spotted the pamphlet numerous times, its purple border peeping out from the array of literature on everything from smear tests to resistance training to food supplements. This was the first time she'd considered taking one.

'Beverley.'

Her hand flew two leaflets to the left and she plucked a page at random. Fiona Murphy had left the studio too, red-faced and sweating in a hot-pink Adidas sports bra that was at least a decade too young for her. Fiona threw the gold chain of her Chanel purse across her chest, like one of the tackier Kardashians.

'I'm with you,' she said, still breathing heavily. 'Any excuse to wrap things up early.' Her eyes tracked down. 'Never too soon to be making plans.'

Beverley looked at the brochure in her hand, an advertorial leaflet for a new eco-cemetery in east Cork. She stuffed it back into the display. 'What do you want, Fiona?'

'Just checking in. You've been quiet on WhatsApp. And you didn't sign Lorna's petition for Woody Whitehead's expulsion. Fair enough, I didn't sign it either. It's amazing Cooney hasn't been submerged into the Atlantic with the weight of all these petitions.' She pulled at the strap of her bag. 'So, how are you? How's the musical? I heard Woody's gone. That's quite the mess they've left you in. The lion, wow. Tough role to replace.'

'We'll manage.'

The rest of the class flowed out of the studio now, chatting and fanning their hands in front of their faces. Beverley waited for Fiona to stand to one side, then she did the same.

'I was thinking this might be a chance for Ciara to move up a bit. You remember we were looking for a bigger role for her?'

'And we found one. She's the Wicked Witch of the West.'

'The Witch of the West,' she corrected.

'I have to go now, Fiona. I need to get ice water on my face before it sucks up all these awful toxins.'

Fiona pursed her lips. Beverley felt the twitch, but she didn't blink.

'Now that the lion is available, I was thinking Ciara could move up again,' she said, readjusting her gold chain. 'I was also thinking that since Amelia has the perfect hair to play a lion – all yellowy and coarse – she'd be better suited to that role, while Ciara would work perfectly as Dorothy. Her hair is so fine, it looks great in pigtails, and she knows most of the lines.'

'*In-croy-able*,' said Beverley, throwing her head back and laughing, though what she really wanted to do was smack this pathetic cradle-snatcher hard on her inflamed cheeks. 'I think the heat might have gone to your head.'

'You just need a minute to think it over.'

'I really don't.'

Fiona frowned, or tried to. 'I think you're forgetting what I know, Beverley.'

Beverley stood straighter and relaxed her shoulders. She was always an inch taller after yoga and she used it to her advantage. Fiona didn't balk.

'I was actually out at Tamara's house this morning,' she continued, 'and she was talking about Malachy, your Malachy, of all people. It seems she knows him, too. Which I didn't realise. Did you realise?'

Beverley had had enough. 'And I heard about you and Arlo Whitehead.'

Fiona smiled modestly, flapping a hand, as if batting away a compliment.

'He's a child, Fiona.'

The woman rolled her eyes. 'He's eighteen.'

'You should be ashamed of yourself.'

'Oh, come on,' she scoffed. 'Anyway, it's got nothing to do with you. Worry about your own relationship. And let's not get off subject here. Ciara is playing Dorothy. Or else.'

Two regulars from the class passed them and Beverley cracked a smile.

When they were gone, she moved closer. This time, Fiona's chin betrayed her. She tried to point it upwards, but there was a hint of a tremor.

Beverley thought of Ella sobbing through the ceiling; of all the untouched trays of food that had sat outside her door; of how deathly lonely it felt to be betrayed. If Beverley could get

305

away with it, she'd have pulled that bag strap up and wrapped it around Fiona's neck.

'If you utter one word about my family or me, I'll tell everyone about you and that *child*.'

The woman shrugged. 'He's eighteen, and he's hot.'

'I'll tell Ciara.'

Fiona's eyes narrowed, or tried to.

Beverley, who paid twice as much for her Botox, widened her own.

'You wouldn't dare.'

'And Butcher.'

Fiona looked worried now.

'I'm not sure how he'd feel about his ex-wife taking up with a teenager, but I guess we'll find out. Do you remember that time he thought Mr Peoples had the hots for you? Arlo will have a lot more to worry about than a pig's head on his car bonnet.'

'It's not true, okay?' Fiona hissed, looking over her shoulder. 'We kissed, just about, but he – I mean, I was just about to stop it, but he chickened out first. Not that I was actually going to *do* anything. It was just sort of a joke. Nothing happened.'

'That's not what I heard. That's not what everyone is saying.'

Fiona sighed. 'I can't help it if people are obsessed with my love life. They're trying to live vicariously through me. But I never actually said anything happened; Lorna Farrell heard what she wanted and ran with it.'

'And you didn't think to correct her?'

The woman shrugged.

Beverley could imagine exactly how it had gone down: the teenager shunning Fiona's advances and, not taking this slight well, her allowing everyone to think something had happened between them. It was pathetic, but it was very Fiona.

'Goodbye, Fiona,' she said coldly. 'I really can't allow my pores to suck up any more of *this*.' She looked her straight in the eye. The woman inhaled loudly but said nothing. Then she turned on her heels and walked to the exit.

Beverley headed for the bathroom. If she didn't get water on her face stat, her skin would get even worse. But first, she leaned back and grabbed the *Recovering from Eating Disorders* pamphlet.

....

Mrs Rodgers had waited patiently by the back door for almost twenty-four hours. She'd arrived home from her Tidy Towns committee meeting yesterday afternoon to find the house empty. She'd thought Albert had been suitably fattened so he could no longer fit through the cat flap, but she must have been mistaken. She had the back door wide open now and she was sitting on a low stool ready to greet him, but still he didn't return.

She didn't know how Albert would have coped last night. He'd never been out alone in the dark. Come to think of it, he had never been out alone. She'd done a thorough tour of the house, checking every window, and giving the front and back doors a good once-over. Of course, her mind had sprung to the neglectful family up the street, but there was no way they could have got in to steal her cat.

A thought occurred to her. The only other person with a key to her home was Father O'Shea. As far as she knew, he was still in Medjugorje, hunting for the spectre of Our Lady. Still, it was worth a shot.

To her surprise, he answered on the third ring.

'Blessings upon you, Father Brendan O'Shea speaking.'

'Oh, hello, Father, it's Rita Rodgers, from number one. I wasn't expecting you to be home.'

'Hello, Mrs Rodgers. Yes, I flew in last night. Turned out it wasn't the Blessed Mother up on the hill at all, just some kids playing a practical joke, Protestants probably. So, I said I'd get back before All Saints' Day.'

'I'm sorry you had a wasted trip.'

'Not at all. Didn't I get a beautiful new halo in the apparitions' gift shop? Fits perfectly on my Blessed Mother shrine and phenomenal wattage. You must call and see her, Mrs Rodgers. She'd bring the most lapsed believer to his knees.'

'Sounds lovely.'

'What can I do you for? Another few prayers over an animal grave?' The priest chuckled, but when she didn't immediately correct him, he grew sombre. 'Oh, I am sorry, Mrs Rodgers, don't tell me you've lost another cat? Of all the bad luck. How many is that that have gone and died on you this year?'

'Still just the three, Father. And I don't know what happens; I feed them so well.'

'You need to stop adopting such hopeless cases.'

'That must be it,' she said gravely. 'But no, no funeral required today. I'm calling about the spare key to my house. I wanted to check you still have it. Nobody has come looking for it?'

'Not that I know of, but as I said, I was away until last night. Hang on just a tick and I'll check.'

'Thank you, Father.'

As she waited for the priest to pull out the old tea tin where he kept the keys, Mrs Rodgers gazed out onto her vibrant rose bushes. While

308

every other garden on Seaview Terrace was muted in the autumn months, hers retained colour. She never bothered with coffins. At least that way their lives had not been in vain. Their lovely, overfed bodies were the greatest fertiliser her plants had ever known.

'Still there, Mrs Rodgers?'

'I am, Father.'

'Well, so are the keys. I've got yours right here.' The soft jangle travelled down the receiver.

'Okay, Father, thank you for checking. I'll see you at mass on Sunday.'

'By the grace of God,' said Fr O'Shea, in what was more Irish pessimism than religious blessing.

Mrs Rodgers walked out into her back garden and looked up in the direction of the Maguires' home. If Albert was there, could it be that he'd gone of his own volition? When she thought about all their evenings, eating meat and cheese boards in front of marathon runs of *The Chase* – well, it was almost too much to bear.

....

'Two minutes. Literally, two minutes and then you get the fuck out of my house, boy.'

Ella wrapped her arms tightly across her chest as she stood in the middle of her bedroom. She'd never cursed at him before, not in a serious way. He stayed where he was, right inside her door, arms hanging uselessly by his side. He didn't dare go any further. He was so glad to see her, even if she refused to look at him, even if he'd just risked being shot as she snuck him up the stairs. Ella's father had inherited a military collection of guns, and you could just tell Beverley would have a killer aim.

'Thanks for seeing me. I really appreciate it,' he said, like she was a doctor who'd fitted him in for an early check-up.

'One minute, forty-five seconds.'

She'd finally answered one of his calls. He'd promised it wasn't about him. He needed to talk to her about Woody. He was worried, and there was nobody else.

'You're not wearing your A and E necklace.' He looked around the room, deciding that if he could see it, if it was still here, then all hope was not lost. He scanned the bedposts, the hooks above her desk, but nothing. 'It's not what you think with Mrs Murphy, Fiona, your mom's friend. I barely kissed her – I mean, I didn't kiss her at all. She kissed me, but barely. And I didn't kiss her back. I couldn't. It was barely a second and then I pushed her off.'

'One and a half minutes.'

'I should have messaged you back straight away, I know, but I wanted to tell you about it and I was just trying to figure out how, and then I had to visit my dad and there was all this stuff with Woody, and then your mom came to my house' – her eyes widened at this, but he ploughed on; he didn't want to miss his one chance to explain – 'and she seemed to think something more had happened, like maybe we slept together or something mental like that, but I don't know where she got that idea, because I would never, I could never ...'

Sweet Jesus, Arly, do not cry.

Leo's voice righted him. He hadn't heard from him in days.

'I wouldn't even have let her get that close, if it wasn't for Woody. She knew he'd been sexting other girls in the class and I wanted her to keep it to herself. I mean, it's too late now because everybody knows, but that's the only reason I let her, even for a second ...'

Eyes cold, she didn't budge.

'I'm so sorry, Ella.'

'You promised you were here to talk about Woody.'

'I am.'

'Well, if you don't start talking about him, I'm going to open that door and scream down to my parents that there's a boy in my bedroom – a *Whitehead* boy.'

The scorn hit him in the chest, and it was worse than people phoning their house and telling them to move, worse even than being spat at on the street. He wanted to sink into the carpet and disappear.

'Did you hear about the pictures? About all the other girls, not just Amelia? Woody was exchanging nudes with all these girls in his class. I mean, I know you and me sent ...' She was looking at him now, but it was not a regard he welcomed. He cleared his throat. 'But he's twelve, and so many girls. That's not normal, is it? And he's always on his own, in his room, playing computer games. Why wasn't I more alarmed by that? My dad asked me to look after him and I'm fucking up, Ella. I am fucking everything up.'

There was silence, and he thought she was going to leave it there, his desperation hanging in the air.

'Talk to him.'

'I don't know how.'

'Of course you do. You're close.'

Arlo shook his head.

'You said he was the most important person in your life.'

'When did I say that?'

'In your fifth-year religion essay. You said you knew him better than anyone else.'

311

He blushed at the memory of that essay being read aloud in school. He couldn't believe she remembered. 'Not any more. I've been avoiding him for months – I've been avoiding everything and everyone in my house. What am I supposed to do? Just waltz into his bedroom now and ask him why he's become some sort of weird sex fiend?'

'I wouldn't phrase it like that but yeah, basically.'

'I can't. I know it's pathetic, but just thinking about it makes me want to die of embarrassment. I can't do it. I'm too much of a wimp.'

'You're not a wimp, Arlo,' she said reluctantly, her arms loosening slightly. She sighed. 'Look, what you need to do is channel Bev. Whenever I have to do something I don't want to do, I just pretend I'm my mother. She sees the thing that needs to be done, and she does it. She can be rude, but she gets shit done. And she does it straight away. She says you should start the day with the task you least want to do and, loath as I am to ever take her advice, it's a pretty good philosophy.'

'So, talk to Woody in the morning?'

'Not just any morning; tomorrow morning. If it wasn't so late, I'd say go home and do it now, but yeah, first thing in the morning. Now get out of my house.'

Arlo knocked on the bedroom door and waited. It was barely 7 a.m. and already the low rumble of gunfire and general warfare emanated from the other side. He knocked again. Then he let himself in.

His little brother was in his pyjamas, sitting in his usual position, on the carpet with his back against the foot of the bed, eyes focused on the lifelike military forces doing battle on the Whiteheads' old TV set. He leaned slightly to the right, pressing down hard on the controller, and furrowed his brow.

'I don't think you're supposed to be playing games this early.'

'I'm not allowed to play them before school,' corrected Woody, leaning forward now. 'But I'm not going to school today. I'm off all week.'

'You're not off. You're suspended.'

'Yeah, I know.'

'Well, it's a bit different.'

The boy made no further sound until something exploded on the screen, the muted colours reverberated, and the action stopped. 'That's so sly! I almost had him!'

'Can I talk to you for a minute?'

'Yeah, I just have one more life left and then ...'

The screen burst into motion again, text appearing at the top as the man in camouflage began to jog. Arlo could feel his insides tensing. It would be too easy to turn and leave, to say he'd be back into him later.

He walked across the room, so he was standing to the side of the old television. 'Now, Woody.'

'It'll only take two secs—'

'Now!'

His brother looked up at him, mouth slightly open. This was not a dynamic they were used to. Even when they had been closer, he had always been Woody's ally, not his disciplinarian. Arlo wasn't a father figure; he was a big brother.

Woody hit a button on the remote and the whole screen went dark.

Arlo pushed some of the clothes, including the Glass Lake uniform, from the armchair in the corner of the room and sat. Woody scrambled up on to the bed, his legs tucked under him.

'Is – is everything okay? Did something bad happen? Is it you? Is it Mom?'

'No, it's you, Woody. I want to talk about you. Okay?'

Arlo was stalling, trying to figure out how to address the matter. He tried to imagine what his father would say, but all he could hear was Charlie Whitehead's instruction, that Arlo look after his mother and brother. This was his responsibility. He couldn't channel his father any more than he could channel Beverley Franklin.

'I want to talk about the photos of the girls in your class and the graffiti on your teacher's coat. I don't understand why you would do those things. It doesn't make sense to me.'

Woody regarded him blankly.

'Why did you do them?'

'I just did.'

'You just did? That's it? No greater reason than, 'cause I felt like it.'

'Not really.' Woody picked up the controller and turned it around in his hands before tossing it aside again.

'You just really wanted to see the other kids in your class naked, your friends?'

Woody cringed.

'You wanted to see them all naked?'

'No,' said his brother.

'Well, that's what you got. Do you fancy them? I didn't even think you were into girls yet. And now apparently you're into them all.'

'I'm not.' Woody's face started to go that familiar shade of red.

'Well, why else would you send them a nude of yourself and ask them to send one back?'

'Stop.'

'What? I'm just asking a question. And why would you write something so cruel on your teacher's jacket? Do you even know what "pedo" means?'

'Yes.'

'Well, why would you write it, then? Do you think it's true? Did your teacher do something to someone that he shouldn't have? Did someone say something?'

'Stop.'

'I just don't understand. And I have to say I'm worried. I am. How could I not be? This isn't the kind of person I thought you were.'

'Don't be worried,' said Woody, starting to look worried himself.

'I can't help it. It's been a shit year, for all of us, but you're not making it easier. I'm ashamed, to be honest. It's hard for me in this town, for all of us, and you're not making it easier.'

'I'm sorry.'

'I thought you were a kind boy.'

'I am.'

'So then why did you do it? You're better than this.'

Woody's eyes were wide. He blinked and Arlo waited, but no explanation was forthcoming.

'Why did you do it?'

'I didn't want to.'

'So then why did you?'

'I had to.'

'Woody,' he chastised.

'I did. She told me to.'

'Who did? Who's she? Amelia Franklin?'

'No, not Amelia. Ruth.'

'Who's Ruth?'

'This woman I do missions with sometimes. On the PlayStation.'

'But who is she? How do you know her?'

'I just know her from the games. She told me to send a photo of myself to the girls in my class and to get them to send me one in return. I didn't want to, but she made me. I said they wouldn't do it, but she said they would. She said they liked me. I didn't even look at the photos, not really. They made me feel bad. I just sent them to her.'

'Sent them to her how?'

'By email.'

'So, you have her email?'

Woody picked up the remote and the screen came alive. He manoeuvred his way into the settings with the controller. 'There. That's it.'

Arlo stood up from the chair to get a better look at the screen:

| BabeRuth_66@eircom.net

'That's how I know her name's Ruth.' The boy shrugged. 'And I guess she's a babe.'

When Arlo didn't respond immediately, Woody took it as him being out of complaints. 'See?' he said, happier now. 'It's not actually a big deal. The pictures weren't even for me. So, you don't need to worry.'

'This is a big deal. A huge deal. A stranger asked you for naked photos of your friends and you sent them to him?'

'Her. It's a girl. Her name is Ruth.'

'Babe Ruth isn't a girl, he's ...' Arlo shook his head. It didn't matter. He couldn't even remember what sport Babe Ruth was famous for, but he was fairly sure he was dead.

'And it's not a real person,' enthused Woody. 'It's just someone on the internet.'

'Of course it's a real person!' Arlo's mind was racing, trying to piece it together. There was something familiar about this. *Babe Ruth* ... 'Why would you do it? Why would you do something so irresponsible and dangerous just because some stranger asked you to?'

The relief left his brother's face.

'Woody?'

'I can't tell you.'

'What do you mean you can't tell me. Of course you can.'

He shook his head.

'Tell me right now, Woody.'

But the head just kept turning.

'All right, grand. I'll just go call Mom and get her to turn around. She's probably not at work yet. You can tell her.'

'No, don't tell Mom!'

Arlo had no intention of telling their mother. She wouldn't know what to do with this information. She wouldn't be able to handle it. There was a good chance it would break her.

'If you don't want to tell Mom, then you better tell me.'

Woody winced. 'You'll get mad.'

'I won't,' he said, convincing neither of them.

'I really don't want to ...'

'And I really don't care.'

Woody groaned. 'Babe Ruth said that if I didn't get the photos and send them on, she'd tell the police who was really driving the night Mike died. She'd tell them it wasn't Dad and that he was just covering ... for you.' Woody looked up at his brother, eyes cartoon wide again.

Arlo felt dizzy.

'I did it for you,' clarified Woody.

'Please don't say that.' *Please don't let that be true.*

'Babe Ruth said you'd go to jail, and so would Mom for perversing the course of justice ...'

'Perverting,' Arlo corrected, pointlessly.

'And then I'd be on my own and I'd probably be put into care and I really don't want that. I don't want you or Mom or anyone else to go to jail. I don't want to be on my own.'

'You won't be, Woody. Why would you believe what some crazy

person on the internet says? Why would you believe there was anything to what they were saying?'

'Because I know it's true. I heard you all talking the morning after the crash. I was getting ready for school and I was at the top of the stairs and you didn't know I was listening, but I was. I heard you arguing with Dad. You were begging him to tell the truth, that it wasn't fair for him to go to jail for someone else's mistakes, for your fucked-up judgement – sorry for cursing, but that's what you said – and Dad said he was confessing and that was the end of it. I heard it all.'

The frantic energy had pushed Woody further along the mattress, inch by inch, and he was now perched on the edge of the bed.

'But how would *they* know that?' Arlo turned his attention back to the computer screen, where the email address shone in white. Only five living people knew that Charlie Whitehead had gone to jail for an offence he hadn't committed, and none of those people would breathe a word about it. 'How could some stranger possibly know what happened that night?'

Unless they weren't a stranger.

Arlo worked his way through the five people who knew the truth: him, his Dad, Leo—

Six.

His former best friend's voice rang in his ears.

What are you on about, boy?

Six people know what happened on Reilly's Pass. It's six now. You're forgetting about little Woody here. He doesn't have all the facts, but he has enough.

He wouldn't tell anyone.

Eh, I know he's your little bro and all, but he sent those images of children across the internet without a second's thought. I think it might possibly be a question worth asking.

His brother was still perched on the edge of the bed, watching him.

'Woody, did you tell anyone else about what you heard me and Dad discussing the morning after the crash? That Dad wasn't the one driving that night?'

'No.'

So then how? Had someone just taken a lucky guess? It would still have to be someone who knew Woody, who knew about the crash, that he was vulnerable—

'I only told one person, and that doesn't count because they're a responsible adult.'

Arlo looked at his brother, whose face contained none of the confidence of his voice. 'Who?' he asked.

'He said he wouldn't tell anyone. It was when Dad went to jail and I was extra upset. I was in school, waiting for Mom to collect me, but it was one of the days she forgot, and I might have been crying, maybe, and he asked what was wrong, and I told him. I didn't want you to go to jail, Arlo. He was really nice about it and he said he wouldn't tell anyone. He was a responsible adult. In fifth class we did this thing about stranger danger, and the teacher said if we were worried, about anything, we should identify a responsible adult to tell.'

'Who was it, Woody?'

His brother looked at him and swallowed. Arlo felt a dull thud in his stomach.

'Was it your teacher?' he asked.

Woody winced.

'Was it Mr Cafferty?'

'No,' said the boy, his still-forming Adam's apple quivering. 'And anyway, Babe Ruth definitely isn't Mr Cafferty using a fake name, if that's what you're thinking, because this person hates Mr Cafferty.'

'What? How do you know that?'

'They made me do all that stuff about the coat and being mean to Mr Cafferty and getting the other kids to be mean too, like Maeve making prank phone calls ...'

Arlo hadn't a clue what his brother was on about.

'Babe Ruth said I had to send on the photos and I had to make Mr Cafferty quit his job, or else they'd tell everyone about the crash and you and Mom would go to jail and I'd be to blame. I felt bad about the pictures because they're my friends and—'

'Woody!'

'What?'

'Who was the person at Glass Lake that you told about the car crash?'

Woody blinked, so far forward on the bed now that he had to hold on to the edges to stop himself falling onto the floor. And suddenly, Arlo realised.

All those drawings on Seamus's workshop walls, several of him playing games consoles, because the caretaker bonded with the kids over a love of Xbox and PlayStation, and the baseball cards framed around his kitchenette, all depicting images of the same man, dressed in stripes and wearing a baseball cap.

He remembered then what sport Babe Ruth had played.

'It was Caretaker Seamus,' said Woody, just as Arlo could have said the same thing. 'I told Caretaker Seamus about the crash.'

....

321

Supplementary questioning, conducted by Garda Joey Delaney

Frank Cafferty, teacher

I was at the school all day yesterday. I was doing some additional movement work with some of the kids after classes, and that ran right into all the parents arriving. I never left the building.

Garda Joey Delaney

I heard you handed in a letter of resignation yesterday. Is that true?

Cafferty

You heard about that? Already? Jesus, I'm used to living in towns where people talk, but here, you all have access to so much information. Yes, I gave a letter of resignation to Principal Patterson yesterday morning and she asked me to take the week to reconsider.

Delaney

Why did you resign? You haven't been in the job long.

Cafferty

Personal reasons.

Delaney

Did it have anything to do with Seamus McGrath?
A couple of witnesses have suggested there was
animosity between you two.

Cafferty

It wasn't to do with Seamus. Well, maybe a
little bit, I'm not sure, but no. It was
personal. Is it relevant?

Delaney

Potentially.

Cafferty

It was … I'm … Well, if you must know, I'm gay.
I don't tend to shout it from the rooftops, but
if it's really relevant … My husband, Jess,
would say I'm ashamed of my sexuality. That's
not true; I just don't always feel the need to
correct people if they make assumptions that
aren't entirely accurate. It's not like I call
him 'my wife' but Jess is a unisex name, you
know, and if people think one thing, what do I
care? I'm not ashamed of myself, or of him, but
when you've been a teacher in a tiny country
school that feels like it's stuck in the 1950s
… Did you know that over 80 per cent of LGBT
teachers in Ireland keep their sexuality a
secret? That's an official statistic. I'm in a
few online support forums and even there, most

of us use pseudonyms. People think things have
changed in Ireland, and maybe they have in the
big cities, but not everywhere, and definitely
not at my last school. It was only about 200
miles from here, but it was decades away too.
I was practically chased out when the parents
found out I was married to a man. I thought
Glass Lake would be different, but similar
things started happening. I was getting prank
phone calls and one of the students wrote 'pedo'
on my coat and, not to sound too millennial
about it, but it was fairly triggering. So, I
decided to leave. I mean, I'm reassessing that
now. Jess thinks I should stay and Principal
Patterson wants me to, which is nice, and the
phone calls have stopped, and Woody, the kid
who wrote on my coat, sent me a really lovely
apology note, which I received this morning.
That was great because we did get on well, at
the beginning. I don't know what happened there.
And I really do love my job, the kids are great.
So anyway, we'll see.

Delaney
And what was the connection to Seamus McGrath?
You said it had something to do with him.

Cafferty
No, I said maybe it did. I don't know, and I
have zero proof. But I got a feeling off him

324

… that he didn't like me, I guess. The first time we met, it was fine, but then one day I was queuing behind him in Regan's Chemist, to print out some photos. They have one of those booths where you connect your phone and it will print out whichever images you select. Seamus was using the machine and I was waiting. I was looking through my phone; I wasn't looking over his shoulder or anything. But when he was done, I looked up, and he was glaring at me. He snapped at me for standing so close, even though I was metres behind. Ever since then, he's been cold with me. He's made it clear he's not comfortable with my sexuality. I know you're supposed to be the bigger person and rise above bigotry, but have you ever tried it? It's exhausting.

Delaney

Did you argue about this?

Cafferty

No, never.

Delaney

Did you argue about anything else?

Cafferty

Not at all. It was clear he didn't like me, but I never challenged him on it. I hadn't a thing to do with his drowning. He was a bigot and

paranoid – what photos could possibly have been
that frickin' private? – but I am sorry he's
dead. It must be very hard on his family.

36

ONE DAY EARLIER

Beverley had delivered the second wake-up call of the morning and now had her laptop and tablet out side by side on the kitchen's central island as she waited for Amelia to appear downstairs. She was comparing two near identical, and pointedly negative, Facebook reviews for Sneaky Sweets. The timing of the reviews – shortly after yesterday's yoga class – and their personal nature had her suspecting Fiona Murphy.

Amelia's footsteps on the stairs told her she did not need to disturb herself to answer the door. It was probably the DPD man. Beverley was a staunch supporter of shopping local, but if Gerry Regan refused to stock non-comedogenic facial cleanser, she didn't see what choice she had.

She added her phone to the tech hub and began scrolling through old WhatsApp messages to see if her fellow Laker had form on using the word 'omnishambles'.

'Mum!'

Still scrolling, Beverley slid off the stool. All the child had to do was sign for the package.

'Mum!' Amelia called again when she was halfway across the kitchen. 'Arlo Whitehead is at the door!'

Beverley paused, then powered ahead, cutting the kitchen-to-front-door journey time to what might be expected in a basic semi-d. She yanked the door away from her daughter. She could barely believe it, but there he was, standing on her doorstep with that eyesore of a van back up and running and blighting their driveway. He may not have been a complete gigolo after all, but he was still a Whitehead.

'Are you lost?'

'No,' he began.

'Or have you suffered a concussion? That's the only reason I can think for why you would be knocking on my door.'

'Mrs Franklin—'

'Ella isn't here, if that's what you're after.'

'I'm here to see you.'

Beverley hooted. 'You are not. And if you don't leave now, I'll phone my husband.' An empty threat, of course. Malachy would tell her to take the boy in from the doorstep and stop making a scene.

'Mrs Franklin, could I just talk to you for a couple of minutes? Please.' The teenager glanced down at Amelia, who was watching the exchange like she was umpiring a particularly embarrassing tennis match. 'Just you, if that would be okay.'

He was paler than usual, none of his rosiness, and he was looking her in the eye – something she wasn't sure he'd done before. Against her better judgement, she opened the door a fraction more.

'Go into the kitchen and get some breakfast, Amelia.'

She waited until her daughter had crossed the foyer and disappeared through the door on the far side. Then, reluctantly, she took a half-step backwards. Arlo stepped inside.

'Shoes off. Actually, no,' she said, as he bent down to undo the laces. 'Keep them on.' She believed Fiona when she said the whole thing with Arlo had been one of her fabrications, but that didn't change the fact that Ella was barely sleeping. She'd heard her daughter pottering around on the top floor last night, and this morning she had left for university about an hour earlier than usual. This lad had the gall to think he was good enough for Ella – and then he had the audacity to break her heart. There was something far too intimate about him walking around their home in socks. 'You can step into the drawing room. It's this way,' she said, veering him to the left. 'Although, what am I saying? You could probably give me a tour of my own house at this stage.'

She closed the door behind him, checking before she did so that Amelia had not reappeared from the kitchen.

'So, what is it?' she said, positioning herself in the centre of the room. She didn't invite the teenager to sit. He wouldn't be staying.

'I'm not sure where to start ...'

'I've got ten minutes before I drop Amelia to school, so you'd better figure it out.'

'It's about the photos Amelia and the other girls sent to Woody – except they weren't sending them to Woody, not really ...' And then he told her the worst thing she had heard in a long time. He talked quickly and clumsily, falling over certain words and abandoning sentences only to start them again, but he got the details out.

'Seamus McGrath?' she echoed.

'Yes,' he said uncertainly, and she realised she was a few sentences behind him.

She nodded and he continued. He told her how the school caretaker had come to contact Woody, that he had blackmailed him with some unspecified threat, and made the child send on all the photos of the girls. Seamus McGrath was looking at those photos. Seamus McGrath was looking at a naked photo of her beautiful, ambitious, confident daughter. Seamus McGrath, the school caretaker, a man well into his fifties, had all those photos.

The teenager explained how he didn't know what to do, how he was technically an adult but didn't feel like one, and how Ella had told him that Beverley always knew what to do. His dad had been like that, he said, but since he wasn't around any more, he'd come to her. He thought Beverley was the kind of person he needed. He knew she wasn't his biggest fan, but Glass Lake was important to her and obviously Amelia was important to her and maybe she'd know what to do.

'Do you know what to do?'

'I just have to think ...' she replied, though instinctively she knew exactly what to do. She would get in her car and drive around Cooney in circles until she saw Seamus McGrath crossing the road on Main Street or pulling into the hardware shop down by the pier, then she would mount the pavement and run him over. Or perhaps she would wait until he was at the top of a ladder, fixing the spotlights on the auditorium stage, and she would charge across the stage and topple the thing, sending him crashing to his death. The details were vague, but the outcome was clear: she would kill him.

'I thought about going to the guards but they're not big fans of our family. A lot of them are in the GAA club and they weren't too happy when Mike Roche Senior moved away. Anyway, it would be too hard to prove. It's just an email address – how can I prove that Seamus was the one operating it? Even though I know he was. Maybe we could get a confession? What do you think about that? Mrs Franklin? Do you think we could get him to confess?'

'I'm thinking ...'

It was not the photo she had walked in on Amelia taking that she saw in her mind's eye, but rather the framed one in the living room, the one of Amelia in her school uniform, her navy stockings pulled right up to the hem of her skirt, and grinning so widely you could see her missing tooth. Seamus McGrath had taken that.

Arlo ran through their various options, but none fit the bill. There was nothing for it but to get rid of the depraved man. It was almost serene, this visceral realisation. She'd gone from nought to ready to kill in a matter of seconds, and she was fine with it. She knew now that this was what her mother was talking about. This was the defining point in her life, the one she would recollect on her death bed and know she had done what was right, the one where she was led by love for her children and a desire to protect the vulnerable.

'Mrs Franklin?'

'Yes,' she replied in that same sharp, defensive tone she used when they were at a Lakers meeting and Claire caught her daydreaming.

'What ... what should I do?'

'You'll leave it to me.'

Arlo nodded, waiting for her to say more.

'It's Wednesday now so ... today. I'm at the school this evening. It's the last night of preparations before opening night tomorrow.'

'I'll be there too,' said Arlo. 'It's my last few hours' work with Glass Lake. Seamus has me helping with lights and some other bits. Will we talk to him then? But there'll be a lot of other people around. Maybe it'd be better to confront him somewhere more private? If we want to get a confession? But then I don't know where. He's not at the school today. He's out collecting some final set pieces. I'm not sure where he is exactly ...'

'This evening at Glass Lake will be fine,' declared Beverley.

Amelia was in danger of being late for school, and she had a lot to organise. 'I'll see you then, Arlo.' She stood from her stool and walked the teenager to the door. 'We'll keep this between ourselves, all right? It's only another few hours, and it won't help to tell anyone else. Is that—' She peered out the glass panel, but she had imagined the sound of her daughter's hand-me-down banger pulling up. 'So, we're agreed? We'll keep it between us?'

So used was she to getting her own way that Beverley took this to be a closed matter. Nobody else was to know. She didn't notice that the teenager hadn't responded; she didn't know that Arlo had one other confidant in mind.

37

......

ABERSTOWN GARDA STATION

Joey had felt sure today would bring a development, maybe even a resolution, but there was fifteen minutes left in his shift and he was no closer to understanding why Seamus McGrath had ended up in the River Gorm than he had been this morning. He'd chased his one lead and it had led to nothing. Frank Cafferty had been at the school all yesterday and he'd been surrounded by witnesses the whole time. What had he expected? That the mild-mannered teacher had pushed the unremarkable janitor to his death because they hadn't gotten on particularly well?

The clock above the station exit ticked loudly and Joey watched the second hand make its journey around the face. The sergeant still wasn't back from visiting Miriam McGrath and Joey had done every scrap of work he could think to do. He was just reaching for the pen jar – a few biros were wearing the wrong colour lids – when the phone rang. Joey dived for it.

'Aberstown Station,' he said breathlessly, just as the double doors pushed open and Whelan lumbered in from the cold.

'This is Sergeant Mulhern. Is Sergeant Whelan about?'

'He's ...'

333

Whelan was about two feet from him now, slowly removing his hat and reaching up to the coat stand.

'I'll just check ... Can I tell him what it's about?'

'News on Seamus McGrath.'

Joey's heart soared, then sank. Couldn't this man have called two minutes earlier? Or couldn't his sergeant have stopped for another sandwich?

'Are you phoning from pathology?'

'Forensics. Is the sergeant about or not?'

Reluctantly, Joey held out the receiver. 'A call from forensics, sir. News on Seamus.'

His boss took the phone. 'Sergeant James Whelan,' he said, lowering himself into the chair.

The younger guard tried to hear what was being said down the line. But all he got was the creak of the sergeant's battered chair as he rotated it towards the desk.

'And they've done a thorough search?' said Whelan, after an eternity of listening. He swung the chair again, so he now had his back to Joey. 'No, I understand. Yes, I agree. Not what you'd want, but still. That does seem to settle the matter.'

38

THE EVENING BEFORE

On her third visit in almost as many weeks, Christine Maguire found the Glass Lake auditorium to be in a whole new state of disarray. It was the evening before opening night – officially the worst time of year to find yourself in the place – and the parents were frantically charging about the hall just as their children had done a week ago. Claire Keating's husband was arguing with Mr Peoples, the choirmaster, while banging something out on the piano, and Beverley was lecturing several sheepish-looking parents on the stage. They may not have been dressed head to toe in the same colour, but the scene was oddly familiar.

She glanced around the auditorium, but there was no sign of Connie Whitehead. She had been feeling uneasy since Maeve's confession on Monday afternoon and while she wanted to make her daughter own up to the prank phone calls and apologise, she also couldn't help thinking about the why of it all. What had Mr Cafferty done that Woody was so eager to get rid of him? She didn't want to add to Connie's hardship, potentially over nothing, but it would be irresponsible to not at least voice her concerns to an adult member of the Whitehead family. She had been hoping to mention it to her, in a semi-casual way, this evening.

There was a roster board in the middle of the hall, but there was no sign of Connie's name. Christina found her own name and headed over to Mrs Walsh. Glass Lake's oldest staff member was standing before six towering stacks of plastic chairs and two towering mothers.

'If you could just start to place some of these in rows ...' the Junior Infants' teacher was saying, in what was clearly not her first plea.

'I'm not putting out a single chair until someone gives me a good reason why my son can't be the Munchkin mayor.'

'My God, woman. There is no Munchkin mayor,' snapped Lorna Farrell. 'Beverley made it clear that this production is based on the book, not the film. There is no mayor in the book.'

'I do not see the harm in letting my son wear a gold chain on stage,' said the other woman, ignoring Lorna and beseeching Mrs Walsh. 'We ordered it especially, paid for fast-track delivery and everything, and we've been doing character development for weeks now. He's sitting on the floor at dinner time because, as a Munchkin, he's too short to make it on to the seats, and he's dreaming about chairing council meetings. The child is committed!'

'Sounds more like he should be committed,' muttered Lorna.

'Ladies, please, we need to get these chairs out and in rows,' begged Mrs Walsh. 'I'd lift them myself if it wasn't for my trapped nerves. Christine, dear! Hello! Could you start putting out the chairs ...? Please?'

'Of course, Mrs Walsh,' she said, pulling a plastic seat from the top of the pile. She placed it down beside her and gave the auditorium another quick search. 'Has anyone seen Connie Whitehead?'

'Thank you, Christine, but the row actually starts at the other—'

'Connie Whitehead doesn't volunteer,' scoffed Lorna. 'Especially not now her son has been kicked out of the musical.'

'So she's not coming?'

'The chairs, ladies, please!'

Christina took a chair from a separate pile and started a row going in the other direction. She had about five of them lined up when the double doors opened at the back of the hall and Arlo appeared, looking slightly frazzled.

He was an adult, technically – and speaking to him about it was better than nothing.

Mrs Walsh blocked her path. 'Don't go.'

'I'll just be a minute. I'll be back.'

'If you go, they'll go. Please. I can't put the chairs out myself. My back can't handle it.' The teacher looked up at her imploringly.

'I ...'

The double doors opened again, and she glanced over in time to see Arlo disappearing back out into the corridor. Beverley was down off the stage and hot on his heels. Whatever set design drama she wanted him for could wait until Christine had had a quick word.

'I'm sorry, Mrs Walsh, I really am. I'll be right back,' she called as she jogged off across the hall, side-stepping an argument about camera positions as she made her way out into the corridor.

'Arlo!' she called.

The teenager, who was halfway down the corridor, stopped. Beverley also turned. Then, Beverley started moving again, pulling the teenager with her. This was not a pairing Christine had expected. Just that afternoon, when she called to Butcher Murphy's to get some lamb, she heard that Arlo and Ella Franklin had been

337

secretly dating for months and that Beverley had just found out. So, unless Beverley was leading the teenager somewhere to do away with him ...

She ran to catch up with them. 'Can I speak to you for a minute, Arlo?'

'Is it about your cat?'

'Hmm? Oh no, that's all fine. It's about Woody, actually, and my daughter ...'

'Photos?'

'No ...'

'Come on,' said Beverley, pulling the teenager again. 'We haven't time.'

'This is actually quite important, Beverley. If I could speak to Arlo in private for a minute ...'

'And what we're doing is actually quite important too. Come on,' she said again.

'Can I find you later, Mrs Maguire?' the teenager said, turning so he was walking backwards away from her.

'This isn't really the sort of thing that can wait,' she said, following them.

'I'm sorry, but we are in the middle of something.'

'Maeve has been prank phoning Mr Cafferty,' she said, annoyed that she'd been given no option but to have this conversation in front of Beverley. 'She's been doing it at Woody's behest. She said Woody was trying to get Mr Cafferty to quit his job.'

'Please, Mrs Maguire, could we talk about this later?'

'Don't you think that's worrying? That your brother would want his teacher to quit his job that badly? I mean, what could he possibly have done?'

She couldn't be sure, but she was pretty sure Beverley rolled her eyes.

'Arlo!'

The teenager stopped again. 'I'm really sorry Maeve got caught up in this. It won't happen again.'

'I'm not worried about Maeve. I'm telling you because of Woody. You don't seem concerned. Would I be better speaking with your mother?'

'No, don't do that!' Arlo glanced at Beverley. What was going on with these two? 'I already knew about the calls. I only found out this morning, and I am sorry Maeve was involved, but it's not what you think, and … we're taking care of it.'

'That's enough,' muttered Beverley, as they came to a halt outside Caretaker Seamus's workroom.

'I have to go,' he said apologetically. 'But thank you for letting me know. And you don't need to worry. Thank you but—'

'Ready?' asked Beverley, hand on the knob. Then she pushed the door and disappeared inside.

'Sorry,' said Arlo again. 'Thanks for the heads-up.'

And he, too, was gone.

Christine looked back down the corridor, then peered through the small window in the workroom door, but there was some sort of translucent paper stuck to the other side and she couldn't see in. She felt a wave of irritation at the entitled way Beverley was commanding the teenager and (in spite of her commitment to never becoming too interested in Glass Lake goings-on) an itching curiosity to know what exactly this unlikely duo were up to.

She might not be up for writing sensationalist news stories, but she was still a journalist. It was her job – no, her *duty* – to be nosy.

'Feck it,' she said under her breath, and she pushed the workroom door open.

....

'Where is he? Where's Seamus?'

Beverley had stormed through the door, all guns blazing, ready for an almighty showdown with the Glass Lake caretaker.

Instead, she was faced with the Glass Lake principal.

'What are you doing here?'

Nuala Patterson barely blinked. 'This is my school, Beverley.'

The door opened behind Beverley, and the principal's face changed. It didn't make sense – because it was Arlo Whitehead who had entered the room – but she could have sworn it softened.

'Where's Seamus?' the teenager demanded, coming to a stop between her and the principal. Whatever about the tone Beverly had used, Nuala wasn't going to accept *that* from a Whitehead.

But when the principal spoke, she sounded apologetic. 'He's not here,' she said. 'I already spoke to him.'

'But we agreed.'

'I know. I'm sorry, Arlo. But I didn't want you getting mixed up in anything else. I took it upon myself. I've dealt with Seamus.'

'What does that mean?'

'He won't be coming back,' said Nuala.

Even though Beverley had been on the verge of murdering the man this morning, she felt a shiver run down her spine. This whole bizarre situation had gone up a notch. Arlo had told someone else about what was going on, despite her ordering him not to. And he'd told Nuala, of all people. Since when did these two speak to each

340

other, let alone in courteous, apologetic tones? Nuala was talking like she was the one who owed Arlo something.

Beverley looked at the teenager, waiting for him to ask some of the many, obvious, follow-up questions. When he did not, she took it upon herself to interrupt this bizarrely cosy chat.

'Okay,' she said, raising a hand, like she was back in school, 'someone needs to fill me in on what's going on here – and quickly.'

'Yeah,' said a voice from behind her, and she spun around to find that Christine Maguire had followed them into the room. 'I was about to say the same thing.'

39

Nuala Patterson's mind had been racing for several hours now. From the moment Arlo had appeared in her office earlier today, she had felt like she was floating outside her own body.

Seamus McGrath. The Glass Lake caretaker. *Her* caretaker. The man she had hired and trusted with so many jobs at the school. Seamus who opened the school in the morning and locked it at night, who fixed everything that needed fixing, who built the sets for the annual musical and took the class photos. Glass Lake was Nuala's school, it was her responsibility, and she had taken her eye off the ball. Had she been so distracted by her personal dramas that she hadn't realised what a perverted man was working under her roof?

There was a chance, she had told herself when Arlo had left her office under the false promise that she would sit tight until that evening, that he had got it wrong.

She held out hope as she checked the staff location planner, told Mairead she had to head into town on urgent business, and drove down to the hardware shop on Cooney Pier. It was possible, she told herself as she tapped on the steering wheel, waiting for the caretaker to appear, that Arlo had put two and two together and come up with the most unsavoury number.

But in her heart of hearts, something about it rang true.

Seamus's van pulled in about three cars down and Nuala hopped out. The caretaker had just shut his own door when he clocked the principal heading towards him. He was carrying a large empty paint tin and splattered crowbar.

'Everything all right?'

'I need to speak to you.'

Seamus kept his eyes on her as he locked the van. 'Beverley finally signed off on a yellow-enough yellow for the brick road, so I'm just picking up another couple of tins for the final coat.' She must have looked how she felt because the man stuffed his keys into his pockets and, face sombre, stepped away from the road and into the narrow laneway between the hardware shop and the credit union. He placed the crowbar and tin at his feet. 'Everything all right, Nuala?' he asked again.

Her plan had been to tell him what was alleged and to ask if it was true. But now that she was here, and she was regarding him in a whole new light, she abandoned that tack, and went instead with foregone conclusion.

She told the caretaker that she knew what had been going on. She made it sound like several concrete sources had come to her, as opposed to one uncertain teenager, and she put forward the extrapolations as facts. They knew he had been messaging Woody and befriending him under a pseudonym; they knew he had blackmailed the child; they knew he had instructed him to pose nude and to use that image to solicit similar photos from the female students in his class; and they knew the photos were being sent on to Seamus for God knows what purpose.

'Who told you that?'

343

'Like I said, several people.'

A woman with a buggy passed about five feet from them and Seamus turned away from the road. 'Was it Frank Cafferty?'

'I'm not naming names, Seamus.'

The caretaker's temper flared. 'It was, wasn't it? You can't believe him. He's a fairy, Nuala. Did you know that about him?'

Nuala had been hoping for speechless shock, extreme outrage, dogged denial. Even a threat to sue her for slander would have been welcome. If his aim was to come across as innocent, his focus was in the wrong place.

'He might think he saw me printing out certain photos, but he's wrong,' Seamus continued, his face red. 'He was too far away. He couldn't have seen anything. He's let his imagination run away with him. That lot often do. It's for the best he's leaving, if he's going to spread such awful rumours as that.'

'Mr Cafferty never told me anything.' The sixth-class teacher had handed in his resignation that morning but she had yet to accept it. 'Though I do also know you were instructing the boy to make his life difficult. I believe you gave Woody the teacher's mobile phone number. And you told him to write "pedo" on his coat.'

'I never – I – I never ...' Seamus's foot started tapping the damp concrete. He took another couple of glances over his shoulder. 'Prove it,' he said suddenly, defiantly. 'Do you have proof?'

Not 'You don't have proof' or 'You couldn't possibly have proof because it's not true' but 'Do you have proof?'. A self-incriminating question.

'I stopped by your workroom before coming here. I was looking at your framed cards over the kitchen counter.'

'My baseball card collection. So?'

'Babe Ruth,' she all but spat, finding it difficult to look at the man that she had thought was an ally at least, but often a friend. She'd never noticed the cards before and wouldn't have if Arlo hadn't mentioned them. 'I trusted you. I gave you a job and I confided in you. I would have trusted you with anything at this school. Our students, Seamus? It's ...' She flinched. 'You disgust me.'

His foot stopped tapping. His body slumped. His whole demeanour changed.

'I'm sorry. I'm really sorry. I didn't mean to hurt anyone. I didn't hurt anyone. I never touched Woody or any other child. It was all harmless, a sort of joke.'

'A joke? Naked images of our students are a *joke*?'

'No, not a joke. But they weren't ... I wasn't ... I didn't do anything with them. They were only for my use. I printed them off and that was it. I'm rubbish with technology. I didn't upload them to the internet or anything like that. I just ... There's something wrong with me, I can't help it, I know it's not right, but—'

'Enough!' she spat. Even the idea of the photos made her feel physically ill. She did not need to know what went through Seamus's mind when he looked at them. 'You're gone, Seamus.'

'Please, Nuala, no; you can't fire me. I love this job. What would you do without me? Who would build the sets? Opening night is tomorrow and—'

'Of course you're fired! That's the least of it. I'm going to the guards.'

All anger gone from him now, his face drained to white. 'No.'

'Yes.'

'No, no, no, please, please, don't do that. Don't tell anyone. My wife – she wouldn't – it would kill her, and my sister ... I couldn't

345

handle it – all our neighbours, my friends. Oh God. You can't ...'

'I trusted you – with my school, with my students!'

'No, no. I'll ... You can't. Please. My wife has a bad heart, you know that. She couldn't ... The neighbours. She couldn't stand them all talking. I couldn't stand it. You know this place, everyone would know, and they wouldn't even care about the truth, I'd never be allowed to explain my side!'

A heat began to rise. The flames started in her diaphragm and whooshed into her chest, her shoulders, up into her head. Her gaze fell on the items at Seamus's feet. It would be so simple to lift up the crowbar, to swing for the man in his flummoxed, panicked state and send it flying on to the side of his head.

'Please, Nuala. It would kill me.'

She felt her hand relinquishing her waist, reaching down. It was not something she would have thought herself capable of, but now it seemed perfectly reasonable. None of us know the extent of our abilities, until we are pushed to the limit.

•••••••••••••••••••••••

'Jesus Christ, Nuala! I was tempted to kill him myself this morning but come on – what were you thinking?!'

'Oh relax, Beverley,' the principal snapped. 'I didn't bludgeon the bastard! I just contemplated it. I'm only telling you what I was thinking, not what I did.'

'Well, it sounded very convincing from where I was standing.'

'So, what did you do?' asked Arlo, keen to bring this whole thing to a conclusion and get out of here. Nuala had put some sort of baking paper over the small window in the door, but any parent or teacher could easily walk in on them, looking for Seamus to help with some staging issue. Christine Maguire was still standing against the back wall. They'd given her a summary of what was going on and she looked mildly ill. Already far too many people knew. Now they'd thrown a journalist into the mix.

He returned his attention to the woman he'd once thought of as a sort of second mother and asked, yet again: 'Where is Seamus?'

'He's gone to the guards,' replied Nuala. 'I told him I was going to Aberstown Station and he begged me to let him do it.'

'So he's gone by himself? You just took his word for it?' came a voice, Christine's, from the back of the room. 'What if he makes a run for it?'

'He won't.'

'Because he's such an upstanding, trustworthy member of society?'

'Where would he go? And even if he did do a legger, what then? He knows I'd go to the guards and they'd find him eventually.'

'Why are we getting the police involved?' demanded Beverley. 'If the police know, there'll be a full investigation and then everyone in town will know where the children's naked photos really ended up. What good is that going to do anyone?'

'Of course the police have to know,' said Christine.

'Easy for you to say,' Beverley shot back. 'Your daughter wasn't caught up in this thing. How do you think Amelia is going to feel when she finds out the image she thought she was sending to a boy in her class was actually going to a near sixty-year-old man who she thought was an adult she could trust? She'll be scarred for life!'

'If there was another way, I'd have taken it,' began Nuala.

'Of course there was another way!'

'What were you planning to do, Beverley? Hmm? Kill him?'

'I was going to record a confession,' the woman retorted, waving her phone at the principal, 'and use it as blackmail. I was going to run him out of town and ensure he never came back.'

'Oh yes. So just make him someone else's problem?'

'Rather that than it being our children's problem.'

Arlo wasn't particularly thrilled about the guards getting involved either – he didn't want Woody to know who he'd really been sending the photos to and, once they knew his brother was being blackmailed, they'd want to know what information 'Babe Ruth' had on Woody and his family. None of them wanted the investigation into the crash resurfacing.

'When did he say he was going to the guards?' he asked.

'Right after I spoke to him,' said Nuala. 'Around two p.m., I'd say. I watched him jump in his van and go.'

They all glanced towards the clock.

'And have you heard from the guards yet?' asked Christine.

'No,' conceded Nuala. 'But I'm sure I will ...'

Beverley guffawed.

And then, right on cue, the unmistakable wail of a siren began to gather in the distance.

40

'**N**uala.'

Sergeant Whelan was striding down the corridor, hat hanging from his left hand, and his shirt its usual amount of crumpled.

She raised her hand in greeting, turning once to check the others had obeyed her request and were staying put in the workroom. Of course, there was a good chance Sergeant Whelan would want to inspect the workroom, lest it contained some sort of evidence.

'I'm here to see if the school might have a phone number on record. One for Miriam McGrath.'

'Miriam,' repeated Nuala. It made sense they'd want to speak to the wife, but surely Seamus could have given them that. 'Seamus's Miriam?'

The sergeant nodded. 'We swung by the house but she's not in.'

'Doesn't Seamus have a number for her?'

He gave her a peculiar look then he dropped his eyes and fed the rim of his hat through his hands. 'I'm afraid Seamus is the reason we're looking to contact her.'

Nuala nodded, not quite getting what the problem was. If Seamus was in custody then surely they could just ask for the number, or take his phone and retrieve it if he wouldn't oblige.

'I'm sorry to be the bearer of tragic news, Nuala, I know you two were close, but Seamus is dead. His body has just been taken out of the Gorm.'

'His ... He's *dead*?'

The sergeant nodded. 'We've just come from the scene. Pathology are working on an initial assessment now, but his car was spotted out near the bridge on the edge of town about 4 p.m. He must have gone in then ...'

Nuala's head was shaking, while Sergeant Whelan's was nodding. 'Was it ...?' she began.

'We don't know what happened. We're investigating. Foul play looks unlikely and it's possible he fell, it is windy this evening, but it wouldn't be that easy to fall ...' He caught her eye in a way that confirmed the guard's suspicion but didn't force him to speak ill of the dead. It was a lot more noble to have fallen than to have jumped.

Nuala thought back on her conversation with Seamus, on how sure he'd been that he should go to the station alone, and how incapable he'd been of accepting a reality in which he would be known as the man who had done such a terrible thing.

'I should clear the school,' she said, thinking aloud.

'It's not strictly necessary ...'

'We won't be doing the musical now. We can hardly open a show the day after the set builder has died, can we?'

'I suppose not.'

'I'll get you that number from my office,' she said, as she turned and started walking, the sergeant following after her. She glanced in through the double-door windows as they passed the auditorium. 'Then I'll send them all home.'

'You don't have any idea why he might have done this to himself, do you?'

Nuala paused at her office door. This was the moment. This was the point at which she should tell the gardaí exactly what she had been planning to tell them a few hours earlier – she should tell them the very things Seamus had promised to relay before he took the easy way out. But she thought of the others in the workroom, about what it would do to Woody, and the other children, and all their families. What good would it do them to know where their photographs had really ended up? What purpose could it possibly serve now that the person who needed to be punished was no more? What would be the benefit in punishing everyone else instead?

'If he did do it,' the sergeant added. 'Hypothetically.'

'Not an idea,' she said, holding the sergeant's gaze so firmly she almost believed herself. 'I am as shocked as it is possible to be.'

41

ABERSTOWN GARDA STATION

'**That was** Sergeant Mick Mulhern from Cork City forensics,' said Whelan, having hung up the receiver and studied it for a good three seconds.

Joey nodded, hands instinctively going to his belt and hoisting it up.

'He was calling about our DOA ...'

'Yes, Sergeant,' replied Joey, desperate for any information he didn't already have.

'... Seamus McGrath.'

Joey waited.

The sergeant sighed.

Joey waited some more.

'Yah.'

He was doing it on purpose.

Joey forced his hands away from his belt and did his best to look relaxed. *Tell me, don't tell, it's all the same to me.*

He had barely finished thinking this mantra when he was opening his mouth to beg for information. But the sergeant got in just ahead.

'They found a suicide note, in the car. They're sending it through to us now.'

Joey clamped his mouth shut. His hands flew back to his belt. He was ready for action.

'It's short. Addressed to his wife and scrawled on the back of a discarded envelope which, judging by the footprints, had been sitting on the floor of his car for a while. It was the only thing he had to hand, I suppose, but that suggests it wasn't premeditated; that he hadn't gotten up that morning intending to take his own life.'

'What did the note say?'

'I'm sorry to leave you. Please forgive me. I didn't mean any harm.'

'That's it?'

'That's it.' The sergeant made a sound somewhere between a sigh and a growl. 'Didn't mean any harm ... in topping himself? Scant comfort that'll be to his missis, all alone in that house now. She's the nervy type, you know. Doesn't seem to have much of a life, no real friends, doesn't even appear to have full access to their bank accounts. When I was out there today, she told me he couldn't swim.'

'Oh,' said Joey.

'Never learned. She bought him lessons when they first got married, but he didn't go. Too proud, I suppose.'

'So that's why he threw himself in the river? He knew he'd have no way out?'

'Suppose so,' said the sergeant, groaning as he stood from the chair again. 'I guess I'm heading back out to Cooney, amn't I? I'd almost rather be telling her he was pushed. You'd be less likely to take that personally. Can you hang on a few more minutes until Corrigan comes on shift?'

Joey nodded as his superior removed his hat and coat from the stand once again.

'And Delaney?'

'Yes, sir?'

'Put your last few minutes to good use.'

'Yes, Sergeant. Whatever you need.'

'Get a screwdriver from the back office and put another notch in your belt. All day those goddam trousers have been falling down.'

....

Arlo Whitehead, temporary employee

I was working with Seamus for the past couple of weeks. I didn't notice anything out of the ordinary. I can't think of a single reason he might have jumped, or a reason he might have been pushed. He was a very popular man. As far as I know, nobody had a bad word to say about him. Has anyone said a bad word about him?

Beverley Franklin, parent

The last thing he said to me? Mmm ... Oh, yes. He apologised for messing up the paint on the Yellow Brick Road so many times. That was it. He said I was right, and he was wrong and that the colour hadn't been correct, but now it was. I thanked him for the apology and for all his work. We parted on excellent terms.

Christine Maguire, parent

I went looking for him in his workshop yesterday evening, yes. It was for an article I was planning to write on the musical. But he wasn't

there. A few people were looking for him. Which
just shows you how valued a member of our
community he was. Drownings are so tragic. Poor
Seamus. It couldn't have happened to a nicer
man.

Christine Maguire piled costume fabric into her boot as the wind continued to howl. The parents had all left the hall on Principal Patterson's instruction and, around her, they were clambering into their own cars. She saw Beverley approaching from a couple of metres away.

'Don't you think that was strange?'

The wind caught the tail of a roll of blue satin and she grabbed it just before it went sailing out of the boot and across the car park.

'I think I made it clear I thought it was all very strange,' replied Christine.

'It was the best possible outcome,' said Beverley matter-of-factly. 'That barbarian is no more, and my daughter doesn't have to be subjected to police interrogation and neighbourhood gossip over something that was entirely not her fault. It's always the victims that suffer. At least this way, justice was still served.'

Christine continued to stack the material, doing her best to keep it apart from Conor's mucky hiking boots that had been living in the boot for several months.

'Anyway. I'm talking about Arlo and Nuala Patterson,' said Beverley, lowering her voice. Orla and Rodney Smith were heading for the car beside Christine's.

'Can't wait for the show tomorrow!' enthused Orla.

'We've been watching the film in preparation,' added Rodney.

Nuala had sent the parents home, but she hadn't told them why. Only the few who'd been present in the workroom knew about Seamus's death and that there would be no show tomorrow, or at all. Beverley nearly had a fit when Nuala told them the plan – 'The TV producers are already in town!' – but even she accepted there was no way around it.

'It's not based on the film, you ignorami,' she muttered now after the Smiths shut their doors and started their car.

Christine slammed the boot. She was jealous of the Smiths. She was jealous of everyone who had already left this car park and who hadn't been bound for life to Beverley Franklin over a deeply uncomfortable secret.

The sound of the boot shutting focused the other woman's attention. 'Don't you think it's strange that Arlo and Nuala, of all people, were in cahoots?' said Beverley. 'They usually go out of their way to ignore each other. And you couldn't blame Nuala for that. Imagine your child was in a horrific accident and you have to risk meeting the people associated with it every time you walk down the street?'

'What's your point, Beverley?'

'Why did Arlo go to Nuala for help? And why did Nuala give it so readily?'

'I don't know,' admitted Christine. As surprised as she'd been to see Beverley and Arlo chatting civilly, she'd been even more taken aback to find Nuala apologising to the boy. There were rumours out of Aberstown Garda Station after the crash, inconsistencies in the forensics reports, heavy suggestions Charlie hadn't really been driving that night, that he was covering for his son. They were only ever rumours, nothing she could report. But still, if there was even a possibility that Arlo had been the one to injure her son, how could Nuala be so civil to him?

'I can't think of a single reason for it,' mused Beverley, as Christine opened the driver's side of her car. 'It just doesn't make any sense.'

....

'Everything looks perfect,' said Arlo, as he and Nuala stood at the back of the auditorium, surveying the impeccably straight rows of chairs, and the picture-perfect cornfield that occupied the entire stage. There was bunting streamed around the perimeters of the hall, and a huge banner hung from the vast ceiling: *The Wonderful Wizard of Oz*.

'It really does,' agreed Nuala, her hand hovering over the light switches a moment longer. Everything was ready to go for opening night. 'Pity we won't get to put any of it to use.'

She brought her fingers down and the hall plunged into darkness.

He kept pace as they made their way down the corridor, their footsteps echoing softly. The faint murmur of the last few stragglers travelled in from the car park. They were the last to leave. He pushed his way through the side foyer and out into the blustery night. He held the door for the principal.

'Thank you,' he said, as Nuala turned back to lock the door and the tails of her coat whipped around her.

'You don't need to thank me.'

He wanted to say that he missed talking to her, but embarrassment stopped him. It hadn't even been a year, but he felt so much older, too old for those kinds of declarations. Everything was different now.

The wind whooshed around them and Nuala squinted against it, pulling her personal keys from her pocket now and clamping her fist around them. 'I owe your family,' she said, catching the hem of her coat. 'I told you I'd never forget that. I'm just glad to have the chance to start paying you back.'

EIGHT MONTHS EARLIER

Mike **was** the one who snuck in the alcohol.

Mike was always chancing his arm, and he was a demon for the drink. He had his dad's spirits cabinet watered down to nothing. Luckily for his son, Mike Roche Senior still treated his body the way he had when he played GAA. But some day he would open the mahogany sideboard in his study and wonder why his eighteen-year-old bourbon-barrelled Jameson was now the colour of well-hydrated piss.

When Charlie got chatting to someone at the bar before the gig started, Mike pulled his two friends up from their seats. 'Come on,' he said. 'We're going to the jacks.'

'I'm not going to the jacks with you,' said Leo, shaking him off.

Mike winked at Leo. 'I've got something that'll make it worth your while,' he said, whipping one side of his jacket open to reveal a brief glimpse of a Sprite bottle containing a liquid too dark to be Sprite.

'Where'd you get that?'

'Big Mikey's stash, of course.'

'Your auld fella has nothing worth taking any more,' said Leo. 'We're just drinking our own diluted muck at this stage.'

Mike rolled his eyes. 'It's a new bottle, *Leonardo*. Gerry Regan wants his son on the senior team; he dropped this into my dad during the week to sweeten the deal.'

'I've seen Ralph Regan trip over his feet walking down Main Street,' said Arlo sceptically. 'He hasn't a chance of making the team.'

'A total no-hoper,' agreed Mike, patting his breast pocket. 'So, you know this stuff has got to be good.'

There was one other lad in the bathroom, using the urinal. Mike nodded at him – 'A very good evening to you, sir' – then he pulled his friends into the last stall after him.

'I'm not going to bum fuck you, Leo,' said Mike, catching the look on his friend's face. 'And I'll do my best to restrain myself with Arlo, too. He's got a girlfriend now, so I suppose that means he's taken.'

'Arlo hasn't got a girlfriend,' scoffed Leo. 'Unless you're talking about his right hand.'

'She's a secret,' said Mike, climbing up on to the toilet cistern as the other two squeezed in and stood with their backs against opposite stall walls.

'You don't have a girlfriend, do you?' said Leo. The tight quarters meant his face was about ten inches from Arlo's. 'Who?'

'Nobody. I don't have a girlfriend.'

'Your fucking face, Arly, it's on fire,' he laughed. 'Who is she? Do I know her? Of course I know her. Is it someone from school? Rachel Grogan? Kathy Fleming? Who?'

Mike took a generous swig of the whiskey before proffering it forward. 'Gentlemen?'

Arlo shook his head. 'I'm driving, remember?'

'Why won't you tell me who she is?'

361

The bathroom stall was too small to look anywhere but at his friend. 'It's nobody.'

Leo turned to Mike, who was taking a second swig. 'Do you know who she is? Is it someone from school?'

Mike stopped swirling the whiskey around his mouth and swallowed. Then he gave a wide, mischievous grin and nodded.

Arlo threw him a look and mouthed, *Shut up*.

'I don't know any more than that, though,' said Mike. 'Now, does anyone else want this or am I going to get wasted on my own? Leo, here.'

Leo took the bottle, then he held it out to Arlo. 'You have it. You've something to celebrate.'

'Thanks, but I have to drive us home.'

'I'll do it. I'm a better driver than you, anyway.'

'You're not insured on the car,' said Arlo, eyeing the bottle. He felt giddy with the excitement of his secret romance and the fact that he was about to watch one of his favourite artists play live with his two best friends and his dad.

'Do you think Charlie'll give a fuck?'

They all knew the answer to that.

'All right, cheers,' said Arlo, taking the bottle. Leo wouldn't be offering him anything if he knew his mystery girlfriend was Ella Franklin. But as it was, he was looking at Arlo in a way he never did, with something approaching respect.

Arlo brought the bottle to his mouth and threw it back.

Leo liked Ella. Everyone at school knew that. They'd kissed once and Leo said they were taking things slow, but that was about two years ago. They'd been friends since they were kids, though less so lately. Arlo also liked her, a lot. But he didn't do anything about it because Leo was his best friend and he'd made his intentions clear, and also because, as Leo liked to remind him, he was a wimp. Then one day, about a month ago, she caught up with him after school. She walked in the wrong direction, in the rain, just so she could talk to him. That was when she told him she liked him too.

The three of them left the jacks and headed back out to the venue. Arlo felt like he was sailing above the crowd. He hadn't had that much to drink but, as Leo liked to tell everyone, he was a lightweight.

Donovan appeared on stage and they dumped their belongings where they'd been sitting. Arlo waved to his dad at the bar, who lifted his pint in reply. Then they squeezed their way to the front. This was going to be one of the greatest nights of his life. Arlo loved his friends and he loved his dad and it was all very new but fuck it he loved Ella Belle Franklin too.

After the third song, the music stopped and Donovan told a funny story about a misunderstanding with a local taxi driver.

Arlo pulled out his phone.

'Checking for a message from your mystery girlfriend?' said Leo, looking over his shoulder.

'No,' lied Arlo, for once grateful that there was none. 'Just checking the time.'

Mike swooned into them: 'Oh Arlo, I miss you, will you come over and massage me?'

'Massage?' laughed Leo, as Arlo joined in. Mike was always fun, but drunk Mike, when Arlo was also drunk, was the best buzz.

'Oh yes, Ella,' Mike continued. 'I'll be over as soon as the night allows. Leave a light on for me and I will climb the drainpipes of your mansion ... Wait, do mansions have drainpipes?'

Nobody answered his question. Leo looked at Arlo like he might lunge for him, but then the music started again, and the crowd carried them all forward.

'I meant to tell you,' Arlo shouted over the guitar, but Leo turned and pushed a path away from them through the crowd.

'Fuck,' said Arlo, as Mike began to jump and sing along again. '*Ba baa ba-ba-ba!*'

When the gig was over, Arlo and Mike met Charlie back at their original seats. It was a few minutes before Leo appeared. He approached the group and handed Mike his jacket.

'I was wondering where that was.'

'All right, let's go,' said Charlie, pulling on his own coat. 'Jesus, but it's great to have my own personal designated driver now.' His face was flush from the drink as he winked at his son.

'Actually, Dad, I'm not gonna ...' Arlo looked to his friend, trying to confirm if he was still willing to cover for him and drive home.

'Arlo has had a bit to drink, Mr Whitehead,' said Leo loudly. He never called Charlie 'Mr Whitehead'.

'Really?'

'Yes, he and Mike drank quite a lot of whiskey.'

'Fuck, Arlo. Seriously? I don't mind you drinking but how are we going to get home?'

'I'll drive us,' said Leo, still talking in that weird, studied way.

'Are you sure?'

Leo nodded. 'Absolutely.'

They hurried to the car, Charlie walking in front with his head bowed against the rain. Arlo tried to speak to Leo, but his friend wasn't interested.

'Another one for the road, Arlo?' said Mike, reaching into his breast pocket.

'I'm grand.' Now that things had turned sour the alcohol was making him feel ill. He'd been so excited about the gig that he'd barely touched his dinner.

'All the more for— What the fuck?' Mike turned the empty bottle upside down then right way up. 'I had about a third of this left.' He patted his other pockets, as though the liquid might just be sitting in one of them. 'Leo? Did you fucking drink this?'

Leo kept walking and kept looking ahead. He had a hood, but he didn't bother to pull it up. 'My best friend just told me he stole my girlfriend, so yeah, I needed a drink.'

'She's not your girlfriend,' said Arlo.

'Not any more she's not.'

'But did you have to drink it all?' whined Mike.

'She was never your girlfriend. She told me the kiss was a mistake.'

'Oh, she told you, did she? Did you have lots of lovely little chats? Did she tell you that she let me put my hand on her tits?'

'Fuck off, Leo,' said Arlo, banging against his friend.

'No, you fuck off,' he shouted, grabbing Arlo's arm and twisting it back.

'Ow! Fucking ow!'

'Oi! Lads!' Charlie was jogging back to them, his feet sending a gentle spray up onto the cuffs of his jeans. He looked between them. 'Ah, Jesus! Have youse *all* been drinking?'

'I haven't,' said Leo, the stoic tone and raindrops hanging at his fringe really adding to the martyrdom.

Arlo and Mike exchanged a look but neither of them said anything. Arlo climbed obediently into the passenger seat of his mother's ancient Volvo as Leo positioned the driver's chair and side mirror to his liking.

His dad talked about the gig for a while, but Mike was the only one responding, so he soon gave up. He was dozing in the seat behind Arlo by the time they left the city.

They were about twenty minutes from home and Arlo was just starting to relax when Leo suddenly declared 'Music!' and lifted himself from the driver's seat so he could retrieve his phone from his pocket.

'I'll do it, I'll play something,' said Arlo, pulling out his own phone, relieved to see both Leo's hands back on the steering wheel.

Then the rain got heavier.

Arlo's eyes flicked nervously between playlists and the road. He suddenly felt very sober. He wished he was the one driving.

'No Guthrie,' said Leo, as the first chords of 'Dust Bowl Blues' filled the car.

'You're annoyed at me, don't take it out on Guthrie.'

'I'm the one driving and I'm the one you fucked over, so I pick the music.'

'I was going to tell you. I know you like Ella—'

'I don't like her,' said Leo automatically. 'She likes me. She's just using you.'

'What would she be using me for? This car?'

'You're like a practice boyfriend. That's actually exactly what you are. Someone she won't mind messing things up with. You're not threatening. You'll let her do whatever she wants once she goes out with you. It's embarrassing really.'

'That doesn't even make sense,' said Arlo, his tone neutral, though he could feel himself going red.

'You keep telling yourself that.' Leo leaned forward as Woody Guthrie sang on.

'You're being childish now. Slow down.'

Leo sat back, then leaned forward again, foot down, accelerator tearing.

'Stop, Leo. It's too wet for messing. It's too dark.'

'You're a wimp, Arly, a pathetic weasel. Do you know that? You're pathetic.'

'Fuck off.'

'Like a little limp dog or something. How could you think she likes you? You're a fucking wimp. You're deluded. How could you even—'

'Slow down!'

But it was too late. They were coming around the last bend, right at the 'Welcome to Cooney' sign, when the car started to skid out of control. Leo tried to get a grip on the steering wheel, but the thing kept sliding back in the other direction. The car slipped and skated, turning so quickly that it was almost facing fully in the opposite direction by the time it left the road and headed on to the mucky verge. Arlo reached over to grab control – his mom's steering wheel was loose, unlike the one in the van; he should have told Leo that – but he couldn't get a grasp on it. He was sent banging into the passenger door, then thrown forward, wincing as the seatbelt tightened against his chest. The car should have slowed on the grass, but there was a slope, followed by a ledge, and the grass was so wet. The car picked up speed as it fell then tumbled and flew full force into one of Cooney's 200-year-old oak trees.

Next thing Arlo knew it was morning and his dad was calling him for school. 'Five minutes,' he said, turning on to his side. Only he couldn't turn. Something was restraining him. Reluctantly he opened his eyes and saw that he was not in his bed.

'Just hang on, okay? I'm going to open the door.'

Arlo turned the only way he could, towards Leo. His friend was breathing fast, muttering something to himself. He turned further again, wincing at the pain in his shoulder, and saw Mike. How was he still asleep? The windows were smashed and the rain was coming in. How much had his friend drunk that he could snooze through that? And who uses a tree trunk as a pillow?

Slowly, then quickly, Arlo got his bearings. His dad opened the passenger door and pulled him out of the car.

'Dad, Dad! Mike! Stop, I'm all right.' He pushed his dad off. 'Mike is ... We need to get Mike!'

He moved his hands down over his body. A pain in his chest and at the side of his head, but otherwise he was all right.

'Come on, quick! Dad!'

'Stop, Arlo.'

'What? No. Come on!'

'It's too late, Arlo.'

'I can't feel my legs! I can't feel my legs!'

'It's okay, Leo, we'll get you out now,' said Charlie, moving around to the driver's side and reefing the door open.

'Am I moving my feet? Can you look, Charlie? Can you see? There, now, am I moving them?'

Charlie looked down under the steering wheel, then over at Arlo. 'It's too dark, Leo.' But it wasn't dark. The dashboard was lit up and Arlo had a perfect view from the passenger side. The only part of his friend that was moving was his face.

'Take me out,' shouted Leo, his breathing fast again. 'Take me out of here.'

'Hang on, I'm just ...' Charlie trailed off. He was drenched. His hair had flopped forward into a sort of modish fringe and the rain was hitting his face.

Arlo was scared. He couldn't deal with this. He needed his dad to tell him what to do.

'Am I going to go to jail? I am, amn't I? Fuck. Oh God. My mom is going to kill me.' Leo was whimpering now. 'I was drinking, Charlie. I'm sorry I lied, but I was drinking and now I'm going to go to jail. Where's Mike?' Leo strained his head up to look in the rear-view mirror. 'Is Mike still there? Is he okay? He's not ... Charlie! Arlo! Did I kill Mike? Oh fuck, tell me. Did I? I can't—' But the rest of it was lost to incontrollable sobbing.

Arlo was crying now too. He couldn't decipher the snot and the tears from the rain, but he could feel the stinging in his eyes.

'Okay, everyone, listen.' His dad was back in adult mode and Arlo felt himself calming slightly. 'We're going to move you, Leo, okay? But not out of the car.'

Leo whimpered.

'Listen, just listen. We're going to move you into the passenger seat.'

'What? Why?'

'Because I was driving, all right? I was driving us home and I lost control of the car and we crashed.'

'Dad, no, you—'

'Shhh!' Charlie gave him a look that made Arlo feel about four years old. 'I was driving. Leo was in the passenger seat and Arlo, you were sitting behind him, okay? Okay? Repeat that, please.'

'Y-you were driving. I was ... I was in the passenger seat,' said Leo, starting to sob again. 'And Arlo was sitting behind me.'

'Good. Okay. I'm going to call an ambulance and then we're going to move you.'

The doctors had told Nuala what to expect but when she walked into the hospital room and saw her only child shrouded in wires and tubes and imposing machines, she faltered for the first time since her phone had rung four hours earlier.

'Leo,' said her husband Martin, skirting around his frozen wife to move to their son's side. 'How do you feel? Are you in pain? What can we do?'

'Am I moving my legs? Nobody will tell me for sure, but I don't think I'm moving my legs.'

'You need to take it easy now. Don't be pushing yourself to move anything until the doctor asks you to.'

'I'm sorry, Dad. I'm so sorry.'

Her son's blubbering helped Nuala to rediscover her sense of purpose. She crossed the room to stand beside her husband, only now appreciating that she was still in her slippers and pyjama bottoms. How had Martin found the time and wherewithal to get dressed?

'Don't get upset, Leo,' she said. 'You don't need to be sorry for anything.'

'What if I never walk again? What if I can't ...?'

'Shh. It's okay, it'll be okay.'

'Is Mike dead?'

'We're not sure but … we think so,' said Martin, as Nuala reached out for her son's hand. The doctor said Leo had suffered a spinal injury. The first surgery suggested it was incomplete, but they'd need to go back in and examine it again. He had also fractured his left tibia and broken three ribs. But he was still alive. The gratitude almost knocked her to the floor.

'We love you,' she said, careful not to squeeze his hand too tight.

'I was driving,' he whimpered, looking at her as if he couldn't quite believe what was coming out of his mouth.

'No, Charlie Whitehead was.'

'Charlie's taking the blame. He told them it was him. But it was me. And I was drinking. I don't know what to do, Mom. I'm scared. I'm proper scared. What should I do?'

Her son threw his eyes in her direction but the apparatus around his neck and shoulders prevented his head from moving. Just a few days ago, she'd thought it would be good for Leo if something happened to take the wind out of his sails. He was a cocky young fellow. Not that it was unwarranted – he was academically gifted, good at sports, handsome and popular – but it was unbecoming. He could be cruel about his friends without giving it a second's thought. Arrogance was not a flattering trait and certainly not one she had encouraged.

But she'd been thinking of him getting turned down by a girl or dropped from the football team, something like that. She hadn't wanted her son to learn a lesson that he would have to keep learning for the rest of his life.

'What should I do?' he asked again.

'You should tell the—'

But Martin cut in. 'You should do what Charlie said,' he whispered, moving closer to the bed as he looked at the door. 'He was the adult. What was he thinking letting you drink? And what was he thinking letting you get behind the steering wheel? He was probably drunk too, knowing Charlie. Was he? Was he drunk?'

Leo nodded, still whimpering.

'Well, there you are then,' said Martin, as if the whole matter had now been put to bed.

'Mom?'

Nuala felt, as she often did, outnumbered. Leo's personality was closer to Martin's than her own. She knew what her son would do, just as she knew what her husband would do, but still she asked: 'What do you want to do?'

'I don't want to go to jail.'

'And you won't,' decreed Martin, doing a great job of implying he was a legal expert as opposed to a taxation one. 'Not a chance.'

An hour later, Nuala and Martin were gently ushered out of the hospital so Leo could get some rest. There would be another surgery and tests later that day. For it was a new day now. The six o'clock morning news came on the radio as they drove out of the hospital car park.

'Can we really allow Leo to let someone else take the blame?'

'It was Charlie's idea,' said Martin. 'And what's the alternative? Leo goes to jail for a decision he made when he was a teenager? He's probably going to be in a wheelchair for the rest of his life. Don't you think that's sufficient punishment? Charlie was in charge. Either way, he'd probably end up in prison.'

'So why don't we just let the courts decide? At least that way, Leo will have a clear conscience.' She said Leo, but she meant herself. She did all the guilt wrangling in this family.

'I'm not putting Leo through some circus trial, no way. It'd destroy him. It'd destroy us.'

Nuala let her head fall back against the headrest. The rain had stopped, but the roads remained wet. The sound of tyres on water used to make her feel safe and warm inside the car. Now, it made her shiver.

She instructed Martin to drive out to the crash site, where he stayed in the car while she clambered down the muddy slope, past the young guard who was minding the crime scene until forensics arrived. She observed the place where Leo had lost the use of his legs and killed his friend, and questioned if she was the sort of woman who could sacrifice another family to save her son.

Then she climbed back up to the car and told Martin to take her to the Whiteheads' house.

....

Arlo was discharged in the early hours. He'd suffered minor lung contusions, a fractured rib and a head injury. The doctor wanted to keep the lungs and head under observation for twenty-four hours, but when Arlo learned his dad was leaving, he wanted to go too. Charlie's injuries were worse, but nothing could stand between him and the police station. They'd made an appointment for him to come in that afternoon with a solicitor.

Charlie didn't tell his wife the truth. He had been insistent; nobody but him and Arlo and Leo were to know what had happened. As far as Connie was concerned, her husband had been driving the car that killed Mike and seriously injured Leo. They weren't home from the hospital long when the doorbell went. It was Mr and Mrs Patterson.

'Oh, hello,' said Leo, taken aback. ' Come in. Were you looking for ...?'

'Your dad. Is he home?'

Arlo wanted to rescind the offer, but he'd already stood to the side and Principal Patterson had one foot through the door. They stopped in the hallway. Mr Patterson removed his coat, but his wife was wrapping hers tighter. Her slippers left a trail of muck on the carpet.

'Nuala, Martin.' Charlie appeared from the kitchen holding a tea towel. 'I'm so sorry. I'm ... I don't know what to say.' The distress on his dad's face was such that for a second Arlo was convinced he had been driving. But then his own face probably didn't look much different. They were all responsible in their own way.

'If you want to swing for me, do.' Charlie held his arms out like he was going for a group hug. 'I deserve it.'

Arlo cringed. His dad was mad for grand declarations. His mom said this all the time. 'King of the big gesture, but no follow-through.' Although what was taking the rap for manslaughter, if not follow-through?

'We know you weren't driving, Charlie,' said Principal Patterson.

'I was.'

'No, you weren't. Leo told us.'

Charlie gave a half-laugh. 'I don't know why Leo would say that because it's not true, is it, Arlo? Have the doctors looked at his head? Might he have concussion?'

She looked at Arlo. 'Is it true, Arlo? Was your dad driving?'

He didn't know what to say.

What was the right answer? How was he supposed to know? He could feel the tears prickling at his eyes. He hadn't slept in more than twenty-four hours. He couldn't do this.

Charlie ushered them all into the living room and closed the door.

'Please let me do this,' he said quietly. 'The accident was my fault.'

He looked at Martin who held up his hands. 'You won't get any disagreement from me. My son is a child. You're an adult. Shame on you.'

'How is Leo? How are his legs?'

Neither of them said anything.

'I don't want him to suffer any more. I will not be able to live with myself if you do not let me do this. Please, I am begging you. It was my fault.'

'Agreed,' said Mr Patterson.

'I don't know how I'm going to accept this,' said his wife quietly. 'If you go to prison, how will I look at your family?'

'Don't,' said Charlie, as if it were the simplest thing in the world, as if they lived in New York City or London or even Dublin, not the small, intimate village of Cooney, West Cork. 'People would think it strange if you were to talk to them. From now on, you hate me, and you want nothing to do with us. It's the only thing that would make sense. You won't want to look at us anyway. We'll be a reminder.'

Arlo glanced at Principal Patterson, waiting for her to say this was not true. She liked him; he knew she did. They got on great. But she didn't look at him. She hadn't, he realised, since she'd come into the house.

It was easier this way. They were all carrying guilt. They all felt responsible. They hadn't the capacity to take on anyone else's.

She nodded, and her husband placed a hand in her lap, grateful for her acquiescence.

'But I owe you,' she said. 'I owe all of you. And I won't forget that. I promise.'

EPILOGUE

· · · · · · · · · · · · · · · · ·

THREE MONTHS AFTER THE DROWNING

Nuala Patterson had found it surprisingly easy to go along with the whole charade. She had declined to speak at the funeral (a refusal everyone presumed was because she found Seamus's death too upsetting), made sympathetic sounds when fellow mourners said how desperately sad it was, and silently cheered as his body was lowered into the ground.

The initial pathology report had confirmed death by drowning, no signs of foul play. There would be a coroner's court hearing in a few months' time as a matter of procedure, but the cause of death, combined with the suicide note and Miriam McGrath's testimony that her husband could not swim, meant the finding was a foregone conclusion.

She'd lied to the gardaí when they asked if she'd any idea why her colleague might have taken his own life, and she hadn't lost any sleep over it. It was for the greater good of the children involved. With Seamus gone, they would have been the focus of the inevitable scandal.

The whole ordeal had made her less judgemental of her own son. Letting Charlie Whitehead take the rap for the crash had never sat well with her. She hadn't said this explicitly, but her husband and

Leo could tell. They felt she was judging them, and maybe she was. It just wasn't the sort of person she'd wanted her son to be. But she also hadn't wanted him to go to jail.

When Leo and Martin first left for Leo's therapy in Dublin, there was vague talk of her following. But once they got there, the subject never came up again. She couldn't make her peace with Charlie going to jail and it had been easier to avoid the whole situation. Then it was too late. Leo was so angry about what had happened to him, and completely incapable of seeing his own role in it. Speaking to his mother, who he was convinced had disowned him, only made things worse. And then the divorce papers arrived.

But the whole business with Seamus had made her more understanding, and more willing to compromise. We do what we think is best and then we live with that decision. So, who was she to judge anyone else?

She'd been to visit Leo and his father three times this month. She even spent a couple of nights there over Christmas. She was making progress, she thought, drawing him out of himself, helping him to realise the world was not closed to him, and that feeling sorry for himself was not the best use of his time. She brought the divorce papers with her every time she went to Dublin, but they were still sitting right where they always were – on the back seat of her car. She hadn't been asked for them yet anyway.

It was shortly after eight o'clock on a Monday morning and she was on her way to the school. She'd got back late from Dublin last night, but she had plenty of energy. She was through the worst of the menopause, thank God. (That might also have something to do with her increased tolerance for other people, family included.) They'd had to hire a new caretaker at the school, and the Whiteheads had moved into the city, but otherwise things continued as normal. Mr Cafferty had agreed to stay – she'd told him she couldn't go into details, but that she'd got to the root of the problem and it wouldn't happen again.

Arlo had left Cooney before his mother and brother. He relocated to the city not long before Christmas, with Ella Franklin of all people. Apparently, they'd been an item for a while now. She remembered Ella from school. A fine girl, despite her mother. Nuala was delighted for them. She was still so fond of Arlo. It did her heart good to know that he was happy.

....

It was 27 January – exactly three weeks since everyone else on their street had taken down their decorations, and yet a wreath still hung on Arlo and Ella's front door and a Christmas tree sat dying in their tiny living-room-cum-kitchen.

'I like it,' said Ella, feet up on the table as she shovelled cornflakes into her mouth before legging it to her first lecture. 'This is my first home of my own and I want to do things my way.'

'Our way, you mean.'

'Sure.'

'It's starting to smell.'

'And Woody likes it,' she countered. 'Isn't he staying tonight? Just imagine the look on his cute little face when he arrives to find the tree and all the festive magic is gone.'

Arlo sighed. 'Well, when are we going to take them down?'

'February,' she said decisively, throwing her feet back on to the floor and placing her bowl in the sink. 'Just in time for Valentine's Day. I've got my eye on some great 3D hearts in the two-euro shop.'

She scooped her bag up from the floor and kissed him on the mouth. Already the milk tasted sour, and he liked it. 'Gotta go.'

He walked to the door and kissed her again. She waltzed up the street, turned at the halfway point, and waved. In the end, Beverley had been his unexpected knight in shining armour, telling her daughter the truth about how nothing had happened between him and Fiona Murphy, and inadvertently saving a relationship she'd rather not have saved.

His first job wasn't for another hour. He returned to the kitchen and washed the breakfast things. He needed to decide what he was going to cook tonight. Woody was coming over after school.

Days after Arlo told his family that he was moving into Cork city several months earlier than intended, his mom decided to do the same. A fresh start for all of them. Nuala Patterson had helped to get Woody into a good primary school for the last few months of sixth class and, in September, he would be moving up to secondary. Arlo was delighted; it had relieved his guilt about abandoning them, and it meant he still got to see his little brother several times a week.

Arlo often cooked for him now, something he never used to do. He loved eating with him, and chatting to him, and staying up late playing computer games together. They were as close as they used to be, and Arlo grinned every time he realised that.

Tonight, he would make macaroni and cheese, Woody's favourite. His mom was coming for dinner too. She wouldn't care what he made, she was just happy when they were all together.

She thought his new home was cute.

Though she might not be so taken by the browning Christmas tree.

The woman making her way along the aisle slowed as she came to Beverley's table. Beverley had assumed that once the train was moving, she'd be free from the possibility of strangers wanting to squash their bodies up against hers.

She pointed to the two electronic names above the seats: Beverley Franklin, Ella Franklin.

'These are both taken,' she said, before the woman got any ideas. 'My daughter's just in the bathroom.'

When the woman shuffled on, she returned her handbag to 'Ella's' seat.

Her daughter was not in the bathroom, or anywhere else on this train. She was probably sitting in a lecture hall or crammed into that tiny shed of a place she and Arlo Whitehead now called home. But if Beverley was going to get public transport, she'd be damned if she was going to spend the journey wedged in beside a potential psychopath. So she'd booked both seats. It was the logical solution.

She'd been to Ella's house twice now, and while it would not be to her liking – who gets a real tree, let alone still has it up in late January? – she was happy her daughter was happy. More importantly, she was happy she was talking to her. They hadn't had anything worse than a disagreement since she moved out. Maybe absence really does make the heart grow fonder. Or maybe it was easier for Ella to be civil to her mother when she wasn't trying to keep a lover squirrelled away on the top floor of their home. She'd still rather her daughter was dating someone with more prospects than Arlo Whitehead but, after the whole business with Seamus and the photos, she had a newfound respect for the boy. She felt confident, at least, that he'd do all he could to protect her daughter.

Her phone buzzed and she pulled it from her handbag.

'Did you make the train?'

'Of course I made the train, Mother. I'm sitting here now.'

'Wonderful, *a stór*, just wonderful!'

'Are you all right? You sound a bit out of it.'

'No, no,' said Frances, wind chimes jangling somewhere in the background. 'I'm just getting everything ready for your visit. My lovely neighbours heard you were coming and they dropped around a few brownies for the occasion. Isn't that lovely? I may have started on one, but I promise there'll be lots here for you. You know, if you wanted to stay until Thursday, I'm running a beginners' workshop and I think you'd really—'

'I have to be back by Thursday, I told you. The camera crew is coming to film Amelia.'

'Of course, of course. Dorothy finally goes to Oz!'

The musical had been cancelled after Seamus's death, but a few weeks later *The Big Children's Talent Show* got in touch to say they'd still like to feature Amelia, maybe with a solo performance of 'Over the Rainbow'. Naturally, the other Lakers were already clandestinely complaining about nepotism, but their daughters couldn't carry a note between them, and she had little time for shameless jealousy.

'I'm going now, Mother. I'll get a taxi from the station and I'll see you shortly,' said Beverley, pulling a newspaper out of her bag. 'I have the *Southern Gazette* to read.'

Fiona Murphy's estate agency business had appeared on the latest tax defaulters' list – and Beverley hadn't read a single newspaper article so many times since her own heyday in the acting limelight.

....

Christine was working on an article about Bill Farrell's official mayoral bid. His wife was running his campaign and she had Christine bombarded with press releases. If she didn't write something soon, Lorna's accusations of political prejudice would start to have merit. But she didn't care how many times the woman quoted them, she would not be likening Bill to Barack Obama or, and this was a journalistic principle she was willing to go to jail for, Lorna to Michelle.

'Do you think something bad will ever happen again?' asked Derek, despondently, from a desk across the room.

'I don't know, boss.'

Her editor sighed.

A real-life, legitimate mystery had finally happened in Cooney and it had been solved – in so much as a suicide note could solve anything – before he could even get an issue of the paper out of it. The pathologist's report had brought an end to any remaining speculation or conspiracy theories. Derek hadn't felt this short-changed since Charlie Whitehead confessed to dangerous driving causing death, doing him out of a trial.

He was a good newspaper man, but he was not the most sensitive of humans.

'Someone has to be up to *something*,' he beseeched, continuing to make his way through the local phonebook. An 'O'Sullivan' had been added to Interpol's 'Most Wanted' list the previous week and he was cross-referencing the name. For all his news hack cynicism, Derek remained an optimist.

'Post,' declared Amanda, appearing at the entrance to the office. She dumped three envelopes on their boss's desk.

'Hope!' declared Derek, greedily ripping open the first envelope.

'Another bloody complaint about all the Keating twins' photos ...'
He balled that one up and threw it in the bin. The next one, he
waved above his head. 'This is for you.'

Christine walked over to collect the latest Bill Farrell for Mayor
missive.

'Our last shot ...' he said, rubbing the final A4 envelope between
his hands like a man about to roll the dice at a high-stakes craps
table. 'Come on, compromising photographs of a high-ranking
official ...'

He tore the top from the envelope and pulled the single
photocopied sheet from within. It was, at least, a photograph.

'Another missing cat! Who do these people think we are? We
might be desperate, but we'll never be *that* desperate. I spent
seventeen months embedded with a notorious crime gang, and the
subsequent six under garda protection. I do not report on missing
bloody cats!'

The two journalists leaned over their boss's shoulder to look at
the flyer. 'Dr Tickles,' read Amanda. 'Cute.'

Derek slammed the page down on his desk and stormed out of
the office. 'I'm going for a smoke! Call me when someone gets shot!'

Christine dedicated another forty minutes to putting some shape
on the Bill Farrell article, then she grabbed her car keys and bag.
Amanda had already left, and Derek was back at his desk, poring
over the phonebook.

He looked up as she pulled on her coat.

'Didn't you say something terrible happened to *your* cat?' he
asked hopefully. 'Someone stole him or crucified him or something?'

'Our cat was abducted, yes, but just temporarily. All is well now,
and he is safe at home.'

'Oh,' sighed Derek. 'Great news.'

'See you tomorrow, boss.'

He waved a hand distractedly in her direction as she disappeared out the door and down the stairs.

It had taken a while to get the last of the dye out of Porcupine's fur but once they'd achieved it, he had settled back in easily. The children were more besotted with him than before and, with the musical scrapped, Maeve's bedroom noticeboard had returned to being a shrine solely dedicated to the unworthy creature. Even Mrs Rodgers had eventually stopped lingering at their garden gate.

Personally, Christine would be delighted if nothing bad, or even exciting, ever happened in Cooney, ever again. Come back endless petitions and parental tiffs, all is forgiven! She'd seen Principal Patterson and Beverley a few times since the showdown in the Glass Lake workroom, but she hadn't said more to them than a few words. Word around town was the Whiteheads had moved to the city – and Arlo was now sharing a house with Ella Franklin. Good for him.

She turned the car up Seaview Terrace, slowing as she passed Mrs Rodgers' house – a habit she had yet to get out of. The older woman was sitting on her stoop, wrapped up against the January chill in a bulky coat, oversized hat and furry hand muff.

Only, it wasn't a hand muff.

'Is that ...?'

Christine brought the car to a near stop.

Sitting on Mrs Rodgers' lap, blocking her hands from view, was another cat. The woman smiled brightly as she stood from the step. With some trepidation, Christine rolled down the window. The cat had light ginger fur and a crude white stripe running down the centre of its forehead. It was identical to the animal from this afternoon's missing poster ... except for the white streak and about three extra pounds.

'Hello, Christine,' the woman shouted over. 'Have you met Terence? He's my cat. I've had him a long time now.'

Christine looked from the animal formerly known as Dr Tickles to her deranged neighbour. She opened her mouth but the words would not come. The animal stood on all fours and stretched. Unable to tear her eyes away, she felt for the window control.

'Lovely to see you, dear,' called Mrs Rodgers, as the cat nuzzled down to sleep and the window eventually, thankfully, shut.

ACKNOWLEDGEMENTS

This was the first book I wrote after becoming a mother – and the first I wrote during a pandemic – so a lot of the process is a blur. But I must thank some of the people who helped me through it.

I wrote the first draft of *It Could Never Happen Here* in my parents' house – which is ten minutes from my own. Covid-19 had just struck and my son was six months old and at home with his father while I headed off up the road to my childhood home to get a few hours' writing in before breastfeeding called me back again. I was avoiding contact with my parents, bringing my own teacup and water bottle, and all childcare was off the table. It was a mad time.

As things relaxed slightly, my dad started to make me coffee and deliver it to the bedroom where I was writing. It was always served in the same Seamus Heaney mug – which has the word 'Inspiration' on it. I hope it had the desired effect, Dad. And thank you, too, for never asking how the writing was going. This book is dedicated to you.

My mam, a retired primary school deputy principal, inadvertently provided the initial spark for the book. She has given me so many ideas at this stage that she is likely owed a royalty. I am also grateful for the lockdown baking spurt she went through while I was writing in her house. Warm scones went very well with the Heaney coffee.

I'd like to be able to thank my son, but honestly, he was a terrible sleeper throughout the first draft of this and so not of much direct assistance. I do love you though, Ruan, dearly, and I am so very glad you exist. Thanks are, however, due to my partner Colm, who often got up to settle him during the night and was the parent most likely to rise with him in the morning.

To Sarah Hodgson, my editor, thank you for your care, patience and understanding. And to everyone else at Corvus who helps with my novels – I will avoid the temptation to list names, in case I forget anyone, but know that the work is appreciated. A huge thank you to my agents – Liz Parker at Verve, and Sarah Lutyens at Lutyens & Rubinstein – for being invested in the book at every stage. I am very grateful.

And finally, to you, the reader. With every book I write, I grow more appreciative of the people who read them. Without you, these words wouldn't exist. I hope you enjoyed it. (Or if you are one of those people who skims the acknowledgements first – that you will enjoy it.) Thank you, thank you.

What happens when Cupid plays co-pilot?

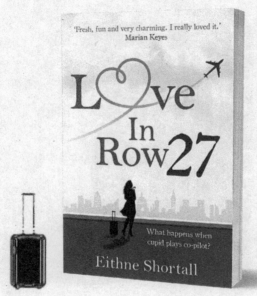

'Fresh, fun and very charming. I really loved it'
Marian Keyes

'This is the perfect holiday romance read'
Red

A poignant, funny and moving exploration of love and loss

'Witty and well written. I loved it'
Louise O'Neill

'Satisfying and warm, and written with humour and heart'
Sheila O'Flanagan

'Engrossing, surprising, and empowering'
Jill Santopolo